Most Likely
to
Succeed

By
Misty Wilson

Chapter 1

Natalie put on her left blinker and listened to the *tick tick.* Sweat trickled down her neck, and slid down her back until she shivered. One hand searched out, groping, until she hit the button, and all four windows descended, letting in the afternoon breeze with its faint aromas of cow manure and freshly cut hay.

Natalie dropped her head and slumped over the steering wheel. The rhythmic ticking of the left turn signal seemed to grow louder and louder, until it filled her ears, blocking out every other sound.

With a flip of the lever, the ticking stopped.

She sat up in her seat and ran a hand over her ponytail, gathering up any clinging blonde strands until it was a smooth single unit she placed on her shoulder.

"You can do this." She willed her finger to move, and the ticking began anew. The arrow blinked to the right.

Natalie opened her eyes. This felt better. She turned down the air a notch, the roar of the fan dropping enough for her to hear the lowing of a cow.

A cow. Natalie dropped her head to the steering wheel again and listened to the turn signal. She hit the lever, and the blinker stopped.

"Then again, I have to go somewhere." She hit lever, and the arrow began ticking to the left. She clenched her fists, and flipped it off again.

"I could live in a box. Add some curtains. It wouldn't be so bad." She closed her eyes and groaned. It felt so good she did it again. Louder. She didn't usually give in to self-pity, but this last month had sucked up every ounce of moxie she had left. Natalie groaned again, getting into it. Surprisingly, it helped.

Tap. Tap. Tap.

Natalie jerked upright, caught sight of a hulking form outside her open window, and jolted back, squealing the high-pitched scream of a movie heroine about to be slaughtered.

"Yeah, I get that a lot." The voice was deep, masculine, and mildly amused.

Behind the man loomed a large, red, rumbling tractor that blocked the left lane. No cars approached in either direction, and even if they did, a tractor in the road was hardly an uncommon sight.

Outside her window, though *was* an uncommon sight around here—a stranger. A man, probably in his early thirties, she guessed, wearing a baseball cap pulled low over aviator sunglasses and a tanned face. He wore a Cardinal's t-shirt, jeans, and work boots—all of which looked a little worn and dirty, as though man and machine had just spent the whole day working in a field.

"How long have you been here?" she asked. She had no idea how she hadn't noticed a tractor pulling up next to her. Probably all that groaning.

"Are you hurt or something? I can call for help." He leaned down to peer in the car, probably looking for blood or broken bones.

"No, I was just...uh, breathing. More like groaning." Natalie cleared her throat and attempted a smile. "Thanks for stopping, but I feel better now."

The stranger straightened and took a step back, obviously convinced she wasn't dying.

"I couldn't help but notice your turn signal going back and forth. You lost?"

Natalie looked around, taking in the familiar surroundings. The driveway on the left led to her parents' home, her old room, three hound dogs sleeping on the porch, and two people who would welcome her home with open arms. They'd been so proud of her for living on her own in the city, but they would be happy she was back—their baby girl finally home to stay—happy until they found out why she was home. Then she would have to watch as their pride changed into disappointment

Another option was her older brother, Brett, who was living in a part of the old barn that had been remodeled into an apartment. He had once told her that each night before bed he went out in his boxers to check on his prize bull. Compared to him, Natalie's modest accomplishments seemed phenomenal.

Sure, she could probably wheedle Brett into letting her sleep on his hand-me-down couch in the barn apartment, but between living with the bull and living with her parents' disappointment...that cardboard box was sounding better and better.

Natalie knew she should turn her wheel left and head on home, help Mama with dinner, come clean about why she was back, and afterward sit next to Daddy on the porch swing while they came up with a plan for getting her life back on track. She could go to bed in her old room and sleep under the comforting warmth of the quilt Mama had made with love.

Natalie blew out a breath and stared down the long drive. She just couldn't face them yet. When she'd turned in her apartment key, gotten into her car and left the promises and heartbreaks of Memphis behind, she'd intended to go home. Now she found that she needed more time to work up the nerve.

Natalie looked at the gravel lane to the right. It was bordered by fields on each side, the grass tall and golden, swaying in the gentle summer breeze. There was a creek running across the lane about halfway down, shallow enough to drive over unless it was a flood year, when only tall trucks could get across. That held another possibility. One she hadn't considered before.

Natalie remembered the man standing outside her window. She blinked a few times and focused her attention.

"I know where I am. I just haven't decided yet where I'm going." For the first time in years, she mentally added.

The stranger nodded. "What are your options? Maybe I can help." He leaned back against the tractor, crossing one booted foot over the other, settling in.

"Disappointed," she said, her gaze on her parents' drive; her eyes turned to the lane on the opposite side of the road, "or crazy...those are my options." She held back a groan, but settled for a loud sigh.

The man nodded, took off the ball cap and ran his hand through his thick, brown hair. There was something vaguely familiar about him, like he was someone she ought

4

to know, but couldn't quite place—a memory that wouldn't surface—but maybe not a total stranger after all. He put the cap back on and looked down each driveway, and Natalie once again focused on the problem at hand.

"Well, I can't tell you what to do. I don't know the whole situation. If it was me, I'd choose crazy." His mirrored gaze settled back on her. She couldn't see his eyes, but a dimple appeared in one cheek. "Crazy is a lot more fun. At least with crazy, you don't always know what you're going to get from one minute to the next." He shrugged. "But then again, that's me. You might see it different."

Natalie looked back at the lane to the right with its idyllic appearance. She sighed and turned on her blinker. Crazy could be fun. It could be hilarious and spontaneous and caring. It could also make her want to scratch out her own eyeballs and slam her head in the door of the deep freeze.

"You going to be alright?"

Natalie turned back to the mystery man and his tractor. She nodded.

"Crazy it is."

He pulled off his sunglasses and blue eyes, the color of the clear summer sky, stared back at her. The niggling feeling of recognition came back. He reminded her of someone. She was sure she hadn't met him, though. In this neighborhood, you were well-known before your first birthday, and every day afterward was spent in the spotlight of small town life. This man, with those blue eyes and that one dimple, would have made an impression on her from age thirteen on up, a fact that she acknowledged with an inward shrug. She wasn't in the market for a handsome face, dimple or no dimple.

"Good luck with crazy." He slid on his sunglasses, climbed back on the tractor, and watched as she raised a hand in a wave, then aimed her car down the lane, leaving the driveway to her parents behind her, untraveled for now.

"I'm going to need all of the luck I can get."

***

AJ had recognized Natalie James the moment he'd seen her sitting in her Prius, blocking the road. She was just as beautiful as he'd remembered, and twice as pretty as the pictures on her parents' walls. It had been about twelve years. After that summer, he had gone away, and though he'd moved on, she had stayed in the back of his mind all those years. Now that he was back in Big Springs, living with Gramps, AJ had started to think about Natalie James more and more.

Just like that, here she was, driving back into town and back into his life. He started up his tractor. He had work to finish. But knowing that Natalie was next door, well, that was something, wasn't it?

Chapter 2

The old farmhouse had been built sometime around the Great Depression by Natalie's great grandparents: one-storied, wood-sided, and built with love and salvaged nails. The old milking barn, now full of sentimental odds and ends, was farther down at the end of the drive. The farm was a relic of days gone by, days when Natalie's own grandmother had helped milk the cows twice a day and had slept outside in a hay wagon on hot summer nights.

Steeling her nerves, Natalie climbed the front steps. She considered knocking, but hearing her grandmother's voice inside, went on inside.

Even at seventy-two, Grandma Gertie, Gigi, had bounce in her step, though that might have to do with the iPod attached to the hip of her hot pink capris, with a white cord stretching up over a bright yellow tank top.

Not for the first time, Natalie noticed her own resemblance to her grandmother. They had the same blonde hair, though Natalie wore hers long and pulled back in a sleek ponytail, while Gigi's hair was cut into a stylish bob, fluffed and teased up like a true Southern belle, "The bigger the hair, the closer to heaven." Then there were the bright green eyes and full lips, though the face that reflected back was aged with lines from a lifetime full of laughter, despite Gigi having been a widow for almost fifty years.

Gigi was in the kitchen rolling out a pie crust, her back to the door. Natalie started forward, but stopped when she heard the familiar lyrics of Dolly Parton's "9 to 5" belted out like Gigi was auditioning for American Idol. It's safe to say that she would not have made it to Hollywood.

"Gigi?"

The older woman shrieked, the wooden rolling pin raised above her head.

"Sorry! I didn't meant to scare you!"

"No, darling. It's alright. Did I scare you with this rolling pin? I've lived alone so long, you bet that I know how to defend myself. You're lucky you weren't a robber."

Gigi pulled down the hem of her tank and smoothed her hair, trailing the cord of the earbuds around her neck like a scarf. While she may have once been a knockout in the traditional sense, she had aged some since then. However, no one with a lick of sense would ever suggest to Gertie Gale that she was anything less than the blonde bombshell she'd been in 1970 when her bikini-clad image had graced the pages of Vogue and the walls of prison cells and garages across America.

"Well, thanks for not rolling me to death, Gigi. What kind of pie are you making?"

"Oh, just a little something to keep me busy. An apple pie. You never know when you're going to need one." Her grandmother peeked out the window at the car in the drive. She narrowed her eyes at it.

Natalie snatched one of the apple slices off of the cutting board. It was crisp and tart. Gigi pulled a pitcher of sweet tea from the refrigerator. Natalie got down two glasses from the cabinet.

Her grandmother sat down at the table and took a sip of her tea. "Are we going to keep dancing around this, pretending you're just here to visit and I didn't see your car full of suitcases and boxes? Because we can talk about the weather if you want to."

"Sure is hot out," Natalie responded. Gigi raised an eyebrow and waited. Natalie heaved a sigh, sat down hard in a kitchen chair, and let her head drop to the table.

"You have no idea." She took a large breath, bracing her hands on the table in front of her. "I got fired. Me! Valedictorian. Most Likely to Succeed. Straight A's in college, well, except for that philosophy class, but the main point is that I am unemployed!" Natalie stood and began to pace, gaining steam. She took another starting breath, only to be interrupted.

"Salutatorian."

Natalie whirled around. "What?"

Her grandmother rolled her eyes. "You graduated second in your class. Technically. If you're labeling your achievements, at least get them right." She took a drink of her tea and reached into the rooster shaped cookie jar for a snickerdoodle.

"You *know* that Jessica Carlisle was disqualified at the end of the semester. They found out she'd plagiarized her final paper for senior English. I was valedictorian. I gave the speech."

"Oh, that's right. Now tell me, I've forgotten, who was it that discovered the girl had cheated on the assignment?" Gigi gave her a condemning stare.

"I was editor of the newspaper. It was my job to investigate pressing issues." Natalie clenched her fists and sat back down at the table.

"Still, some kindness, some forgiveness. Both go a long way."

"I know." Natalie's shoulders slumped. "I felt bad about it. I apologized later. I actually tried to give it back, you know, let her give the speech and all, but the principal wouldn't let me." Her grandmother reached out and patted Natalie's head, skimming her comforting hand over the hair and down the ponytail.

"I know you have a good heart, but you're impulsive sometimes, especially when it comes to opening your mouth so you have somewhere to put your foot. It's a family trait, I'm afraid." She offered a reassuring smile. "So, tell me what you need. A place to stay?"

Natalie nodded.

"If I let you stay—" her grandmother started.

Natalie gasped. "*If?* You'd kick me out?"

Gigi snorted.

"Back to your parents' house across the street? You'd hardly be homeless, doll." Natalie frowned but nodded again. "If I let you stay," Gigi began again, "you're going to have to earn your keep. Until you get another real job or back on your feet or whatever." She sat back in her chair and folded her arms across her chest.

"Earn my keep how?" One thing that she knew for sure about her grandmother was that nothing was ever as easy as it seemed. A simple trip to Wal-Mart to buy pantyhose had once resulted in the entire women's department being shut down and searched by drug dogs.

Natalie knew better than to blindly trust that whatever deal she made should be taken at face value, and no matter the circumstances, she would never, ever shake on it. That was as good as a deal with the devil. Not that she would ever call her grandmother the devil—at least not to her face.

"You won't be my maid or anything, but just help out around the house and the senior center. We could use you down there, getting it all started. You're a lot of things, sweet cheeks, but most of all, you're motivated—at least you usually are when you aren't having a pity party. If I know you, you'll help get the place up and going in no time." Gigi shrugged.

"What senior center?"

"Oh, well, I guess you wouldn't know, would you? When they built that new kindergarten building over there near the baseball field, they turned the old one into a senior center. They had to make some changes, of course. Those toilets were practically on the floor. Henrietta Sellers tried to use one when we were in there scoping the place out, and once she got down there, she couldn't get back up. I had to go get Pastor Matt next door at the church to come help me pick her up. Poor Henrietta hasn't been able to look him in the eye since. She's been thinking of converting, that way she can go to St. Peter's and won't have to see Pastor Matt every Sunday."

Gigi winked, then stood from the table.

"That's the deal. Take it or go across the street to your mama and daddy." With that said, she left the room. The woman knew when to make a dramatic exit.

Natalie wasn't averse to working. She'd been working her whole life—she started out on the farm, feeding horses and cattle. Then she had pushed herself in school to get out of Big Springs, Arkansas and off that farm to a city with an art museum and fancy restaurants and more than one traffic light. No, she wasn't averse to work. She was just disappointed that it had come to this. Nothing was working out the way she had planned.

She allowed herself a final groan before she called out, "I'll do it," then mumbled to herself, "Who's crazy now?"

***

Natalie carried in her suitcases, stacking them on the bed in the guest room at the end of the hall. The room was overwhelmingly pastel with walls the color of pink baby lotion and framed pictures of flower arrangements. One wall was filled by a painted wrought iron daybed covered with a handmade quilt. Another wall held an antique oak vanity with a large three-part folding mirror, two small drawers on each side, and a little tabletop that the padded bench tucked under. Gigi's father had built it for her as a sixteenth birthday present.

Natalie ran her hand over its smooth, well-tended surface. Their family had never had a lot in the way of luxuries. Sad stories had been passed down about the Great Depression and how Natalie's great grandfather had struggled to hold onto the farm and the home he had built for his family, until finally he had gone away to find work with the WPA, leaving his wife and kids to tend the animals and themselves on the small amounts of money he could send back home. They survived the hardest times relying heavily on turnips and prayers, somehow holding on until better days.

Even though they didn't have much in the way of material goods, the family members had cared for what they did have and cherished what was precious to them. She could see their loving touches in this house, in this vanity, and in the way her family continued to take care of each

12

other. Any one of them would have taken her in. Being loved was a given, and Natalie knew she was blessed.

Right now, though, she was trying very hard to feel that way, to find those warm fuzzy feelings down deep in herself. She was hurt, humiliated, and just plain mad.

Natalie left her bags packed. She slipped off her shoes and crawled into the comfort of the bed. The pillow was cool against her flushed face. She didn't want to cry over him. She was a grown woman. She could cry over the loss of her job, over the loss of her apartment, over coming home with her tail between her legs after all the mistakes she had made, but Natalie would not let herself cry over a boy who didn't love her back.

Chapter 3

Natalie definitely smelled bacon and maybe biscuits. There was coffee in the air too. She considered her options. She could get up and investigate the delicious aromas wafting through the house, or she could stay buried under the blankets for the rest of her life. Granted, it would be a short life devoid of bacon and biscuits, two essential ingredients of life in the South, but it would be a cozy existence where she wouldn't have to face anyone or explain anything...except perhaps why she didn't want to get out of bed ever again. Crap. She was going to have to get out of bed, and she didn't even remember going to sleep.

Groaning, Natalie pulled back the covers, discovering she was still wearing yesterday's clothes. At least she'd hung the blazer up in the closet before coming in with her bags. Otherwise, it would be ruined. Her skirt and blouse looked like...well, like she'd slept in them. Her teeth felt fuzzy, and her mouth tasted like Bigfoot's armpits. Or what she imagined Bigfoot's armpits would taste like. She needed coffee. Grabbing her toiletry bag, Natalie headed for the bathroom.

Two steps out, she collided with Gigi in the hallway.

"Oh, sweet heavens, girl! You nearly gave me a heart attack. Don't do that to an old lady!"

"Sorry. I didn't mean to sneak up on you." Natalie pushed her hair from her face.

Gigi smiled sweetly. "I heard you coming. You just startled me with that head of yours. Between the wild hair and not taking off your makeup last night, you look ready for the loony bin. I thought some psycho had murdered my beautiful granddaughter in her sleep and was coming for me next." She patted her chest, her eyes crinkling in amusement at her own joke.

"It's too early for you to be funny." Natalie stepped into the bathroom and closed the door.

She heard her grandmother muttering to herself, "That's what you think. I've been up since four thirty, thinking up that line, and I still had time to make breakfast. "

Fifteen minutes later, Natalie emerged into the kitchen, went to her grandmother, who sat at the table with a cup of coffee and a crossword puzzle, bent and hugged her, kissing the top of her head.

Gigi patted her arm. "Well, now, that makes up for your lack of humor earlier. As soon as you're ready, we will head on into the senior center to get started for the day."

Natalie went to the stove and helped herself to bacon, eggs, a biscuit, and a cup of coffee. She really didn't eat this kind of food anymore, having forced herself to adopt a low-fat, healthy diet when she'd moved out, but she also reasoned that since it had been a rough couple of days, she deserved some of Gigi's cooking. She took a bite and nearly melted with pleasure. Oh yeah, she definitely needed this.

Natalie spoke around a bite of biscuit with strawberry jam. "Gigi, I really know nothing about senior centers. What can I possibly help with?"

Her grandmother frowned. "What can you do? Sweetheart, you can do a lot. We can always use a good, strong, young person to help out with the physical stuff, hanging banners and moving the coolers, but we can also use someone with your unique talents."

Natalie blinked. "What talents? I don't have any talents. I used to ride horses, but I don't think you need a Pony Express rider. I can't sing any better than you can. I am terrible at math, so I can't do your taxes or anything. I can't even juggle. Plus, I always lose at checkers." She frowned into her plate. Where had all the bacon gone? It didn't count if she couldn't remember eating it. She took her plate to the stove and added a few more strips. Crispy, just the way she like it.

Gigi huffed, "We don't need a juggler. We need *you*, Natalie. You're driven, so you'll get things done. You're creative, so you'll have better ideas than just bingo and knitting circles. But most of all, darling," her grandmother paused dramatically, taking Natalie's hand," you're fun. That's what that place needs more than anything else— someone to remind us old geezers how to live, shake it up a little." Her grandmother gave her a meaningful stare, stood up, taking Natalie's empty plate to the sink. "Go put on some make-up, and then we'll go," she said, the matter closed to all discussion.

"I wasn't planning on wearing any make-up today."

Her grandmother's beautifully-coiffed head whipped around, and Gigi spoke through perfectly lined and painted lips. "We are going to see people today. People we know. Go put on your face, so they won't think you've got the flu or a broken heart." She kept staring, her gaze intense and patient while Natalie sat, staring back. Gigi raised an eyebrow, and Natalie sighed and went back to her room to do as she'd been told.

***

Big Springs, Arkansas started growing in the late 1800's after local landowner and entrepreneur Pete Kressner discovered that veterans from the Civil War were flocking to towns like Eureka Springs, which lay a little over a hundred miles to the west, and Hot Springs, which flourished in the southern part of the state. Pete was certain that he could make something big out of the spring pouring from a craggy hillside into the icy, crystal clear stream that flowed through the western edge of his property and wound its way through the Ozark Mountains until it finally emptied into White River a several miles away. He didn't know if his spring held any medicinal healing powers, like those the other towns' springs were rumored to have, but that didn't stop him from advertising that it did.

While it wasn't as successful as the others, possibly because this spring was frigid where the others were steamy, Big Springs did attract visitors who would stay in the cabins Pete had built near the picturesque mouth of the spring. They drank the water, went on walks along the creek, and swam in the deepest swimming hole in the summertime, as young folks still did, despite the chilly temperature of the water. The addition of a rope swing helped to draw the young and the daring there year after year.

Of those visitors, a few stuck around, convinced the spring had worked its healing magic. Those people set up businesses, formed and joined the churches, and had children who had children who had children who inherited and ran the businesses and sat in the family pews.

What the town of nearly a thousand people lacked in change, it made up for in charm. It still hosted tourists,

17

though not for the healing waters. Instead, tourists came to climb the various hiking trails the city had remodeled around the spring, which was now part of a city park. They hiked, camped in the parks or enjoyed the quaint bed and breakfast, visited the natural cavern—discovered in the years after World War II when a veteran who had served in the Navy had gotten lost and used his keen survival skills to find shelter—discovering the cavern entrance in a jagged and ominous-looking corner of a hollow just inside the large park's back border.

The townspeople had never been clear on how a man skilled in survival had gotten so lost, but someone suggested that perhaps Navy men didn't *need* to know their way very often, since they were usually picked up and delivered by a ship. It's the commonly accepted theory today and has become a part of the cavern's history as related to visitors.

The fishing was decent, but not spectacular. The roads were winding and hilly with a few straight stretches on which the local police set up speed traps. It wasn't a fancy town, or a trendy town, or an important town, but it was home to Natalie, and as she rode in, sitting shotgun in her grandmother's Jeep Wrangler, staring out at the scenery that was as familiar to her as her own childhood, she felt like even more of a failure.

She'd always sworn she wouldn't be one of those people who lived with her parents into her twenties, eating in the same restaurants, buying all her groceries at the same store as everyone else, so that everyone knew the time of the month when she bought tampons and chocolate ice cream. She didn't want to follow the trend set by her classmates of selecting a husband from the yearbook because there was no way to meet anyone else.

Natalie looked down at the creek as they crossed the bridge, just as they got into the city limits. It was still flowing, reflecting the blue sky and the leaves of the overhanging trees. Despite her sour mood, she couldn't help but marvel at the landscape, seeing it with fresh eyes.

"Still pretty, isn't it?" she observed.

"Always will be, I expect." Her grandmother crossed the train tracks into the city limits and onto Main Street, which stretched out in front of them. "It's a comfort to have some things you can count on in this world."

Natalie nodded, noticing that Main Street had retained its comforting sameness as well. A quarter mile of shops lined each side of the two-lane road. There was space for eight businesses, four on each side, though they were all rarely occupied at once. Main Street held two of the town's four restaurants, Millie's on one side and Barb's on the other. Millie's sat in line with Blondie's Salon, the pharmacy Big Springs Drug and Dry Goods, and the hardware store. If the hardware store had an official name, only the owners and their accountant were aware of it. The opposing side contained Barb's, two empty storefronts, and the chamber of commerce, which was situated on the corner overlooking the creek. Big Springs citizens, who had called themselves Springers long before Jerry Springer was born, were a close bunch. They shopped locally when they could to support their friends and family members.

Gigi said, "I figured we could take care of some things, and then maybe order carryout from Barb's later. We can eat in the dining room at the center while we make some plans."

Natalie frowned. "Why aren't we eating whatever they serve at the senior center's cafeteria?"

"They don't serve meals there except for when we do a potluck dinner. Before you ask, I don't know why not. That's for you to figure out. If you can get that problem solved, we'd all be pleased as punch." Gigi took a right turn past the hardware store and continued down a steep hill, finally pulling into the parking lot of the remodeled building where Natalie had attended kindergarten.

"There's something else that looks exactly the same," she commented.

"We changed the sign." Gigi pointed toward the small white brick and concrete sign in the green lawn out front. The old blue and green letters had been pulled off, and a white painted sign labeling it *The Big Springs Senior Center* had been screwed down in their place.

"I stand corrected." Natalie pushed her sunglasses up on top of her head and smoothed down her ponytail.

"Come on in and let me show you the new toilets. You'll really be amazed by those."

Natalie followed her in, noting the small changes. The main office looked similar, but now the secretaries' desks and the front counter were clear, but instead of looking clean, it looked like a museum robbed of all its artifacts. A few lonely flyers lay out on the long countertop, and a calendar on the wall exhibited only a few events scribbled next to the dates.

The smell, industrial cleaner with a hint of urine, brought back memories of walking these halls as a five year old. The same fluorescent bulbs reflected long, bright strips on the shiny, waxed floor. A mural of children holding hands welcomed visitors to the school. Truth be told, the painting had always creeped her out. No matter where she stood in the hallway, the kids' eyes seemed to follow her like cheery little demons. Rumor said it was haunted. Natalie shivered and scuttled past.

In the former cafeteria, she found the long lunch tables had been replaced with cast off dining room sets, all mismatched. The placemats and salt and pepper shakers were equally haphazard. Someone had stapled on one wall a quilt with a map of Arkansas, the fabric featuring apple blossoms and honeybees and diamonds.

"See? Isn't it a lot different now that you're in here?" Gigi's excitement poured out with every word. Natalie would almost swear her grandmother was dancing from room to room, hands fluttering and flapping at every small alteration.

"It's great," Natalie lied. "What do you need me to do first?" She hoped it wasn't to clean the bathrooms. The smell of urine got stronger with their proximity to the restrooms, and Natalie was sure that she knew why.

"Come with me." Gigi turned toward the hallway that led to a row of former classrooms. She stepped into the first one and flapped her hands in the air. "I need you to turn this into an exercise room."

Natalie stared. It was a classroom—chalkboard, pencil sharpener, bare white cinderblock walls painted with the alphabet along the top. The desks and cubbies had been removed, but it looked as much like an exercise room as Gigi looked like Jillian Michaels.

"How?"

Her grandmother shrugged her shoulders. "I don't really know. I thought you could figure that out."

Natalie's eyebrows went clear up to her hairline. "Do you have any exercise equipment?"

"Mabel Whitmore is donating her treadmill."

"One?"

"It's a start." Gigi's hands settled on her hips.

"Oh. Oh, no." Natalie sighed. "Are you sure this is what you want me to do? Can't I just mow the lawn or organize the cupboards or something?"

"No. That stuff is all taken care of by other volunteers. What we need is an exercise room where mature adults can get a little activity without busting a hip. We don't want to train for the Olympics or anything, just get our old joints moving a little."

Her grandmother rarely lost an argument, and Natalie could tell that arguing was futile. No matter how much she fought it, sooner or later she'd be working on how to get octogenarians to do cardio without having a heart attack.

"Fine, I'll do it."

"I know you will. Now come on." Gigi started for the doorway. "I'll show you the rest of it, maybe introduce you around a little."

"I know everyone in town. I wasn't gone that long," Natalie said, following obediently.

"I know that, but people change. Henrietta dyed her hair black as pitch and looks like Cher. I want to make sure you recognize her.

"She looks like Cher?" Last time she'd seen Henrietta Sellers, the older woman had been about five feet tall and round as a pumpkin with tight gray curls styled into a helmet framing her aged cherub's face, rosy cheeks and all.

"Well, not exactly like Cher, but that's what we tell her to boost her confidence. After the potty incident with Pastor Matt, we do what we can for the poor dear." Gigi took off down the hall until she reached a dimly lit room. Inside there was a small circle of faded recliners and a worn, floral loveseat set up around a large, flat screen TV that was showing *Days of Our Lives*.

Gigi put her finger to her lips for Natalie to be quiet. They just stood behind the group, watching the television drama unfold until a commercial came on, then Gigi stepped into the center of the circle in front of the television.

"Hey, ya'll," she said, waving for Natalie to join her, "you remember my granddaughter Natalie, don't you?" She put her thin arm around Natalie's waist, almost like she was posing them for a picture.

"Sure, I do, darling. How are you?" Henrietta heaved herself out of the recliner and stepped onto the braided rug at her feet. Natalie had been mistaken in her memories of the woman. In her stocking feet, Henrietta was closer to 4'10". She embraced Natalie, who had to bend over considerably.

"Miss Henrietta, so good to see you again. Your hair is something, isn't it?" Natalie spoke in the sweet, polite voice that was reserved for talking to old people and the credit card company.

"Oh, it's too much for me, but I like it," Henrietta giggled, patting her ebony helmet. It wasn't quite like Cher's, but the older woman beamed anyway.

"Well, self-confidence becomes you," Natalie offered. She stepped back to see the next person in the line of her grandmother's friends, Mabel Whitmore, formerly the head cook for the high school cafeteria.

"Miss Mabel, good to see you too." Where Henrietta was short and round, Mabel was tall and muscular, wrapping Natalie in a firm, but quick hug. Clearly, lugging around those pots of mashed potatoes had built muscle on the woman, and she looked exactly the same as Natalie had remembered her, like a drill sergeant whose only nod toward femininity was a long, gray braid hanging down her back. Though her apron had obviously been left behind in her former profession, she had that cool efficiency of movement that bespoke her ability to prepare a meal for two hundred in under three hours.

Mabel spoke, her voice a little husky, "Just as pretty as ever, isn't she Charlie?"

Natalie turned to the next in line—Charlie Jackson, who lived down the road from her parents and Gigi. He'd always put up Christmas lights on his barn every year. Some years he'd spell out greetings, others years he'd shape a star or a Christmas tree. All year long, he had a smile for everyone and smelled like peppermints.

"Charlie!" Natalie gave him a genuine hug, instead of a polite one. "It's been too long."

"Almost four years," he said, patting her back.

"I was so sorry to hear about Eileen. She was such a sweet, special lady."

"That she was. She thought the world of you too— always said you were like a granddaughter to us." His smile had faded a little, but his blue eyes were shining with affection. "And now you're spending the day with Gertie, who looks lovely today." He winked at the older woman, who was watching their interaction with interest.

"Oh, Charlie," Gigi waved him off, a slight blush coming to her cheeks. "Believe it or not," she went on, "Natalie is going to be staying with me for a while."

Henrietta, Mabel, and Charlie all burst out at once with exclamations of surprise and joy and congratulations to Gigi, who beamed.

"You two beauties will have to come over and have dinner with us single men one of these evenings," Charlie offered.

"Who are you putting on, Charlie? You, cook? If we want to eat more than hot dogs or macaroni, we will have to cook and have you gentlemen over to my house." Gigi nudged Natalie's arm.

"Absolutely! Our pleasure," she said, still confused. This felt weird. Was she agreeing to a double date with her grandmother and Charlie and some other elderly man? Not that Natalie disliked older men. Some were downright sexy: Robert Redford, Sean Connery, and well, surely there were others. But that didn't mean she wanted to go on a date with one.

"Who else are we talking about?" Her voice was timid, carefully polite.

"AJ," Henrietta offered, wiggling her gray eyebrows suggestively.

"AJ?" Natalie asked, looking from face to face. Mabel was blushing and fanning herself in a very un-Mabel-like way. Henrietta's eyebrows were wiggling so fast Natalie was a little concerned she might hurt herself. Gigi and Charlie were grinning at each other, oblivious to the facial acrobatics going on around them. The whole situation had little creeping fingers of doubt crawling up Natalie's spine.

"Uh...I don't know," she said.

Gigi snapped back to attention. "Oh, you know him. AJ," Gigi said, nudging her granddaughter's arm again. All that nudging was starting to hurt. "Andrew Jackson." She spoke slower this time. Natalie shook her head. "Andrew Jackson," Gigi said louder. "Andrew," she repeated.

"The president?" Natalie asked. The older women threw up their hands.

"I don't know how any woman could forget him." Henrietta's eyebrows had stopped wiggling and were now pulled down in a disapproving frown.

"Me neither," Mabel added. "That man leaves an impression."

"But isn't he seeing that sweet girl from the hardware store?" Henrietta asked the room. Natalie shrugged. Most of the older ladies in Big Springs could be labeled "sweet." It was the tea. If you drink enough, it goes to your personality...and your hips.

"They're not married. Not even engaged," Gigi protested. "No harm in inviting two nice gentlemen neighbors over for a fried chicken dinner."

"Fried chicken?" Mabel asked, eyes hopeful.

"You're not invited, dear. You'd be a third wheel," Gigi informed her friend. Mabel deflated. Gigi turned back to Charlie. "Why don't you men come around tonight about six?"

Charlie started to speak, when Henrietta burst out, "Oh, we missed some. Shoo! Shoo!" She shook her hands at Gigi and Natalie, who scurried away from the television. Charlie gave them a thumbs up as they headed out the door.

"Gigi, I appreciate you trying to help, but--" Natalie began. Her grandmother fluttered a hand in the air.

"Oh, shush. I've had my eye on Charlie Jackson since Eileen passed, bless her soul. This isn't about you, dear. I know you're nursing a broken heart." They had been walking down the sterile-looking hallway, when Natalie stopped.

"How did you know?"

"Oh, honey, it's written all over your face. Or, it was this morning when your mascara had run all the way over to your ears from where you'd been crying in bed." She gave her granddaughter a one-armed hug. "You just hang in there. Keep busy. Keep living, and it'll get better." Natalie squeezed her in return, grateful for Gigi's quiet understanding, never intrusive or demanding. "So, let's get you busy turning a kindergarten classroom into a senior citizens' exercise room."

Chapter 4

As they walked in the door of the house a little while later, Natalie could sense trouble...or maybe she could detect the faint scent of White Shoulders perfume. Her grandmother walked in the door behind her and froze.

"Oh, crap! Your mama's here," she whispered.

"Language, Gigi." Natalie's voice was equally hushed. Neither had moved.

"Sorry. I didn't mean to offend your sensitive, young ears." Apparently her grandmother got snippy when frozen with the fear of imminent disaster. Good to remember. She watched as the older woman slipped off her shoes and padded across the floor in her stocking feet, as nimble and silent as any ninja who ever qualified for Social Security.

"I can hear both of you," a curt voice said from the other room. Gigi stopped, wide-eyed. She looked at Natalie then swung her head to look at the doorway to the living room. She gave her granddaughter an apologetic look and ran down the hall to her bedroom, slammed the door, and with a click the door was locked.

Natalie eyed the distance to her own room at the end of the hall. It was pretty far, but if she really committed to it, she could probably get there in less than four seconds.

"I'm waiting, Natalie Ann James." It was a voice which brooked no opposition. The voice that says playtime is over, and you are totally busted.

"Hi, Mama," Natalie said with feigned cheer, as she turned the corner of the doorway. Her mother, DeeJay James, stood in the middle of the room, hands on her hips. If she'd had a death wish, Natalie would have remarked on how similar her mother's actions were to Gigi's—like mother like daughter. They even looked similar, though Natalie's mother was quite a lot taller, having inherited her height from the paternal side. Perhaps that was also where she'd gotten her practical, sober disposition, though that could also be a byproduct of growing up the daughter of Gertie Gale.

"Don't you 'hi' me, young lady. Do you know how I heard you were in town? From Susan Appleby. I'm shampooing her hair, and she starts going on about how proud I must be, what with my Natalie being home and helping out at the new senior center. I had to act like I knew, just so I wouldn't look like a complete fool."

Natalie took a breath and opened her mouth.

"Oh, no. You do not get to talk yet. I'm not done telling you how hurt I am." Her mother paced in front of the window, the afternoon sun setting her blonde frosted hair ablaze. Combined with the intensity of her expression, she had the look of an amazon warrior—if the amazons wore lipstick. "What are you doing here? How long are you here for? Why are you here at your grandma's and not at home with the rest of your family? And what about your job? Are they ok with letting you have time off? And the senior center? What is going on with that?" Her mother's arms had crossed; her toe tapped. "I'm waiting."

"Can I talk?" Natalie asked.

"Don't be smart with me."

"It's a long story." She sat down on the couch. Her mother did not.

"I've got time."

"I was going to tell you eventually. I just needed some time to figure out...well, it doesn't matter." Natalie clasped her hands together until her knuckles were white, and said it quickly. "I got fired."

Her mother gasped. "What did they fire you for?"

"It's complicated, but basically, it was for gossiping."

"That's ridiculous. No one gets fired for gossiping. They can't do that. No one in Big Springs would have a job if that were the case—men included."

"Well, Memphis isn't Big Springs." Natalie winced. That came out a little sharper than she'd intended. "It's really more of a company policy that I broke. I said something nasty about a co-worker over the e-mail. They made an example of me, I guess." She shrugged.

"So what did Brantley have to say about it? He's high up in the company, a vice president of something. Besides, his uncle is the Wallace in 'Baxter-Wallace Marketing,' right? Couldn't he get your job back for you, talk to his uncle or something?"

"No." Natalie shrugged. "Well, maybe he *could*, but he didn't."

Her mother finally sat down hard in a wingback chair... "Did you guys break up?"

Natalie shrugged, reconsidered, and then nodded, her eyes still fixed on her hands. She needed to get a manicure. She sat on her hands so her mother wouldn't notice. No reason to add insult to injury.

"No chance of getting back together?"

Natalie shrugged again, blinked hard, and finally shook her head, turning her watery gaze to the row of African violets in the windowsill. The room remained silent for several long minutes.

Her mother cleared her throat, then said, "Your apartment? The one we helped you move into? It was so cute with the balcony and the swimming pool."

Natalie shook her head again, slumping further into the couch.

"Why are you shaking your head? Are you out of money? I'll need to talk to your daddy about it, but we can probably lend you some money for rent and all. Just until you find yourself another job and get settled on your feet again. Not that I'm sad to see you home, you know that I'm tickled pink that you're back in Big Springs. Why you're at Gigi's and not home with me is another matter. Regardless of that, I know how much you loved living in the city. You can stay here through the weekend, and then after church on Sunday we can drive back to Memphis with you, help you unpack, maybe finally spend the night and take you out to dinner. We can see the ducks at the Peabody. I never have gotten over there to see those ducks."

Natalie took a deep breath and let it out slowly. It had been almost a year since her parents had come to visit her in Memphis. With her mother's salon and the family farm, something always came up that made it hard to get away.

"I don't have my apartment anymore. I gave it up."

"Already? How long ago were you fired? Good grief! You should have called before you let it go. Maybe it isn't too late. Why don't you call the property manager and we can--"

"No, Mama. I can't get it back. I gave it up back in December."

Natalie watched her mother's forehead crease. She blinked several times, her mouth gaping open like a fish flopping around on the banks.

"But that was a full six months ago. How did you...where have you...? Have you been living with Jenn or something? I thought she lived with her cousin, or was it her sister?"

Natalie shook her head. She didn't want to have to say the words out loud. She knew how her parents felt about the matter, and hadn't told them on purpose, to save them the heartache and worry. To save herself from having to feel the weight of their disappointment.

"Well, you weren't living nowhere! You weren't living in your car..." Realization dawned in her mother's eyes. Natalie knew the moment it happened and would carry that image with her always. It was like looking at a house fully lit up with Christmas lights, shimmering, and then one strand goes out. The house is still lit up, still shining, but it isn't as bright as it was before. This was what Natalie had dreaded most, what she'd tried to avoid for the past six months.

"I'm sorry. I thought that Brantley and I—"she broke off. What could she possibly say without sounding pathetic? That she thought that she and Brantley would get married? Where was the ring? Where was the proposal? That she thought he loved her? Where was he now? "I'm so stupid, Mama. I don't know when I got this stupid, or if I was always an idiot, and I just had everyone fooled up until now."

"Don't you talk like that! My baby girl is not stupid." Natalie's mother was by her side in an instant, her arms reaching and pulling her close. Natalie breathed in the floral scent of her mother's perfume and melted into the familiar comfort of the embrace that had eased the pain of a million tears.

"I'm so sorry, Mama. I know you're disappointed in me. I don't know how this all happened. It seemed like such a good idea at the time. His apartment was closer to work, and he said I didn't have to pay rent or anything. I thought I'd save a bunch of money, and besides, I thought...well, you know what I thought. I wouldn't move in with a guy if I didn't think that he loved me."

"Did you love him?"

Natalie wasn't sure how to answer that question. If she'd been asked a week ago, the answer would've been easy. Looking back on it now, though, she wasn't so sure. On one hand, it hurt that Brantley hadn't so much as sent a text message to her. On the other, well...it was almost shocking how unsurprised she was, like she'd always known somewhere deep down that something like this would happen. Brantley had been fantastic on the surface. He was handsome, head-turning handsome. His sandy blonde hair was thick and wavy. His smile was straight and white, as perfect as a toothpaste ad. He always had a little bit of a tan and dressed like he took the pages of GQ with him to the mall. What she hadn't realized was that the gorgeous exterior wasn't anything more than fancy wrapping on an empty box.

After living with him for several months, Natalie had discovered that Brantley bleached his teeth. He had his hair professionally highlighted to look like he'd spent hours outside in the sun. He owned his own tanning bed, and really did take a copy of GQ shopping with him, but he wouldn't be caught dead in a mall. Beyond the handsome exterior, though, Brantley Wallace had been, well...boring. He read fashion magazines, and though Natalie wanted to look nice, it wasn't her passion. He went out, mostly to bars or clubs. She had gone along, but had tired of it after a few times.

They weren't going to any of the music hot spots that Memphis was known for. Brantley preferred to listen to classic rock cover bands in smoky places that served appetizers that cost more than some of her blue jeans. He never wanted to go to the park or to any of the festivals or historic sites. She'd spent more time with her friend Jenn in the past month than she had with her supposed boyfriend. The shine had worn off the relationship a while back, but Natalie sure hadn't thought he'd completely abandon her, especially in her time of need. They had a history and a friendship that warranted more than that. At least she thought so.

"Not anymore. That probably means I never really did love him, but it seemed like it at the time." Natalie lay her head on her mother's shoulder. She closed her eyes and relaxed as she felt her mother's hand start to smooth her hair back. It was just like when she was little. Her mother would run her hand over Natalie's hair, and before she knew it, the world was alright again.

"This isn't going how I planned," her mother said on a sigh. "It doesn't feel right to scold you when you're down. Kind of ruins my day. I'd built up some steam, and was looking forward to letting loose. I haven't gotten to do that in a while."

Natalie let out a sharp laugh, then another. She looked up at her mother, who smiled down at her.

"You're a mess, girl," she said, laughter finally bubbling out.

"I know," Natalie laughed too, though the sound was tinged with sadness.

"Fired for gossiping? Who ever heard of such a thing? Oh, my. You know your father is going to be thrilled to find out this can all be blamed on me. All that beauty shop gossip growing up must've ruined you."

"No, Mama. It was my fault. I shouldn't have said what I did, especially not in an email."

"Those computers aren't nothing but trouble. We've got one in the shop now, but I won't touch the thing." Her mother nudged Natalie up to a sitting position. She slapped her hands across her thighs and rocked herself up off of the couch to her feet. "Ok, well, go get your bags. You can help me with dinner, and we can figure out how to tell your father about this without it looking too much like either of us is to blame. The part about your apartment. Well, we won't lie about it, of course. But there are some things it's just best that your daddy don't know. I've got a roast and potatoes in the slow cooker. We'll eat dinner come up with a plan for how to get you back to Memphis, if that's what you want. Or you can finally settle down here. Susan Appleby was telling me how her sister's boy is single again. You remember Robby. We took you two to the movies one time when you were thirteen. He was such a cutie, wasn't he? The bowl cut was unfortunate, but I'm sure he's got a different style now. He's just down in Conway. That's not too far for a date…or more. No pressure." She stood up, straightened her blouse and looked down at her only daughter expectantly. "Go on and get your things. Why are you just sitting there?"

Natalie didn't move. "Mama, I'm staying here with Gigi."

Her mother's face froze in an expression of open-mouthed horror that would be comical if it hadn't been sincere. She finally sputtered, "But...but...Natalie, you can't stay here. Why would you want to? Gigi's crazy."

"I am not crazy. I'm quirky. And old. You're allowed to be quirky if you're old." Gigi scampered into the room in her stocking feet, screeching with indignation.

"You were listening to our conversation?" Natalie's mother huffed, hands on hips.

"Of course! I was hiding around the corner behind that bookcase in the hallway." Natalie and her mother just stared. "Don't look at me like that! I'm quirky...maybe eccentric. That's different than crazy." Natalie and her mother shared a knowing look. "Besides, Dolly Jean, she can't go and eat *your* dinner. I got company coming, and she's going to help *me* with the fried chicken."

"Mother, please don't call me Dolly Jean. You know I hate it."

"You can't hate the name Dolly. It's just not American!" Natalie and her mother looked at each other again. "I'm quirky!" Gigi scowled. "Fine, DeeJay." She made a face like it pained her to use the abbreviation. "Thank you for stopping by, but we've got to get started on supper. Besides, I've still got to primp some before they come over. My hair's gone flat."

"Who's coming over?" Natalie's mother raised an eyebrow.

"Charlie and AJ Jackson," Gigi answered, her own eyebrow rising in challenge. There was a silent standoff. Neither woman relented, neither eyebrow fell.

"That's Andrew Jackson. Not the president," Natalie added, breaking the tension. Both older woman sighed.

"Of course, not the president," Gigi said in exasperation. "He's dead."

DeeJay pointed at Gigi. "See what I mean? Crazy."

"Quirky!"

Natalie gave her mother an apologetic smile. "I know, but I'm going to stay here for a while anyway, help Gigi out, and be useful."

DeeJay threw her hands in the air. "I don't understand it, but you're an adult, and I will *respect your wishes*." She said the last part loudly.

"I called you by your initials once, didn't I, DeeJay? See, that's twice."

Natalie's mother sighed. "Fine, but, you're coming over tomorrow night—wait, I can't do tomorrow night. We're playing cards at Lila's." Her eyes narrowed. "You're coming to church on Sunday morning. Don't even think you can get out of it. People will be expecting to see you." She gave her daughter a stern look and turned to leave the house. As Gigi was about to shut the door, Natalie heard her mother call out, "Leave that poor AJ alone. He's not on the market. The last thing this family needs is more gossip going around about us. Lord knows I've got enough to deal with as it is." Her words trailed off into mumbling that continued until Gigi made a face and shut the door hard.

"Let's start cooking. Those men will be hungry, and you know the way to a Southern man's heart is with fried chicken."

"I don't want to put any ideas in this AJ guy's head. Tell me. Is he bald? Does he have age spots?"

Gigi burst out laughing, bending over and holding her sides. "Oh, honey, ask me that again in an hour!"

Chapter 5

They had a dinner invitation. AJ had showered, shaved, put on a touch of cologne and his nice jeans. After talking to her yesterday, he had gone to town and bought a new shirt. He'd been told once that he looked good in green. Something about his eyes or some other girly reason like that. Whatever. He'd take all the help he could get. He'd spent the better part of yesterday in the hot, dusty field, and hoped to make a better impression when he saw her tonight.

The last time he'd seen Natalie, AJ had been barely twenty, and she'd been all of sixteen and absolutely off limits. He'd kept his distance, at war with himself between the urge to go and talk to the pretty blonde and the need to stay away, far away, until she was older. Good sense had won out, and he'd barely said two words to the girl who lived down the road from his grandfather.

Instead, he's spent most of that summer hanging out with her older brother Brett, hauling hay and shoveling manure in the daytime—playing basketball, eating pizza, and camping by the creek at night. On the weekends they went fishing or swimming, but he'd always talked Brett into leaving the swimming hole if Natalie and her friends had shown up, feeling guilty for noticing how she filled out that pink bikini. Other boys didn't pay her much attention. She was good looking enough to turn their heads, but they weren't willing to risk their necks with Brett looking out for his baby sister.

AJ couldn't say he didn't feel like hitting Jarrod Ferrell the one time the cocky kid had whistled and mimicked swatting her behind. In fact, he hadn't needed to knock the guy out. Brett had done it in one punch, and Jarrod hadn't looked Natalie's way ever again. Neither did any other boy that summer, which was fine and dandy by him.

AJ hadn't spent the last twelve years pining away over her or anything like that. He'd dated, had two girlfriends he'd cared a lot about. The first had gone off to law school in California after they'd graduated from college, while he headed east to Quantico for the Marine Corps' Officer Candidates School, or OCS. The second serious girlfriend, eight years later, hadn't wanted to stick around after he'd decided to leave the Corps and move out here to help Gramps. She liked towns, loved cities, and wanted a man who wore a soldier's uniform, not the jeans and boots of a farmer. So, they'd gone their separate ways.

But now, there was Natalie. Next door. Waiting for him to come to dinner. Well, him and Gramps. Not exactly a great first date, but beggars can't be choosers.

Gramps called out from the living room, "Boy, you about ready to go? Don't want to keep the ladies waiting." The old man had taken only half the time to get himself ready for dinner, but these days he spent most of his time taking it easy, leaving the dirty work to AJ. It was the way it should be. Though farmers never really retire, Gramps had earned a little rest.

"Hold your horses. I'm coming." AJ checked his reflection one final time. He tugged on his cuffs and sighed. At the very least, he'd be clean this time.

"You're sure slicked up for a simple dinner," Gramps pulled a comb out of his front pocket and ran it through his hair without even looking in a mirror. He replaced the comb, tucking it back into this shirt pocket with an assortment of pens.

AJ looked at his starched clothes in the mirror and cringed. "Is it too much?"

His grandfather snickered. "I haven't seen you this cleaned up since your senior prom, Romeo. Now, get out the door. Punctuality is good manners, and women like good manners."

AJ knew he was making too much of a simple dinner, acting like an idiot, especially given that it was a double date with their grandparents. His Marine buddies used to give him a hard time about being so smooth with women, a real ladies' man. If they could see him now, they'd never let him hear the end of it. Heck, he probably deserved all the ribbing they could dish out, not that this was a story he'd ever share. Charlie and AJ pulled up to the house, the diesel pick-up rumbling as AJ sat, letting it idle, staring at the house.

"Manners, boy. Move it," Gramps said, jumping out of the cab of the truck and walking toward the front door of the farm house.

AJ took a deep breath and let it out slowly. He turned off the truck and stepped down. It was a blonde, not Baghdad. His long stride ate up the distance so that he was at his grandfather's side when Natalie opened the door.

"Charlie, look at you! All cleaned up and so handsome," she gushed, pulling the older man into a hug. "And this must be—" Natalie paused, her eyes widened, and then she looked him up and down. His skin heated. "Andrew Jackson?" she finished, seeming a little unsure.

"AJ," he corrected, putting out a hand. Natalie stared at it for a moment, before she seemed to gather her wits and shook it, smiling politely. AJ noticed how soft her hands were compared to his own calloused ones.

"AJ, it's nice to meet you. I'm sorry," she said. Her eyes narrowed. They were light blue, the color of a cloudless sky. "I was under the impression you...well, never mind. My mistake."

"Not a problem. My given name is Andrew, but I go by AJ."

"Well, it's nice to meet you, AJ. Why don't you both come in?" She opened the door fully, stepping back to let the men pass.

"About time you invited them in," Gertie said behind her. "Charlie, come on in. Can I get you a drink?" The older couple went into the living room to sit in the wingback chairs by the picture window, too wrapped up in each other to take notice of the pair they'd left standing by the open door.

Natalie stood to the side, and AJ entered the house, the delicious aromas filling the house made him all the more pleased to be there. There was something about a homemade dinner. In the past few years he'd come to appreciate them more and more. Since Grand had passed away, he relied on invitations from other people's mothers and grandmothers for real home-cooked meals. They were a rare treat. And a home-cooked meal with Natalie James? Nothing short of a miracle.

Natalie closed the screen door behind him, leaving the main door open to let in the cool evening breeze. AJ watched her move, graceful and just as beautiful as she'd always been. That hadn't changed. In fact, she was even more of a knockout than she had been. While she'd been a pretty girl at sixteen, now she was a woman.

She looked up at him and smiled again, the perfect hostess. "Can I get you a drink?"

"Sure." He smiled back and stuck his hands in his pockets.

"We've got sweet tea, water, lemonade, and Coke." She listed the options as she led him inside.

"What kind of Coke?"

She shrugged. "That's a question you can only ask in the South! I'm not sure. Come and check it out. We'll let the old people flirt in private."

"I heard that!" Gertie called out from the other room.

"Thanks!" Charlie added. AJ grinned and followed Natalie to the kitchen. She opened the fridge door and bent over. AJ stared at the wallpaper. He really did. The temptation to take in the eyeful that she was unintentionally presenting was intense. But the little red cherries on the wallpaper were nice too, and he knew that staring at them wouldn't haunt his conscience.

She straightened, presenting him with the can to inspect, holding it over her arm like a waiter at a restaurant presenting a fine wine. Natalie raised an eyebrow. He nodded, and she stepped back and turned to get a glass down out of the cabinet.

"Oh, I can drink it out of the can," he said.

"Not at Gigi's house, you won't. Didn't you know only heathens and criminals drink out of the can?" She filled the glass with ice and held it toward him.

"No, I can't say as I did know that." He smiled and took the glass from her outstretched hand, his fingers connecting with hers, accidentally on purpose.

"Well, now you do. You wouldn't want to be unfairly labeled." She hesitated, rubbing her fingertips against the pad of her thumb where his fingers had brushed her. "I'd better get this chicken going or we'll never eat, and clearly my grandma does not intend to leave the living room." Natalie gave him another quick smile.

"I think my grandpa's as eager to be there as she is to have him."

Natalie turned on the heat under a large cast iron skillet, and AJ tried to think of something else to say. He'd never had trouble talking to other women. Look at Jamie. They were practically best friends, and he talked to her every day. Natalie got down another glass and filled it full of tea, then leaned a hip against the countertop near the stove. They stood for a long, awkward moment eyeing each other across the kitchen.

"You're tall," she said, her face serious. She seemed to be trying to measure him, gauging his height against the height of the fridge.

"I'm a hair short of six foot five."

She flushed a little and turned quickly away, reaching above her for the Crisco from the top shelf, stretching and not quite reaching it.

"I'm more like five foot five. Whoever invented top shelves clearly didn't have me in mind."

"I'm good with top shelves." He reached up above her and handed it down, stepping back quickly. "It's doorways and stairwells that get me." AJ pulled out a chair at the table and sat. "That better? Now we're closer to eye-to-eye."

She nodded and took a sip of her tea. "I didn't mean to be rude." AJ watched her set her glass down, then reach up to pull on her ponytail.

He cleared his throat and concentrated on the conversation. "Nah. I get it a lot. Six foot four is a little taller than most. Do you know who Laura Ingalls Wilder is?"

"The writer? I read all of those *Little House on the Prairie* books when I was little."

"Have you ever been to her house? It's a museum now. It's in Mansfield, Missouri." He watched as Natalie stirred the shortening around the pan, shifting it so it would melt. She shook her head.

"She was a small gal. Not even five foot, if I'm remembering it right. Her husband wasn't a big guy either."

"I remember in the books where her daddy called her 'Half Pint'. I didn't know she was always small, though."

"When she and her husband built their house there in Missouri, they built everything down to size for her. I visited it with my grandma when I was a kid. The kitchen countertop was about waist high to me. Even when I was small, I wasn't *small*, you know. I was ten or so, and I remember thinking that I could never live in that house. I'd be stooped over and cramped. From then on, though, I've always had this idea of building a house that was me-sized. Everything exactly the right height for me." He grinned at her.

"Less like *Little House on the Prairie* and more like the giant at the top of the beanstalk?"

"Precisely! The doorways would all be seven feet high, and the sinks would hit me where I could wash my hands without having to bend in half. I'd have step stools for guests, of course. I've got fifty acres that connects with Gramps's property. I could do it."

She shook her head and laughed, turning back to the stove to check the heat in the pan by dropping in a little bit of batter. She adjusted the knob and reached for her drink.

44

"How long was your drive into Big Springs?" He leaned back in the wooden kitchen chair and stretched his legs forward, crossing his boots at the ankle.

Natalie's hands flew to her face. "It was you on the tractor yesterday!"

He smiled, but quickly covered it up by taking a sip from his drink. She must be remembering all those groans she'd been letting out. She'd sounded like a cross between a cow at milking time and someone playing tug-of-war. Which she had been, he supposed, only her opponent was herself.

When she lowered her hands, Natalie was cringing. "I knew you looked familiar. I'm sorry for not recognizing you earlier. You looked...different yesterday." She turned back to the stove, her head bent in what he supposed was feigned concentration as she dropped in another little piece of batter to watch it dance and sizzle in the pan.

"I looked dirty." He chuckled. She glanced back at him, then slowly returned his smile. She turned back to the stove and began an elaborate process of dipping chicken into different bowls before putting them into the pan. The sound of frying chicken, bubbling and popping, was music to his ears. His stomach growled, adding its own bit to the melody.

"So are you here to visit or to stay?"

Natalie crossed to the sink to rinse off her hands. "I'm staying a while, I guess. I'm not sure how long, though. I sent my resume out to a few places in Memphis. I'm hoping to hear from some of them." She picked up a set of tongs and lifted a drumstick out of the pan to check how well it was coming along. Clearly it wasn't ready yet, as she set the tongs next to the skillet. She got down a platter from a low shelf in the cabinet and began covering it in paper towels.

"Memphis? I think I remember hearing from your folks that you were in Memphis. That's a long way from here." He tried to keep his disappointment out of his voice, clearing his throat. "So you're going to stay here with Gertie in the meantime? Not across the road with your folks?" She nodded, and he watched her ponytail bounce up and down. "So, you chose crazy after all," he said humorously. Natalie whipped around, horror-struck, hand over her open mouth. "Don't worry. I won't say anything," he promised.

She spoke in hushed tones. "No, that's not it. We call her crazy to her face all the time. I did it today. We just don't usually do it in front of anyone who's not family. She would be mortified. Don't say anything, please." Her eyes pleaded with him.

"I won't," he assured her.

"You won't what?" Gertie asked as she came into the kitchen. Natalie grimaced and turned to the chicken again.

AJ glanced back and forth between the two women. "I won't think badly of her if she burns the chicken."

"What? You'd better not burn that chicken! Let me see that." Gertie nudged Natalie aside and snatched up the tongs.

Natalie gave him a grateful smile and rolled her eyes when Gertie said, "No, it's fine, but I'd better take over, all the same. Natalie, dear, you take Charlie a can of Coke and then help me get the other dishes on the table." Natalie took a glass down, and AJ took it from her.

"I'll get this, and you can do the other."

"Oh? Thanks." She smiled up at him, and he reminded himself to breathe.

"Don't thank me. The sooner it's on the table, the sooner we can eat." He winked at her and took the glass to the other room, saying as he went, "Gramps, did you know only heathens and criminals drink from the can?"

The rest of the evening flew by. The meal was delicious, and Charlie and Gertie kept the conversation lively. AJ thought he saw Charlie reach under the table and grab Gertie's knee when he thought no one was looking. It weirded AJ out a little to think of Gramps touching anyone other than Grand's knee, but he was relieved to see Gramps smiling again. He'd taken Grand's death hard, but that had been a while ago and Gramps wasn't a natural bachelor. He was a husband, and a good one. He just needed a wife, and Gertie Gale seemed like she was interested in the position.

The women put the leftovers away, and the men carried the dishes to the sink, over Gertie's protests. She claimed the dishes could wait, then the older couple took their coffee to the living room.

"Would you like coffee?" Natalie offered. "Gigi has half and half in the fridge."

"No, thank you. I don't know how they do it. If I drink coffee this late, I'll still be awake come daylight."

"Me too. I'm getting a glass of lemonade. Would you like one of those? Guaranteed not to keep you awake all night."

"Sure. That sounds great."

The sound of Gertie giggling drifted into the kitchen.

"How long will they be doing that? Flirting or talking or whatever?" she asked.

He winced. "How about we take our lemonade out on the porch?"

"That long? Ok. Let's go." Natalie handed him a cool glass and carried her own. She called into the living room, "We're going to sit on the porch." She waited. There was no response.

AJ held the door open, "We probably don't want to go investigate. If one of them has a heart attack, I'm sure we'll hear about it. Otherwise, wild horses couldn't drag me into that room."

Natalie laughed and walked past him onto the porch where they settled onto a porch swing. The sun had set while they'd eaten, and the dim porch was lit only by the lights shining in from the windows. As she gave it a gentle push and they settled into a comfortable rhythm, AJ smiled and reminded himself to thank his grandfather later.

"Courting," he said.

"What?" Natalie asked. It was a roomy swing, big enough to seat three adults across, if the middle person didn't mind being glued to the others. So when she turned to him, her face was still a full twelve inches away. It was, however, the closest his lips had ever been to hers. Not that he was thinking about her lips.

"Gramps calls it 'courting.' He's been courting Gertie since about March. Taking her to dinner, BINGO nights at the center, the VFW dance, eating dinner here about once a week, that sort of thing. The two of them have quite the social calendar. Seems like they're always headed somewhere."

"This is the first time I've been invited on one of their dates. Usually, he just runs out of the house without as much as a 'see you later'. I only know where they've been

48

from all the talk going around town. I expect that Gramps doesn't want me knowing where he is. Maybe he's worried I'll want to tag along, ruining his mojo."

"He's got mojo?"

"He thinks he does, and that's good enough reason not to want me hanging around."

Her eyebrows lowered, as though she were working on a puzzle. "But you were invited here tonight. Why is that, do you suppose? Since this is the first time you've ever been invited along, there must be a good reason."

He nodded. "Logic would have me believe that."

"I'll bet you're here tonight to distract me, so they can court in peace, without being rude and leaving me out of the conversation or whatever they're doing in the living room. You're my distraction." She shook her head, amused.

"I'm happy to be of service."

She laughed, a deep, throaty laugh that hit him in the gut. She turned her eyes up to the dark, starry sky and sighed. "I'll say one thing for the country. The nights certainly are beautiful."

He looked out at the tapestry of stars, framed by the lush leaves of tall oak trees. A flashing light flew slowly, seeming to dodge between the stars. A plane full of people all going somewhere else. AJ had been on too many planes like that, headed somewhere he didn't want to be. Not tonight, though. Tonight he sat swinging on the porch, feeling a smooth, peaceful breeze against his skin with only the crickets, the peeper frogs, and the creak of the swing to break the silence. Nights like tonight were not to be taken for granted.

"No moon tonight, though." Natalie's voice joined in with the chorus of the evening. "I hope I'm still here when it's full again. I love to see the full moon." Natalie laughed, shallow and a little self-conscious. "I've been in the city too long, I guess. There's some things the city just can't compete with." She turned her attention to the sky again.

"What about the other things? Is Memphis that much better than Big Springs?"

She was quiet for a few long minutes, and AJ could hear his grandpa's booming laughter inside. "Not lately. It used to be great, but then...well, that has more to do with me than the city itself." She looked over at him then, their eyes connecting. Their gazes held for a long moment, nothing moving around them but the gentle rocking of the porch swing and the gentle breeze ruffling his hair.

"You should stay here." The words were out of his mouth before he could catch them. When he saw her face, he could've kicked himself.

The smile fell away, and she turned her gaze back to the sky. They were both silent for a few minutes. AJ spent the time trying to figure out how to pry his boot out of his mouth.

"Sorry," he finally said. "You know-- if I overstepped there."

"No, it's fine. You're right. It would be easy to stay here. Well, not here with Gigi, but here in Big Springs. But, you probably don't know this about me," she looked him in the eye, "I've worked really hard all my life to get out of this place. I love it here. It'll always be home to me, but I can't come back. Not for good."

"I'm not sure I understand," he admitted.

The swing stopped moving. "That's alright. You don't have to. I barely know you, AJ. Until tonight I thought you were an old man named after a dead president that Gigi was trying to fix me up with." Natalie's face flushed.

"Ah. The kill shot. Good one." She started to speak, but AJ raised a hand. "No, don't apologize. You look like you want to, but it's not necessary. I stepped on a nerve there, or more like a landmine."

"Sorry."

"That's alright. I survived it. Let's backtrack. What do you say?" He nudge the wooden porch with the toe of his boot and set the swing to rocking again. "Wow! That sure is a pretty sky, isn't it? Arkansas is one gorgeous place to live...or to visit. Both are nice. Equally."

Natalie laughed and the awful tension that had grown between them dissolved. "It is a wonderful place to call home."

"Agreed. Speaking of homes, are things much different since you've been gone? If I'm not mistaken, it's been a while since you've been back."

She sighed and considered, obviously pleased with the change of topic. "It's changed a little. The senior center is new."

"Yeah, I'd heard you were going to teach aerobics or yoga or something. If so, sign me up."

"No! I'm just helping to plan and organize and advertise some things. But not teaching the classes."

"You've got to draw the line somewhere, and since it sounds like you're doing everything else—"

"It's not so bad, only one day of it so far, though. Talk to me again after a week." Natalie reached a hand up and smoothed her ponytail.

"Will do." He planned on talking to her more than once a week, though. Once a day, maybe. "Anything else changed?" he asked.

"There's some names I don't recognize, though not as many now that I know who the mysterious Andrew Jackson is," Natalie teased.

"Yep. That's me. You can call me 'AJ'. Everyone does. Though I'd let you call me just about anything that you want. So long as you call me often, that is." Natalie grinned. This was shaping up to be the best first date he'd ever been on. With the exception of that one little snag, and the fact that he was double dating with a pair of senior citizens who were being entirely too quiet inside, it was perhaps the most romantic evening of this life. "Who else don't you recognize?"

"Well, let me think. I haven't seen her, but who is the 'sweet girl' everyone says is working at the hardware store. Last I heard, only Old Harv and Leonard worked there."

"You knew that Little Harv's boy graduated last year? He went off to the U of A to be a Razorback, like all good children do, or so I'm told."

"Don't bring that up around my daddy. He's still sore that neither of us went to U of A."

AJ laughed. Mr. James complained about those "rotten kids" all through football season, but only if the Hogs were winning. If they were losing, well then, "maybe those kids knew something, after all."

"So when the boy, luckily named Brandon and not Harv the Youngest, or something equally bad, went off to school, Old Harv and Leonard had to hire outside the family."

Natalie gasped dramatically, a hand covering her mouth.

"I know. It was quite the scandal. They hired Jamie Griffith. I think you two went to school together. And I would say that the description fits. She is a sweet girl."

Natalie's face lit up. "Jamie Griffith! Of course, I know Jamie. We were best friends in junior high. We kind of went our separate ways in high school, drifted apart, but I always really liked her. Wait. I thought she got married right after graduation? Moved to Harrison or Yellville or somewhere like that?"

"She did, but got divorced a few months later. Seems her ex-husband was fond of…well," he cleared his throat, then lowered his voice, "Have you ever seen the show *Sister Wives*?"

Natalie's eyes widened. "No! I mean, yes, I have, but you're not saying—"

"She left him and came back here. She was working at a daycare for a while, but then Leonard offered her the job. The rest is Big Springs history. Right after I moved to town, I went in there and met her, and ever since then we—"

Natalie interrupted. "Oh, I do remember now Mama mentioning that the two of you--" She stopped and looked down at her drink. AJ couldn't tell what was going through her mind, but whatever it was had knocked her back, stolen away the smile and the peace that had been there only moments before. "I could use some more lemonade. Would you like some?" She stood up and reached for his glass, which he relinquished willingly.

"I don't understand. What did you hear?"

The screen door swung open and a Gertie came out escorted by Gramps. They were holding hands so tightly a tornado couldn't have pulled them apart. Natalie stood behind them, a glass in each hand.

"There you are, boy. You ready to head out?"

AJ stood. "Yes, but—"

"It was so lovely of you to come, AJ. I know you probably had to cancel your plans with Jamie, but I'm so glad you could be here to entertain Natalie while your grandfather and I were—well, while we were—"

"Courting?" Natalie offered with a wink. "Yes, AJ, thank you for coming. Please tell Jamie that I'd like to see her sometime to catch up. It's been too long, and I always did like her." Natalie's smile was polite and didn't reach her eyes. He couldn't read the emotion behind them, but he got the feeling she was holding something back now that she hadn't been before. Like some kind of a dam had been built in a few quick moments, and whatever she was feeling was walled up behind it.

"I will tell her. Maybe I could see you again—"

She cut him off. "Oh, that would be nice. We can all get together. Go to Luigi's for pizza or something. Have Jamie call me here. Goodnight, Charlie." She hugged the older man and went inside, the screen door flapping shut behind her.

That hadn't gone the way he had hoped it would.

Chapter 6

After dropping off Gramps, AJ headed to his buddy Brett's place, also known as the old barn. Brett had been trying to give it an official name—The Barn House, Brett's Bouse—but so far nothing had caught on. Brett may have been in his early thirties, but he lived like a college freshman. Carefree and casual. AJ opened the door and went in.

"Hey, man! You can't just barge in here without knocking or whatever. I could've been with a girl or something." Brett was sitting on the couch in his boxers eating Chips Ahoy out of the package with a mixing bowl full of milk in front of him. A basketball game was on the TV.

"You're eating cookies. What's with the bowl of milk? Are all of your glasses dirty or something?"

"No, this is my cookie bowl. Watch." Brett picked up a cookie from the package and, using two fingers, dipped the whole thing into the bowl, submerging his fingers up to the second knuckle. "You have to let it soak a minute to soften up." They waited, the sounds of the game filling the empty space. "Now you eat it." He lifted the dripping cookie out of the bowl, leaned over the top of it, and shoved the entire thing in his mouth, milk dribbling down his chin. He wiped his face with the back of his arm.

"That's not a bad idea, actually. But, I'm not here to discuss cookies. I've got a problem, or a question." AJ scratched his head, pulling at his hair. "I'm not sure which. Maybe both."

Brett sat the cookies on the coffee table. "Alright, shoot. I'm ready."

AJ stood and crossed to the fridge to grab a bottle of water. He used the seconds to try to figure out how to word the fear that had been creeping up on him in the minutes since he'd dropped off Gramps. The conclusions he'd been drawing about Natalie's comments weren't adding up in his favor. "Want one?" he asked Brett, holding out a bottle of water.

"No. I have an entire bowl of milk in front of me. Was *that* your question? You came all the way over here to get me a drink. How nice." Brett leaned back and propped his feet up on the beat-up old coffee table, one foot on each side of his box of cookies.

AJ scowled. "Don't be a jerk. This is serious." He sat on the other end of the couch, took a long drink, and then put his elbows on his knees, hands massaging his brow. He'd given up drinking alcohol a long time ago, but this was one of those instances when if he'd been a drinking man, he'd be taking shots of whiskey to ease the pain and loosen his own tongue. As it was, he had to rely on his own strength to get through it.

"I just heard something tonight. About me and…about me and Jamie. I was wondering if you'd heard anything. You know, about us." AJ dug his hands into his hair again.

"No, man. I haven't." AJ sighed. That was good. Then Brett added, "Except of course, that you two are seeing each other most nights, and that last week you didn't get home to Charlie's until morning. I heard that. But nothing too awful bad. Most folks figure you're as good as engaged anyway."

Panic seized him. He'd experienced panic before, too many times to count. But his training had always carried him through. He knew how to keep a clear head with the world began to shatter into a million splintering shards. He breathed deep and let it out slowly before he began to speak.

"I'm not seeing Jamie. Not like that."

"Seeing. Dating. Sleeping with. Engaged to. Whatever you want to call it. Not my business."

AJ took in another deep breath and focused on choosing his words wisely.

"No, I mean, we aren't romantically involved. At all. I don't see her that way, and I'm pretty sure she doesn't see me that way either. We're friends."

Brett nodded. "Hmm. You're just friends. You're sure you don't have feelings for her, but are you certain that she doesn't think it's more than that?"

"I'm pretty certain," AJ said.

"You put that word 'pretty' in front of it. Makes you not sound really certain at all." AJ's could feel his pulse behind his eyeballs. "Tell me one thing. If you two aren't, you know, 'involved,' what were you doing at her place until the wee hours? Just playing gin rummy or Monopoly or something?" Brett wiggled his eyebrows.

"No!" AJ stood, pacing to the other side of the room. "We were watching a movie. It was one of those girly things that she picked. All top hats and long dresses and stuff. I fell asleep on her couch."

"Yeah, but—"

"By myself!" AJ roared.

"Ok, ok. I believe you. But what's the big deal? You know people talk. Why do you care?" Brett leaned forward and took a cookie from the box.

"I don't care what everyone thinks. Forget them. I just care what one person thinks."

"Jamie?" Brett gave a knowing smile and put his milk bowl back in his lap.

The magnitude of Brett's words sank in. This was about more than just Natalie, the beautiful girl who had walked back into his life after so many years away. It was about more than the slim chance that she'd want to see more of him, to spend time with him, to give him the chance he hadn't been able to take when he'd fallen head over boots in love with her so long ago.

No. This was also about Jamie, his best friend. Watching as Brett sat his milk bowl back on his lap and sank a cookie in, he acknowledged that while Brett was his best buddy, Jamie had been his truest friend this past year. Ever since they'd started talking at the counter of the hardware store, they'd been nearly inseparable. No wonder folks thought there was more going on than there was. They went to the county fair together, were each other's Valentine's dates this past year, went to dozens of movies and restaurants side by side. They even sat by each other in church half the time, depending on whether or not Jamie was helping out with the nursery. But in AJ's mind, they had been nothing more than friends. Not quite brother and sister, but more like first cousins. Definitely not kissing cousins. The closest they got to romance with each other, was a hug once in a while when Jamie was feeling down—usually something some busybody had said about her divorce and her status as a "fallen woman". That kind of hurtful nonsense needed a hug.

"Maybe there are two people whose opinion matters to me."

"Two? Who else? Another woman?" The milk bowl clattered back to the coffee table, milk sloshing over the side, and Brett dropped his feet to the floor, leaning forward in interest.

"Yeah. And no, I'm not telling you who. I've barely spoken to her. We've had one date. A sort of date." He clenched his fists, crushing the now empty water bottle. It probably didn't count if Natalie didn't consider it a date, but considered it being distracted. "I'm counting it. It felt like a date to me."

"Did she dress up?" Brett asked.

"No." But she had looked pretty.

"Did you kiss her?"

"No." But he'd wanted to.

"Did you pick her up at her door and take her out? Buy her flowers? Hold her hand?"

AJ shook his head.

Brett blew air out his mouth in exasperation. "Did you even ask her out? Did you physically say the words, 'Will you go out with me?' and did she respond in the affirmative?"

AJ scowled.

Brett smirked. "Not a date. Also, a little sad. You might need to see a psychologist about those delusions you're having."

"I'm leaving."

"Ok, well, thanks for stopping by," Brett said, taking up his cookies and milk again.

AJ growled as he closed the door behind him. He could hear Brett's laughter all the way to the truck. It was too late to call tonight. She had to work in the morning and would already be in bed, but tomorrow he had to talk to

Jamie. He had figure out if she was his girlfriend. That was one thing a man ought to know.

Chapter 7

The next morning, Natalie woke up much earlier than normal and was surprised to see her grandmother already drinking coffee in front of *The Today Show*. Natalie shuffled in, barefoot and groggy, unashamedly wearing her flannel pajamas with snowflakes on them. It didn't matter that it was summer. Comfort knows no season.

"Good heavens, Gigi, what time did you get up?"

"I get up at four-thirty. Every morning."

Natalie poured herself a cup of coffee.

"What do you do? Wait. Never mind. I don't want to know." She settled in on the couch, pulling her legs up under a knitted afghan.

"Want to talk about Brantley, then?" her grandmother asked. Natalie pulled the afghan up over her head, but her grandmother's words carried into her knitted cocoon. "I met him at Christmas," Gigi reminded her. "He seemed like a nice enough boy. What happened there? You were saying his name in your sleep."

Natalie snapped the throw back down, giving the older woman a wary once over. "When you get up at four-thirty you don't stand over my bed and watch me sleep do you?" She looked innocent enough. If you didn't really know her, that is.

"Sometimes I do. You'll understand when you're a mother. But not last night. No, you called out real loud and angry-like. I hopped right up out of bed and brought along my baseball bat, but you were sound asleep. Not an intruder to be found. Don't you remember me shaking you?"

"I don't remember that at all. I guess I had a bad dream," Natalie admitted, a little embarrassed, a little ashamed.

"I'd say so. I peed my jammies. Had to change my britches."

"Did you really?"

"No, I was just trying to make you feel bad, maybe guilt you into telling me what's going on." Gigi leaned over and covered one of Natalie's hands with her own. Her touch was cool, but comforting. "You weren't—"she began. Her grandmother cleared her throat. "Honey, what I'm trying to ask is, well, did he hurt you? The way you called out, you sounded so sad and so helpless. I can't help but wonder if maybe he hit you? If he did, you need to know, it's not your fault—"

Natalie turned her hand over and gripped her grandmother's. "No. Nothing like that. No man has ever laid a hand to me, Gigi." Tears welled in her eyes, and she blinked them back. "Thank you for asking, though. And for bringing the baseball bat. It means a lot to me that you'd take on an intruder to save me."

Gigi squeezed her hand. "Honey, I'd take on the fires of hell if I had to." The older woman sniffled and released Natalie's hand. She turned away, swiped at her cheeks and took a sip of her coffee. "Well then, now that that's settled, I think it's about time that you told me the whole story. Don't think it's slipped my mind that you haven't filled in all the details yet. You told your mama some of the story, but not the whole thing." She held up a hand. "I know. I know. It's bad to eavesdrop. I wouldn't do it if I didn't have to. No one tells me anything. If I didn't listen at keyholes, so to speak, I wouldn't ever find out anything. So, out with it, little missy."

Natalie stared down into her coffee, its dark surface still and calm, not at all how she felt right now.

"You aren't going to like parts of it, Gigi."

"I don't expect that I will, dear. I'd like to hear it anyway. And more than that, honey. I think you need to tell the whole thing. It'll make you feel better to get it all out of you. It's no good, holding it all in like that. It'll start to fester."

"Some parts of the story, some parts about me, aren't very good. I've made some mistakes."

"All the more reason not to hold them in. Best to get them all out of you. Be rid of them."

Natalie nodded her head. She knew her grandmother was right. Crazy as the woman could be, she was as wise as King Solomon. So Natalie sat there in her snowflake jammies, clutching the knitted afghan around her and poured out the story, detail by detail. Even the parts that hurt to say aloud. To know how far she had fallen from the idealistic girl with the drive to move mountains to what she had become. Lost.

"So you really called her that? In an email? You typed out the words and everything?" Gigi asked. She may be a bit eccentric, but even Gigi was too prim to say the name out loud. That was one line she had never crossed for as long as Natalie had remembered.

Natalie nodded, ashamed. She'd spoken the words, said them in front of her grandmother. It had been so easy to type the nasty name out, one letter at a time, but to say them for the ears of this woman who had bought Natalie her first Bible. It had torn a piece out of her heart knowing what she must think of her granddaughter now.

Gigi rubbed her fingers over her lips, deep in thought. She nodded and closed her eyes. If Natalie didn't know better, she'd think that the older woman was napping. It wasn't sleep that Gigi was retreating into. It was prayer.

After several minutes, her eyes opened, and she focused her gentle gaze on Natalie's worried face.

"We all do things that we regret, baby girl. In my generation, we were more apt to say them out loud or write them in a letter. Even if we didn't do that, I know that I thought them in my heart more than once." Her eyes crinkled as she smiled. "I thought something terrible about that Susan Appleby just last Sunday. And at church of all places. I had to pray for forgiveness right there on the church steps." Natalie's lips quirked into a small smile. "Now, I have never called anyone that name that you did, but it's not because I wouldn't. It's just that your particular turn of phrase isn't in my naughty vocabulary. I'm more likely to call someone a 'dirty harlot' or a 'scheming old slut' or a 'loose-legged tart'."

Natalie covered her ears with her hands. "Gigi! I can't believe you said those! I've never heard you say anything like that before!"

"Oh, you stop it now. I don't say them out loud. I think them, though, and that's just as bad as saying them. So, don't you be thinking that this thing you've done is anything worse than what anyone else has done. Not really." Gigi shrugged her shoulders. "Except the part where you got caught and they fired you for it. That's pretty bad. Does that go on some kind of permanent record?"

"Like in the principal's office or something?"

"Or the internet," she offered.

Natalie considered. "I don't think so. A future employer might not like it. Might not hire me because of it. It's a mark against me, but more like one of honor, I guess."

Gigi nodded her head, satisfied that there was no large record book of offenses hiding on the web somewhere, logging each person's offense and punishment.

"I guess you learned a lesson from all this, didn't you?"

"I did." Natalie looked down into her coffee. It was cold now. That was fine. The sun had come up and was starting to heat the air for what would surely be a scorcher of a day. "I learned more than one lesson, I think."

"Have you prayed about it?"

Natalie shook her head.

"Would you like me to pray with you?"

Natalie shook her head again. It didn't feel right going to God with the mess that she'd made all on her own, asking for His help and guidance when she'd been the one to get herself in this situation in the first place.

"Do you want to talk about how you came to be living with a man without a wedding ring on your hand?" Gigi asked, sipping her own coffee and raising a challenging eyebrow.

"Not at all." She'd hoped Gigi hadn't caught on to that part of her story.

"That's what I thought." Her grandmother reached over and patted her leg. "We'll save it for another day, but I'll be praying about it, and there's nothing you can do about that." She smiled and a light came into her eyes. "Tell you what? Today let's go to a bunch of garage sales and buy a lot of useless junk. It'll make you feel better. Why just last week, I found an old Thighmaster at Geraldine Everly's. It's not hardly been used."

Natalie stared at her in horror. Then someone knocked on the door and called out as he entered.

"Gigi, you here?" Brett walked around the corner into the living room and stopped with his mouth ajar.

"I'm here, handsome boy," Gigi said, the Thighmaster forgotten for now.

"Hi, Brett."

"Hey, Gigi. Hey, Sis. How long you been home?" He moved to give her a one-armed hug. "I didn't expect to see you here."

"Yeah, well, I am living here for a while, I guess. It's a long story, but the gist is that I'm back for a while. I'm staying with Gigi to avoid seeing Mama every day or I'd eventually have to flee the country to avoid the murder charges."

"Why don't you have a seat, Brett, and I'll make you two a nice breakfast. Bacon and eggs ok?" Gigi asked.

"Now, don't go to any trouble, Gigi. I can eat a Pop-Tart." Brett winked at Natalie, who rolled her eyes.

"Don't you dare! It's no trouble at all to cook a simple breakfast for my only grandchildren. A Pop-Tart! For shame!" Gigi began to bustle around the kitchen, opening and closing the fridge, pulling pans from cabinets, and waving away any and all offers of assistance.

Natalie could tell this had been her brother's plan all along. Mooching meals was an art form with him. He never asked. He never had to. People just offered him a meal every time he entered the room. By all rights, he ought to weigh three hundred pounds, instead of looking as trim at thirty-two as he had at his high school graduation. It would be so easy to resent him, but she just didn't have the heart.

"So you got a job in the works or anything?" He shoveled sugar into his coffee cup.

She shrugged and said, "Helping Gigi at the senior center in return for room and board."

Their grandmother sat the salt and pepper on the table. "Not weekends, though. You get weekends off. I'm not a slave driver. In fact, since it's a Saturday, I was just telling Natalie how we should go to some garage sales today." She walked back to the stove where the sizzling bacon was beginning to fill the air with its delicious aroma.

Brett's eyebrows went up in surprise. "You want to go to garage sales with Gigi?" he asked.

Natalie check to see her grandmother's back was turned and shook her head violently, eyes pleading for salvation, while saying, "If I'm not needed anywhere else instead, I'd love to check out some garage sales. Why just last week, Gigi found a used Thighmaster at one."

Brett nodded in comprehension. Then he got a look in his eyes. A look she had seen many times over the years. One she didn't like or trust. It was the sort of evil look only an older sibling could get.

"You know, dear sister, I was just going to go out looking for someone to help me today. I'm in a bind. I'm not sure what I'll do if I can't find someone to help me out." His face appeared both innocent and desperate. The Academy Award would be sure to follow.

Their grandmother placed a plate in front of each of them, both heaped with two fried eggs each and what appeared to be a half pound of bacon per plate. Then there was the buttered toast and jelly to the side. Natalie didn't know which worried her more—Brett's obvious scheming or what her butt would look like if she actually cleared her plate, though she was tempted to try it out and ignore the consequences. With the way her life was going lately, she really shouldn't chance it.

"Let's pray," Gigi said, holding out a hand for each of them. They clasped hands around the table, and the older woman voiced their gratitude for the food in front of them and the family beside them.

"Amen. Now, kids, there will always be other garage sales. I'm sure Natalie would love to help. I'd offer myself, but I've got plans for later on this morning. Now you two be sure to clean your plates. You'll need all the energy you can get." Gigi took a seat at the table, her own plate containing one lonely piece of toast. Natalie briefly considered sneaking some of the bacon off of her plate onto her grandmother's, but then decided that might gain attention. Moving her toast over to Gigi's plate, though, might just work. Maybe her grandmother wouldn't remember she'd only gotten herself one piece. She was old after all. Blame it on her memory. Bacon, though? Bacon was hard to forget.

Brett, however, wasn't worried about his weight, and when Natalie turned her attention back to him, she was amazed to see that he'd somehow already eaten most of his bacon and was eyeballing hers. She subtly nudged her plate toward him, but took one piece for herself. She wasn't trying to be a supermodel or anything. One piece of bacon wouldn't kill her. Neither would two, she decided, and took another.

"So, are you in?" Brett said, his mouth full of eggs.

"In to do what, exactly?" Natalie had learned the cardinal rule of sibling negotiations by age four. Never agree without knowing all of the conditions and keep an eye out for loopholes.

"Drive the truck in the hayfield."

"No way. I hate that job. It's hot as Hades in the truck, so I'll get all sweaty, and then all that dust and grass will stick to me." She pointed a finger at her brother. "Plus you'll just yell at me the whole time like you always do. Find someone else to sucker into it."

He pushed out his bottom lip, pouting. "Please. Pretty please."

She shook her head and threw a piece of toast at him. He caught it and started covering it in homemade grape jelly. While her grandmother's attention was turned, her face scolding Brett for his overuse of the jelly, Natalie slid her other piece of toast onto Gigi's empty plate.

Brett's face turned serious. He leaned his elbows down on the table and said, "I really do need someone, Nat. I don't know what I'll do if you don't help. There's no one else around today. Wyatt Arnett was supposed to help, but his parents took him on a camping trip to celebrate his eighth grade graduation."

She scowled, knowing the serious plea was just another of his tricks. "Is this a paying job?"

Gigi took up the jelly and carefully used a butter knife put a thin coat on the piece of toast that had been resting on her plate, as if to show Brett how toast should be properly prepared, saying, "Like that. That's all the jelly you need. Now, Brett, it's only fair that she get something for her time." She held up the toast, "and look, completely covered, and I only used a tiny little bit. Jelly doesn't grow on trees, you know." She winked.

"Sure," he offered his sister, "I'll pay your old salary."

Natalie gasped, dropping her fork and in the process dropping one of her eggs onto the table next to Brett. He slid it onto his own plate and dug in. It's a good thing she didn't like hers runny, or that hand-off would've been a lot more noticeable.

"There is no way I'll drive the hay truck for two dollars an hour. I was thirteen when I was tricked into agreeing to that. Absolutely not." She began eating her remaining egg before Brett got carried away and decided to make a go for that one too.

He stroked his chin. "I can see your point. Inflation. Cost of living increase. You do have a valid license now, I'm assuming." Natalie stuck out her tongue at him.

"Not at the table, young lady. Wait until after breakfast to do that," Gigi admonished.

Brett chuckled, spitting out little pieces of egg whites onto the table. When he'd calmed down, he wiped his face with a napkin and conceded. "Alright. You drive a hard bargain. In addition to five dollars an hour, I'll buy you pizza at Luigi's. A night on the town with the most handsome man in Big Springs." He leaned back in his chair and put his hands behind his head, preening.

"Like a date with my brother? I don't need your pity favors—hanging out with your poor, loser sister."

"Now, Nat, don't call yourself poor. That's not fair. The loser part, though, well that—" He jumped back a little bit. "Ouch! That hurt. What did you kick me with? You're not even wearing any shoes."

Natalie smiled sweetly and took a sip of her coffee. "I don't know what you're talking about. Gigi, did you see me kick him?"

Their grandmother shook her head. "I didn't see a thing. Where's the proof of this alleged kicking, young man?" Gigi gave Brett the same innocent smile and said in her sweetest voice, "I wouldn't recommend calling your sister a loser. We Southern women are tougher than we look."

"Sorry I called you a loser, Natalie. And I'm sorry if my shin hurt your foot when you kicked me so hard." He crossed his arms, pouting again. "I guess if you don't want to go out to Luigi's with me tonight, you can stay here with Gigi." He turned to their grandmother, "What did you say you were doing tonight?"

"Poker night. The girls are all coming over to get sugared up on virgin daiquiris. Except for Henrietta who is diabetic. We'll tell dirty jokes and gamble away the change from the bottoms of our purses." She grinned at the two shocked faces. "What? We old ladies know a *lot* of dirty jokes. We've had a long time to collect them, after all."

"Are these the same women I see in church every Sunday?" Brett asked, his forehead wrinkled in surprise.

"Oh, don't give me that. No one loses more than five dollars. And we aren't drinking real alcohol. But calling them virgin daiquiris for poker night just sounds better than saying that a bunch of old ladies are going to get together and drink slushies and slide nickels across the table at each other for three hours. Now you shoo and let us have our fun. I've got to go to the farmer's market and buy some strawberries."

"I'll drive the truck," Natalie said with quiet desperation, "but you've got to get me out of here tonight." She stuck out her hand to shake, but just as Brett was about to take it, she added, "And you've got to make sure I've got a ride home from Luigi's."

"I only forgot you that one time," he protested.

"Twice."

He shrugged his shoulders. "Whatever. I guarantee that you'll have a ride both ways."

They shook on it.

"I'll be ready to go in ten minutes." Natalie stood up, put her plate and cup in the sink and headed down the hallway to her room.

"Dress for the hayfield. No high heels or glitter or anything. And remember, we can't run the air, so it'll be hot."

"Like I could forget," Natalie shouted back before shutting the door.

Chapter 8

Fifteen minutes later they were pulling into the field behind the old barn, a gooseneck trailer attached to the old Ford farm truck. The barn was an older, rustier version of the barn Brett lived in, but instead of having living quarters, it had a large, empty space where they stored the small square bales of hay. The field stretched out into about 40 acres of pastureland. Most of it was dotted with newly-made round bales, five foot tall cylinders of rolled-up hay that would be picked up by a tractor with a prong on the back. Many would be sold, and the rest would be stored outside near the barn in several long rows.

Natalie took in the picture and smiled to herself. When she thought of home, she thought of scenes like this. The contrasting gold of the hay against the brilliant green of the fields was pretty in a way, but it was also peaceful to see what it represented to her family. Security. They'd store up the hay for the winter ahead, and their animals would be fed and cared for. One summer when she was about ten, her father had lifted her up onto the row of round bales and explained that to her. He'd told her how each bale was valuable in a way that had nothing to do with money. Each one had value because each one was useful. And that the same could be said about each of us. He told her that while they didn't have much money, they were still valuable, special people, and that it was up to each of them to decide how to be useful in this world. It made a soft glow of affection build in her chest to remember it. It also stirred some pangs of guilt. She hadn't seen her daddy yet since she'd been home.

The square bales, though, gave her an entirely different feeling than the round bales prompted. It was not so much a feeling in her heart as one in her gut. A feeling that was a lot like that one you get when you're so hot you think you're going to puke, but you never do. You just keep on sweating and wondering why in the world you would *ever* have agreed to do this.

The truck and trailer bumped along through the field, headed toward the five acres of square bales that looked small and insignificant compared to the round bales in the rest of the field. Their small appearance was deceiving, she knew. They were heavy and scratched exposed skin, leaving long red welts. Worse yet, they seemed to stretch out for miles in long rows to be picked up by hand and thrown onto the trailer.

Natalie turned her attention away from the hay and toward the maroon Dodge truck she'd just noticed parked at the edge of the field. "You expecting someone else?"

"Oh, yeah, that's AJ. He's Charlie Jackson's grandson. You probably don't remember him. When we were younger, he came during the summers sometimes to give Charlie a hand. He didn't live around here, but he moved back a little over a year ago. He's helping me with my hay today, and then next week, I'll help him to get his in. He's got little land right down the road."

"I met AJ actually.   I just didn't recognize his truck." Natalie watched AJ as they approached. He was sitting on the tailgate, elbows on his knees. He was dressed the same way he had been the first time she'd seen him—jeans and boots, a blue t-shirt that, while not fitting skin-tight, definitely showed off his muscular chest and arms. She'd bet he would have no trouble picking up those hay bales. Would probably have no trouble picking her up either, not that she was planning on falling at his feet or anything.

Natalie wasn't in the market for a new boyfriend, even if he wasn't spoken for. Unlike a former co-worker of hers, she would never go after another woman's man, but it didn't hurt to look. Like admiring a piece of art. Just because you noticed that the statue of the Greek god was handsome, didn't mean you were going to touch its butt, did it? Nope. So there was nothing wrong, Natalie told herself, with admiring her brother's friend. It would probably be wrong not to. Sort of like bypassing Michelangelo's David.

"You getting out of the truck, Natalie?" Brett asked.

They'd stopped. Her brother had turned off the engine and exited the truck, and Natalie hadn't even blinked, hadn't even noticed.

She was glad she had on her sunglasses, so neither of them could see that she had obviously been staring at AJ. That would have been crossing a line, she was sure. This wasn't really a museum, after all. Real life art appreciation has to be covert.

"Yeah, sure. I was just calculating how many hours it's going to take to get all those bales picked up."

"Probably about four hours. Maybe a little longer." Brett pulled out a small tube of sunscreen from his back pocket and began smearing it on his face in white streaks.

"Hi, Natalie. I didn't expect to see you here." AJ's baseball cap and aviator sunglasses hid his eyes, but his lips were turned up in a grin.

She smiled back at him.

"When did you two meet? I thought you said you'd never really talked to my sister." Brett looked at each of them.

"Oh, he and Charlie came over to dinner last night. Gigi and Charlie are courting, as they call it." She snatched the sunscreen from his hand and began applying it to her arms.

Brett's eyes narrowed. "Last night?"

AJ quickly hopped off the tailgate, slammed it shut, and said, "Let's get started before it gets too hot out here."

"Alright. Which way first?" Natalie put the cap back on the sunscreen, tossed it at her brother, and walked around to the driver's side of the truck.

Brett stood stock still and serious another moment. Natalie had no idea why he was acting so weird. AJ had jumped onto the trailer and was standing there, looking down at him. Brett was staring back. Neither man so much as blinked an eye.

"You ever get hold of Jamie today?" Brett asked him.

"She's not answering her cell. She works on Saturday's. They must be busy."

"You've got to get some stuff straightened out there."

"I know I do. I'm working on it." AJ never broke eye contact.

Brett walked to the edge of the trailer, still frowning. Natalie had no idea what was going on. They were obviously in the middle of some kind of a situation. The tension between the two was palpable, but she had no clue what it was about.

"Everything ok?" she asked. Everything had been fine a minute ago. She had no idea what had happened. Brett looked ticked, and she didn't know AJ very well, but he kind of looked like he was expecting Brett to take a swing at him. As angry as Brett looked, he just might.

Then Brett looked down at his boots, nodding to himself. He looked at Natalie, then at his friend. "You tell me, AJ. Is everything going to be ok?"

AJ nodded once. "I'll make sure it is." He stuck out his hand to Brett, who hesitated a moment before he took it, put a foot on the edge of the trailer, and hopped up. They each nodded at the other, then sat down to ride to the hay bales.

Natalie threw up her hands. "You guys are weird."

"Just get in the truck," Brett snapped at her. He sighed, bowed his head, and when he looked back up at her, he spoke in a gentler tone. "We'll pick up the bales on the east side first then work our way back. And go slow. I know how you usually drive."

"You aren't allowed to yell at me until I've actually messed up. That's the rule. Daddy said so way back when. No preventative griping."

Natalie climbed into the truck, rolled down the windows to let in the breeze, and took off at a snail's pace, aiming the truck and trailer between the rows of bales that lie on the ground. Her brother jumped down and began tossing the bales up to AJ, who stacked them on the trailer. They would switch positions at the end of the row.

Natalie played the radio and zoned out, singing quietly to the music. All she had to do was keep the truck and trailer between the rows and not go too fast or hit any bales when she turned a corner. It was an easy job usually relegated to those too young to throw the bales, but old enough that their feet reached the pedals. She had begun to qualify at age ten. She and Brett had both learned to drive this way, at eight miles an hour with nothing to hit but hay. It was only thrilling to those who weren't allowed to drive anywhere else.

Good grief, she was bored. She couldn't remember a time when she had been this bored. She starting turning radio stations, flipping from country to pop to oldies and back again, until she found a song she could sing along to. It didn't matter what station or style, if she halfway knew the lyrics, she belted it out. Anything to pass the time crawling down the endless rows. She even sang along with a classical song, improvising a little by making up her own words, most of which were about how bored she was, all of which she sang as loud as she could. Nothing else to do but steer the truck and sweat buckets.

Brett's face appeared, red and dirty. "It's full, I said!"

Natalie eased on the brake. "You don't have to yell."

"I said it like twelve times." He was sweaty and winded from jogging alongside the truck. Gross.

"I never heard you."

"Because you weren't paying attention. You were singing too loud. You're the worst at this job because you don't pay attention. Now scoot over, I'll drive us to the barn. You suck at backing up the trailer." The last part he mumbled under his breath, but Natalie heard him. As much as she hated to agree with her brother, especially when he was in a snit, he was right about that. She could hardly back up her little car, much less a long trailer filled with hay.

He took the vacated driver's seat, and she slid all the way over to the window. Natalie looked back and saw AJ climb in the back of the truck and sit on the edge of the bed, holding on to the cab. Looking out the back glass, her eyes were level with his chest. She blinked a few times in surprise. He was sweaty and his shirt was clinging. On him, the look wasn't gross at all. Kind of the opposite.

The truck hit a hard bump, and Natalie saw a few hay bales fall off.

"Who needs to slow down now?" she asked her brother. He scowled and turned the radio up, easing back on the gas as he did. She turned the radio back down.

"I haven't seen Jamie in a long time. I'm looking forward to catching up with her. I was sorry to hear that her marriage didn't work out."

Brett didn't say anything, merely worked a muscle in his jaw and kept an eye on the hay in the rearview mirror.

"So, tell me, are AJ and Jamie serious?"

Brett scowled. "I don't know."

"Have they been dating long?"

"I don't know."

"Are they coming to Luigi's with us tonight?" Natalie could feel her frustration building. Seriously? She thought AJ was her brother's best friend. How could he not know how long he and Jamie had been seeing each other? Guys talked about that kind of thing. She was pretty certain they did anyway.

"I don't know, Nat. I don't know anything about their relationship or friendship or whatever it is. Leave me out of it. I've got to concentrate." Despite his irritation, he took his time to expertly back the massive trailer through the doorway of the old barn, leaving just enough room on each side to walk between the sides of the trailer and the door. Irritation not entirely gone, he set the emergency brake, opened the truck door, jumped out, and slammed it behind him as he took off to the trailer to unload the bales.

Natalie sat there, pondering the strangeness of her brother. She knew every guy that her best friend in Memphis had gone on a date with in the past two years, and she could tell you why Jenn had dumped each of them. One had owned nine cats. One had gone to tanning beds regularly. One had a weird eyebrow she couldn't quit staring at. One had come to pick her up for a date, then spent the whole evening playing Mario Kart with her brothers in their apartment. But then again, maybe guys didn't actually discuss their relationships. That in itself was strange to her. But men are from Mars or whatever, right?

"Everything ok with Natalie?" she heard AJ ask her brother, and listened intently for more, refusing to compare herself to Gigi.

"I don't know. Would everyone stop asking me so many stinking questions!" Brett picked up a hay bale and threw it against the wall of the barn, the aluminum siding ringing with its strike.

"Alright, man. No problem." AJ told him, backing away to pick up a bale on the other side of the trailer. He carried his over and stacked it against the wall. It didn't make a sound.

While the men continued carrying and stacking, Natalie climbed down from the truck to stretch her limbs. She felt like she'd been in that truck for years. Worst of all, they were only starting. There were still acres and acres to go.

She lifted her hands above her head, then reached down to touch her toes. When she looked back up, she saw AJ standing on the trailer above her, his leather-gloved hands hooked into the baling twine of a bale above her head. Their eyes met. It felt to Natalie like something passed between them. Not sparks or electricity or anything like that, but what felt to Natalie like a quiet, mutual understanding that her brother was acting like an idiot.

Their eyes still locked, Natalie smiled. AJ smiled in return, and Brett threw another hay bale against the wall, the deafening ring striking like a gong. She turned away to dig a bottle of water out of the cooler in the back of the truck, and AJ picked up another hay bale.

A while later, Natalie stared in the side mirror at AJ working, tossing those heavy hay bales like they were nothing. It was hot in the truck, her tank top was soaked through with sweat, but it must be even hotter working outside in the sun. AJ had taken off his shirt, and Natalie was pretty sure her heart had stopped.

Sweet heavens, but that man was nice to look at. He was the polar opposite of Brantley, not that Brantley was ugly. Next to AJ, Brantley looked like a weenie. She'd once thought of her former boyfriend as having aristocratic, elegant features. She had once thought his artificially tan skin was attractive, complementing his sharp features and soft, blonde hair. But the sun-tanned chest and shoulders of the man she was seeing now completely changed her opinion. Brantley was slender, opting for running or biking for his exercise, which was great. It just didn't build muscles like she was admiring now. Watching AJ pick up a bale of hay, she could see the muscles in his arms work, each muscle in his arm was delineated and hard. As for hands, Brantley had the softest hands. When Brantley had touched her, she had felt cherished under his silky caress. Natalie would bet that AJ's hands were roughly calloused and strong. She let herself dream for a moment about what it would feel like to have hands like that holding hers, then touching her face, her neck...She sighed.

"Dang it, Natalie! What do you think you're doing?" The truck door flew open, pulling her out of her mirror-induced fantasy, and dropping her firmly back into the real world. It was only then that Natalie noticed that the truck had veered off course.

Brett stepped onto the running board and turned the wheel of the truck, steering it back between the hay bales.

"What were you doing, sleeping?" His face was red and a vein in his forehead pulsed.

"Sorry. I guess I wasn't paying attention," Natalie began.

Brett interrupted her. "I'd say. You ran over two hay bales before I could run up here and stop you. How do you not notice that? The bump about knocked me off the trailer. One of us could've been hurt, Natalie. How hard is it to steer a truck at five miles an hour?"

Natalie felt her own face reddening. She slammed the truck into park, causing it to lurch and a few hay bales to topple off the topmost layer, hitting the ground in soft thuds. She reached out the window, put her hands on her brother's chest and pushed, shoving him off the running board, causing him to stumble for his footing.

Natalie leaped from the truck, slamming the door hard behind her. She stepped up toe-to-toe with him, and poked him hard in the chest.

"You don't get to yell at me like that, Brett. I'm not some twelve year old nuisance of a sister anymore. I'm a grown woman. I have a college degree, and the states of Tennessee and Arkansas have issued me driver's licenses. I'm not some pesky little brat you can push around anymore. I'm here doing you a favor. If you don't start to act like it, cut out the nasty attitude, you can drive your own stinkin' truck for all I care."

"If you're not a pest, then why are you acting like one? What kind of a lady yells like that? You're a spoiled brat if I've ever seen one. Just spending all day sitting inside in the air conditioning, lying around watching your stories and eating chocolates. That's all you ever did when we were kids, and it's what you're used to now. Any time you have to get out and do a bit of work, you mess it up as soon as you can so you can run back home to the air so you can lie down with a washcloth on your head and— " Brett pointed at her, his own voice rising louder and louder, the same old accusations she'd been getting year after year.

AJ got closer, standing beside the siblings, as though he were ready to step in and separate them if need be. Like prizefighters in the ring, they ignored the ref and kept on swinging.

"You don't know what I've had to deal with, Brett, what I've had to do. I may not work outside in the heat and the dirt, but I've worked my butt off my whole life. You have no idea."

"What have you ever worked hard at? Everything has always been just handed to you. Baby Natalie treated like a princess."

"Treated like a princess? I studied my tail off all through high school. I was in every club, president or vice president of most, editor of the paper. I took all the honors classes and hardly ever went out. Not like you, just coasting by on your looks and football. I didn't get to go to parties after the game, or run off with friends on Saturday nights. In fact, I didn't have any real close friends. Even Jamie Griffith and I drifted apart. I spent all my time studying so I could graduate first in my class to get scholarships. I didn't have time for friends."

"You only graduated first in your class because—"

Natalie cut him off with a screech. "I apologized! I've apologized and apologized and apologized. Am I never going to live that down? For crying out loud! What do I have to do?" Brett crossed his arms as Natalie continued, her voice calming, quieting. "I went to college, and the whole high school process repeated itself. I studied, and I worked, and I tried and tried to make something of myself, to get out of here." Brett had fallen silent, and Natalie's vision had become blurry.

"All that work and where am I now? I'm here. In the stupid hay field being yelled at by you, accused of being....being....lazy of all things." Her voice was breaking up now, growing softer. "I should've just stayed in Big Springs. I should've gone out to the parties. I should've made time for friends. I wanted to, but I just never had time. If I'd known I was going to end up back here anyway--" Natalie's voice broke, and Brett wrapped her up in a tight hug and held her until she'd calmed down.

"You done?" he asked her in the same voice she'd heard him use with a horse that had spooked. It soothed her in a way that only her family could.

Natalie nodded.

"Alright then. Get your butt back in that truck and keep the wheels between the bales this time. Can you do that?"

Natalie nodded again. In his own way, Brett was apologizing. He wasn't the kind of a guy who would come right out and say he was sorry. He never had been. When they'd fought as kids, he'd always make it up to her in his own way. He'd bring her a candy bar or let her ride in the front seat of the car even though he hated the back. The apology wasn't in the words, not with her brother. It was in his tone, and the pat on the back, and his willingness to let the awkward moment drop away unmentioned.

Natalie remembered AJ and felt the heat creeping back up her neck. She looked around for him and found him sitting on one of the toppled hay bales drinking out of his water bottle. He poured some of it in his hand and scrubbed his face. Natalie put the truck in drive and focused on the space between the rows. AJ was Jamie's boyfriend anyway. It didn't matter that she'd just made a fool of herself in front of him. It didn't matter, she repeated to herself over and over, hoping that she'd start to believe it eventually.

Chapter 9

Natalie had showered off the sweat, dust, and bits of hay from her long day of sitting in the truck bored to tears. It was amazing how dirty a person could get just sitting there making sure the vehicle didn't hit anything as it crept along slower than a snail, or a slug, or dial-up internet, or very sleepy sloth. While her brain had been occupied dreaming up all the things that moved faster than the hay truck, her eyes had been busy watching AJ load hay bales onto the trailer.

He was handsome, definitely, but there was something else about him. Something magnetic. It was more than those blue eyes that she'd seen watching her from beneath the brim of his hat, more than those shoulders.

She took a good hard look at herself in the mirror. Natalie knew she had her faults. Some had been highlighted lately with her recent fall into loser-dom. One thing she wasn't, though, was disloyal.

While she and Jamie Griffith hadn't been close friends in years, she still felt as loyal to her as if they were still having sleepovers, staying up all night eating candy, painting their nails, and wondering what it would be like to kiss a boy.

The bonds of friendship still bound her. A friend never went after another friend's crush, boyfriend, or husband. Natalie never had. In fact, it made her happy to know that deep down, she still counted Jamie as a friend. It would be good to have a friend in Big Springs, for however long she stayed, someone besides her grandma or her brother, especially since Brett had been acting like a beast all day.

Staring into her own eyes with new determination, Natalie made a promise to herself. She would ignore whatever she felt for AJ because Jamie was her friend, or at least, Natalie hoped she still was.

"Nat, let's go!" Brett called from the living room, where he'd been cornered into moving furniture around to make room for Gigi's poker table, which was pink and purple with ivy stenciled around the edges. "Seriously, Nat, I will leave you here, and you'll have to play poker and drink slushies with Gigi and her friends. I don't want to do it, but I will leave you behind. Gigi has started talking about moving the china cabinet, and you know that thing weighs—"

"Hold onto your panties. I'm ready. Let me tell Gigi goodbye, and I'll be out the door." Natalie found her grandmother in the kitchen mixing a pitcher of virgin strawberry daiquiris and sampling from the spoon every few swirls. "I'm headed out, Gigi. Are you sure you didn't put any booze in that? I don't want to hold your dentures while you puke."

Her grandma slapped Natalie's arm and laughed a little too loudly. "I'd just put my teeth in a cup by the bathroom sink, like I do every night." Her eyes twinkled.

"Too much information. See you later." She kissed her grandmother's cheek and came out just as Brett laid on the horn. "I'm here! Knock it off," she yelled as she rounded the truck to the passenger side.

"My bad. I was already in mid-honk when you came out the door."

She buckled her seatbelt, and Brett took off down the drive. It felt oddly tense, but then again, they'd never been really close. The four year age difference combined with drastically different interests had kept them from being close friends. Most of their relationship was built around either bickering or surviving the familial weirdness. There had never been this strange tension like there was now.

"Everything ok? You mad at me or something?" she asked. He looked startled.

"Why do you think I'm mad at you?"

"Because you're acting weird, and you keep snapping at me. I thought maybe you were mad."

"Nat, you just got home. You haven't been here long enough to make me mad at you yet. I mean, I snapped at you in the hay field and everything, but that's just the hay field, you know. It doesn't really count."

"So, are you mad that I didn't call you when I came back? That I went straight to Gigi's instead of coming home? Mama was a little steamed about that."

"No," he paused, "it would've been nice if you'd told me, though. Texted or something."

"I know. I was just, I don't know, sad and embarrassed that I'd gotten fired and dumped and had needed to move back to Big Springs."

They were pulling into town now, passing the darkened windows of Main Street, which closed down early on the weekends. The truck turned, and they drove past the senior center and a gas station. Natalie noticed that Brett's hands had clenched harder on the steering wheel.

"What's wrong with living in Big Springs?" Brett asked, his jaw muscle twitching.

"Nothing. It was a great place to grow up. I just always thought I'd get out. Move to a city, any city, and have a successful, glamorous life. It's just not what I had pictured for myself."

When Brett spoke again, his tone was gentler than it had been before. "You know that we don't care if you're some fancy city lady or whatever. We're just happy when you're home, Sis."

Her gaze shifted to him. Her brother patted her shoulder and smiled. "I mean it, Nat. I'm glad you're home, no matter how long you stay or the reason you came for. I know Dad and Mama feel the same way." She nodded, feeling tears prick the back of her eyes. "But don't cramp my style in here. A little sister tagging along--not cool." He winked.

Natalie rolled her eyes and got out of the truck to go inside.

Luigi's was a pizza joint that was open for lunch and dinner every day of the week, but didn't deliver, instead doing a steady carryout business and cramming as many people into the building as the fire codes would allow, especially on a night like tonight when it seemed like all of Big Springs ages two to eighty-two were here to eat the thin crust pizza and to play a few rounds of pool in a family atmosphere. Theirs was a dry county, after all.

Luigi's was owned and operated by Louis and Gina Larson, who were third generation Big Springers. When they'd started their pizza place, they had decided to spice up Louis's name to make it seem more Italian. Plus "Luigi" was sort of a combination of their names. Strangely enough, the townsfolk had just kind of accepted their change in heritage from German to Italian for the sake of good pizza. No one but out-of-towners called Louis "Luigi," which was one way the regulars could spot a newbie.

"Oh, man. The place is packed. We'll never get a table." Brett half-shouted to be heard over the din.

Natalie searched the room for empty seats, and she locked eyes with the one person she was most excited and most dismayed to see sitting in a booth in the back corner with empty seats all around him.

"AJ is back there," she pointed out.

Brett took off for the back of the crowded restaurant with Natalie following. As they weaved around tables, she saw faces she recognized, and smiled, nodded, and waved a few times. It was an unspoken rule at Luigi's that no one stopped to visit until after pizza orders were in. Manners went out the window in favor of good food.

"Do you mind if we join you?" Brett asked his friend.

"Yeah, I was hoping you guys would make it before Gina made me give up the table."

"Blame Nat. She took forever getting ready." She scowled at her brother, but slid over into the booth across from AJ. Brett kept standing, scanning the room until he saw Gina. He waved two fingers and threw her the time out sign before he sat down. Gina nodded in understanding from behind the bar at the long end of the room. Two iced teas would come their way as soon as Gina could manage it.

Natalie avoided looking straight at AJ, opting to scan the room instead. She saw her fifth grade teacher, who waved. Natalie waved back. Her mother's friend Tina with her husband Jerry were seated several tables down. Tina smiled broadly and waved her whole arm above her head. Natalie waved back, though less enthusiastically. There were other faces she knew well, though they'd aged, grown up in the years since she'd seen them in the hallways at school or in the stands at ball games. Several openly looked, nodding her way. A few only sneaked sly glances over shoulders, or peeked over the backs of booths. She felt a little self-conscious, like everyone was staring at her and wondering why she was at Luigi's with her brother on a

Saturday night when she ought to be in Memphis with the boyfriend she'd been showing around last Christmas.

"We're really getting a lot of attention tonight," AJ said. He was bending a straw between his fingers, twisting it into a shape.

"Must be my handsome looks finally getting the notice I deserve," Brett said, puffing out his chest dramatically. AJ threw the straw at him, and Natalie elbowed her brother in the ribs. "Or I guess it could be that everyone's looking at Nat here." Brett looked around, nodding at people he knew. He winked at someone, but Natalie couldn't tell who. With Brett it was just as likely to be a hot babe as it was to be the eighty-four year old great-grandmother of a hot babe. His charm did not discriminate.

"They all look happy to see you," AJ said. Natalie finally looked up into his face. The corner of his mouth tilted up in a half grin. It made Natalie wonder if he was happy to see her, even though he was off limits. She told herself it was still alright to hope that he was pleased to see her tonight. It would be good if she and Jamie's boyfriend were friends too.

Natalie shrugged. "I'm sure they're all just curious what I'm doing back here when it's not a holiday. Wondering how long I'm here for or what scandalous thing might have happened to drive me home again."

"Maybe," AJ said. "But that doesn't mean they're any less happy to see you."

Natalie was skeptical, but she let it go since Gina had brought their drinks.

"Any preferences in pizza toppings?" Brett asked them. They shook their heads, so he went ahead and ordered the house special for the table.

"You guys expecting anyone else?" Gina asked.

"Jamie might be by later," AJ told her.

Gina nodded, then gave Natalie a quick smile, saying, "I'll bring you guys some buffalo wings too, on the house, in honor of Natalie here's return. Good to have you home, doll. Gotta run." Gina tucked her notepad in an apron pocket and rushed back to the kitchen.

Natalie relaxed into the booth, wondering if AJ might have been right. Maybe people were more than merely curious. Maybe a few really were happy to see her.

"No poker tonight?" AJ asked Natalie, who had picked up her own glass.

"Not tonight. I'm not quite that wild." She took a sip, then blurted, "Or maybe I am. When I was fired the words 'sexual harassment' were thrown out at me, so that's just one step away from the big house, right?" She looked at the men's faces. Brett's drink was halfway to his mouth, his arm frozen in place. AJ's eyebrows were almost hidden in his hairline, they were lifted so high in surprise. His mouth was slightly ajar.

Finally, AJ gathered his wits and asked, "Who did you harass?"

"A girl I worked with named Vanessa."

"Nat! You sexually harassed another woman?" Brett exclaimed a little too loudly. Several heads jerked their direction.

Natalie whispered and slouched down in the seat. "Shut up, Brett. It wasn't like that."

"Let's talk about this, Nat. You're still my sister and all, and no matter what you do—"

"Brett! Knock it off. I'm not attracted to women. Thanks for your support, but I didn't harass her like that." Natalie could tell her face was red, and she was so embarrassed that people in town may take Brett's words out of context. Or in context, even. It was bad either way. By tomorrow morning, people would be saying she was a sex offender on the run from the law.

"How was it, Natalie? What happened?" AJ asked calmly, his eyes intent on her, compassion shining out. She relaxed a little and told them the short version, figuring her brother deserved to hear about it, and since AJ here, he might as well hear it too. Somehow, his knowing didn't bother her. She gave them the short version, telling about how she had sent a nasty email detailing the other woman's attributes and calling her a few unflattering names.

"So, how big were her new boobs?" Brett asked. Natalie elbowed him again. At this rate, he'd have a broken rib or two by the end of the night.

"It was all my own fault. I can't complain too much. Oh, look, here's our wings." She was happy to put everyone's focus somewhere besides on her. "I don't care what Mama and Gigi say, I'm eating with my fingers."

"Thirty years old and still rebelling," Brett proclaimed, using his hands as well.

"Speak for yourself. I'm still in my twenties." She raised her wing in the air, and toasted, "To rebellion."

"To boobs," Brett said, raising his wing.

"To both of those." AJ raised his wing. The three smiled at each other and took huge, messy bites. Natalie giggled. It was a great moment.

"Have room for one more?" a female voice asked from over Brett's shoulder. Everyone froze, startled by the arrival of Jamie Griffith, who stood smiling down at them.

"Sure!" Natalie was the first to speak, hand covering her mouth.

Both men were still paralyzed, holding their wings to their mouths, making eye contact, some kind of silent conversation happening between them. Natalie saw AJ give the slightest shake of his head. Brett huffed and threw his wing down on the plate in front of him.

"Hey, Jamie." Brett stood up. "I'll be back," he muttered through clenched teeth before he stalked off toward the pool tables in a side room blaring country music.

"AJ, are you going to let me sit?" Her voice was as sweet as molasses. He cleared his throat and scooted over, pulling his drink and plate with him. Jamie sat down, snatched his tea, and stole a drink. She gave Natalie a wink and returned it to its place in front of him.

"Natalie, it's good to see you again. You look fantastic. I love your hair that long." Jamie was sincere, not at all like the women Natalie had worked with in Memphis. Now here was a girl, she told herself, who would never be accused of sexual harassment.

"Thanks. You look great too." She really did. Jamie had one of those faces that hardly aged. Her pale skin with a splash of freckles across her nose, the deep copper color of her hair that was piled high on her head, and her thin frame gave her an almost elfish, fairy type quality. She fairly radiated energy and goodwill. Her wide, guileless, hazel eyes and even wider smile made Natalie wonder why they'd ever drifted apart.

"So," Jamie began, "I hear you're a certified yoga instructor and have all the old folks putting their feet behind their ears." She took a wing from the basket. "Last I heard, you were in Memphis at a marketing place, though. So I told everyone they must be mistaken, and that you were probably just helping out over at the senior center, and it got all blown out of proportion."

It was Natalie's turn for her mouth to fall open in surprise.

"I hear all the gossip at the hardware store. Men gossip worse than women do. They don't call it gossip though. They call it news. It makes them feel superior." Jamie winked.

"Yeah. You're right." Natalie filled Jamie in on her own recent gossiping misadventures while they ate. It felt good to tell the story to her old friend, like old times. Jamie nodded as Natalie spoke, gasping in indignation over her losing her job.

"I don't understand. It's not like you were making up lies or telling people she was screwing the boss in the break room or anything," Jamie exclaimed. Natalie looked down at her tea, stirring the ice with her straw. "Uh-oh, was she doing that?" Jamie whispered, looking side to side like she might get caught.

Natalie shrugged. "It looks like it."

"That's so unprofessional," Jamie said in a prim voice. Natalie kept her gaze on her wings, then covered her plate with a paper napkin. "Uh-oh. I've stepped in it, haven't I?"

Natalie looked back toward her, their eyes locking. The friends shared a look, one that still resonated from a childhood spent reading each other's thoughts.

That was all it took. Jamie switched seats, sliding next to Natalie, taking her into a tight hug. She petted Natalie's hair.

"He was my boyfriend, or at least, he was supposed to be. They were the ones sneaking around, but I was the one who got punished. Though I know now that what I did was wrong too. Maybe not as wrong as what she did. It doesn't matter. But you know what? I don't even think she likes Brantley. I think she wanted him just to show that she could have him."

"Just like that Dolly Parton song. What's it called?"

"Jolene," said a masculine voice from across the table. Both women snapped their heads up in surprise. "You forgot I was here, didn't you?" AJ asked, shifting uncomfortably.

"I figured you had gone to play pool with Brett a long time ago," Jamie said. "You're not one for girl talk."

"I was sitting right beside you," AJ reminded her, his face betraying no emotion.

"Am I supposed to keep track of where you are every minute of the day?"

"I'm going to go find Brett." AJ edged out of the booth and headed toward the pool room.

"Men. I tell you what," Jamie said as she handed Natalie a paper napkin for her nose, "sometimes they're so dense. And AJ is better than most." Jamie stuck out her tongue in his direction, and then shot Natalie a grin like she'd just gotten away with something.

"Yeah, AJ seems like a pretty good guy." Natalie turned aside to wipe her nose, and when she turned back she saw a familiar, mischievous glee in Jamie's eyes. "Uh-oh.

What are we going to do today that we're going to get in trouble for tomorrow?" That was the look that had gotten Natalie grounded more often than not.

"I think you and AJ should go out. You'd be perfect for each other. Hear me out! You're both so good looking, neither would be jealous. You both like the same kind of TV shows—those lawyer shows where they have to figure out who the serial killer is. Also, you both grew up in the country. Similar roots. That counts for something." Jamie was ticking the reasons off on her fingers, gaining speed as she went.

"Wait! Wait! Wait!" Her voice finally cut through Jamie's list-making momentum. "Why are you trying to give me your boyfriend?"

"AJ's not my boyfriend."

"I have had multiple people tell me that he is. My mom, my grandma, the folks at the senior center, Brett." Natalie paused. "Actually, I'm not sure about Brett. He's been weird today."

Jamie pulled a stick of lip balm out of her pocket and carefully twirled the end to let up a small amount. She applied it with the precision of a brain surgeon. Natalie watched her, recognizing the tell. This was one girl who would lose at poker every time.

"Jamie? What's going on?"

Jamie shook her head, her lips pressed into a thin line. She spun the balm back down into the tube and replaced the cap, then proceeded to roll the tube between her hands.

"You can tell me. What's up?" Natalie leaned in close, her voice dropping to barely a whisper. Around the restaurant, people continued to eat and talk and carry on.

They were alone in the crowd, just two old friends catching up.

Jamie opened her mouth to speak, then shut it again. Natalie took the lip balm from her hands and sat it on the table.

"Go on. Just tell me. Quick. Like pulling off a Band-Aid. Out with it."

Jamie lowered her eyes and spoke in a rush. "I sort of...well, I didn't mean to at first, but then it just kind of happened, you know? I mean, I've known about it for a while now, but I didn't plan for it to be like it is. An accident really, that's all it is."

"Jamie--"

"I let people think AJ's my boyfriend so they won't feel so bad for me." Jamie blurted the words out. Her eyes darted to Natalie's face, searching for the accusations she thought might be there.

Natalie leaned back in the booth. Nothing about this made sense. Why would anyone feel sorry for Jamie? Cute, fun, caring Jamie? Just about every nice word she could think of applied to Jamie. She was the sweetheart of Big Springs.

"My divorce," Jamie supplied. "Has anyone told you about it?"

Natalie cringed, and the pieces fell into place.

Jamie took hold of her lip balm again. She rolled it between her hands as she spoke. "I thought so. It's pretty juicy gossip or news or whatever." She shrugged. "I'm not into sharing my man. At least, not when he's mine for real. But you could have AJ. He's like a brother to me. There's nothing between us, nothing romantic at least. As long as I get to keep being his friend, though. And maybe I could be your friend again too?"

Natalie watched the rolling lip balm, and wondered how it had ever come to this. The girl she had spent so many years beside--playing, crying, growing up—asking to be her friend.

She pulled Jamie into a hug. "I don't think I deserve a friend like you. But if you're willing to put up with me, who am I to call you crazy?"

Chapter 10

AJ stood at the bar and raised a hand for Gina, who was busy at the other end. When it looked like it would be a minute, he turned his back to the counter and looked toward the booth where Natalie and Jamie sat talking. Even just looking her way, he felt like a cow patty. It wasn't like he didn't want to see Jamie. He was happy to see her—she was fun to have around, always smiling and joking around. He never felt uncomfortable around her. Until now, that is. But he hadn't been able to get in touch with her for two days, the two of them leaving each other a series of voicemails and text messages. That was how she had known that they would be here at Luigi's tonight.

But when she had walked in, he'd wanted to crawl under the table and hide. It wasn't that he was cowardly in general. He'd been a Marine, after all. He just dreaded the conversation he knew he'd have to have with her. He loved Jamie like a sister and would rather take on a rattlesnake than break her heart—if her heart was truly at stake here. It was just so hard to tell how she felt about him. He'd thought she thought of him like a brother, but now? It was so confusing.

One good thing did come from Jamie's chatterbox tendencies and innate ability to squirrel out information from people. He now knew the full story of what had made Natalie run home. He had figured it had been more than just losing her job that had made her look so distraught that day on the road when she'd chosen to face her grandmother rather than her parents. He could see how she'd prefer to face one person's constant attention than two, especially when one of those people is DeeJay James, who had decided opinions on what her daughter's life ought to be like and wasn't afraid to share those with anyone willing to listen. AJ had heard a rant or two himself about what Natalie needed in her life, though the ranting was usually aimed at Mr. James or Brett.

AJ pondered this as he stood at the counter to get another iced tea, since he'd left his sitting on the table.

Heaven knew he wasn't heading back in there right now. When Gina had served him, he took off toward the pool room in search of Brett. While Brett may not be the sharpest tool in the shed, he knew Jamie and could possibly offer some insight into how to ask Jamie if they were accidentally dating. Crap. That sounded bad, even in his head.

He found Brett with a pool cue in his hand, leaning over a table with only a few balls left. A few of the guys they played basketball with sometimes were playing against him. Judging by Brett's swagger, AJ figured that his buddy was winning.

"Left pocket," Brett called. AJ waited until after Brett had sunk the 8 ball before he approached; he was panicked, not stupid.

"Hey, man. Can we talk a minute?" AJ gave the other guys a nod, and they nodded in return, raising their glasses in hello.

Brett rolled his eyes, called out a quick goodbye and followed AJ outside to the parking lot, which was crammed full of empty cars. A few kids were hanging around the back corner, sitting on a tailgate and ignoring the rest of the world.

"Alright, you got me. What?" Brett crossed his arms over his chest, his expression stony.

"I still can't tell if Jamie think we're dating," AJ winced at his own words.

"Are you kidding me?" Brett shouted in frustration, pacing away from AJ, then coming back quickly. "Man, just ask her. Pull her aside and say, 'So, Jamie, are you my girlfriend or, for God only knows what reason, can I chase after Natalie?' Easy as that." He spat on the ground and put his hands on his hips.

"I'm not usually like this, you know," AJ said voice rising. He pointed at the restaurant. "Those girls got me all twisted up, so I don't know which way is up."

Brett took a step closer. "That's not my fault, and I don't want to have to be your wingman so you can hook up with my sister, you idiot."

AJ stepped toward Brett, his volume increasing as his tone darkened. They were nearly chest to chest now. "I'm not asking you to be my wingman. And I don't want to just hook up with Natalie. I like her a lot. I have for a long time, so leave me alone about it and deal, you moron."

"You deal, man, and stop telling me how you like my sister. I don't like it. Do you remember what I did to the guys who chased her in high school?" Brett added a poke to AJ's chest. He was several inches shorter than his friend, but that didn't keep him from going toe to toe with the guy who was after his little sister.

AJ's eyes narrowed. "I know I haven't acted too manly today, but I can still kick your butt, and if that's what you want me to do, you just poke me again."

Brett's chest puffed out. AJ's chest followed. Brett pulled his arm back, his index finger jutting out from a tightly balled fist, prepared to issue one more poke.

"What are you two doing? Are you going to fight?" Jamie's voice cut through the tension.

The men both took a step calm back. Their gazes were locked, and it was several moments before the dark tension around them eased.

AJ stuck out his hand.

Brett shook it, maybe squeezing a little harder than necessary, and mumbled under his breath, "Talk to her." He walked toward Jamie and put a hand on her shoulder, giving her a friendly pat. "I'm going to see where Nat is."

"She got held up by Gina. Comparing restaurants in Memphis, I think. We had the pizza boxed up. You might want to save her or she could be there all night," Jamie offered. Brett sighed and went inside.

When they were alone, Jamie took a step toward AJ. "Why are you so weird tonight? And why all the mysterious voicemails and texts the past two days? Are you dying or something? You kept saying how you need to talk. I've been worried about it all day."

AJ swallowed hard and cleared his throat. "You know that I've—"He coughed and started over. "I mean, I heard something yesterday about you and me... I'm not sure--" AJ broke off, rubbed the back of his neck with his hand. "I'm not sure if you think it's true. I mean it was a surprise to me."

AJ watched Jamie for signs of distress—tears, a gasp, a trembling bottom lip. None were visible, but there was an odd look coming over her face. Like he was a newborn puppy.

"You are adorable when you're trying to break up with a girl." Her lips were definitely not trembling. In fact, she seemed to be holding back a smile.

"Am I breaking up with you?" AJ asked, uncertain.

"You're looking at me like I'm a ticking time bomb." Jamie started giggling.

"I'm so sorry to hurt you like this," he continued, trying to take their relationship seriously, even if she wasn't. "You know I value your friendship," he took a deep breath to continue.

"Stop! Stop!" She waved her hands in front of her. "I don't know why you're under the impression that you're my boyfriend, but I never thought--" she stopped laughing, her expression turned serious. "Oh, no! Do you think I'm your girlfriend? What have I done?"

"No! I don't think that." AJ said. "I thought maybe you did."

Jamie scrunched up her nose. "Why would I think that? We don't kiss or hold hands or stare into each other's eyes. And we've watched movies on my couch on at least three occasions, and I have never once tried to make out with you." She shuddered, and AJ tried not to take it personally.

"I guess I freaked out over nothing. I didn't want to hurt you, though."

"This is why I told Natalie you two would be perfect together. You're so thoughtful. She needs someone like you. All manly, but also pretty nice."

He grabbed Jamie in a big bear hug and gave her a smacking kiss on the forehead.

"You're the best friend a guy could have," he told her.

"Thanks. I'm sorry everyone in Big Springs thinks we're dating. I knew what people assumed. I never went out of my way to correct anyone. What with you being so handsome and all," she nudged him in the arm with her elbow, "it made me look good to have people think I was your girlfriend."

"It's fine. No sweat. Can we not talk about it tonight? I mean, if you want to grovel sometime, that's fine by me, but let's not do it tonight. There's something else I'd like to do instead."

Chapter 11

Natalie followed her brother out the door. In the parking lot, the voices of crickets and bullfrogs took over, their noise rivaling that of the din from inside. Outside the air was cool, but not chilly. A couple of street lights lit up the darkness, and underneath one Jamie and AJ sat on the tailgate of his truck, their legs swinging as they chatted. AJ laughed at something Jamie said. It was a bellowing chuckle that made Natalie smile.

Brett put hand on his sister's arm and directed her between two pickup trucks. He looked around to see that no one was listening, like a spy on a mission. Though judging from his grim expression, Natalie would say it was a mission he'd rather not be taking on.

He rubbed his forehead. "Nat, I don't want to get involved, but AJ and Jamie..." He stopped, looking at the sky like he was hoping for some kind of divine intervention.

"They aren't dating. I know. Jamie told me."

"They aren't?" Brett asked, his eyes going wide.

"No. She just let people draw their own conclusions to save face. She and AJ are good friends. That's what Jamie told me."

"Oh. So, she's not really his girlfriend?" Brett asked. Natalie shook her head. "Good. That's really good." He breathed an audible sigh of relief.

"Why good? You interested in Jamie?"

Brett pulled a face. "She's pretty and fun and all, but she's like a sister. You two were together so much when you were younger, you were practically the same person. I can't think of her like that!" He stepped out from their hiding place and started toward their friends. Natalie jogged to catch up.

"Brett, why is it good that they aren't together?" she asked, pulling on her brother's arm until he stopped and looked down at her. He blew out a big breath and looked at his boots.

"Why am I in the middle of this?" he mumbled under his breath, before nodding his head toward AJ. "Because of the way he looks at you," Brett scowled and shook his head, obviously disliking the notion of anyone being interested in his baby sister.

Natalie followed Brett's gaze across a short stretch of parking lot to see AJ, his gaze intent on her. Their eyes met. His were warm and friendly, maybe even hopeful. It made her heart beat faster. He stood up and walked slowly toward her, his powerful body moving with surprising grace. She'd never paid much attention to how a man moved, but the way AJ strode across the parking lot made her feel all buttery inside.

"Can I give you a ride home?" His voice was deep, sending shivers down her spine.

"I'd like that." It didn't seem real, but like a scene from a movie. She followed AJ to the passenger door of his truck, where he opened it and waited for her to climb in before he shut it behind her. He raced around the back, closing the tailgate as he went. Like a matchmaking little fairy, Jamie had vanished. AJ hopped up into the truck, the dome light flickering on briefly before it dimmed with the close of the door. The darkness inside of the cab intensified the feeling that it was only the two of them in this world, everything else having fallen away. His blue eyes locked on hers once again, and he grinned.

She was lost. At least for now. In the back of Natalie's mind, she could hear niggling doubts. She'd just gotten out of a relationship. It had ended badly, and if her heart wasn't exactly broken, it was at least disappointed.

She'd only known AJ a short time, and they needed time to get to know each other. The small doubts flew at her consciousness, but they had all of the impact of a bug hitting the windshield. Barely noticed, but not stopping her. Because in the front of her mind, she could reason it out. There was nothing to keep her from accepting a ride home from a guy like AJ, who was friends with her brother and everyone else in Big Springs. It wasn't like he was putting a ring on her finger or sweeping her off her feet and into his bed. It was a ride home. Nothing more.

As AJ pulled out of the parking lot, Natalie saw Jamie waving to her and throwing them a thumbs up. Natalie waved back, and AJ gave a two fingered mock-salute.

"Jamie's great, isn't she?" Natalie broke the silence that hung over the dark cab of the truck.

"She's been a good friend to me. I can't imagine the last few years of my life here without her."

Natalie watched him, the street lights illuminating his face. Now that she didn't feel guilty for appreciating his handsome features, she wanted to stare for a while, to soak him in. His jaw line was highlighted by a five o'clock shadow. When she'd seen him earlier that day, he'd been clean shaven, but now the added hair outlined his sharp features. The only feature of his face that seemed to be slightly imperfect was his nose, which had a bump in the middle, like it had been broken at one time. She wondered if he'd gotten it in an accident, or if he boxed, or if maybe he'd been a brawler in his younger days. She realized a minute or two later that had been staring at him as they drove along in silence. Natalie shook her head a little, hoping to wiggle some focus back into her overwrought brain.

"What's happened in the last few years?" she asked.

"Oh, I just mean with me moving here, starting over and all that. When I came here, I really only knew Gramps and Brett and a few others." They crossed the bridge, lit up with orange lights across the length of it. Underneath, the creek reflected back the moonlight. On either side of the bridge, the surface stretched out in inky darkness, light glinting off the water. The countryside, the bluffs and the fields on top of them, were all obscured by the dark. The mountains in the distance were nothing but smudges against the starry sky. Even in the nighttime, it was beautiful, though that might be because it was home.

"Where were you before? I know Charlie is your grandpa, but where did you grow up?"

AJ ran a hand through his hair and sighed before answering.

"I grew up in Missouri, near Jefferson City, so in the middle of the state. My parents had a farm, crops mostly. Corn and soybeans. A good size spread."

"So why did you move here to be a farmer? Couldn't you have stayed there to do that? Not that I'm complaining or anything," she added with a smile.

He kept his eyes on the winding road, but his mouth tilted up at the corner.

"My parents sold the place several years ago. They used the money to buy a condo on a lake. It makes them happy, and that makes me happy."

"Sounds nice," Natalie said. Her parents would never do that, she knew. Even if her mother wanted to live on a beach half of the year, Natalie knew her father would never sell their farm. It had been passed down to him from his father, who got it from his own. There had been a James family on that land for almost a hundred and seventy-five years, and there would be for generations to come if he had any say in it. Natalie couldn't imagine a father selling the farm away from the family name, and she said as much, mentioning her own family.

AJ nodded. They'd left town and all of the streetlights. His face was dark again, lit only by the dash lights, but Natalie could tell by the way he clenched his forearms and stiffened the muscles in his back that he didn't really want to talk about it, and that maybe she should back off.

"They would've kept it for me if I'd asked them to. At the time, though, I didn't think I'd ever want to settle down and farm. I had—" AJ broke off and cleared his throat, then shifted in his seat. He turned on the air conditioning, the cool air rushing into the cab. "I had other plans at the time," he finally finished over the gentle whir of the fan.

"Funny how plans change, isn't it?" She understood that completely. She was living it.

"I'd rather not talk about it tonight, if that's ok?" AJ asked, his eyes darting from the road toward her. "I'll tell you all about it, the whole sad story, sometime, but not tonight, please. I don't want to ruin this." He reached out a hand, and Natalie hesitated only a moment, looking down at his big hand, before she put her own into it. He squeezed, and she squeezed back, though she wasn't quite sure how she felt about holding his hand. It felt nice, this connection.

"What exactly is *this* that you don't want to ruin?" she asked.

"This is me getting to take you home. Getting to talk to you with no one else around. Maybe even kissing you goodnight." AJ raised an eyebrow at her. She let out a quiet laugh.

"Maybe."

His smile widened so that, even in the darkness, he was fairly glowing with happiness.

"Maybe ain't 'no'."

The truck turned into the drive, and AJ still held her hand snugly in his. Natalie noted how strong his hands felt, wrapped around hers. The calluses were rough against her smooth palm. Rough, but not bad.

They pulled up to the house, the truck bouncing over the creek, their hands jostling, but not letting go. Along the front of Gigi's house, a few cars were still parked, lined up in the grass with spaces in between, like more had been there and gone, indicating that the poker players had begun leaving, but many remained inside.

"I forgot that Gigi's got friends over." A quick worry flashed through her mind that maybe she'd get teased for kissing a man on the porch—if he decided to follow through on the earlier comment and if she decided to kiss him back. She might shake the hand she was currently holding and head right on inside without another thought, his lips and the feel of his skin against hers forgotten completely.

"I can see that. So what do the matriarchs of Big Springs do on a Saturday night?"

"You don't want to know."

The truck came to a stop in one of the empty spaces between two cars. He turned off the headlights and killed the engine.

"Wait there," he told her before circling the truck. When she turned toward the door he opened for her, AJ put his hands on her waist and helped her down, lifting her slightly so that she was suspended for the merest instant before her feet touched the ground.

"Can I see you this week? Soon?" he asked, still holding on, his fingers warm where they lay spread across her lower back.

"I'm going to church tomorrow. It's mandatory in Big Springs," she joked. "No way around it unless you're on death's door, and even then they say it's better to die inside the church as out."

"I know." He smiled down at her. "I'll be there. How about after? You busy? Maybe we could go out to lunch or drive around?"

"I promised Mama I'd eat lunch with the family. You can come if you want, but I can't imagine why you'd want to."

"I could do that. I go over for lunch after church once a month or so anyway. It's been a while, and I guess I'm due," he teased.

"The rest of the week, I don't know. I'm at Gigi's mercy."

He nodded. "I'd like to take you out on a proper date. Soon." He leaned an inch or so closer. "That is, if you want to go out with me sometime."

"Alright." Natalie tilted her head up to look into his eyes.

"Alright," he said, his gaze shifting from her eyes down to her lips. His gaze darkened, and his fingers gripped her tighter, drawing her closer until they were only a hair's breadth apart. Close, but not quite touching. AJ's gaze went from her lips back up to her eyes, the intensity in them sending ripples of goosebumps across her skin. She saw him close his eyes and lick his lips. Natalie closed her own eyes and a moment later felt his lips on hers, soft but firm, the kiss slow, as though he was taking his time to draw the moment out, to make it last. Natalie let her arms wrap around his waist, holding on to him as he held on to her. Their kiss deepened, and they were lost in each other, learning the taste and feel of each other, feeling their breath mingle, breathing each other in.

When the kiss ended, his hands remained around her, holding her tightly to him while she tried to erase the fog from her mind. Natalie breathed deeply, pulling in the scent of him. It was distinctly him, smelling of hay and cedar and something unnamable and masculine. She let go of his waist, and he let go of hers. He took a deep breath and let it out slowly, running a hand through his wavy hair.

"I should go," he said, his voice low and quiet.

"Yes, you should," echoed a shrill voice from the front of the truck that didn't sound at all like her grandmother.

Natalie jumped back and screeched, heart beating fast for an entirely different reason than before.

"Gigi?" she asked between gasping breaths. The porch light flipped on, and the glare nearly blinded her. She put a hand up to her face and squinted into the light. It was only then that she was able to make out the small army of angry-looking women closing in, all elderly and all fierce.

"What are you ladies doing out here? Can I help you with something?" AJ asked the crowd gathered around his pickup.

"You can step away from our Natalie and high tail it out of here." Natalie couldn't see clearly, but she thought the speaker might be Barb, from the restaurant of the same name.

"You no good, cheating rascal!" Natalie had no idea who that was. She could only see a little tuft of gray hair poking up from where the voice had come.

"Rascal?" AJ asked, looking from one face to another. "Wait. What's wrong? Is this because I kissed Natalie?" He looked at her for help.

"It's ok. I kissed him back," Natalie assured the hostile group.

"We know, dear, we saw you. But you couldn't help it. You're in a fragile place right now," Henrietta reassured her, then turned and shot a mean glare at AJ.

"And that silver-tongued devil lured you in!" came a high-pitched voice from the crowd. That was definitely Millie, whose restaurant had the best muffins around. What in the world was going on?

Natalie looked at AJ in bewilderment. He looked even more confused than she felt. Even worse, he looked a little heartbroken, being accosted by the queens of the community in such a way.

"I thought you all liked AJ. What's going on here?" She turned toward her grandmother's friend, "Henrietta, you were singing his praises the other day. Mabel, you too. Not to mention some of the comments you made, Gigi," Natalie said, giving her grandmother a look that spoke volumes.

Mabel stepped forward. "That was before we caught him stepping out on Jamie. Our opinions have changed now." A sea of nodding heads affirmed her statement.

"Oh, Jamie and I aren't dating. So, my kissing Natalie is perfectly fine. I'm not cheating on anyone."

"You broke that sweet girl's heart?" screeched Millie, who was beginning to quiver in indignation.

"Rascal!" came from the gray tuft in the back.

AJ threw up his hands in defense. "Wait! Ladies, you've got it all wrong. Jamie and I were never dating. We're just friends. That's all we've ever been." Natalie was a little impressed with how well he held his calm under fire.

"You've been leading her on all this time?" asked Henrietta, her hands fluttering in the air around her, like angry little hummingbirds bent on attack.

"That poor thing!" Barb wailed, clutching her sizable bosom.

Gigi stepped in front of the crowd, her presence calming the angry masses.

"AJ, I think it's time you went on home," her soft voice suggested.

Natalie watched as his gaze flickered from face to face of the women of the town gathered around him. With each angry expression, the disbelief and hurt grew in his eyes. When his gaze landed on hers, she tried to look reassuring.

"I'll see you soon," she said.

His eyes searched her face for a long moment, and clearly he didn't find what he had been hoping to see there, because she saw his jaw clench. It was as if his face fell, though his expression never changed. Natalie saw a shift though, as if he had lost something precious.

She didn't know what to do. Fight for him? Take on all these women on the strength held in one really great kiss and a few conversations?

Truth was, if she had been in their position just now, she'd be angry right there with them, probably leading the pack.

But she wasn't in their position. She was in hers, and she felt just as misunderstood and confused as he did.

"Yeah," AJ nodded. "I'll see you."

With that vague promise, he crossed to the driver's side of his truck, fired it up, and pulled slowly away into the dark of the night, red tail lights disappearing down the drive.

Natalie turned to the women gathered around her. They were a motley collection of women from her past—her grandmother's close friends who had been surrogate aunts for all of her life, two of her former teachers, and Mrs. Lansing, who played piano in church. There were Barb and Millie who always brought her special treats from their restaurants, and now that the crowd was moving, Natalie could see the owner of the tuft of gray hair who had so fiercely come to her defense. It was sweet, old Mrs. Talburt, propped up on her walker. She had made the doll Natalie had carried around from ages four to nine. The woman must be in her nineties by now, but here she was, calling mountain of a man a rascal on her behalf.

They were staring at Natalie now with such intense protection in their eyes, having gone to battle to save her, even when she didn't need saving. Natalie looked into their loving faces and felt her heart fill up in return, until it was so full that tears fell down over her cheeks.

"Oh, sweetie!" Gigi gathered her into her arms.

Natalie was passed, tearful but laughing, from one bosom to another as everyone in the crowd took her into her arms for a hug.

"Dear, you go on in to bed. It will all look better in the morning," Henrietta told her, nudging her gently toward the porch.

Natalie passed through the crowd, her back patted and shoulder squeezed all the way to the front door. Natalie let the momentum carry her forward. She knew she should set them straight, tell them all about how AJ and Jamie had never been together and how it had all been a misunderstanding, but she found herself unable to say the words, to tell them that they'd all stood up for, fought for her even though she'd once left them behind for bigger dreams in a bigger city and had not even thought about most of them in years.

Natalie stopped at the door and turned back to them. "Thank you," she said softly, the emotions she hadn't expected sticking in her throat. "It really isn't what you think," she started, but stopped when she heard a loud snort and the outraged clicking of a tongue. "Well, it isn't, but thank you for coming to my rescue. It means more than you'll ever know."

She put a hand to her heart and made eye contact with Gigi, whose smile seemed vaguely understanding, as though she had seen and heard it all.

"Go on in, dearest," Gigi told her. "They're all just leaving. I'll see them off."

Natalie suddenly felt exhausted, and it took all her strength to open the screen door and walk down the hallway to the waiting bed.

Chapter 12

"You're driving too fast! We're going to wreck. You haven't driven on these roads in ages. I think you plumb forgot how." Gigi had a white-knuckle grip on the handle above the passenger's side window of the Prius like she could be ejected from her seat at any moment. Her polyester skirt was bunched up around her knees, her high heels pressed into the floorboard as she braced herself.

Natalie sighed. "I'm only going forty." The road was twisty, but she'd driven it thousands of times from age fourteen on up. For crying out loud, the suggested speed limit on the curves was forty-five.

Gigi whimpered, "I'm too young to die."

"I slowed down. Now I'm only going thirty-five." Natalie pointed to the speedometer, but Gigi refused to look, instead keeping her eyes trained on the road.

"You've been watching too much NASCAR. This isn't a race. We'll get to church either way, of course, but I'd rather not go there in a coffin."

Natalie pulled over to the side of the road. "You drive." She opened her door and came around to the passenger's side just as Gigi was opening her own door.

"Oh, no. I couldn't. You go on ahead and drive, honey. I hate to complain so much, but I think your driving is making me nauseous." Her grandmother stood up and rubbed her stomach, then took in dramatic gulps of air like a catfish thrown onto the bank.

"Please drive. I insist." Natalie scooted around the older woman and sat down in the passenger seat of her own car—a place she'd never been before. It felt weird, but it probably wasn't safe to drive when she was rolling her eyes that much.

Gigi took her time, looking both ways fifty or so times before walking around the car to the driver's seat. Natalie took advantage of the time by mumbling to herself.

"Crazy old bat. I have never watched NASCAR in my life. Thirty-five! Why did I ever agree to drive her to church? I swear, I must be as loony as she is."

Gigi closed the car door. "Were you saying something dear?'

"Nope. Let's go. At this rate we'll be lucky to get there for the closing prayer."

"I've just been itching to give this car of yours a spin. How fast can she go?" Gigi strapped on her seatbelt and gripped the wheel with both hands.

"Forty." Natalie put on her own seatbelt and pulled on it a few times to make sure it would catch.

"Then hold on. Let's see if I can get her up to forty-five." Gigi hit the gas and gravel from the shoulder flew out behind them. She took the winding curves at fifty and sailed across the straight stretch pushing seventy.

"Jesus, slow down! You're going to kill us!" Natalie's heart beat in her throat as Gigi inched the speedometer up higher and higher, each corner feeling like a rollercoaster nightmare just before the wheels jump the track and everyone careens down to their deaths.

"Don't take the Lord's name in vain, missy. We're on our way to church." Gigi's eyes were glinting with the glee normally only associated with psychotic murderers.

Natalie conceded that her grandmother probably had a point and closed her eyes and began to pray instead.

Lord, forgive me for calling Vanessa from the tech department a slut, even if she is one. I probably shouldn't have said it. Forgive me for calling Gigi crazy, even though she obviously is and even though we're probably going to die when this car flies off the road on a corner, and we roll down into the ditch just before it explodes. Forgive me for fighting with Brett all those times, though he did deserve it. Forgive me for lusting after a man I thought was my friend's boyfriend, even though he wasn't, and forgive me for kissing him when everyone thought he was her boyfriend, but he wasn't. Though that one isn't actually bad at all. So never mind on that. Forgive me for being a big fat failure and having to move home to live with my grandma. Forgive me—

"You coming in?"

Natalie opened her eyes and saw that the car had stopped and was parked in the side lot of the church. Gigi sat beside her, a flush on her wrinkled cheeks and a smile on her face.

"Um. Yeah. Sorry." She unbuckled her seatbelt. Her grandmother put a hand on her arm.

"Wait. Before we go in there, maybe you ought to kind of lay low about AJ today. You know, not push things." Her grandmother's expression was concerned now. Her former glee dissipating.

"What do you mean?"

"Well, I know you'd never go after another woman's man. You aren't like that. But not everyone in this town knows that. After all, you've been gone a while, and living in the city no less. I think last night's little situation showed that emotions are running hot right now. Maybe you and AJ ought to back off of each other for a bit, give the town some time to catch up."

Natalie nodded. That idea had some merit. After she'd gone to bed last night, she'd lain there staring at the ceiling trying to figure out what to do. It was hands down the best kiss she'd ever had. It was short and relatively innocent. Something about that kiss, though, had turned her inside out. It had felt so…right. Electric, but also like two puzzle pieces that just fit, easy and perfect. Then the old lady circus had begun. But until that moment, it had been…almost magical, and she had replayed it in her mind again and again until she'd finally drifted off to sleep.

Then Natalie had woken up this morning. In the harsh light of the morning, she felt kind of dirty about the whole thing. She'd just left Memphis under the impact of a scandal. She didn't need another one. There was nowhere left to run to.

"I can do that."

"Good girl. Let's go." Gigi turned to open the door. "Oh, dear, it looks windy out. I hope my hairspray can stand up to it."

Natalie rolled her eyes for the twentieth time that day, tightened her ponytail, and climbed out of the car. Gigi was already ahead of her, the wind blowing her skirt around. She had a scarf wrapped loosely around her head and was trying to hold it in place with two hands. Natalie used both of her hands to keep her own A-line skirt from blowing up. She'd seen the pictures of Marilyn Monroe, and sex icon or not, Natalie had no desire to emulate her. For starters, her underwear weren't that great—plain pink cotton. Nothing worth showing off.

Gigi, however, had no such concern. Her peach colored skirt was airborne, billowing up around her thighs.

"Mother, your skirt. Grab your skirt!" DeeJay yelled from the church steps, where a small crowd was standing shaking hands and waiting for approaching members of the congregation.

"I paid twelve dollars for this hairdo. I'll be darned if I let it get messed up." Gigi kept her hands firmly planted on her scarf as her skirt took flight and rose up higher and higher until one final, cursed gust blew it up clear past her shoulders.

A gasp went up from the crowd on the church steps. Pastor Matt winced, clearly having seen too many elderly female bottoms recently. Henrietta cackled, finally glad to have company in that small club of pastor flashers. DeeJay groaned, and Natalie's father threw his hands up over his eyes like he'd been doused with acid. Brett screamed and ran inside the church. Charlie Jackson watched with fascination as Gigi ran up the stairs into the sanctuary, showing clearly that her red satin panties were indeed a thong. Come to think of it, that thong looked pretty familiar. It looked just like one of her own that she remembered unpacking just a few days ago. Oh, no! It just got worse and worse. And to top it all off, Natalie didn't think she'd ever get the sight of those pruney cheeks out of her brain, and if Charlie's wolf whistle was any indication, neither would he.

Natalie ascended the stairs at a slower pace than her grandmother, and decided to keep the ownership of the offending underwear to herself. She had enough trouble as it was. Her parents greeted her at the top.

"I would have fixed her hair for free," her mother informed her. "It's not my fault she insists on paying Lila. In fact, I think she does it just to irk me." Deejay gave her daughter a hug and clucked over the ponytail that Natalie had pulled over her shoulder. "I'd do yours for free too if you'd come down to the salon one day."

"I know, Mama. But no, thanks. I'm fine with this." Natalie turned to her father. "Hi, Daddy. How are you?" Her father wrapped her up in a hug and held on to her.

"I'm a little ticked that you haven't been by to see me yet. How long you been in town? Three days? And still my girl doesn't come by."

DeeJay swatted his arm. "Don't say 'ticked' at church."

"I'm not at church. I'm outside of it. It doesn't count." He kept one arm around Natalie's shoulders as they started for the door.

"Sorry, Daddy. It's been a busy few days. I'll come over for lunch after church, spend the afternoon. That sound alright?"

"Sure." He gave her arm a squeeze, then dropped it to reach out and shake the preacher's hand. They men greeted each other, then Pastor Matt turned to Natalie.

"Well now, here's someone I haven't seen in a while. Natalie, dear, you just get prettier and prettier every time I see you." Pastor Matt was nearing forty, with salt and pepper hair and a genuine, friendly smile. He had moved to town when Natalie had been a teenager, and while he wasn't truly a local, he was still an Arkansas boy. In no time, he had fit in and become part of the community. She thanked him for the compliment, and her father beamed with pride and patted her on the back.

Pastor Matt continued, "I hear you're helping out at the senior center these days. If there's anything we can do here at the church, you be sure to let me know. We do a lot with the seniors around here. In fact, we're taking a trip to Branson, Missouri to see a gospel music show in a few weeks. You ought to advertise it down at the center. The more the merrier—all faiths invited."

Natalie smiled. "That sounds like a good idea. I'll be sure to do that."

"Information is in the bulletin. We're having a pie auction to pay for it. I'd love to have your help. We always need more hands."

Natalie agreed to look into it, and then followed her parents into the sanctuary. It was a small church, seating only about a hundred and fifty people, though that many only ever showed up at Christmas and Easter. The windows were stained glass, though nothing terribly fancy, and an organ and a piano sat on opposite sides of the dais.

Her family sat all in one long pew, about halfway down, in the exact center of the church. Gigi and Brett were already seated, though not next to one another. Years ago they had adopted a sort of birth order seating arrangement. Gigi on one end and Natalie on the other. The remaining members of the family filed into the pew and took their respective seats just as the doors closed and the piano began to play.

The Jacksons were seated to the right of them. Charlie and AJ were shaking hands with the couple in front of them. Natalie watched as AJ smiled politely and presented his hand to greet one of the women who had been at Gigi's the night before, and saw as the woman frowned at him and gave him her back, turning away to whisper something into the ear of the woman in front of her. They both turned back to him to give him a glare, and then proceeded to whisper again. Natalie saw AJ's face as he took this in, putting the rejected hand into his pocket. Her heart hurt for him.

He must have felt her gaze, or maybe he'd been waiting for her to come in, because he turned back to look her way and caught her eye. She gave him a little wave. He stared for a moment without responding before he nodded briefly then resumed facing the front.

Surely not everyone would treat him like that, would they? This was church. Judge not and all that. But Natalie watched as lips turned toward ears and whispers passed from person to person, and their eyes always turned first to her with a look of pity and then to AJ with condemnation. Natalie felt her face heat up. Then she saw a separate wave of whispers start on the other side of the church, only this time the scandalized looks were directed at Gigi. They must've heard about the thong. Natalie leaned forward a little to peer over and see her grandmother's reaction. The older woman beamed and held her head high, even winked at Henrietta, who turned pink and giggled.

Natalie had forgotten about this part of small town life—the part where everyone knows your business and considers it fair game for gossip and judgment. She watched as AJ stood next to his grandfather, weathering the stormy looks aimed his way. It wasn't right.

An open hymnal was pressed into Natalie's hands. She looked up at her brother, who rolled his eyes before returning to the song. Natalie squared her shoulders, reached one hand up to smooth her ponytail, and opened her mouth and sang out in her best and loudest voice. The fact that this had heads turning her way again—this time in shock and horror at the sounds she was producing—meant nothing to her. Who cared if she was a terrible singer? She'd had quite enough of feeling embarrassed today.

After the song was finished, Pastor Matt took approached the pulpit, a grin on his kind face, "Well, thank the Lord for that joyful noise."

Brett snickered, so Natalie elbowed him in the ribs, giving all of the eyes that had turned her way a beaming smile.

Pastor Matt went on with the announcements, the offering was collected, and a few more hymns were sung, though with less enthusiasm from Natalie than before. The sermon was given. The pastor spoke about God's unconditional love, and described the prostitute who came to Simon's house and fell at Jesus' feet, weeping on him and drying the tears with her hair. It was a story that Natalie had heard often, and even though she knew she should follow the message more closely, Natalie's mind wandered away from the sermon into her own troubles. God's love may be unconditional, but the love of the townsfolk seemed to come with quite a few conditions. In Natalie's own case, that was great news as she was accepted back into the fold with open arms. AJ wasn't so lucky. After the final prayers were spoken, the congregation was dismissed, and everyone stood to leave.

Charlie Jackson made a beeline for Gigi. He leaned in and whispered something in her ear, causing her to blush and giggle. Natalie noticed his hand lingered on the older woman's back, almost caressing.

"Well, I don't think that's entirely acceptable in a church, do you?" Natalie's mother asked. Natalie's father shook his head.

"Oh, let the young lovers have their fun, DeeJay. They're doing nothing wrong," he told her.

Natalie agreed, "I think they're cute."

"You, young lady, don't get to talk about *cute* today. You are the expert on what is *not* cute today. I want to speak with you at home, at *our* home. Go right on out and get into that truck. You're not sneaking out on me today."

Natalie protested, "Mama, I drove here in my own car. I'll meet you there." Her fingers were crossed behind her back. There were thousands of places she could hide out until her mother's mood had passed, and she intended to find one.

"In the truck. Two minutes." The most unsettling part of the conversation, for Natalie, was how her mother's face continued to look pleasant. They could be discussing their plans for lunch or the pie auction. No outsider could tell that Natalie was seriously beginning to fear for her safety— or at least her sanity.

"I already promised Daddy that I'd come to lunch, Mama. You can trust me." Her father raised his hands in surrender, backing away and heading up the aisle toward the exit. Natalie's mother didn't say a word. She just raised her eyebrow, the only outward indication that she was fed up with her youngest child.

Natalie let out a breath. "Let me tell Gigi I can't drive her. There's no way I'm giving her my keys."

Gigi beat her to the punch, however, flitting over in a rush, "I'm going to lunch with Charlie. I'll see ya'll later." With that, she rushed to Charlie's side and they exited the building into the sunshine.

"I hope she holds onto her skirt this time," Natalie mumbled. DeeJay turned her eyes to heaven and whispered a prayer.

Natalie started toward the open church doors, stopping for a moment to search the room for AJ. He was nowhere in sight. Too bad. She would've liked to talk to him for a minute. See how he was holding up after last night's geriatric ambush. He had mentioned coming over for lunch after church, but now Natalie figured the plan was off, though she would've liked hearing the words.

Her daddy chose to catch a ride with Brett back to the house. Smart man. The whole ride to her parents' house, Natalie got an earful on how the members of the family must be in on some kind of a secret plot to ruin DeeJay's life, to bury her in embarrassment, how she didn't know how she would show her face in town on Monday. Natalie tuned it out and focused her attention on the scenery instead. She'd heard her mother's rant a thousand times. It seemed like someone was always doing something to embarrass her mother. Usually is was Gigi, but occasionally Natalie or Brett would do something to set her off. It was rarely Natalie's father. Natalie was pretty sure that DeeJay Gale had married Danny James simply because, being quiet and reserved, he was guaranteed not to embarrass her, and he usually didn't.

The May sun had brought out the flowers. The dogwoods and daffodils had already lost their blossoms, but the irises and lilacs were gorgeous. Natalie pressed her forehead against the cool glass of the window and watched the familiar countryside passing by. She knew what those fields and hills looked like in the winter with snow piled up on the cedars. She knew what they looked like when the autumn winds blew the red and yellow leaves around in waves. It filled her with warmth to think of those postcard images that she had grown up seeing every day. Then again, Memphis was nice. It had a lot of trees and parks, and then there was the Mississippi River, of course, but all that concrete and asphalt couldn't hold a candle to Arkansas in May. Then again, Big Springs did have something else that Memphis didn't...her family.

"And then there's that poster of hers. I don't know why I was so surprised to see her flashing her behind at church today. You know she's got copies of that one stashed away in tissue paper. It's that one of her in the yellow bikini with her legs up in the air. I don't know how I show my face in this town when everyone in the world has seen almost all

128

of my mother's goods." DeeJay made the turn into the driveway.

"It shouldn't be such a shock for everyone then, since they've already seen her booty before," Natalie offered.

DeeJay scoffed. "That's hardly reassuring, honey. Did you know she got one of those posters laminated? Took it right up to the post office to get it done where everyone could see. No shame at all. You know, I think she's proud of it."

Natalie laughed. "It's not like it's Playboy, Mama. It was an ad for a swimsuit. And just so you know, it's hanging on the wall in her bedroom."

"Thank heavens your father hasn't seen it. He has a hard enough time as it is having a mother-in-law like her." The car pulled into the carport, and DeeJay cut the engine. They sat in the car, the silence weighing down the moment. Natalie's mother sat staring forward, her private struggles playing across her face.

Maybe it was the angle, maybe it was the years that had passed since Natalie had just sat looking at her mother, but Natalie saw now that her mother looked older. The skin under her neck hung a little more than it used to. There were laugh lines, the accumulation of happier moments written on her face, but there was also a crinkle between her mother's carefully plucked eyebrows that hadn't been there before. It made Natalie sad to see it, made her wonder if some part of that worry line hadn't been made by her.

"She means well, Mama. You know she doesn't embarrass you on purpose. It's almost like she can't help it, like some kind of a personality handicap that makes her a little stranger than the rest of us."

"Don't you dare suggest that to her. She'd take it as license to be even more outrageous." They laughed together, but the laughter had a sad tinge to it.

"I'm sorry. You know, for all the times I've embarrassed you. I don't mean it either." Natalie reached over and squeezed her mother's hand.

"Oh, honey," her mother said, pulling her into her arms into an awkward car hug, the gear shift digging into their sides, seatbelts still on and holding them back. "I want you to know, Natalie, that you have never embarrassed me in the way that my mother does. You never could, because under it all, I'm just too proud of you to ever be truly ashamed."

Natalie closed her eyes tight and soaked in the moment. She hadn't had such an honest, soul-bearing moment with her mother in years and years. It was overdue.

"We better go in soon," DeeJay said as she pulled away. "Your father will be starving to death. If we don't get lunch ready soon, he'll decide to *cook*, and that means we'll all be eating bowls of cereal."

"You ladies coming inside?" Natalie's father shouted from the open front door. "I'm wasting away. Do you want me to make something?"

"No!" both women shouted, then laughed and got out of the car.

After a quick lunch of chicken salad sandwiches with chips and sweet tea, the men settled down in the living room for their weekly Sunday nap. Brett stretched out on the loveseat, a mountain of throw pillows piled up under his legs to prop up his bare feet. Natalie's father reclined in his favorite chair, tipped back with an arm covering his eyes. DeeJay sat down on the couch, her legs curled under her, and Natalie sat on the floor, her back resting against the loveseat.

"Tell me about AJ," her mother prompted.

Brett groaned. "No. No more talking about AJ."

Their mother frowned. "What's wrong with you? I thought AJ was your buddy."

Brett huffed, eyes still closed. "He is, which is why I don't want to talk to him, and I *really* don't want to talk about him kissing my sister. Yuck." Natalie elbowed him hard in the hip. He grunted in pain. "I don't know why he'd even want to, mean as you are. I think you broke something. I'll probably walk with a limp from now on."

Natalie gave a satisfied smile and said sweetly, "Why brother dear, whatever are you talking about? I didn't hit you. Maybe you're having a bad dream."

He took a throw pillow from his cache and shoved it over his ears to block them out. "I'm sleeping."

Natalie rolled her eyes. "Why doesn't he sleep at his own place? It's not like it's far away."

Her mother shrugged her shoulders. "He says our house is more comfortable. He's almost as weird as your grandmother. No wonder he doesn't have a girlfriend. Spends all his time with that bull of his. I wonder sometimes if he isn't spending *too much* time with the bull— if you know what I mean." She winked at Natalie.

"I always thought there was something special between him and Cupid. The way that bull would follow him around everywhere," Natalie added.

"I can still hear you, and you two are sick." Brett threw the pillow at his sister, stood up, and stormed out of the house, mumbling to himself the whole way.

Natalie and her mother giggled. Natalie thought she even saw her father chuckle a little before his breathing smoothed back out into the easy rhythm of sleep.

"Now that he's gone, tell me the truth, what's going on there? I never took you for the kind of woman who'd go after her best friend's man—even if Jamie isn't technically your best friend anymore." DeeJay sipped the tea that she held in her hands, waiting patiently for the response Natalie wasn't sure she could give.

"It's complicated," she began.

DeeJay raised an eyebrow. "Try me."

Natalie filled her mother in on the made-for-TV-movie style drama that had unfolded over the past few days, glossing over the kissing part, not mentioning how the kiss had felt like more than just a simple meeting of lips. Natalie had kissed her share of guys over the years, a few boys in high school, a handful in college, then her relationship with Brantley, which she'd thought had been something special. None of those kisses had ever made her feel like AJ's did. It scared her a little, though she'd never admit it to anyone. She hadn't even really admitted it to herself. It had turned her inside out and outside in.

"It isn't that big of a deal, Mama. Nothing serious to get too worked up about. After all, I'm not here to stay, you know. I don't want to get too involved with someone from Big Springs, not when I'm heading back as soon as I get a few things lined out. I'm certainly not planning on staying here forever."

Her mother frowned, the crinkle between her eyebrows appearing again. She stared down into her tea, swirling the ice. "Would it be so bad to stay? I can understand wanting to move away from your grandmother, but what about the rest of us? What's so bad about Big Springs?"

Natalie felt lower than dirt. She wished she could call the words back, bottle them up and bury them somewhere so they'd never be able to hurt anyone ever again. But she couldn't. They were out there, and now her mother was hurt...crushed if the expression on her face was any indication.

"That's not how I meant it."

"Yes, it is. You've been trying to get out of this town since the day you were born. I've been trying to keep you here for just as long, but I know that's selfish of me. I just can't help but want you here, honey." Her mother turned her face toward the wall, and Natalie thought she saw a tear or two fall onto her shirt.

"I want you here too," her father spoke, his deep voice startling both women.

"Daddy, I thought you were sleeping," Natalie said.

He still lay stretched out and reclined back in his comfortable old chair, arm thrown over his eyes. "Impossible to sleep with you both yammering like that. Thought that if I couldn't sleep, I might as well toss in my two pennies."

Natalie smiled. "Thanks you guys. I love you both."

"We'll convince you to stay. One way or another," her father said seriously, still in his napping position. "We have our ways."

"What are you going to do tie me up and keep me in the barn?" Natalie asked, laughing a little.

"Won't need to. You'll see," he promised her. "Now hush up and let me nap."

Natalie left shortly thereafter, walking down the drive and across the road to her Gigi's house. She knew every footstep by heart and thought about the thousands of times she'd taken this same stroll. It did feel good, but it wasn't good enough reason to stay in Big Springs, though if her father's words were any indication, she might decide to stick around after all.

Chapter 13

Natalie spent the next several days working her tail off at the senior center. She woke up at seven each morning, "nearly noon" according to Gigi, and spent her days ordering and installing the exercise equipment, stacking yoga mats in bins, and organizing DVDs that promised to tone and tighten through yoga, dance, stretching, or kickboxing. They'd amassed four treadmills, two stationary bikes, several sets of hand weights, and a large flat screen TV, courtesy of an anonymous donor.

Natalie kept expecting to see AJ, but he appeared to be avoiding her. He hadn't come by, even when Charlie had stopped in for dinner. When he and Brett hauled the hay off of the Jackson place, Natalie had expected to be hassled about driving the truck, but no one said a word. Later on, she'd heard that they'd gotten thirteen year old Reggie Lamb from church to do it. She wasn't disappointed to miss hauling hay, but it didn't feel good to be replaced.

Yesterday when she'd been standing at Barb's waiting for her carry-out lunch order, she'd seen AJ stop just in front of the big picture window, look in, then turn away and keep on walking. The worst slight, though, had been on the road. She'd passed him on her way home, and while she'd given him a big wave and a smile, he'd raised one finger in greeting. Granted, it had been his index finger and not its less popular brother, but in this part of the country, the single finger wave might as well have been the royal brush off.

It was fine with her, though. She barely knew the man. Yes, she would admit quite freely that he was handsome, hot, hunky, and every other yummy description a woman could think of. She would probably even admit that he was interesting to talk to and kind of fun to be around. But she would never, ever, ever admit...not even to herself...that their kiss had meant anything at all. It was just a kiss. She'd had dozens, maybe even hundreds of kisses. His was nothing special. That was what she told herself every time she thought about it, which was hardly ever...or a couple times an hour, if she was honest with herself, which she rarely was lately.

Natalie taped the new fitness schedule to the window of the front office, then set about straightening up the various brightly colored sign-up sheets that lay neatly on the countertop in the front office. It made her happy to see this formerly empty stretch of space filling up. It made her even happier to see so many names already written on the sign-up pages, though Gigi, Henrietta, and Mabel were listed on nearly every single one, which was sweet. She'd bet those three would be sleeping like babies and trying to erase their names after a full week of the fitness classes.

"Knock, knock," Jamie said from the doorway. Her slight frame was clad in yoga capris and a modest tank top, showing off her trim figure and some surprising biceps. "I know we said four, but I thought I'd come by a little early. It's my day off, and it was either come early or start cleaning my bathroom, so here I am!" Jamie's top knot was jiggling as she bounced with anticipation.

"Great! I'm so glad you came. I was just finishing up here, anyway. Let me get changed into my workout clothes, and we can try out all the new equipment." Natalie was claiming organizer's privileges and had invited Jamie over to check out the new Mature Athlete's Fitness Center, as the seniors called it. "I'll just grab my bag and go to the restroom to change. Why don't you head on in? It's that one down there with the schedules taped next to the door. I think Gigi might already be in there."

Jamie took off for the room, water bottle swinging as she skipped down the hall. Five minutes later, Natalie had just finished tying her shoes when Jamie came back, walking sedately, her lips pressed into a thin line, her expression inscrutable.

"Oh, no! Are you ok? Is someone hurt?" Natalie asked her, looking her over for injuries.

Jamie shook her head, then nodded in the direction from which she'd come. Her eyes were wide, but her lips didn't move.

"What is it?"

Jamie shook her head again and indicated for Natalie to follow her, which she did, her heart beating heavy in her chest. What if something was broken? What if *someone* was broken?

Jamie stopped at the door to the fitness room, and waited for Natalie to step in. As soon as Natalie rounded the corner she understood Jamie's grim expression. What she saw inside that room would haunt her nightmares for years to come. It would pop into her head at inconvenient times, distracting her while she was driving, causing her to swerve. It would never leave the recesses of her brain. All this she knew in an instant.

There were probably a dozen older women working out. The treadmills were full. One biker was spinning vigorously. Several ladies were gathered around the remote, trying to figure out how to work the new DVD player. Then there was Gigi, Henrietta, and Mabel…all bending over stretching their hamstrings. Each and every single woman was wearing a Jane Fonda style workout outfit. There were brightly colored tights with leggings and tennis shoes. There were terry cloth headbands and wristbands everywhere. Then, of course, there were the leotards. Neon colors with belts. Leg holes cut high over hip bones and tops cut low into the cleavage. The worst, though, the primary image that would keep repeating itself in Natalie's mind, was the thongs.

Gigi, Henrietta, and Mabel…all bent over…all in a thong leotard. Gigi with her meatless bones, Henrietta with her boneless meat, and Mabel with her miles and miles of long, muscular legs and…the horror, the horror.

Natalie nodded, raised her hand in a wave, and backed out of the room slowly. Why she didn't turn around she couldn't say. It was like the sight had entranced her, and she couldn't stop looking. Finally, Natalie cut her eyes to Jamie, then back at the scene in front of her. Jamie had tears running down her face, which was now a color beyond pink, crossing into reddish purple. She tugged on Natalie's arm.

They pair bolted down the hallway and into the blessedly empty TV room. Natalie fell onto the floor in a heap, Jamie shutting the door behind them. Both lay on the rugs, laughing until they held onto their bellies with tears running down their faces until they gasped for air.

"My abs hurt," Natalie said, wiping her face with her hands.

"My eyes hurt." Jamie wiped the streaked mascara from under her eyes.

"I don't think I'll ever get that image out of my head." Natalie sat up and started to redo her ponytail, which had tilted askew.

"Do you think they called each other and planned out their outfits for today? Like, 'Good morning, Henrietta. What do you say we wear some thongs?'" Jamie started giggling again.

"Or, 'Don't worry, Mabel. You can borrow one of mine, just be sure to wash it before you give it back.'" Natalie pulled her ponytail tight, then smoothed it out over her shoulder.

"Let's make a pact. Someday when we're that age and coming here, or wherever, to workout, let's wear something a little less...um…"Jamie struggled for the right word.

"Up our butt cracks?" Natalie offered.

"Exactly. Deal?" Jamie stuck out her hand, and Natalie shook it.

"Deal," Natalie agreed. She thought about what she'd just shook on, and deep down, kind of hoped she and Jamie would be back here in another thirty or forty years, still friends and still close enough to want to work out together. It sobered her.

"I don't know if I'll be here. I mean, if I go back to Memphis like I planned, I don't know… I mean…I hope we'll still be friends then."

"I hope we are. I'll plan on it. Even if you go back to Memphis. I've missed you, you know. Then back in high school, I still thought of myself as your friend, but you were just so busy. It was hard to find time to hang out. You were always either studying or picking up trash for a club or working a fundraiser to go to some kind of camp. I just kept waiting for you to slow down." She shrugged. "Then you moved away. All those years you were gone, I still missed you." Jamie reached over and took Natalie's hand. "Another pact. Friends, no matter what?"

Natalie squeezed Jamie's hand. She didn't know how she'd gotten so lucky, "Friends."

**

AJ was avoiding Natalie. He'd seen her waiting next to the counter in Barb's and had decided to just grab a hot dog from the gas station. He'd convinced young Reggie to drive the truck in the hayfield, which turned out to be a disaster. Reggie had been playing games on his phone and had nearly run into a fence before they'd gotten him stopped, because he'd also worn his headphones so loud that he hadn't heard them call out. Yesterday when AJ had passed her on the road, he'd waved to her when she did, but his heart just wasn't in it. Now here he was, doing his least favorite job on the farm, fixing fence, because he knew that there was no chance he'd run into her out here in the back field.

That was the problem. His heart. AJ had kicked himself after that kiss—that night and every minute since then. What had he been thinking? With everything he'd been through, he knew better than to get in too deep with a girl like her. He wasn't looking for a fling or whatever people called it. A short term deal. He wanted a woman who planned on sticking around a while. But he'd had a thing for Natalie for so long, he just hadn't been able to help himself.

But that had been some kiss. She'd looked beautiful. Like she always did, but there had been something special about her that night. Maybe it was just proximity. Then when she'd told Jamie all about Memphis and why she'd left...well, his heart had starting beating a different way. That was the thing about Natalie James. She just did it for him. Everything about her. Everything except that she was leaving, and AJ had lost enough people he'd cared out in his life. He didn't want to lose another.

He wanted to see her, though. It wasn't like he could avoid her much longer. Big Springs was a small town. In fact, it might be better if he went ahead and got it over with. Said what needed to be said about that kiss. Tell her that he had enjoyed it...understatement...and then explain that he wanted more than just a temporary thing. Sure, if given half a chance, he'd love to kiss her again, maybe see about some of those fantasies he'd had about her, some of which involved her in that pink bikini again, and others involved her in a white dress holding a bouquet of roses.

AJ flexed his hands over the handle post-hole digger he'd been using, resting it on the ground to lean against it. He was nearly finished in this field. Set the post, attach and stretch the fence. By the time he was done, got back to the house and cleaned up, she'd be back from the senior center. Not that he kept track of her schedule. Gramps kept track of Gertie's schedule, and Gertie's schedule was the same as Natalie's. So, yes, AJ knew what time Natalie usually got home. That didn't mean he had been thinking about heading over there every day around this time. At least, that's what he told himself.

By the time AJ crossed the creek in Gertie's drive, he'd worked out exactly what he wanted to say. He'd explain that he didn't want a casual relationship, and that if she planned on sticking around Big Springs, he'd like to pursue something serious with her, but if she was returning to Memphis, he hoped they could remain friends.

AJ saw Natalie's car parked in front of the house. His heart began to beat faster, and he reminded himself to be cool. As his truck approached the turn in the drive, he saw someone crouched at the far edge of the garden. He slowed to a stop and parked, planning his strategy as he exited the truck. If it was Gertie, he'd say 'hey' and search out her granddaughter, but if it was Natalie, it might be easier to have their talk out here away from Gertie's ears.

A row of corn stood chest high, and from the road he couldn't make out much more than a large floppy straw hat. He ran a hand through his hair and stepped carefully between the rows of the garden, doing his best not to let his massive feet crush anything edible. Even though he wasn't trying to be quiet, whoever it was must not hear or see him, because she was still crouched down digging in the dirt.

"Hello?" He stepped between two thick rows of corn. He went to separate the stalks to step into sight, when he heard soft singing, if it could be called that. It was a song he knew from high school. A song about women's underwear.

AJ clamped a hand over his mouth to keep from laughing out loud. That was definitely Natalie. He'd heard her singing off key in church on Sunday, but had assumed she'd been trying to detract attention from her grandmother's latest scandal. He grinned. Obviously, it hadn't been an act. Her voice was atrocious. Beyond awful. He'd heard crows carry a better tune. Not that he'd ever tell her that, of course.

He parted the corn and stepped through. "Is that the *Thong Song?*" he asked Natalie's crouched figure.

She squealed, dropping her hand trowel in the dirt, and jumped up, white earbuds falling to the ground beside her. Her hand flew to her chest, and she was breathing heavily.

All these details flooded into AJ's brain at once, but they were in the periphery. His entire mind and body were focused on Natalie's gorgeous, slim figure in a pink bikini: long legs that led up to curving hips, a nipped in waist, then higher a pair of truly magnificent…He took a deep breath. He could feel his mouth hanging open, knew he was staring, as focused as a scud missile, but had absolutely no control over himself at that moment. She was hot. Hotter than hot. The years that had lapsed between his last sight of her in a bikini had been extremely kind to her. Adoring. Devoted. Those years had lavished her with love.

A large, straw hat covered the expansive skin he'd been admiring, and AJ felt the crush of disappointment. He was a man, after all. Then realized what had just happened, where his gaze had been, and snapped his eyes up to meet Natalie's.

142

"Hey," he offered lamely. Not cool. Not cool at all.

"I'm gardening." She kept the hat in front of her. Too bad.

"I can see that. I didn't mean to sneak up on you. I called out, but—"

She spoke over him, "I was listening to my iPod."

"You were singing."

He saw the blush begin creeping across her chest from the edge of the hat, spreading upward into her cheeks. AJ employed superhuman willpower and didn't let his eyes linger down to try to peek behind the hat.

He went on, adding, "I've always liked that song. Superb artistry in it. Lyrical genius that expresses exactly what a person would expect in a song about underwear. "

Natalie rolled her eyes. "It summarizes a large part of my day today." AJ raised his eyebrows. Now this sounded promising. "Gigi," Natalie said, mischief in her eyes, "in a thong."

AJ threw his hand over his eyes. "I already have that image in my head from church last week. Did she do it again? Someone really ought to make sure that woman wears pants. Only pants, no skirts, no dresses."

Natalie laughed. It was a nice sound. Musical almost....definitely more musical than her singing. "In her defense she did have on tights underneath it. She was working out down at the senior center, and all the old women made a pact to pull out their old exercise outfits from the eighties to sort of christen the place."

"I don't want to know. You should stop there."

"All of them, every single one wearing leotards," Natalie said. Her face had taken on a kind of devious charm. He could easily envision her as one of those Sirens from Greek mythology, only without the singing. All she'd have to do is talk. He couldn't stop her, couldn't turn away.

She continued. "Henrietta Sellers was wearing a leotard cut up so high on her thighs, I could see her bikini line."

"Please stop."

"Mabel. You know, lunch lady Mabel, Gigi's friend? Hers had normal thigh cut outs, but the top dipped down so low, her breasts were—"

"No. I draw the line at Mabel's breasts. Oh, man. There's something I never thought I'd say." AJ rubbed his face with his hands. "The image is already there. Why, Natalie? Why?"

She laughed again, and it sparked something inside of him. "I've got the real images in my mind, the memory of it." She went on dramatically, "and it will haunt my dreams for years to come."

He chuckled. "So the song was appropriate. I get it now." She nodded. He cleared his throat. "Not that I'm complaining, but where are your clothes? Do you always garden without them? If so, I'm going to start planning my visits accordingly."

Natalie's blush, which had receded during their conversation, crept back up. He was starting to hate straw hats. She still held hers in front of her.

"No. Well, I'm not sure. I haven't gardened in years, and I thought that since I was working outside, and since it was so hot, I thought I might get a little sun, start getting a little bit of a tan. It's not all that I imagined it would be, though," she admitted. "Turns out," she leaned in conspiratorially, hat in place, "gardens are dirty. I think I need the protection that pants provide."

"I can't tell you how sorry I am to hear that." He said with complete sincerity. She shrugged her shoulders.

"Did you come over for something? I haven't seen much of you lately. Not since Saturday night." Her eyes stared straight at him, not blinking, not turning away. AJ shifted his weight from foot to foot.

"Yeah, I've been busy. Farm work. Gramps keeps a list of repairs and such." He rubbed the back of his neck and looked at the field where the sun was lowering toward the horizon, but not yet a sunset.

"That's bull crap and you know it."

AJ's eyes snapped back to Natalie. He nodded. "I wasn't sure what to do about you," he told her honestly.

"Have you decided yet?" She kept her gaze on him. He could sense the tension in her, just as he could feel it in his own.

"I'd like to take you out, if you'll go." he said. "Will you go out with me?"

It was Natalie's turn to look off into the distant field. She sighed, and seeming to forget herself, put her hat back on her head, "I guess so."

"You've just made me a very happy man." AJ didn't ogle her this time. He smiled, and kept his gaze trained on her face. "How about Saturday night? We could go to Knight's."

It was commonly known that Luigi's was for families, friends, and casual dates. Knight's was for lovers, anniversaries, first dates, and prom nights. It was situated just over the springs, having been added a while back as an upscale restaurant for tourists and for the locals celebrating special occasions. It overlooked the springs and was near the swimming hole, which could be reached by trekking down a long, winding wooden staircase that was built into the side of the hollow.

"That might be a little too *public*, you know. Considering that most of the town thinks you've thrown Jamie over for me. Maybe not the best move. You know, if you want to continue living in this town without being ridden out on a rail."

He nodded. She had a good point. "What does that leave then? Driving to Harrison for dinner?"

She scrunched up her nose. "No. How about a picnic? Maybe we could pack something up and go down to the creek somewhere and eat? Someplace less conspicuous. That way no one has to know. We could each say we were going out to meet Jamie, then meet up."

"That makes us sound like a couple of teenagers sneaking around. I don't know." He rubbed his neck again. "I don't like it. I'd rather take you out somewhere nice. Not lie and sneak out like we're doing something wrong."

"Think of it this way. We don't know if *this*," she motioned to the two of them, "is anything or not. It could be the start of a beautiful friendship, or it could be..." She bit her bottom lip, which was pure torture.

"Could be more?"

"Why don't we just lie low until we know a little more? I mean, I barely know anything about you."

"I know a little more about you, but that's mostly from your folks and your brother."

"None of which can be trusted."

"So we'll do it your way? Keep it on the down low until we know more," he said.

She stuck out a hand to shake on it, and he took her hand in his. It seemed to him, as sappy as it sounded, that something passed between them. Maybe not, but there was definitely a moment there between them.   And even though he wouldn't admit it to anyone but himself, he already knew. At least he knew how it was with him. It could be more.

Chapter 14

When Natalie woke up on Friday morning, she lay in bed and reveled in the idea that her date with AJ was only one day away. She stretched her toes down toward the bottom of the bed and slid down under the covers. It felt nice to have a date coming up. When Brantley had betrayed her, Natalie had thought her heart was broken, but now it felt fine. Pretty good, actually. Maybe even bordering on great. Brantley who?

"Girl, you going to wake up any time today?" Gigi stood fully dressed, cup of coffee in her hand, leaning against the doorway.

"Your face is red. Did you get sunburnt yesterday when you were outside gardening in your swimsuit? I told you to put on sunscreen. Blondes like us gotta wear sunscreen all summer long. I buy it by the gallon at the Sam's Club."

Natalie felt her face. It did feel hot.

"I put on some SPF 30 before I went out, and I wore a big hat." She got out of bed and went to the vanity mirror, then turned her face each way and sure enough, without a doubt, she was burnt. "Oh, no. What happened? I shouldn't be burnt. What about my back and shoulders?"

She lifted up the back of the t-shirt she'd worn to bed. In the mirror, Natalie saw Gigi wince.

"That looks like it smarts a little. Does this hurt?" Gigi touched Natalie's back.

"Not really." That was a good sign.

"What about this?" Gigi asked before she used the edge of her fingernail to gently scratch Natalie's shoulder.

"Holy cow!" Natalie jumped back and threw her hands up defensively. "Don't do that!"

Gigi took another sip of her coffee and leaned back against the door frame. "Your shoulders are burnt pretty good."

Natalie scowled. "You think?" She turned back toward the mirror and pulled down the neck of her shirt until she could see the deep red of the skin on her shoulders. It felt hot to the touch. "How did I not know I was burning?"

"Were you distracted? I always burn the worst when my mind's on other things. Say, a handsome man, for example. Were you thinking about a handsome man while you were working in the garden?" Gigi's mouth twitched like she was holding onto a secret.

"Maybe," Natalie said carefully. "Why do you ask?"

"I talked to Charlie yesterday. He said AJ left yesterday headed this direction, thundering around and moody, and then came back about fifteen minutes later whistling and looking like the cat that got the canary."

Natalie turned away and smiled to herself. If her face hadn't already been red, she would have been blushing.

"I can see you smiling, smart girl. You're facing the mirror," Gigi pointed out. Natalie's smile disappeared. "Just be careful. It'll take people a while to get over The Jilting of Jamie Griffith. You push it too far or too fast, and they're likely to start talking."

"The…what did you call it?" Natalie asked.

"The Jilting of Jamie Griffith. I got up early. Had some time to think of a name for it."

"You need a hobby."

"That fact aside, did you pay attention to the rest of what I said?" Gigi raised an eyebrow.

"Yes, ma'am. He and I already talked about it. We're going out tomorrow night, but we're just going on a picnic, not into town. We don't want to make things difficult for you or Mama or Jamie or Charlie or anyone else who'd have to listen to all the gossip. You know, this kind of a problem would never happen in Memphis."

Gigi nodded. "That might be true, but on the other hand, think of all the people in this small town who care enough about you to wonder what you're up to, and to repeat a story about something that happened. In this town, dear, you are a celebrity. Like Kim Kardashian and Taylor Swift combined."

"I don't know that that helps, Gigi."

"Suit yourself. We need to get moving. I've got a hair appointment in forty-five minutes, and I want to be sure to get there early so I can spend some time with your mama. I swear, if it weren't for me going up there to get my hair done once a week, I wouldn't see that woman."

Natalie rolled her eyes. "I'll be ready to go in ten minutes."

"Make it fifteen and put some makeup on. If you're going to look like a tomato, you might as well look like the prettiest tomato in the garden."

Gigi drove, but she insisted that they take Natalie's car so the ride back wouldn't mess up her hair, which didn't make sense, but having grown up around Gigi, Natalie knew better than to argue. Gigi went to town every Friday morning and to have her hair redone. She'd fluff it up and comb it into place Saturday, Sunday, and Monday morning.

Then when her scalp started to itch, she'd wash it and "do the best she could" for the next few weekdays. This was why she rarely had any plans for that part of the week. Gigi saved all of the best activities and outings for Friday through Monday and went very few places Tuesday, Wednesday, and Thursday. Those were her so-called "home days."

All this she explained to Natalie on the ride to town. Natalie had observed these behaviors over the years, but she'd never had such an extensive explanation before. It crossed her mind more than once that her grandmother was a little nuts, and as a relative, especially one she was living with and tagging along with everywhere, Natalie must be a little nuts also. It wasn't a comforting thought.

Gigi pulled into an open space on Main Street. "I'm going to go on in, so I can get my dryer reserved. I like to sit under the one on the end. I hate that one in the corner. Can't see a thing from there. Why don't you run in Millie's and get us some Cokes? Get your mama a diet, or she'll fuss." She handed Natalie a ten and set off across the street to the salon.

"It's come to this," Natalie mumbled to herself, looking at the cash in her hand. "Errand girl. Great use of my college degree." She groaned and got out of the car. When she stood, she came face to face with Tina Rasmussen, her mother's best friend since high school. "Oh, hi, Tina! I'm sorry if I knocked into you. I wasn't paying attention when I got out."

Tina's face was bright with a huge smile. "Not at all, you pretty thing. I was just coming over here to talk to you. You opened the door just as I was about to knock on your window. How are you?" She pulled Natalie into a big hug. Tina was a tall woman, almost six feet, thin as a reed, and had a chestnut colored pixie cut with highlights streaking down the longer side. DeeJay had always loved to experiment with Tina's hair, and Tina loved to be her test subject with her hairstyles changing with nearly every season.

"I saw you at Luigi's last week, but you left before I could say 'hey' to you," Natalie told her, returning the hug.

Tina waved her hand in a shooing motion. "Oh, we snuck out of there. I didn't want to interrupt you young folks while you were out on the town catching up. I knew I'd see you again soon, since you're back for a while. Then sure enough, here you come driving up right in front of me."
Tina's smile was infectious, and Natalie felt her sour mood evaporate. "Now where did Gertie get to?" She looked from side to side.

"Oh, she was going to get her hair done. I'm supposed to take some drinks over. Bring Mama a Diet Coke as a peace offering, I think."

Tina laughed, throwing her head back and chuckling loudly. "That woman! Why she won't let her own daughter fix her hair, I'll never know. Orneriness, I imagine. Drives DeeJay crazy, she does. A peace offering is probably right."

"She told me it was because she let Mama fix her hair once when Mama was about sixteen, and it was so 'God awful' that she hasn't let her near her head ever since." Natalie used air quotes over her grandmother's words, garnering another chuckle from Tina.

"It was the late seventies! I remember that hairstyle. I had the same one--Farrah Fawcett's hair. It was so cool and trendy. Looked just like Farrah, she did!" Natalie raised an eyebrow at that image. "Oh, I know. Your grandmother is just not the Farrah type. She's a classic kind of woman. You know, she's had the same hairstyle for forty years."

Tina gave Natalie a one-armed hug. "It's so good to see you again. You should stop by the Chamber sometime. Maybe put up some of those flyers for the senior center activities. I'm sure some of the people who come in would want to see them. Besides which, having active seniors is going to be a big draw for Big Springs. Who knows? We might draw in retirees. Wouldn't that just be fantastic?"

Tina ran the Big Springs Chamber of Commerce, humble as it was. She made the most out of what she had, planning community events and sending out brochures about the spring to travel agencies and nature organizations across the country. She'd even started a website a few years ago.

She continued, "I tell you what, I'm just about run ragged over there. I've been trying to take a little time off, but it's hard. You know I put up new pictures every week. Try to show off the area, draw some people in."

Natalie had seen the website. Tina, on behalf of the Chamber, ran the weather report every week as well, suggesting activities and advertising the local businesses. She had even talked one of the local fishing guides into starting a blog where he gave the fishing report and shared tips to reel in the big ones. For all her efforts, the town had seen only a small increase in tourism from her efforts, but in Big Springs, every little bit counted.

"I've seen the website. It's amazing! I don't know how you do it all," Natalie said.

"You know Jerry had a little health scare last winter, and I've been trying to slow down, spend some more time with him. He wants to spend all his time up at his hunting cabin, but it's just hard for me to get away. Things are just starting to pick up, and if I stop now, I'm afraid it'll just all fall apart, you know." Tina's smile had dimmed to a polite grin, a sure sign she was worried. Then the woman visibly shook herself, like a dog coming out of the water. "Oh, well." Her thousand watt smile was back. "It was so good to see you. You have got to stop by and see me sometime. Maybe I can pick your brain some…get some of that marketing genius to rub off on me, huh?"

Natalie promised to stop by, hugged her again, and took off to get the peace offering for her mother from Millie's. Tina's worries still hung in the back of her mind. Natalie didn't know if she could do anything to help her, but hoped she'd be able to think of something.

When Natalie entered Blondie's, her mother's salon, she could hear the bickering over the whir of the dryer chairs. Natalie always loved the smell of the salon. It was the combination of shampoo, hairspray, and perm solutions. To her, it was the comforting smell of her mama. Whenever she was sick or sad, DeeJay would gather Natalie up into a hug, holding her on her lap and running her hand over the girl's hair, smoothing it back. Natalie would press her face into her mother's shirt and breathe in the scent of the salon. To this day, the smell was comforting to her. She'd never tell her mother, of course, but a few weeks ago, right after she'd had a fight with Brantley, Natalie had gone in for a trim, not because she needed it, but so that she could breathe in the smell of home. Crazily enough, it had helped.

"Mama, you can't buy a motorcycle. At your age, you'd be dead by the time you got to the bridge." DeeJay was working on the hair of someone whose face Natalie couldn't see because it was covered with a towel as DeeJay carefully doused perm rods with a pungent solution. It was enough to make most people's eyes water, but Natalie didn't mind it at all.

She approached with the Styrofoam cups, straws already in place, sides labeled in black Sharpie. "Morning, Mama," Natalie said as she held the cup up for her mother, whose lips grasped the straw. She took a long pull on the drink, and then sighed in pleasure, her face relaxing a little.

"Did your grandmother tell you she's thinking about buying a motorcycle? Go talk her out of it. I've got to get Mrs. Robertson finished up here. You doing ok, Betty?" DeeJay leaned in and listened to the mumbled response. Natalie gave her mother a puzzled look. DeeJay spoke loudly and deliberately, cueing her daughter. "You remember my daughter Natalie, right Betty? I'm sure she remembers you from the library. Seems like that girl was there every day during the summertime!"

Natalie nodded. "Hey, Mrs. Robertson. I didn't recognize you under that towel. It's good to *almost* see you again." The woman's shoulders shook with muffled laughter, and she wiggled a few fingers in Natalie's direction, but didn't lower the towel from her face.

Natalie took Gigi her drink. Her grandmother was sitting in one of the dryer chairs. It wasn't running yet, but she'd set up her station around it, claiming it for her own. Her purse was on the floor next to it. Gigi had draped a sweater over one arm and a headscarf over the other. She had a book in her lap, which Natalie knew her grandmother didn't intend to read. She'd been carrying around that old copy of *Gone with the Wind* for years, and Natalie had never seen it out anywhere except the beauty shop, where the massive novel would rest, open to a random page and sitting face down in the dryer's seat while Gigi was up getting her hair rolled onto curlers. As soon as she returned to her chair, the massive book would be tucked into the purse.

"Hey, Gigi. Here's your Coke. I also got you a muffin. You want it?" Natalie took the empty dryer chair next to her, since it was unclaimed by old lady paraphernalia.

"No thanks, darling. You can have it. I figured you wanted it anyway." Gigi drank from her Coke, her face showing the same rapturous expression DeeJay's had only moments before. Natalie briefly wondered if that was an issue of nature or nurture, then forgot about it as she took her own sip and felt the ice cold liquid slide down her throat.

"Oh, that's good. God bless Coca-Cola." Natalie turned to her grandmother, "Are you really thinking about getting a motorcycle?" She bit into the muffin. There was a reason everyone went to Millie's for breakfast. The woman was a genius with baked goods.

Gigi scowled. "Why in the world would you think that?"

Natalie rolled her eyes, but refused to be baited. "You told Mama you were going to get one just to rile her, you devil. You're not going to get me. I refuse to be riled today. I'm rile-less." Gigi's eyebrow lifted. Sometimes Natalie hated that eyebrow. "Nothing special, I'm just in a good mood." Gigi's eyebrow remained. "It's not going to work this time. I've got my Coke and my muffin, and I'm not going to talk to you. I told you, I'm rile-less." Natalie gave her a triumphant smile, and Gigi's eyebrows both furrowed.

"What aren't you going to talk about?" DeeJay strolled over and snatched the last bite of muffin from Natalie's hand, popping it into her mouth before her daughter could react. "Sweet heavens, those are good. What in the world does Millie put in those things?" DeeJay studied Natalie, glanced at Gigi, and then asked, "What's going on? Why are you two having a staring contest?" When neither answered, DeeJay turned to her mother, and eyed her suspiciously. "What are you up to?"

Gigi was outraged. "Me? Why do you assume that *I'm* the one up to something?"

"Experience," Natalie's mother replied.

"Well, I never. I don't know why you treat me this way. I go out of my way to get to my hair appointment early just so I can spend some time with my sweet, darling daughter, who I love more than just about anything else, except my grandchildren and the Lord, of course, and how am I treated? Like a pest. I have feelings too, you know. You can't just ignore me and then stomp all over my emotions like this." Gigi rested her head against her hands and sighed loudly. She waited a beat, and when neither DeeJay nor Natalie said anything, she sighed again, louder this time.

Lila, the other hair stylist in Blondie's, scurried over in a flash of red hair. "Gigi, you gorgeous woman, I'm ready for you. Can I get you anything, doll? Something to drink? A cookie?" Lila winked at DeeJay, then sent Natalie an air kiss as she led Gertie off toward her station. Natalie heard Gigi request a cookie, oatmeal if they had it, and they usually did.

Natalie and DeeJay locked gazes a moment. They each shrugged.

"So what's going on with you? I haven't seen you in a couple of days," Natalie's mother told her as she moved the giant novel to sit down.

"That's my seat!" Gigi called from across the room.

"I know, Mama. I'll get out of it when you're ready. I'm just keeping it warm for you," DeeJay called back. She rolled her eyes.

"Not much. Mostly working at the senior center. I did some gardening yesterday, though, just to shake things up."

DeeJay took her daughter's face in her hands and gently turned it to one side. She tugged the loose neck of

Natalie's cotton t-shirt. "Did you forget to wear sunscreen? I've got some aloe at the house. You should stop by and grab it later. It's in a blue bottle under the sink in the bathroom."

Natalie promised she'd stop by and get it, and she fully intended to do so. The sunburn was sore. They spent a few minutes chatting about the people in town: babies being born, kids graduating from high school, a girl Natalie had known from high school with had broken her arm in a water skiing accident. These little bits of news would be considered gossiping to some, but to the people of Big Springs they were just pieces of news. The next time Natalie saw one of the new mothers, she could ask about the baby. She could congratulate a couple at church on their son's graduation, and maybe send a card to the girl who broke her arm. This was exactly what Natalie had been complaining about earlier, but now that she was on the other side of it, discussing the happenings around town felt alright. She genuinely cared about each one of them, and felt their pains and joys with them. All in all, it was a nice conversation.

"DeeJay, how much longer? You didn't forget me, did you?" Mrs. Robertson, who had been flipping through a *National Geographic* waved her hand to get their attention.

DeeJay rushed to reassure her and to show the older woman the kitchen timer, which still held another eight minutes. She returned to Natalie's side, and turned the dial on Gigi's chair dryer before she sat in it. Gigi waved in acknowledgement, knowing DeeJay was warming it up for her.

Natalie watched as her mother's eyes roamed over her daughter's sunburnt face, then strayed and fixed on Natalie's hair, dismay written all over her face.

"I like it," Natalie protested. The best defense was a good offense, after all. "It's easy and classy, and I don't have to worry about keeping up with it. It's always fine."

DeeJay scowled. "A ponytail? It's boring. You look like a tomboy. Your hair is so beautiful when it's down. It's so long and silky. I'd kill for hair like that." Natalie closed her eyes. She'd heard this speech a million times before. "If you'd let me put in a few highlights, just in the crown and around your face, the light would catch and it would really bring out your eyes."

"No, Mama. I like my hair the way it is. It's easy to fix."

"I could do one of those adorable pixie cuts. You saw Tina's hair. I could do it like that, but longer on the one side just a little, about eye level." She held up her hand to show Natalie the length, then proceeded to move her hands around her own head, illustrating the cuts she would make, and how easy it would be to fix in the morning. "Really, you'd hardly have to do anything. Five minutes and you'd be set for the day," she promised, her fingers crossed under her leg.

"I see your fingers," Natalie pointed out. DeeJay uncrossed them.

"Ok, ten minutes, fifteen tops. You'd love it, though. You'd be happy to spend the time fixing it, knowing how great you'd look. You have the perfect face for it." DeeJay clasped her hands as if in prayer, her eyes pleading.

Natalie shook her head. "No. That's my final answer."

DeeJay threw up her hands just as the timer dinged. She hopped up to take care of Mrs. Robertson, who had grown nervous that she'd be sitting there with the perm on her hair until the chemicals fried it and the rods fell out on the floor. Natalie knew this because Mrs. Robertson had begun explaining it to DeeJay as soon as the perm rods had started coming out, one by one unrolled and tossed in the sink.

Gigi tottered over, cape still draped around her front. She sat down in her seat, and Lila fitted the top of the dryer down over the older woman's head. When they'd agreed on the height, Lila went to grab a chair. She set it down a little ways in front of Natalie, and settled in with her can of Diet Coke.

"So, tell me, did you really kiss that hunky AJ Jackson?" When Natalie nodded, Lila sat back and fanned her face. "Oh, you lucky, lucky girl. What I wouldn't give for looks like yours, I'd have that boy eating out of my hands." Lila giggled.

Natalie had known Lila forever. Lila, Tina, and DeeJay had been best friends for years, despite the fact that Lila was eight or so years older than the other two. She'd started out as kind of a mentor to DeeJay during her early years as a hair stylist, but they'd grown as close as sisters over the years.

Natalie's father affectionately referred to the three women as the Amazon Queens, as in the Amazon warrior women of Greek mythology, not the online store, though that might be fitting as well. They all stood over five foot nine, with Lila as the tallest. Her flame red hair flowed behind her in corkscrew curls. They always joked that it was ironic how Lila was a hair stylist, since she didn't have to do a thing to her hair but let it go wild. Her curls were glorious when left to their own devices. If they were cut, they fluffed out like Orphan Annie. So, Lila let them grow long and just added a little product to them on humid days to contain the frizz.

"Your mama already talk to you about changing your hairstyle?" Lila asked. Natalie nodded and rolled her eyes. "Alright then, I won't mention it. But if you're worried about turning out like Farrah Fawcett, I'd be more than happy to do something for you."

Natalie thanked her and assured her that Farrah's hair was the last thing on her mind. They chatted about the same babies, graduations, and broken arm that Natalie had just learned about from her mother. Then they chatted about Jamie, since Lila was her aunt, the older sister to Jamie's dad. Natalie told her all about the Jane Fonda workout outfits she and Jamie had walked in on, and Lila laughed so hard that Gigi poked her head out from underneath the dryer and demanded to be let in on the joke.

When Natalie told her, Gigi scowled and said, "You should respect your elders, you sassy child," and returned her head to her dryer, her eyes closing as she dozed off again.

The conversation turned toward men once again.

"Are you dating AJ Jackson? I know he and Jamie weren't really an item, by the way. She called me yesterday and confessed all, rotten girl that she is. I swear, if I didn't love her so much..." Lila shrugged her shoulders.

"I haven't gone on a date since my boyfriend and I broke up a while back," Natalie told her truthfully. Her date was tomorrow, after all. "I don't know about getting involved in anything too serious. I'm not sure how long I'll be here. I wouldn't want some guy to get his hopes up, thinking I was staying, then get his heart broken." That was true also, and Natalie was considering it.

"Well, if you want to be set up—"Lila began. Natalie shut her off with a raised hand.

"I don't, but thank you for thinking of me."

"I wasn't, dear, I was thinking of your poor Mama without any grandbabies to rock."

An hour later, Gigi was curled and fluffed, sprayed and double sprayed, and they headed back toward home. Natalie stopped by her parents' house for the aloe, and once she was back in her room at Gigi's house, she slathered it over most of her body and after changing into a pair of leggings and a loose shirt, she took a nap.

When Natalie awoke, she could hear Gigi moving around in the house. Her grandmother was humming to herself, though Natalie couldn't identify the song. She cautiously touched her shoulders, and was relieved to find they felt much better. She took her time getting out of bed and going to the restroom, brushing her teeth and combing her ponytail back up.

By the time Natalie made her way to the living room, she couldn't find her grandmother anywhere. She called out and went from room to room, but the older woman was nowhere in sight. Natalie heard the rumble of an engine and looked out to see AJ's truck rumbling down the driveway. She rushed to the mirror to be sure she looked like the prettiest tomato, as Gigi put it, before heading to the door and stepping out onto the porch.

The truck rolled to a stop, and AJ smiled to her from the driver's seat. Charlie opened the door and climbed out, coming around the front of the truck to give Natalie a hug.

"Oh, be careful! I'm sunburnt," she warned him. He backed up a few steps, hands in the air and apologizing.

"Weren't you wearing sunscreen yesterday?" AJ asked as she got out of the truck.

"I was, but not enough, I guess." She felt her face heating up, and turned back to the older man. "To what do we owe this pleasure?"

He turned and pointed toward the field behind him. "Oh, we're just checking in on that hay field there. Trying to decide when we'll cut it. Don't want to cut it until Monday or so at the earliest, since it's supposed to rain over the weekend. Can't let it get wet on the ground." Charlie continued on for a few minutes on the subject.

Natalie looked at AJ, who silently mouthed the words, "We still on for tomorrow?" She nodded. He grinned. He held up six fingers, and she nodded again. They smiled at each other silently after that, letting Charlie ramble on, until they heard a commotion coming from the gardening shed Gigi used.

There was the sound of a flower pot breaking, something thudding against the wall, and then Gigi emerged. She was wearing a yellow bikini with large black polka dots, the strings that tied behind her neck not quite up to the job of hefting the woman's sizable bosom up from where nature and gravity had placed it, which was closer to her belly button than her collarbone. The bikini bottoms, however, were having the opposite problem. The bottom bagged out, the extra fabric hanging down as though the woman had dropped a load in her drawers. Clearly Gigi's bottom had gotten smaller since the last time she'd worn the suit. If Natalie wasn't mistaken, she'd seen that bikini before—on a poster where a lithe, young Gertie lie posed, her legs together in the air, slightly bent at the knee as she smiled back at the camera.

She employed that same smile now, as she waggled her fingers at the gentlemen who stood stock still gaping in the driveway. AJ made record time crawling in the truck and putting his forehead on the steering wheel, rubbing his temples with his index fingers. Charlie had the opposite reaction. He waggled his fingers back at her, then ambled over for a long chat.

Natalie knew there were some sights a granddaughter shouldn't have to witness, and she cut out for the house. How her mother wasn't a raving lunatic was a complete mystery. A week with her grandmother had Natalie questioning her own sanity for living with the woman.

Chapter 15

As Natalie set about getting ready for her date, she considered her mother's comments from the day before. She brushed her hair down over her shoulders, its dark blonde length smoothing out silky and straight, her brush leaving furrows that opened and closed as it moved through the hair again and again. Maybe her hair style was boring, like Mama had said.

When she wore it down, though, it seemed like her hair was all anyone noticed. She got compliments from all of the older women. The ones closer to her own age gave her envious looks and whispered catty remarks. She'd experienced it often after she'd moved to Memphis. The men's eyes tracked her every movement, following the shine of her locks like moths drawn to a flame. With certain men, it was great, made her feel sexy and desirable. But it wasn't like being charming or sending a seductive smile to a handsome man. It wasn't particular, instead casting out its allure across every man in her path indiscriminately. More times than she could count, she'd been uncomfortable, had seen lust in the eyes of a man old enough to be her father, or even her grandfather. She'd gotten looks from men wearing Armani and men wearing black leather with tattoos of the devil on their necks.

Natalie used the brush to smooth her hair up into her trademark ponytail. People took her seriously with a ponytail. She was someone to listen to, not just someone to look at. She had always been proud of her mind, which she made the most of with her strong work ethic. The ponytail helped other people to see that too.

Brantley had seemed to see both, but when it came down to it he was more attracted to the packaging of a woman than the quality of what was inside--thus the debacle of the e-mail and Vanessa of the fabulous new boobs. As Natalie turned her head back and forth, checking her hair for any missed strands, she felt pretty good about the way things had ended up there. A little wounded, sure, but tonight the hurt of that broken romance was healing under the balm of a promising first date.

"I think your date is pulling up the drive," Gigi shouted from the living room, where she sat in her own Saturday night outfit watching the drive for the gentlemen callers. "It might be my date, though. Hard to tell since either one could be driving that truck."

Natalie came into the living room to look out the big picture window. She was wearing the picnic version of a date outfit: dark brown shorts that showed off her legs and a fitted tank top that she usually wore under her suit jackets. She'd thrown a cardigan over her purse strap in case it got cold later on. "You're not supposed to know about our date," she reminded her grandmother.

"I know that, but since you know that I know, I figured it was alright to mention, given that we're the only two here right now. Unless you think someone is bugging the house." Gigi's hand flew to her mouth dramatically. "*Do* you suppose someone is bugging the house? Listening in on our conversations? Maybe taking pictures with a hidden camera?" Her eyes flashed with excitement.

"No. Why would someone want to listen to *us* or take pictures? That's crazy, Gigi." Natalie couldn't yet tell who was driving the truck. Gigi had been right about one thing. Charlie or AJ either one could be driving it. Both were expected, and both drove that pick up. Natalie didn't even know whose it was officially.

"I can think of four people off the top of my head who might want to bug our house. Especially if they were taking pictures. I used to be a famous model, after all. Pictures of me in my underwear would be worth a pretty penny, let me tell you." Gigi patted at her hair, fluffing the blonde bob.

"That was a long time ago, though. You think they still want to see you in your underwear?" Natalie tiptoed around the subject, not wanting to wound her grandmother's pride, though a small wound or two might bring her ego down to normal size.

Gigi tossed her head back and laughed. "Yesterday afternoon, those boys were all big-eyed at the sight of me in that old bikini, weren't they? I've still got it, and there's your proof."

Natalie had to admit, they had all been big-eyed, just not in the way that Gigi supposed. Well, Charlie had. She considered trying to explain that to her grandmother, but decided it wasn't worth it. Besides, it looked like the driver was AJ, and Natalie could think of better things to do than sit around here trying to convince her grandmother she wasn't still a sexpot pinup girl.

Natalie met AJ on the porch. He looked pretty great in his khaki cargo shorts and dark blue t-shirt. His hair was still damp from a shower and curling around his ears and at the nape of his neck. He was smiling broadly as he stepped onto the porch.

"Hi," he said. They stood face to face a moment, Natalie's head tilting up to see into his, their height difference more apparent at this angle. His eyes darkened, and his gaze flickered to her lips once, twice. He cleared his throat and took a step back. "Uh…Gramps is on his way over. He said he'd give me a five minute head start, so he wouldn't have to actually see us leaving together. Deniability. His word, not mine."

Natalie nodded. "Gigi is staying inside for the same reason. She's looking through the window at us, though.

No," Natalie whispered sharply, "Don't look. We're not supposed to realize she's there. Something about how if we don't know she can see us, then she can't tell anyone about seeing us. Like witnessing a mob hit, but lying low so you won't be a target. I think she's been watching too much TV." Natalie shrugged and held up her hands.

"That actually kind of makes sense."

"I thought so too. When the crazy starts to sound normal, that's when you know you've got a problem." They both laughed quietly.

"We better get out of here before Gramps shows up and feels forced to rat us out. I'm not sure who he'd rat us out to, but I'd rather not find out," AJ told her as they descended the steps. He went to the passenger side and opened the door for her. "Need a boost?"

"You'd like that, but no. I've got it," Natalie said as she took hold of the seatbelt with one hand and put the other on the door to boost herself up into the tall truck. AJ shut the door behind her.

"A guy can still try," Natalie heard him say before he rounded the truck.

They pulled out of the drive just as Charlie reached them to turn in. Natalie ducked down, tucking her head between her legs so he wouldn't see her.

"You think that's necessary?"

"Just keeping up the ruse," she said, keeping her head low until they were about a half mile down the road.

"Coast is clear," AJ told her, smiling. His eyes darted from the road to her and back to the road several times.

"You drive," she told him. "Let me worry about the covert ops, soldier."

AJ nodded and took a gravel road, giving the road his careful attention, though Natalie saw him looking at her out of the corner of her eye. She, on the other hand, had nothing else to occupy her attention, so she stared at him unabashedly, taking stock of the edges of his jawline, the curve of his ears, the strength of his forearm as it shifted gears.

"See anything you like?" he asked her.

"Maybe," she admitted. "We'll see. Tell me about yourself Andrew Jackson. I know very little about you."

"AJ, not Andrew," he corrected, his brow furrowing. So, he didn't like being called Andrew. With the name of a dead president, she didn't blame him. Still, there were worse names to be saddled with than Andrew Jackson.

"What's the 'J' stand for?"

"Jackson," he told her, and then shifted gears. Those forearms were a wonder to behold.

"Your name is 'Andrew Jackson Jackson'?" Natalie asked.

He grinned, his brow smoothing back out. "No. Andrew Charles Jackson. The 'AJ' just caught on, for some reason." Natalie must've made some kind of a noise, because he added, "Really. I didn't give myself the nickname. Gramps did. Just started calling me AJ when I was a kid, and then before long everyone else did too." He shrugged. "My turn to ask a question."

"What? Why do you get to ask questions? You know all about me already," she protested. They were turning onto a different gravel road. Natalie knew there were a few farms out this way, but not a lot of traffic. He was keeping to the back roads, per their agreement to keep their date quiet. It actually felt kind of nice this way. Like there was less pressure without the eyes of the town watching their every move. Like this date was all about them getting to know each other as they really were, not about how the rest of the world saw them: the James girl back from Memphis or Charlie Jackson's grandson, newcomer to Big Springs.

"I want to know more. That ok?"

"Alright. Ask away." She tensed, waiting. Unlike her grandmother, Natalie wasn't a big fan of talking about herself.

He frowned and seemed to consider his options. "Hmm...what's your favorite color?"

Natalie burst out laughing. "That's your question?"

He gave her that grin. "I'm starting small. I'll build up to the hard ones. Besides, I want to get to know you, and the first thing I want to know is your favorite color."

"Ah, a man of strategy. Fair enough. Blue. I like blue. Does that surprise you? It's the boring, common choice."

He shook his head. "Not at all. I like blue. It's the color of the sky, the color of the ocean." His gaze flickered to hers again, and then returned to the road, where he was making a turn onto a dirt path that couldn't be called more than that. It definitely wasn't a road. They bumped along, and Natalie gripped the handle above her window to steady herself.

"Yeah, it's a little rough," AJ told her. "We're almost there." Calling the road "a little rough" was a massive understatement. It had giant holes that they sank in then popped jarringly out of, a few tree roots they bounced over,

170

and branches and leaves that fell across the windshield, brushing the truck as it plowed through.

"Is this the entrance to your secret lair?" Natalie asked, her grip tightening as they started up a hill at an angle that seemed impossibly steep. "You sure this is safe?"

AJ laughed, and the deep, warm rumbling comforted her. If he could laugh like that, it couldn't be too bad. "Just wait a minute. You'll see."

"I don't like the sound of that," Natalie said. A few moments later, she knew what he'd been talking about. The truck's upward angle tilted, and they started down the other side of the hill. Natalie was glad she had on her seatbelt, otherwise she'd be lying on the dash.

"Hold on. We're almost there. Just around that bend." AJ concentrated on his driving, and Natalie concentrated on not falling out of her seat, going so far as to put one foot on the dash.

True to his word, the road evened out to a gentle slope as they made the corner. The truck pulled up next to a large oak tree, and AJ cut the engine. He turned to her and grinned.

"We made it. Did you survive?" He laughed when he saw she still held tight to the handle above her window. "Ok. Let go now. It's only scary the first couple of times." He reached up and took her hand from its position, loosening her fingers with his own. After he'd pried her fingers loose, she relaxed a little. She looked down at their hands, just as AJ was, seeing her small, pale hand in his larger, tan one. He gave her fingers a gentle squeeze then let go, opening his truck door and coming around to open hers.

"I take it you've never been here before?" he asked. When she shook her head, he continued, reaching into the back of the truck for a picnic basket, which he held in one hand. His other hand held her hand to help her navigate the massive tree roots and exposed bedrock that marked their descent farther down the hollow. "Brett showed me this place back when I visited when I was younger. He said he came camping out here with some of his buddies a few times. It was far enough away they could each drink a beer, or share one if that's all they'd managed to steal from the fridge, and would fish and swim and talk about girls."

AJ gave her that grin again before he jumped down a three foot drop, sat down the basket, and turned around to reach up for her. Natalie put her hands on his shoulders, and he gently grasped her waist and easily lifted her to the ground beside him. He looked into her eyes, and she could feel it, a tension between them. She watched as his gaze shifted to her mouth, as it had done several times since he'd arrived for their date.

"Chemistry," he said. She nodded. "I want this to be more, though. You know that, right?" She cocked her head. "I don't want this to just be about a physical connection, about attraction. I want to know you. I didn't bring you out here to make out or to try to get lucky, so I'm going to kiss you this one time." His gaze flickered to her lips, then back to her eyes. "After that, I won't kiss you again until I drop you off to say goodnight. I'll want to. I'll think about it every minute, but I won't. I'll talk to you. I'll listen. I'll hold your hand, but I won't go any further. Is that ok with you?"

Natalie breathed deep, and then let it out slowly. "I'm good with that," she said, leaning into him almost unconsciously.

"But we get this one kiss first," he told her, his expression questioning. Natalie tilted her face up to his, and he leaned down toward her.

Their lips met. Her eyes closed, and she could feel his heart beating against her chest where she was pressed against him. He held her to him, his hand at the small of her back, drawing her in. They breathed together as the kiss deepened, AJ pulling her closer until she was flush against his hard chest. She changed the angle and felt herself melting, both inside and out.

AJ stiffened, pressed his mouth hard to hers, like a man taking a final drink before walking into the desert. He pulled back and moved his hands to her waist, loosening his hold on her, but keeping his forehead pressed to hers. Her eyes were closed, and she tried to catch her breath.

"That was some kiss," AJ said. Natalie nodded, her forehead rolling against his. "Need another minute or are you ready to go on?"

Natalie breathed steadily in and out, regaining her composure. She had kissed her share of boys and men throughout the years. But she'd never, in her entire life, felt anything like that. She didn't want to examine it too closely, a little afraid of what she'd find if she did. Instead, Natalie straightened, tightened her ponytail, and held out her hand. "Ready."

They made their way down the hollow until they reached the flat gravel bed next to the creek, which was only about ten feet wide in this spot, and about four feet deep. There was a small rapid just downstream whose rushing filled the space with a relaxing hum. The area where AJ put down the basket was a few feet back from the water on a sandy stretch of land. The creek was surrounded by large, looming trees on all sides, secluded and secret. The sun was shining down on only the middle portion, like a spotlight setting the water ablaze, as the shade had taken over any places farther back.

Natalie took it all in, turning in a small circle. She closed her eyes and listened to the rushing water, heard some frogs in the distance, heard the buzz of dragonflies. She could feel the sun on her face, and was glad she'd put on sunscreen, so she could tilt her face to its warmth and not worry about getting burnt again, the previous sunburn having faded somewhat. When she opened her eyes, she discovered AJ watching her, his expression one of wonder.

"It's a great spot," she told him. "What do you want to do first?" She laughed when she saw his eyes flicker to her mouth, remembering his promise that he'd be thinking about kissing her.

He cleared his throat. "We could walk around, explore the creek a little, or we could eat first, or we could just sit and talk. Whichever you'd prefer."

"Can we eat? I'm starving," she admitted. "I'm getting used to eating on an old lady's schedule. We usually have dinner by five thirty."

He laughed, sitting down on the sand by the basket. "It's over an hour past your dinner time, so let's get to it. What do we have?" AJ began pulling items out of the basket, stacking them around as he listed them. "Plates and forks. Potato salad. Fancy little breads."

"Baguettes," Natalie supplied.

"Yep. Fancy little breads. Cheese and deli meat. Sliced tomato in this container. Watermelon in that one." He handed Natalie a plate. They ate quietly for a while, their conversation mostly commentary on the food, where he'd gotten the baguettes, whose basket he'd had to borrow and what excuse he'd had to come up with for using it. He'd claimed it was for his grandfather who was taking Gigi out for a picnic dinner.

"He's going to do it, too. After church on Sunday, he's taking her out. I'm packing the basket for him. He said it was my penance for telling a sort-of lie." AJ smiled. "Worth it."

Natalie filled him in on her uneventful day. Since it was Saturday, she'd had the "day off," according to Gigi. Taking advantage, Natalie had slept in, then spent the day reading a novel, watching a little TV, and talking to her friend Jenn in Memphis, who was over the moon about Natalie's date. Natalie left that part out when she told AJ about her day, though. No need for him to know how she'd gone on and on to Jenn about him until finally Jenn had made her promise to call and replay the whole thing later on that night.

When they'd tossed their watermelon rinds into the weeds, AJ stood up and reached a hand down to Natalie.

"Exploring?" she asked.

"Exploring. Let's go this way first." He pointed upstream. "There's this big rock up there. I think we can climb it." He eyed Natalie's sandals. "Maybe."

They walked along the creek bank, tossing stones in the water, pointing out sunfish. It felt comfortable. Right. Natalie couldn't quite pinpoint what it was, but when she was with AJ, she didn't feel like she had to try. She talked, and she listened, and it wasn't hard.

"I think it's my turn to ask a question," she said. They'd come to a bend in the creek, and she could hear more rushing water up ahead, signaling some rapids.

"Alright," AJ agreed, attempting to skip a flat rock across the water. "Dang. It sank again. I'm out of practice." He looked down to find another rock. "What's your question?"

She held a flat skipping rock in her hand, testing the size and shape of it, but not tossing it out quite yet. "What did you do before you came to Big Springs? You don't seem like the typical farmer to me. Not like my brother."

AJ threw his rock, getting two skips before it sank. "What do you mean? You think I'm a bad farmer?" He gave her that grin, letting her know her observation hadn't bothered him.

"No, it's not that. You just seem," she paused, looking at him, searching for the right words, "I'm not sure. You seem like you've done something else. Something bigger. College probably. Traveled some. You've got a way that you speak, a look in your eye. I can't really say what it is. Am I right? Please say I am, or I'll feel like an idiot." She turned away and threw her rock, getting five skips before it sank below the shimmering surface.

"Good one. And yeah, you're right. I've only been here with Gramps for the past couple of years. Almost two." AJ kicked at a few rocks, turning them over, choosing one to pick up.

"And?" Natalie prompted. "Before that? How did you fill your years? College, right?"

AJ threw his rock, sinking it on the first skip. "I'm terrible at this. Let's walk a little while. My ego can't take much more of this failure." Natalie tossed the stone she'd found, getting six skips. She shrugged. He smiled at her, and they took off upstream again. "I did go to college, yes."

"What did you study?"

"Psychology?" He spoke the word almost like he was uncertain.

"So, did you finish? Are you on your way to being a psychologist? Or psychiatrist? Or therapist? I'm not really sure what a psychology major does. Sorry."

AJ rubbed the back of his neck, but he kept his gaze in the distance, his eyes not darting to her face like they had earlier. "I did, actually. Finish, that is. But I went into the Marines right after graduation."

Natalie stopped walking. He stopped too, turning back to look at her. The sun struck his face, and he squinted in the bright light. She looked at him, trying to picture the AJ she knew, AJ the farmer, as a man in uniform. Surprisingly, it fit. She could easily picture him in uniform, holding a rifle, saluting his superior, going into battle.

"Thank you for your service," she said sincerely.

He shrugged. "It was my pleasure." They began walking again.

"So how does that happen? How does a psychology major end up as a Marine? Don't most people go in straight out of high school?" A few of her classmates had entered the armed forces. They'd gone to boot camp a few weeks after graduation.

"I never really thought about enlisting when I was in high school. In fact, I never considered it until after 9/11. When the Twin Towers were hit, I was a college junior sitting in the dorm cafeteria eating breakfast. Pancakes and scrambled eggs. I still remember what I was eating. Isn't that nuts? I went upstairs to my dorm room where I watched the news all day, and I went to the recruiting office later that week. I knew that the world I lived in after that day was completely different than it had been before, and I couldn't just ignore it. So, I signed up." He shrugged, like joining up at that unsure and terrifying moment in American history was the most natural choice in the world.

"But I thought you said you finished college? How did that work out?" Natalie stopped to pick a yellow flower that was growing between two rocks on the bank. They were getting closer to the rapids now, and the sounds around them were getting louder.

AJ had to speak louder to be heard, his deep voice easily carrying over the rush of the water. "I signed up, did summer school to make sure I'd graduate the next year. Then after graduation, I went to OCS, Officer Candidate School, in Quantico. I went through the training, became a Marine." He shrugged his shoulders again.

"That was a scary time to become a Marine, wasn't it? I'm a little fuzzy on some of the details about exactly where our troops were around that time, but I do know the broad strokes." Natalie watched AJ as they walked. The muscles in his back had tensed, and his jaw was tight. He wasn't smiling any more.

"Were you overseas?" Natalie knew she was pushing him, but it wasn't the kind of thing she could let lie. She had downplayed her knowledge of the war. She had corresponded with one of her classmates who had gone into the Army and had been sent to Iraq. She knew what it had been like over there.

AJ grabbed a stick from the ground and threw it into the creek, watching it speed past them on the rapids. "Yeah, I went to Iraq. Did three tours. First time was in 2005. It wasn't a good time to be there. The last time was in 2010. It was still a mess, but not as bad as the first time." He scowled.

From where she stood, Natalie could see his eyes. They'd gotten hard. She'd seen an article once about photographs taken of soldiers' eyes before the war and then after. The images had stuck with her. At the time, she'd imagined her classmate's face in the pictures she'd seen.

178

Now, though, she didn't have to imagine. She saw the same hardness there in AJ's eyes. Her heart broke a little, and she blinked fast.

"I didn't know that about you." She took his hand in hers, squeezed. He squeezed back. "Thanks for telling me."

AJ nodded. "I don't like to talk about it. You know, about what it was like and all that."

"I understand." She leaned in and put her face against his side in a small hug. When she looked back up at his face, it had softened, and he once again looked like the AJ she'd come with on a picnic today. "So what about that degree? You planning on doing anything with it, other than psychoanalyzing the cattle?" He smiled, and Natalie warmed somewhere deep inside her that she hadn't realized had grown colder as they'd been talking.

"I might open up a clinic for cows. You never know. Do I look like a cow whisperer?" He laughed, and Natalie laughed with him. "Actually, I just finished up my Master's. I'm starting my counseling internship this fall. It'll take two years, but after that I hope to be a therapist. I'll focus mainly on patients with post-traumatic stress disorder, for obvious reasons." He winked at her.

'Well, well, well, AJ Jackson. I am seeing you in a whole new way now," Natalie said teasingly. It was true, she was sad to admit. She'd seen him differently when he was just a farmer than she did now that she knew he'd been in the military and was going to be a therapist. When he was only a farmer, a neighbor, and she'd been attracted to him, drawn to him in a superficial way. Now that she'd gotten to know him, to know more about where he'd been and where he wanted to go, she felt a deep down pull that she'd not experienced before. Being such a driven person, she had been struggling with the version of AJ that she'd known before. Now he fit. He made sense to her. He was driven too.

They rounded the corner, and Natalie saw the rapids that had been making so much noise. They were no Niagara Falls, but they were tall and fast. Boulders lay scattered throughout the creek, the bedrock cliffs along the sides of the creek showing the scars of where the rocks had previously held strong to the sides before they succumbed, crashing down into the water ages ago. The creek water rushed, beating against the rocks in swirling white currents.

AJ looked down into her face, his eyes dark when they flickered over her lips. She put her arm around him, and he pulled her to his side. They stood there watching the creek for a long time, enjoying the feeling of being side by side, connected.

Chapter 16

By the time they drove back, it was dark out. AJ was reluctant for the night to end, but anxious for the kiss that was awaiting him. He hadn't lied when he'd said that he would be thinking about it all evening. The urge to pull her into his arms and cover her mouth with his had been nearly overwhelming, but he'd held back. He couldn't regret the decision, though, since they'd spent so much time talking, sharing their lives with one another, discovering.

What he'd discovered was that he was even crazier about Natalie than he had been before. He felt more comfortable with her than he had with anyone since before he'd left for Iraq. He couldn't believe he'd talked about it even as much as he had. In typical fashion, he liked to listen to other people talk about their own experiences in war, but didn't want to discuss his own. What he'd told her had been more than he'd said about it in several years, and he felt like he could tell her more eventually.

AJ glanced at the woman sitting in the passenger seat of the truck, the glow of the dash lights faintly illuminating her face. She was beautiful. She took his breath away sometimes. He focused on the road ahead of him, otherwise he'd start at the top of her head and start working his way down, enjoying the view every inch of the way. If he started that, they'd end up either wrecked in the ditch with the truck wrapped around a tree, or he'd wind up driving to a secluded spot he knew about down near the spring, where he'd start trying to explore where their chemistry would lead them.

AJ rolled down the window and let the cool breeze inside. Natalie smiled and did the same, closing her eyes and letting the wind hit her face. AJ reminded himself to keep his own eyes on the road. As much as he wanted to, he wouldn't take the physical side of their relationship much further. He'd had girlfriends in the past, had relationships with women that could hardly even be called relationships, really.

He'd slept with a few women he barely knew. AJ didn't want it to be like that with Natalie. Besides the fact that this was a first date, that they were keeping it secret from everyone, AJ felt like he was a different person now than he had been before he came to Big Springs. Now that he was here, he went to church every Sunday. He was trying to do more than be a Sunday pew filler. He wasn't perfect, but he wanted to live the Christian life in all aspects, not merely the ones that were convenient. Right now, temptation was staring him in the face, which wasn't really fair to Natalie. She was so much more than her body, and he was more than the physical draw, the lust, that he felt tugging at his insides. He wanted to appreciate her completely, but the physical part could wait. As much as it would kill him, he knew he had to wait. For her, as much as for himself and for God.

"What does your week look like?" he asked her. "Think you can sneak away again?"

"Let me think. Church tomorrow. Then Monday I'm working at the senior center all day, and then I'm supposed to bake that night. Tuesday is the pie auction. I told Pastor Matt I'd help out with it, and I got Gigi talked into helping me bake a pie. I'm working at the center during the day the rest of the week, but I'm free in the evenings."

Her driveway was coming up. AJ couldn't see any lights on in the house, which meant, hopefully, that Gramps and Gertie were still out. He hoped they weren't alone in the dark house. The thought that they might be inside in the dark made his stomach hurt a little. What he'd seen yesterday had been more than enough for him to decide he didn't want to see any more of their courtship than he had to. Bikini gardening on Natalie, well, that was another story entirely. He'd dreamt about her in that bikini, and kicked himself for it afterward.

He needed to focus. He had to get out of the truck soon. He remembered Gertie in the bikini, and made himself picture it again, and a by the time he turned off the ignition, he opened the door and stepped down, knowing he had his body firmly under control.

"Want to sit on the porch for a little bit?" Natalie offered. "It's still early. Gigi said she wouldn't be home until after 10. She took a nap today so she could stay out late." Natalie looked up at him and gave him one of her smiles. It made her eyes dance. Oh, yeah, he had it bad.

"Sure." They sat down on the porch swing, and AJ set it to swaying gently. "I had a great time today. Thanks for coming with me." He watched her legs extending when the swing went back. Her shorts were the perfect length to show off her legs. He forced his eyes up to the sky, searching the stars, not sure what he was looking for exactly. Self-control, maybe.

"I had a great time. I'm glad you asked me." Natalie bent her knee and pulled her leg up on the seat, turning to face him. "I'm glad you told me about you, about being a Marine and getting your Master's. I don't want to sound weird, but I enjoyed getting to know you better. You're different than I originally thought."

"Is that good?" He searched her face. He'd found that it nearly always broadcast her emotions. She'd be a terrible poker player. Right now she looked a little confused, but happy.

"It's not good or bad. Just different." She looked up at his expression. "Alright, it's good! Maybe that sounds bad, but I *like* knowing that you're not just a farmer. There's nothing wrong with being a farmer. My daddy's a farmer, and he's amazing. It's just that I never wanted that life, dependent on the land and the weather, worrying every year about rain and the price of beef and corn and all that." He watched as her eyes went wide. "I'm not saying that I'm thinking about us being…well, what I meant was that I like knowing that we have a lot in common—college, a professional life, all of that."

He couldn't tell really, since she was still a little sunburnt, but he'd swear she was blushing. It was like someone lit a candle deep down in his soul, he felt warmed from the inside out. She had thought about the two of them, about a possible life together. It was too early in their courtship, as Gramps would say, to make any plans, but it was never too early to daydream. He'd done a little of that himself.

"Come here," he said, pulling her close to him, putting his arm around her. He rested his head on top of hers. "I know what you mean. I'm glad we have that in common too." He chuckled a little, and she must have deduced that he was laughing at her, because she smacked his chest.

"Knock it off. I get tongue tied around you sometimes."

AJ sucked in a breath and held it, then let it out slowly. "I know what you mean about that too." He closed his eyes and breathed in the smell of her hair. It smelled like a floral shampoo and faintly like the outdoors, that woodsy scent that perfectly complemented the scent that was all Natalie. "I'm not ready to say good-bye yet, but I'm going to go ahead and kiss you now."

Natalie went still in his arms, then tilted her face up to his. She was smiling, and his heart beat faster. He slid his hands around her face and bent his head down to hers.

Their lips met, and all of the attraction and chemistry came back to him in one sweet rush. Along with it, though, came the new familiarity of the evening spent together, getting to know each other. It felt like more than their kiss from earlier—much more.

He let his lips explore hers, slowly at first, nibbling and soft. It was magnificent. AJ could feel his heart beating fast and strong. He let his thumbs brush across her smooth cheeks and deepened the kiss. He kissed her the way he'd been fantasizing about all day—deeply, thoroughly, and continuously. He didn't push to take it any further, but he let his hands drift down from her face to her arms and her back. When he heard her moan softly, he pulled her close until he could feel her hands close around his neck. AJ let himself revel in the feel of her for a few minutes longer, before he forced himself, through some strength he'd never known he had, to stop the kiss.

He kept her held against him a while longer, though, her face pressed into his chest, and his head resting on top of hers once again. He kissed her hair.

"I feel comfortable with you. Close." Her voice was barely audible above the sound of the wind in the leaves overhead and the frogs singing their night song in the distance.

"I know. I feel it too." He did. He had never felt like this before.

"I just got out of a relationship, though." He could hear the hesitation in her voice. He closed his eyes.

"What are you trying to tell me?" He kept his voice deliberately neutral.

Natalie sighed, her body rising and falling in his arms. "I don't know. My heart's not broken or anything, but I felt like you should know."

AJ relaxed and held her tighter. "Alright. I'll keep it in mind."

"I don't know how long I'll be in Big Springs. It could be weeks or months. Probably more like months, but I haven't worked it all out yet." Her voice shook a little. He wasn't sure why, not without looking at her face to see what she was feeling, but he knew for sure what the thought of losing her made him feel, even at this early stage of still getting to know each other.

"I'll keep that in mind too" He kissed her head again.

They sat like that a while longer, snuggled on the porch swing, swaying gently, watching the stars and breathing in each other's presence.

"I think that Charlie and Gigi just pulled in the drive," Natalie said, breaking the silence.

AJ saw the headlights too. "I guess that's my cue to go."

Natalie stood with him and walked to the edge of the porch. He went down one step and turned back to her.

"What are you doing after church tomorrow?"

She shook her head. "I've got plans with my parents and Brett."

"What about the pie auction? What are you doing after that?"

"It depends on who buys my pie, I guess." She smiled at him, one corner of her mouth pulling up. She raised an eyebrow.

"And if I buy your pie?"

"I get to serve you a piece, and sit with you while you eat it. That's the tradition."

He looked behind him to see where the headlights were. Seeing them crossing the creek, he leaned in and kissed Natalie one last time, this final one tender and soft. He broke off and jogged around to the door of his truck.

"I'll be the one eating that pie," he promised.

Natalie smiled and waved as he pulled away, watching in the rearview mirror to see her standing there on the porch, leaning against the post and watching him go.

Chapter 17

Gigi had cherry pie filling in her hair, and Natalie didn't say a word. It was only Tuesday afternoon, and if her grandmother realized that her hair hadn't made it through the evening, she'd refuse to go to the pie auction, depriving Charlie Jackson of her company, and most importantly, driving Natalie insane with her whining, bemoaning the subject repeatedly until Natalie was forced to desperate measures, like sleeping outside or, God forbid, going across the street and staying with her parents for a few days.

"Why don't you let me do that?" Natalie took the rolling pin from her grandmother, who promptly wiped her hands across her apron, smearing flour across her chest like the Pillsbury Doughboy had been getting fresh. Natalie shook her head and rolled out the last pie crust, her arm muscles aching from her workout at the senior center. "So what's this pie auction for, again?"

Gigi fluffed her hair, some of the bright red filling attaching to the back of her hand. She took a drink of her sweet tea, oblivious. "We senior citizens are taking a trip up to Branson. We're going to go see one of those music shows, stay in a nice hotel with a continental breakfast, and then do some shopping at the outlet malls. We're taking a bus…" Gigi held her hand up, the sign that the best part was coming, then revealed, "a bus with its own *bathroom*." Her eyes were wide as she waited for the shock and awe that would surely follow.

Natalie set the rolling pin aside. "Wow. A bathroom? Is that even possible?" She turned away to get a pie pan, and to hide her amusement. "Does…you know…it… just fall on the pavement behind the bus? Is that sanitary?"

When she turned back around, Natalie saw that Gigi was shaking her head, her brow furrowed in thought. "I don't know. Maybe. That certainly changes how you look at the highway system, doesn't it. I wonder if it's considered littering or just fertilizer for the roadside plants."

"I'm not sure. But it sounds like an important question. You know, you should ask Pastor Matt." Natalie's voice was perfectly sincere. "I'll bet he'd know the answer. If not him, then you should ask the bus driver."

"Oh, the bus driver would *have* to know, wouldn't he?" Gigi jumped up to grab a pen and paper from the shelf next to the refrigerator. "I'll just write myself a note so that I remember. Ask. About. Potty. On. Highway. Litter. Or. Fertilizer. Question Mark. Got it."

Natalie knew she should feel guilty. Clearly her grandmother was insane, but after the past two days, her patience for her grandmother's shenanigans was running thin. In fact, Natalie had considered whether or not she was insane herself several times. So far she'd hadn't come to any solid conclusions, but she was starting to sympathize with her own mother more and more.

It had started at church. This was natural, since most of her grandmother's high jinks occurred in public places. Gigi had insisted on driving again, only this time she'd also created and invoked a rule that the driver got to choose the radio station. It was only right, since she had to endure the chore of driving, obviously. Natalie had volunteered, quite emphatically, to take the wheel, but Gigi would have none of it.

That was how they wound up rolling into the church parking lot, windows down, bass booming, and the unforgettable rhymes of Kanye West bumping out. Not only had everyone who stood on the church steps turned to watch them, Pastor Matt's mouth ajar, but much of the congregation who were already seated came back out to see what the commotion was. The Little Tots Sunday school class started dancing, shaking their heads and stomping their tiny feet. Natalie had distinctly seen Henrietta Sellers bounce along with them. And of course, Susan Appleby, busybody extraordinaire, had pursed her lips and looked down her nose at them, all while shooting video on her smartphone.

Natalie had buried her head in her hands and ducked down in the seat. She hadn't even taken her seatbelt off yet when her mother had approached her door asking just what in God's name was she thinking, *letting* her grandmother play that music in the church parking lot. Natalie had shaken her head, unable to speak.

After church when the family had gone back to Natalie's parents' house for lunch, Gigi had continued her performance, which was clearly meant to do nothing more than irritate her daughter. It was the issue of the motorcycle. Only in this conversation, Gigi was insisting that if the car, with its multitude of radio stations, was such a problem, perhaps she should just ride a motorcycle to church. She went on to explain how refreshing it would feel to have that breeze up under her skirts.

At this point Natalie's father and Brett excused themselves to go to do farm work in the barn. When she'd tried to join them, her mother had clamped a hand around her arm and refused to let go. There might be bruises.

Fifty minutes. That was how long Gigi went on and on about the benefits of getting a motorcycle at her age. It would increase the muscle tone in her legs. It would make her legs look sexy, not that they needed any help, thank you very much. All that fresh air on her lady parts had to be beneficial, especially if she wanted to keep them ready for action someday. She could ride double with Charlie, and wouldn't that be intimate. They'd probably be married in a few days if she got him on that bike, got him to feel that rumble down in his...

DeeJay and Natalie had both stopped her. Natalie's mother told her to take her grandmother home and not to return for two days. They'd been exiled. Natalie could stop by if she wanted, but DeeJay did not want to set eyes on her mother until Tuesday night at the earliest. Gigi had carried on like she'd been mortally wounded, grabbing her chest and claiming she needed to lie down with a cold cloth on her forehead. After getting Gigi settled in her own bed, Natalie had taken two aspirin and a long nap.

Monday morning at the senior center hadn't been any better. Gigi had insisted that Natalie show her how to use each piece of gym equipment, which took almost an hour. Then Henrietta had come in insisting on the same. When she'd finished, Mabel and a few other friends had shown up wanting to try out some of the DVD's. They demanded that Natalie show them how to do the moves, since they couldn't follow that skinny girl on the screen. All in all, Natalie had exercised for about six hours. When Jamie had come in asking if Natalie felt like hitting the treadmills, Natalie had almost cried. She'd wound up lying on a yoga mat on the floor next to the treadmill, talking to Jamie while her friend walked. It had been the best part of her day.

And now they had to *remake* two pies. When Natalie and Gigi had come home from the senior center, Natalie had decided to reward herself with a tiny spoonful of pie filling. After checking to make sure the coast was clear, she'd gone to the pies they'd made, poked a knife in the slit used to let the steam out and widened it slightly. She then inserted her spoon, and carefully lifted out the shining, bright red cherry filling. It looked delicious, and the very thought of it made all her trouble from the past two days fade away.

Then she put it in her mouth and gagged. Then gagged again. She gagged all the way to the sink. She spit out the gorgeous filling in the sink and turned on the faucet, sticking her mouth under the running water, tongue out. She used the spoon to scrape her tongue again and again.

When Gigi had come in to investigate, they'd determined the flaw. The sugar and the salt were in similar canisters, and instead of adding a cup of sugar to the homegrown cherries, Gigi had added a cup of salt. Natalie nearly puked.

So here they were, making two cherry pies with sugar instead of salt, two hours from auction time.

Gigi licked the pie filling off the back of her hand. "Mmm. That's good. We definitely got it right this time. How you got the salt mixed up with the sugar, I'll never know."

"Me? That was your job. You wouldn't let me touch the filling, said it was your specialty." Natalie pinched the edges of the top crust to seal it to the bottom one.

"It doesn't matter who is to blame. All that matters is that we have two homemade pies to take to the auction tonight. There are men who want to buy these pies just to enjoy our company, after all."

"I don't like the way you say 'enjoy our company.' Makes it sound like they're getting more than just a pie at this auction."

Gigi waggled her eyebrows. Natalie rolled her eyes.

"The auction would make enough money for sure that way, wouldn't it?" Gigi suggested.

Natalie put the pie in the oven, leg muscles screaming as she bent over. "Yeah, you ask Pastor Matt about that too. Please?" She set the timer and waddled off toward the bathroom. "I'm going to soak my muscles before the auction. I feel like I'm going to collapse any second now."

"I don't know what you're complaining about. I did the same workout as you, and I feel fine. Great, even."

Natalie growled, but didn't stop. There was no way she was turning around and walking all ten of those steps again just to set the old lady right. At the end of this hallway was a medicine cabinet with some ibuprofen, and it was calling her name.

"Same workout, my foot. You old bats tried to kill me today," Natalie grumbled as she ran the water. She lowered her body into the steaming bath carefully and rethought all of the decisions that she had made in her life that led her to this moment. If nothing else, this pain made her realize the idiocy of so many of her recent choices.

She sat in the tub, eyes closed, and numbered them off to herself, beginning with sending the infamous e-mail and ending with the decision to get out of bed that morning.

"Girly, you going to stay in that tub all night? The auction starts in forty minutes, and you still have to brush your hair and slap some makeup on that face. I'm not taking you anywhere looking like you did earlier." Gigi knocked on the bathroom door. "Besides, I've got to tend to my own needs in there, and unless you want to watch an old woman sit on the toilet, you'd better get to moving."

Natalie was out of the bathtub and heading down the hall less than a minute later. Even in a life that had started to resemble a bad reality TV show, there were limits to how much she could endure.

The auction was set up in the fellowship hall of the church. A hundred people had piled into the room, and Natalie surmised that they must be approaching the limit for the fire code. Tables had been arranged along the perimeter, each holding at least a dozen pies, all wrapped up with cellophane and tied with a bow and a tag that advertised the name of the baker and the flavor of the pie.

"This is a madhouse," Natalie muttered.

"Isn't it great?" Gigi was beaming. "Look, I've got to go and find my honey, so you go amuse yourself. Play with your friends or whatever you all do, but scram. I don't want you cramping my style. Here, take these pies." The older woman pushed the pies into Natalie's hands and took off into the chaos, calling out in her high pitched voice to people she knew.

"Alright. Sure. I'll just figure out what to do with these," Natalie said under her breath. "Oh, great. Now I'm talking to myself. Before you know it, they'll be shipping me off to the looney bin."

"They don't do that much these days. They'll just give you the good drugs and send you back out into society." The voice that spoke into her ear was deep and masculine, and if it hadn't been giving her mental health advice, she would have appreciated it even more.

"I don't always talk to myself. Gigi would make even the most sane person turn to drugs." Natalie turned and looked up and into the smiling, blue eyes of AJ.

"Is one of those for me?" He licked his lips, and her stomach did a backflip.

"If you are the highest bidder, it is." She licked her own lips, and watched as his eyes followed her movements. "Now, any idea where I take these? Use your tallness and see if you can find where they go."

He grinned, and looked around, finally indicating a table set up at the front of the room. He took one of the pies, and they carried them over to be checked in. Along the way, they discovered Jamie and a few other girls who had gone to school with them, but who had been a several grades below. Natalie didn't know them very well, but they said they'd already found a table with seats and had a few empty places. A couple of the girls eyed AJ up and down, a predatory look in their eyes. Natalie rolled hers and sat down at the table.

"I'm supposed to save a spot for your brother," AJ told her. With those magic words, the girls nearly fell over themselves scooting around, switching places, each vying to secure an empty seat next to her for Brett.

"It's like musical chairs," Natalie whispered to AJ.

"Do you think it'll resort to a catfight? I haven't seen one of those in ages."

"Surely it wouldn't come to that. We're in a church, after all." Natalie saw one woman pull the chair out from under another, who fell on her bottom, legs sprawled, hair falling over her reddened face.

"I wouldn't rule out the possibility of a slap fight," AJ whispered in her ear.

"Do they ever do this over you?"

AJ grinned and winked, which wasn't an answer, but Natalie let it go. She really didn't want to know.

Somehow, Jamie won the battle. The other girls' faces fell in despair, but they quickly overcame when they saw Brett enter the room. Natalie knew without even looking that her brother had come in when the gaggle began to covertly fluff their hair and tug down the front of their shirts, revealing more boob action than had probably ever been seen, or should ever been seen, inside the church fellowship hall.

There was something disturbing about watching a group of women in their mid-twenties preen for the same man. This was double when that man was your brother, who, let's face it, wasn't so much a man as an overgrown boy.

Natalie tried to look at him objectively, to see what these women saw, but try as she might, she still thought he looked like the eight year old boy who had stolen her Barbie and tossed it onto the roof, and then had cried when she did because he hadn't meant for it to get stuck and didn't want to make her sad. He leaned down and gave her a one-armed hug, nodded at AJ, then sat down in the empty seat between Jamie and his sister.

"Did you guys notice some of the nasty stares you're getting? I hate to point it out, but your seating arrangement has some of the old bitties whispering," Brett said, leaning in toward Natalie. "If you two are meaning to keep this thing quiet, you're not doing a very good job of it."

Natalie sighed. AJ scowled.

"I'll trade places with you, Natalie," Jamie offered. "Then you're still sitting next to AJ, but also next to your brother. That can't be scandalous, can it? But let's go get some glasses of tea, so it won't look so obvious that we're switching. Plus, you know, we'll have tea."

Natalie smiled apologetically at AJ and went to get the tea, giving her brother a pat on the back as they went by. He was still looking out for her. Once a big brother, always a big brother.

They resumed their seats a few minutes later, handing drinks to the men. The auction was beginning. The first pies to go were some made by the older women of the community whose husbands dutifully bought the pies they usually ate for free at home. It was cute all the same.

The first major upset of the night came when Mabel's pie was up on the auction block. Most of the crowd had tasted her heavenly desserts as students in the public schools, and it stood to reason, that if she could work wonders with school cafeteria cobblers, any pie she made at home would be food for the gods, though no one would make that kind of comparison in the church, of course.

Her chocolate pie went for fifty dollars, a fortune in a community pie auction. The roar that filled the hall after Richard Larson won the bidding was deafening, especially since he'd only paid five dollars with his wife's coconut cream a few minutes earlier. Mrs. Larson, red faced, walked quietly out the door, coconut cream in hand, while Richard rubbed his sizable tummy in anticipation.

Mabel beamed with pride.

After forty-five minutes of pies being sold for anywhere from five to twenty dollars, Gigi's and Natalie's pies were up. Gigi's was first.

Charlie Jackson won the bidding, of course, but only after fending off a dozen or so other prospective, though elderly, suitors. The pie went for a respectable thirty-five dollars. Gigi fluffed her hair and gave Charlie an air kiss, which he caught in his fist and put in his front pocket.

"We're going to have to keep a close eye on those two," AJ said in Natalie's ear just as her pie was brought up.

The auctioneer, a professional who volunteered for community events, began to speak. "Next we have the pie of Natalie James. Raise your hand and wave Natalie. It's my understanding that the pretty young lady is just home from the big city of Memphis, staying with her grandmother, Gertie Gale. Now, who wants to bid on this delicious cherry pie and the pleasure of eating a slice in the company of the beautiful Natalie, the spitting image of her gorgeous grandmother?"

Natalie blushed. She didn't remember those kind of introductions being a part of the auction before. Clearly the auctioneer had a thing for Gigi. He was winking in her direction.

"I'll start the bidding at twenty dollars," he called out.

That seemed a bit steep. What if no one—

"Twenty-five!" a voice called from the other side of the room. She was pretty sure it was her dad, God bless him.

"Thirty!" AJ raised his hand.

"I've got thirty dollars, who'll give me thirty-five?"

Natalie shook her head. There was no way anyone would pay—

"Thirty-five!" her dad called out again.

"Forty-five!" AJ responded, hand in the air.

Brett was making funny hand motions, Natalie noticed. Subtle neck slashing motions.

"What?" she asked.

"AJ can't get your pie. Everyone will know you two are together. He needs to cut it out. I told Dad to buy yours, and Romeo over there is ruining it. Elbow him or something."

Natalie tried to get AJ's attention, shaking her head and frowning his way. He gave her a confused look, not understanding. His attention snapped back to the auctioneer, who had called out a new bid.

"Fifty dollars. I've got fifty, who will give me sixty dollars for this pie?" Natalie could see the flush crawling up the auctioneer's meaty neck, nearing his bearded face. He was loving this.

"Fifty," AJ called.

Natalie elbowed him in the ribs.

"Sixty dollars!" Natalie's father called out from the other side. She saw her mother pop up at the table where her father's bids were originating. DeeJay was scowling and shaking her finger at AJ.

"Seventy dollars," AJ said, obviously not seeing the death stare DeeJay was sending his way. She turned her steely gaze on Natalie, who shrugged, then to Brett who sighed, defeated.

Brett stood up. "One hundred dollars." He turned to AJ and gave him the masculine equivalent of their mother's death stare.

AJ did what most people did when confronted with that stare. He froze, paralyzed, like a man facing the hypnotic eyes of a cobra.

The auctioneer called for bids, and then pronounced, "Sold! To the young woman's brother. What a waste!"

There was a great deal of nodding and sounds of agreement from the audience as a whole when Brett walked up to claim his pie and part with a hundred dollar bill from his wallet.

While he was gone, Natalie explained the situation to AJ, who flushed with embarrassment. Deception was clearly not his strong suit, which in normal circumstances would be great news. Definitely un-Brantley-like.

"Just don't ever try to become a spy, alright?" she teased quietly.

"No problem. I was a Marine. We're much more direct."

Brett returned to the table and set down the overpriced pie. Natalie and AJ thanked him, and the other girls at the table nearly swooned when Brett smiled and shrugged it off.

"That's alright. I can afford it. But AJ, you have to buy Jamie's pie now. We had a deal, right, Jamie?"

Natalie frowned. "How can you afford to spend a hundred dollars on a pie?" As far as she knew, her brother was broke, or close to it, all the time.

"Don't worry about it, Nat. I'm going to stick around until Jamie's pie is safely purchased, then I'm headed out. I want to eat my pie in peace." He cast a look at the preening women around his table.

Natalie rolled her eyes. "Do you might if I walk out with you? I rode here with Gigi, but AJ is going to give me a ride home."

"And I'm your cover? You are going to start looking like a real loser. Your brother had to buy your pie, now has to give you a ride home. Poor girl. If only you had—Ow! Did you kick me?"

Natalie winced. "That hurt me more than it hurt you."

"Yeah, right. You're wearing boots." Brett rubbed his shin.

"No, seriously. You have no idea. Those old ladies are awful. They had me doing exercises all day long." She reached down for her purse and winced. "I don't know if it's because I've been sitting here for so long, or if my medicine is wearing off, but I think I might have a problem here."

AJ and Jamie were distracted with the auction. Her pie was coming up for bid, and AJ was determined not to mess it up this time.

Brett leaned in, whispering, "What kind of problem?"

"I don't think I can pick up my bag."

"I can carry it."

"Can you carry me?" Natalie felt tears welling up. "I'm not being overly dramatic here. I may need a little help. I've never hurt this much before."
"You're a wimp. You'll be fine."

"Brett, I'm no football star like you were. I've never worked out this hard before. You probably don't need to carry me, but maybe walk beside me, let me hold onto your arm. Please?"

Brett sighed, pushed back his chair, and held out his arm like a martyr. "You owe me." Natalie leaned her weight on him, and it was a good thing. Her legs were shaky. They felt about as solid as the meringue on top of Jamie's pie.

"Let's get out of here fast. I'm afraid I'm going to have to throw you over my shoulder." Brett carried her purse and his high-priced pie in his other hand, the other wrapped around Natalie's waist as she leaned heavier and heavier on him.

She blinked back tears. "I can make it. The last thing I want is my behind up in the air for the whole town to see." She kept moving, one unstable foot in front of the other until they were mere yards away from the door that led to the darkened parking lot where she would gladly let her brother carry her to his truck.

"Natalie, sweetheart! Leaving so soon? You haven't even served Brett the pie that he bought!" Lila stepped in front of them, blocking the exit. Her mother's friend and co-worker teased, "You can't get out of serving the pie! It's part of the tradition."

The momentum lost, Natalie's legs buckled. She sank down to the floor, pulling her brother's arm along with her. He lost his balance, falling to the side. The cherry pie slid across his palm. It felt like slow motion, and lying on the floor with both hands under her, Natalie was powerless to stop it as the pie fell.

Lila shrieked. The auctioneer quieted. A collective gasp went up from the congregation. Susan Appleby snapped a picture on her smartphone of Natalie sprawled out, red cherry pie filling splattered across her face, chest, and lap.

Chapter 18

Natalie wasn't so much given the day off, as much as she'd demanded it. She slept a good portion of the day away, waking up to eat a piece of toast for breakfast, then a few pieces of cheese for lunch, all of which had been delivered by Gigi, and by dinnertime, was feeling better—except that her muscles required monumental strength to get them to work, and even when they did, they screamed in agony.

"Natalie?" Jamie's soft voice came from the doorway along with a faint knock. "You awake?"

"I am, but I don't think I can move," Natalie groaned from the bed. She'd been contemplating getting up for a while now, but didn't think she had the courage to try.

"Do you want some help?" Jamie asked, coming into the room. She was dressed in her uniform from the hardware store, a pair of jeans with a blue Big Springs t-shirt. "I can pull on your arms, maybe, and you can just sit up real fast. Do it like a Band-Aid, all the pain at once, you know?"

Natalie nodded and stuck out her hands, even that much motion causing her to wince.

"One," Jamie counted. "Two." Natalie grimaced in preparation. "Three!" Jamie pulled, and Natalie put to use her tortured ab muscles. She squealed in pain, but made it to a sitting position.

"Are you ok?" Jamie asked, helping Natalie sit up so her back was to the wall.

Natalie nodded. "I hate exercise."

"I don't think that what you did yesterday could be called 'exercise'. It's horrific."

Natalie groaned. "Horrific like being publicly shamed and humiliated?" She closed her eyes and let her head fall back against the wall. It was cool to the touch. Maybe if she could put her entire body against it, the cool surface would make her muscles feel better. But that might require standing, which was entirely out of the question.

"Yeah, everyone feels awful about that. Aunt Lila stopped by earlier with a coconut cake. It's in the fridge. She remembered that it was your favorite. Kind of a pity cake." Jamie shrugged her shoulders.

"I get those all the time," Natalie said, chuckling, then wishing she hadn't. "Ow," she cried. "No joking."

"You made the joke, not me," Jamie protested. "I was talking to myself," Natalie assured her. "I've got to get up." She started pushing herself away from the wall.

"I can bring you some cake," Jamie offered.

"Can you bring me the toilet?" Natalie asked.

"No, probably not. But I can help you get to it," Jamie offered. Natalie declined, and moved slowly, a little hunched, to the bathroom. She even used superhuman strength to brush her teeth and pull her hair back up into a ponytail. But nobody, not even Gigi, was going to force her into putting on makeup. She just didn't have the muscle control for it today. She'd end up looking like a preschooler's art project.

"I got you some cake out," Jamie told her when Natalie shuffled into the kitchen.

"Thanks. Let's sit on the porch to eat. I feel like I ought to see the sun for at least a few minutes before it goes down today." Natalie grabbed a cup of coffee from the pot, cold, but whatever, who cared if your coffee was cold when you'd spent the night wallowing in self-pity and the day sleeping off the worst case of sore muscles known to mankind.

"How was the hardware business today?"

"Pretty good. All anyone wanted to talk about was the pie auction tragedy. It's a sad what passes for news in this town." Jamie took a bite. "I've eaten more desserts in the past two days than I ate all last year, I think."

"What did you say?" Natalie asked, her own dessert forgotten on the seat beside her.

"That's an exaggeration, I know. But definitely more desserts than I ate last week."

"Not that part. The part about everyone talking about last night."

Jamie winced. "Yeah, I guess that Susan got the whole thing on video. Then there's the picture." Jamie took another bite of her cake, not making eye contact.

Natalie dropped her head in her hands, which hurt. This was awful. Not only was she the girl who couldn't make it in the city, coming home jobless and hopeless, but now she was also the town joke. If she wasn't so sore, she would be really upset about it. As it was, this kind of news just added to the pain she was already feeling.

"So I guess some of the people in town are feeling pretty bad about it," Jamie went on. "Pastor Matt's Bible study group prayed for you this morning, and some people have been saying that we need to do something to make it up to you."

"What? Why?" Her head was starting to hurt. She probably needed to eat cake. Cake tended to make things better, and this coconut cake could probably perform miracles the likes of which hadn't been seen since the apostles were healing people with their sweaty handkerchiefs.

"That doesn't matter. These people are all concerned for you. It could've happened to anybody...maybe."

"Whatever," Natalie said around a mouthful of cake. "Not their fault. Well, except for Susan Appleby. It's at least partly her fault."

Jamie nodded in agreement. "So, they're all tossing around ideas. They're supposed to have a meeting about it tomorrow morning to decide."

Natalie began planning how to murder Brett, but also how to avoid seeing anyone in Big Springs for the next decade or so. Short of hightailing it back to Memphis, which she was too broke to do, there weren't a lot of options.

She was pretty successful for a few days, though. Natalie worked on the computer for the senior center, scheduling events and creating flyers. She sent notices to Tina at the Chamber of Commerce of their dates and events. Natalie discovered that if she wrote up nice little blurbs about their events, coupled with photos she'd taken on her phone that Tina would post them on the town's website, gaining some publicity for the senior center. While she was sorely tempted to send the picture of the ladies in their leotards, she didn't, opting to send one of Jamie helping the ladies select a workout DVD, which was a chest up shot. The unsuspecting public didn't need or want to see anything below that. It might drive people away, instead of bringing them in.

Natalie made phone calls on behalf of the senior center, acquiring a musical group who would come and perform bluegrass, a local barbeque champion who offered to teach them how to grill the best burgers and ribs but refused to share his secret sauce recipe, and a hypnotist who could convince the patrons that they were Lady Gaga or Kermit the Frog, or whatever he wanted. It was a successful work week overall, even if it was accomplished from the kitchen table while she wore sweatpants and ate ice pops.

Avoiding AJ, though, could not be done, not that she'd wanted to. He'd called Wednesday night and had let himself be put off. He stopped by on Thursday, causing Natalie to rush around to change out of her chocolate-stained oversized t-shirt and gym shorts and into a pair of khaki capris and a cute t-shirt with a little flowers sewn into the sleeves. It had taken her ten minutes, as her rushing was about the speed of a tortoise on tranquilizers, but he had waited for her. They had sat on the porch, drank sweet tea, and talked about everything and nothing for two and a half hours. Gigi ran him off when she got home, telling him she had to wash her hair. He'd insisted that was just a clichéd excuse from movies, but Natalie had explained about the weekly hair rotation, and he'd finally caught on and had left.

Friday he came to take her out to lunch. When she'd balked at the idea of ever showing her face in Big Springs again, let alone going out to lunch when they were supposed to be keeping things quiet, he'd driven thirty minutes to a small family-owned diner in a nearby town. He pulled out the chair for her and had gone in search of ketchup when their waitress had gotten distracted and forgotten to bring her any…Romance at its finest.

Friday night Gigi and Charlie had gone out to Knight's for a fancy dinner, leaving their grandchildren unattended. AJ and Natalie had used their time alone to cook a simple dinner for just the two of them, making and later cleaning up a mess in Gigi's kitchen. They'd eaten their pasta and salad in the kitchen, drinking cans of Coke, and making eyes at each other over the table top. They spent the remaining hour on the front porch swing, cuddled up watching the sunset and what Natalie described as "low impact kissing" in deference to her lack of pain-free mobility and the weirdness of making out with a guy on her grandmother's porch.

The more time they spent together, the more right it felt. When he wasn't there, she felt like something was missing. When he was by her side, she felt whole, like what she had been searching for had shown back up and slipped smoothly into place. When she had been living with Brantley, they had been lovers, a piece of her past that she wasn't proud of and had spent some time praying about in church. But when AJ held her hand, it felt more intimate than anything she had done with her former boyfriend. In fact, if it hadn't been for her regular phone conversations with Jenn, she might have forgotten about her life in the city entirely. She refused to let herself think about what that might mean, instead choosing to focus on today, and this week.

Despite the terrible way it had begun, Natalie's week had turned out pretty well. That is, until she was summoned down to the church on Saturday afternoon to be the recipient of the church's first and only pie auction pity gift--two tickets to a show in Branson, accommodations included, along with two seats on the senior citizens' bus, set to roll out the following Friday morning. Her cup overfloweth.

Chapter 19

The next week passed in a blur. Sunday's church service had been accompanied by an announcement of the trip participants' meeting place and time, along with a brief mention of Natalie being included. She had buried her face in the church bulletin, unwilling to make eye contact with anyone. When she had seen AJ in the parking lot later on, she'd begged him to come on the trip with her. It hadn't taken much arm twisting, though they'd have to reassess their plans to keep all that was going on between them quiet, which was getting harder and harder to do. But that was a wasp's nest to be tangled with another day—Friday to be precise.

Monday through Thursday, while normally passing at the pace of an elderly snail, flew by in a hurry. Natalie attended most of the events she had helped to schedule. She ate barbecued ribs in the cafeteria of the senior center and went to two yoga classes, participating only in the beginning stretch and final relaxation portions of the class, claiming she'd done all of her workouts for this week during the week before. The older ladies had patted her head and blessed her heart. She sent pictures from the events to Tina for the website and tacked schedules up in windows and on bulletin boards all across town, mostly in an effort to escape the senior center, which she was affectionately calling the "loony bin" as the excitement over the Branson trip had escalated to an arthritic frenzy.

The morning of the trip dawned with clear skies and the promise of record-setting heat later in the day, which Gigi deemed a good sign. When Natalie had reminded her that they'd be walking around to shop later on, Gigi had brushed her off as gloomy and still pouting over her short-lived walk on the wild side. She'd acquired her own copy of Natalie's video, and swore that if Natalie didn't "cheer the heck up" she would hook it into the charter bus's TV system and show it to everyone, never mind that she had no idea if it was possible. She'd find a way. Natalie put a smile on her face and offered to drive them to the church.

Surprisingly, Gigi didn't do anything embarrassing as they pulled into the parking lot and unloaded the trunk. Natalie pulled out her one small suitcase and Gigi's large one, along with her two smaller cases: one for pills and one for beauty products. From the rattle of each, Natalie couldn't tell which one had the medicine, but both were suspiciously heavy.

"Here, let me help you out," Pastor Matt said, rushing to her aid. Natalie had always liked him. He was fairly young, as far as ministers went. He had come to the church straight out of seminary when she was about thirteen. Natalie had enjoyed a massive crush on him for a few months before moving on to the dreamy boy who sat next to her in science class, but maintained an admiration for his clean cut good looks, but primarily appreciated his endless patience with the crazies that populated his small congregation.

"Thanks, Pastor Matt. Also, thanks for inviting me." Natalie handed over one of Gigi's rattling cases with a polite smile.

Pastor Matt placed the case in the storage bin under the charter bus, which rumbled loudly and churned out exhaust. "It'll be nice to have some other young people on the trip." Natalie felt her eyebrows shoot up, completely on their own. Her brain told her face not to act surprised, but it happened anyway. "Oh, I know," Pastor Matt chuckled, "but I'm closer to your age than theirs, so I'm considering myself young this weekend."

Natalie smiled, a little ashamed that her face had been read so easily. She placed the rest of her load of baggage under the bus and straightened, tugging her ponytail into an almost painful tightness. Not even out of the parking lot, and she was already embarrassed.

Then she saw AJ drive his big truck into the lot, and her cheeks reddened for a reason entirely separate from the embarrassment she'd been feeling before. Just the sight of him made her feel all melty and hot, which was a feeling that was fairly new to her, but not unwelcome. Sure, she'd lived with Brantley, but he'd never made her feel this way. As soon as the truck was parked, Natalie saw AJ's eyes scan the parking lot, stopping when they rested on her. He smiled, and she felt her stomach drop down to her knees.

"Ah, there's the Jackson boys," Pastor Matt said genially. "You know, I'm glad you asked AJ to come along. I was going to suggest it, actually, before I'd heard that you'd already asked him. Nice guy, that one."

Natalie could hear the minister talking, but his words didn't entirely sink in. AJ was getting out of the truck, reaching into the bed for one small suitcase and one camouflage backpack. He wore blue jeans that were a little weathered around the pockets, and the hem was shaggy where it covered his shoes. He'd traded out his usual boots for a pair of running shoes, and while it was unexpected, it worked on him. Natalie had a feeling that AJ could wear anything from a tux to a bath towel and still look like a movie star.

"I was just telling Natalie here that I'm glad you're coming along," Pastor Matt was saying, shaking hands with Charlie then AJ, whose gaze only briefly met the minister's before returning to Natalie. "Maybe you two could sit together, get to know one another better," the pastor suggested, perhaps a little louder than necessary. This gained the attention of both AJ and Natalie, along with that of a few of the senior citizens gathered around them.

"Sit with AJ?" Natalie asked, eyebrow raised. She looked around at the crowd. "You think that's alright, Pastor

Matt? You don't want us to mingle with the others?" She saw AJ's wary, yet hopeful face.

"Oh, yes, I it's a great idea, don't you, Mabel?" Pastor Matt winked at Gigi's friend, who nodded emphatically. "And you, Henrietta, what do you say?"

Henrietta nearly squealed with delight. "I think it's a perfectly magical idea for those two to sit together!"

AJ grinned. "Well, if it's ok with you all, I'd be happy to sit by Natalie and keep her company."

The nodding heads made the decision unanimous. Pastor Matt had paved the way for them to take their relationship out into the open. Natalie looked up at AJ, who was beaming. He shook hands with Pastor Matt, hugged Mabel and Henrietta enthusiastically, and shook the hand of a few more people who happened to be in the vicinity. When someone yelled for the group to load up, AJ returned to Natalie's side, took her hand in his and squeezed it too—not quite a handshake, more of a caress that she felt all the way down to her toes. She laughed and climbed aboard.

Natalie noticed Gigi and Charlie sitting close to the back, their heads together as if conspiring. She saw Gigi look up at her, eyes going wide, and then ducking down again into a whispering huddle. Natalie nudged AJ, who was behind her, and nodded toward their grandparents. He shrugged.

They found seats in the middle, where there seemed to be a gap between those who needed to sit near the toilet in the back and those who needed to sit near the front to avoid motion sickness. Several rows were unfilled between the groups, and AJ and Natalie took two empty seats next to each other. She stowed her tote by her feet, and AJ sat beside her, wincing as he folded himself into a space more appropriate for someone of Natalie's stature.

"You going to be alright?" she asked him, seeing how he pulled his knees up to fit his legs under the seat in front of him.

"Yep. Just trying to figure out how to get all of me into this seat and out of the aisle." He grunted a few more times, adjusting his feet, crossing one knee over the other until his knee jutted out into the aisle, then returning his feet to the floor. He put his elbows on both armrests, then realizing Natalie may want it, retracted it to lean into the aisle. He saw how far into the aisle he was leaning, then pulled in, finally folding his arms across his chest, like a bouncer outside a club.

"You sure you're going to be alright?" Natalie asked.

"I'm good. I've been in worse positions," he assured her as the bus churned forward.

Pastor Matt stood up and addressed the bus, saying, "We're about two hours away from Branson right now. We'll be making our first stop in about 45 minutes to eat breakfast. Use the bathrooms sparingly, as what odors you make in there tend to spread to the entire bus, so try to hold it until we stop." He shot a few warning glances around, clearly having experienced this problem on previous trips. Natalie tried to see who he was eyeing, but couldn't make out any guilty expressions.

"So, I guess we can officially start dating. If you want to be my girlfriend." He nudged her with his knee, leaving it to press against her leg warmly.

"Oh, I don't know. I might need to think about it," Natalie teased. "I saw Mr. Dewey giving me a look earlier, and I think he's got his own house and everything."

AJ laughed out loud. "I think he shares it with his wife, who might have a problem with you two hooking up."

"I forgot about Mrs. Dewey. Maybe she won't mind, though, if it gets him out of the house more."

They both looked over at the Deweys, who were both working on word searches. Looking around the interior of the bus, Natalie saw several others working puzzles, Henrietta and Mabel were craning their necks to look at Charlie and Gigi, who were still huddled together whispering.

"Aren't you worried about what they're talking about?"

"We're going to Branson, not Vegas. How bad can it be?"

Natalie's eyes went wide. "Don't say that. Quick! Knock on wood or something."

AJ laughed again and nudged her with his shoulder, letting it rest against hers.

"Are you trying to take my seat? Conquer it slowly? I'm on to you," she said, nudging him back. He edged closer, his warmth heating her skin. "Tell me about some of the places you've sat that were more uncomfortable than this." Her request was softly spoken, knowing she was prying into a time he would rather leave in the past.

For the next half hour, he told Natalie about riding into Baghdad in the back of a truck packed with other Marines. He downplayed what she suspected were the worst parts, and she listened as much to what he didn't say as to what he did. AJ didn't mention car bombs or roadside bombs or explosions of any kind, but Natalie saw his brow furrow and his lips frown when he mentioned passing by the ruins and rubble of the city. He didn't mention his own fear, but she watched him clench his jaw when he talked about riding, knee to knee, shoulder to shoulder, breath to breath, with his fellow soldiers into the unknown depths of a city known for its terrors and high death toll.

"So this seat here?" Natalie asked, when he'd breathed deeply and continued to stare straight ahead, as if he wasn't really seeing this highway anymore, but was seeing another road entirely.

"This seat is fine." He turned to look at her, his face softening, the faint hint of a smile on his mouth. "Sitting here next to you...is, well, I can't quite think of the word," he nudged her and grinned widely, "I might call it magical."

Natalie laughed and nudged him back, letting her head rest on his shoulder briefly. She didn't care if the whole bus or the whole town saw it. She felt him kiss the top of her head, a whisper of breath and lips on her hair that filled her with an emotion she couldn't name, but that brought tears to her eyes nonetheless.

"Breakfast stop!" Pastor Matt called out, when they pulled into a Shoney's. "The breakfast buffet is included and paid for courtesy of our fundraisers, so fill up. Lunch is on your own."

"We've barely made it out of town," AJ murmured to her under his breath.

"They're old. They need to stop often. I don't know why. I guess we'll figure it out when we get to be their age." The idea that she might still know AJ then, might still be sitting by his side flitted through her mind, but she let it pass, unwilling to dwell on big questions and enormous decisions when faced with a smorgasbord.

The group swarmed the breakfast buffet, leaving behind only the stems from grapes and a few remaining lumps of sausage gravy in the bottom of the vat. They'd even emptied out the jelly packets that sat on the tables, though Natalie suspected there were a few packages of jelly in the purses and pockets of the diners.

All in all, it was a nice break from the bus, and even more shocking, Gigi was behaving herself, sitting between Charlie and Henrietta. Natalie even saw her grandmother give her girlfriend a biscuit that she'd already covered in butter and jelly. Maybe she'd underestimated Gigi, and she was much nicer and better behaved than Natalie had been giving her credit for.

When they piled back on the bus, Natalie checked her phone for messages. There was one from her mother, reminding her to keep an eye on Gigi for mischief. Natalie typed out a positive report in a text message, happy to be able to set her mother's mind at ease. She looked back over her shoulder at Gigi, who was smiling angelically, eyes forward, hands crossed in her lap like the primmest of church ladies, almost like Susan Appleby herself, who had chosen to remain behind to pray for their safe travels. Gigi gave Natalie a sweet little finger wave. Odd. It almost gave Natalie shivers, like the feeling of electricity in the air before a storm.

Natalie had another message from Jenn saying that she hoped Natalie was well, and that Natalie was missed, and that there was a sale on Coach bags at the mall, and wasn't she so sad she'd missed it? Natalie turned off her phone. She'd reply later.

"Do our grandparents look strange to you?" AJ asked, leaning in to ask quietly. Natalie looked back between the seats to inspect the older couple.

Gigi was still sitting, quiet and sweet, the picture of a perfect little grandmother. It was disturbing, really. Charlie was next to her. He had put on his reading glasses, which sat low on his nose. He appeared to be reading a book of some kind, but Natalie could see his eyes darting around the interior of the bus, like he was watching for something to happen.

"Weird. What do you think they're up to?"

AJ shook his head. "I don't know, but I don't like it."

They didn't have to wait long. Within a few minutes, a smell drifted up from the back of the bus. It had the distinct stench of sewer and stuck to the interior of the nostrils like tar. The passengers looked side to side, as if assessing to see if it was their own body making the odor, and sensing that it wasn't, attempted to assess whether or not it was their seatmates'. It would have been funny if it wasn't so putrid.

"I think I can taste it." AJ covered his face with his t-shirt. Natalie followed suit.

"Yuck. Now I think I can too." Both were trying to be discreet, as were the other passengers, not wanting to offend the offender, in case it was a friend.

There was a small moan from the back of the bus. Natalie and AJ looked back at the same time, eyes locking on the grandparents. Gigi and Charlie were the only two on the bus seemingly unaffected by the stink. Gigi still smiled sweetly, and Charlie concentrated on his book more than ever. No darting eyes anymore, which told Natalie that they were the two behind this.

The moan returned, and this time Natalie looked beyond her grandmother. She saw Henrietta, poor, sweet, un-Cher-like Henrietta. Her skin was chalk white, and her black hair was sticking to her face with creamy rivulets of makeup running down her cheeks and dripping off her chin. Henrietta winced and moaned again.

She pushed herself up out of the seat, stooped over clutching her stomach, and hobbled the few feet to the bus's toilet. The other passengers heard the ominous click of the lock with a feeling a dread. Natalie turned quickly to her phone, pulled up the first song she came to, and cranked up the speakers as high as they would go. Though the voices of Hall and Oates came through, covering up the worst of the awful noises coming through the door, it wasn't until the song reached the chorus that Natalie realized her mistake. She was playing the song "Man-eater," whose lyrics implied that perhaps Henrietta had, or was going to, chew them up.

Two dozen pairs of eyes turned from the door to the toilet to Natalie, their expressions ones of shock and condemnation.

"Sorry!" She hit skip and Beyonce's "Single Ladies" bounced out, garnering the approval of the crowd. A few of the more hip individuals raised their hands to do the dance. Natalie eyed Gigi, who had risen to look out the back window of the bus, her silver bob distinctive as her head turned from side to side, watching the road behind them. Presumably, Natalie decided, to see if the toilet really did empty out onto the road.

It was Natalie's turn to face the front, folding her hands primly in front of her, feigning innocence the rest of the way to Branson.

Chapter 20

The bus rolled into town with the windows down, the wind blowing out most of the odor. The smell of exhaust filled the interior now. The traffic was bumper to bumper on 76 Country Boulevard that ran through the "Live Entertainment Capital," showing off a myriad of tourist stops, from souvenir shops and home-cooking restaurants to massive theaters hosting minor country music celebrities to a wax museum housing replicas of the major ones. The bus crept up the hills slowly enough that a few of the passengers began to offer pointers to the mini-golfers playing at a pirate-themed course next to the road.

Their hotel was located at the fringes of the country music mecca near a newer part of town that had been built up along Lake Taneycomo. Within walking distance were a large selection of restaurants, and about a million stores, or at least it seemed that way to AJ when they passed by, and he envisioned having to accompany Natalie to every single one. Though if he was going with Natalie, AJ admitted to himself, it wouldn't be too bad.

He saw a small train station across the street and wondered if they'd be able to take a ride. He had been in armored trucks and convoy vehicles, a few tanks, dozens of airplanes, and all the normal methods of civilian transportation, but he'd never been on a train. It could be fun.

Natalie had been pretty quiet since the "Man-eater" incident. She'd turned red and stared out the window the rest of the short journey. AJ hoped she wasn't feeling too bad about the looks some of the old people had given her.

As soon as the bus, stopped and people began to unload, she turned to AJ and said, "I'll catch up with you inside. I need to do something."

Natalie exited the bus, but stood waiting next to the door. AJ watched her out the window. The moment that Gertie and Gramps stepped off, she nabbed each one by an elbow and escorted them around the front of the bus. AJ stood up to watch. He couldn't tell what she was saying to the older couple, but she alternated between wagging a finger at them, putting her hands on her hips, and crossing her arms and tapping her toe. Gertie began the conversation shaking her head and shrugging. She ended it slumped over and nodding. Gramps responded the opposite way. He began by looking at the ground, but by the time Natalie was finished with him, the Vietnam Vet stood at attention for his dressing down. He all but saluted her when Natalie was finished with him. AJ wasn't certain what the pair had done, but he had a pretty good guess.

He watched as Henrietta slipped out of the restroom, seeing only him on the empty bus, the other occupants having gathered up their belongings and entered into the air conditioning of the hotel lobby. She grabbed her purse and slipped a pair of oversized sunglasses onto her face. As she passed him, she mumbled a quiet apology.

"Think nothing of it. These things happen. I hope you're feeling better." He helped her down the steps and out into the sunshine, then picked up both of their bags. She held onto his arm, like a princess being escorted into a ball, until he deposited her in a lush armchair on the far corner of the lobby.

"You be sure and tell me if you need anything, Miss Henrietta." He kissed her hand before leaving her to sit, resting after her ordeal.

Natalie entered the lobby, Gertie and Gramps walking on either side of her, heads down, faces red. They separated inside the doors, the troublemakers joining Henrietta, Natalie finding him.

"Everything alright?" he asked her. She heaved a sigh.

"Laxatives."

"What? Are you sick?" He looked down at her stomach.

"No. Gigi and Charlie gave Henrietta laxatives. It's a long story, and I play a very small part in it, but let's just say that it was an experiment gone wrong. They've been lectured and instructed to treat their friend like a queen for the rest of the trip." Natalie walked over to her suitcase, which had been wheeled in on a cart, and extended the arm to pull it behind her. AJ slung his own backpack over his shoulder.

"I also told them that under no circumstances are they to tell her what they did. Thinking she has food poisoning is one thing, but knowing that two of her friends poisoned her on purpose? Put her through that humiliation on purpose? Bad idea. She might never get over it." Natalie's face was tight with concern, and AJ hoped they'd be able to relax later on, without Gramps or Gertie around to spin every event into chaos.

Pastor Matt waved a hand, and their group congregated and lined up near a two-story, rock-lined fireplace for their room assignments and plastic key cards. AJ had been holding out hope that there would be some kind of mix-up, and he and Natalie would have to "whoops" room together. Not that he intended to take their relationship to the next physical level, especially not on a church trip, but he wouldn't mind her face being the last thing he saw at night and the first that he saw when he woke up. He wondered if she snored, or sang in the shower, what she looked like saying her prayers before bed. All of those small intimacies that he wanted even more than the intimacy of lovers. No such luck. He was stuck with Gramps, and she with Gertie.

They were conveniently across the hall from one another, though.

Pastor Matt gathered the senior citizens, Natalie, and AJ around him. "Ok, folks, the plan is to take some time to get settled into your rooms, rest up for a bit, and then we'll walk down and explore the shops at Branson Landing, which is just down the street. Of course, you're welcome to walk down there on your own, or you can wait and walk over with us in an hour."

AJ looked around. Was he the only one who saw how ridiculous this was? "It was only a two hour trip."

An older gentleman wiped his face with a hanky, saying, "I know. I'm beat. I need to lie down for a while, take my medicine, and find my walking shoes." Several heads nodded and there was some discussion about what pills were in what suitcases.

In the hallway outside their rooms, Natalie turned to him, "Want to meet me here in about 10 minutes? We can get the old folks settled, then maybe head out to see what we can find."

They agreed, and AJ spent two minutes helping Gramps figure out how to work the remote control for the flat screen, then took the elevator down to the lobby. In one corner was a wooden case advertising area attractions, including old time photos, an IMAX theater, and a brochure for the train. There was one leaving in about thirty minutes, and while he waited, AJ called to see if there were still tickets available. Just out of curiosity.

When Natalie appeared, still looking tense and tired, he pulled her into his arms, holding her tightly against him. He felt her relax only slightly. He stepped back, but kept hold of her hand as they walked toward the elevator.

222

"I don't know why I ever thought living with Gigi was a good idea. What was I thinking?"

"You were thinking you wouldn't have to sleep in the same room as her."

"Oh, yeah. That makes a difference."

"Did you want to go shopping? Would that make you feel better?" he asked her warily. He would do it, of course, if that's what she wanted. AJ had a feeling in his gut that he'd do just about anything Natalie wanted. Anytime. Anywhere. It was a little frightening, but in the way a roller coaster is scary, but thrilling too.

Natalie chuckled lightly, "You should see your face right now. Such a brave expression." She squeezed his hand. "No. I'm operating on a very small budget right now. Miniscule." She held up a finger and thumb to show him how small. "No shopping for me. Though if you want to go, I'll go along with you. Bravely, of course. I hear there's a Bass Pro."

He shook his head. "I don't need anything. I'm not operating on a small budget, but I'm a pretty simple guy. I don't need a lot of stuff, you know?" He held up his brochure for the train. "But I have an idea. Want to go for a ride instead? It'll take a few hours, but no one will miss us."

"Do we have to come back?"

He chuckled. "Tempting. Let's see where it goes, then we'll decide."

"I'm in. When can we go?"

They purchased their tickets and boarded the 11:30 train just as the conductor was yelling his final "All aboard!" Natalie and AJ settled into two plush seats in the dome car, which had a transparent top to better see and appreciate the beauty of the Ozarks. The train took off slowly, its wheels whirring. The ceiling view changed from the awning of the train station, to a brilliant blue afternoon sky complete with a shining sun and birds flying overhead.

"And we're off!" Natalie called. She leaned in to AJ's side. "Thanks for this. I haven't been on a train in ages. I took the Amtrak to New Orleans once for Mardi Gras, but that was a few years ago. And I have to admit," she said as she looked around, "it wasn't as cool as this. Very utilitarian, like a rolling airplane. This is really nice."

AJ looked around him at the reclining blue seats with raising armrests and the glass dome overhead. "I've never been on a train, so I have nothing to compare it to," he confessed. "I'm pretty pumped, to be honest. I know I've been on lot of bigger and faster methods of transportation, but there's something about this old fashioned way of travel." He shrugged his shoulders. Part of the excitement was doing something for the first time with Natalie.

The seats across from them were empty, but a quick look back told him there was a family behind them, composed of a couple in their forties with a pair of sullen-looking teenage boys who were riding in rear-facing seats, each with his headphones in his ears and a scowl on his face. Their parents had clearly given up on trying to engage them and were pleasing themselves by pointing out various types of trees and calling them out to each other.

AJ looked in front of them and saw that the next several rows were taken up by a group of friendly-looking bikers who appeared to be in their late fifties, and looked more like a group of accountants than Hell's Angels. They wore leather vests over ironed t-shirts with bandanas wrapped around graying, business-like haircuts. The women looked more like Natalie's mom playing dress-up than like

224

hardened biker chicks. One woman was standing, adjusting her leather vest, and she gave AJ a sweet smile and a wave. He waved in return before she sat down, turning back to face the front of the train.

"You know," he whispered in Natalie's ear, "it's nice to ride next to each other with no one watching us."

He let his lips linger on her earlobe, breathing out and feeling her shiver next to him. "No one checking to see if we're holding hands," he squeezed her hand, then let go, "or if I've got my arm around you." He put an arm around her then, and pulled her in close.

Natalie nodded her head and tilted her face up. Her eyes were the most beautiful color of blue he'd ever seen. The very color of the sky they'd been watching rush by outside the glass dome of the train. It was enough to take his breath away. He bent his head down to brush a kiss across her lips. She sighed in pleasure, and he forced himself to pull back and sit up straighter. They may be on their own, but a train full of tourists and families was hardly the place for long, drawn-out kisses.

They settled back in their seats, and let themselves be soothed and awed by the landscapes rushing past. All the while, he had his arm around her. While he admired the mountains, he admired the curve of her neck, so graceful. AJ let his finger slide across her skin, tracing from her ear lobe to her collarbone. While he watched a heron take flight from the shore of the lake, he noticed the shine and silkiness of her hair, and he wrapped a lock of it around his hand, letting it slide through again and again. While he marveled at the high cliffs over a river, he explored the canyons between each of her fingers, amazed at the soft perfection of her skin.

"You know," Natalie said after a while, "I think I'd like a snack. It's almost lunch time. Do you want to see what's available in the dining car?"

He stood and extended a hand to help her out of her seat, which could be a little tricky on a moving train. She stepped around him, and walked down the small aisle to the door at the end of the train. They had entered a small hallway outside the restrooms when she spun around to face him.

"AJ..." she whispered, her voice low and husky. She kept her eyes on his, and he saw in them the same wonderment he felt. AJ slid his arms around her, pulling her against his chest, heart to heart and breath to breath.

Holding her tight, he leaned his face down to kiss her, using the moment of privacy to take his time. He couldn't say in words how he felt about her, it was too soon for her, but instead let his kiss express it for him. He poured out his heart in that kiss, telling her without words that she was all he ever wanted, the answer to a thousand prayers. Her kiss spoke back. The rocking of the train made it feel as if they were dancing, swaying together, connected in ways beyond the physical. His heart felt near to bursting with overwhelming joy and love for the moment, but mostly for the woman who was moving against him, her beauty, her wit, her compassion, and her adventurousness. It all hit him as he stood with her.

The sound of a door opening brought them back to reality. One of the bikers came through the door behind them, passing by with a polite smile and an, "Excuse me, folks." They broke apart, faces flushed with embarrassment.

"It's not very romantic, is it?" AJ asked her when they were alone again. They took in their surroundings and heard the voices of people in the dining car, their conversation about what was showing at the IMAX Theater clearly audible. Now that he was noticing, the hallway outside the restrooms smelled slightly like disinfectant and armpits. Definitely lacking in romance.

Natalie looked up into his eyes again, their gazes locking. He kissed her lips again, gently, her forehead, her hair. He straightened, and the world around him came into focus again.

"I know," she said, her gaze following him. "And we've got two perfectly nice hotel rooms back there just waiting for us." She smiled, and the worry that had started building in his chest faded.

"Only one problem," he replied.

"Two," she corrected with a raised eyebrow. "The same problems we've got in Big Springs."

"Do you think we can convince them to swap roomies with us? They can be in one, and we can take another?" He comically waggled his eyebrows at her, like a lecher in a cartoon.

"Believe me if I thought we could talk them into it, I'd try, but seeing as how this is a church trip, I just don't think it's going to happen." Natalie bit her lip, indecision written across her face. She took a large breath and began, "Really, though, AJ, we should discuss—"
"It's alright, I get it."
"Get what?"
"You don't want to go any further."
Her face flushed again. "It's not that I don't want to, not really. I mean, I really like you. I like you a lot, and I'm attracted to you—"
"I hadn't noticed."
She narrowed her eyes and slapped him playfully on the arm. "It's just that I want to do things differently from now on. I went down that road before." She swallowed hard and looked down. "I know you know that, but..." She cleared

her throat. "Anyway, I've made mistakes in the past. Mistakes that I don't want to repeat. I want to be sure. The next time I give my heart away, give my body..." She flushed clear out to the tips of her ears. "I want it to be forever. Does that make sense?"

AJ reached out and pulled her into his arms, needing to hold her close, to ease her fears and erase her insecurities. "It does more than make sense. I think it's a great idea. We'll take this one step at a time." Even as he said the words aloud, he sent up a silent prayer, because holding her in his arms already felt like forever to him.

Chapter 21

The rest of the train ride was peaceful and relaxing. After their interlude in the hallway outside of the restroom, they really had gone to the dining car. By the end of the train ride, they had enjoyed a fair amount of the breathtaking scenery of the Ozarks, and even more, Natalie felt the relief of knowing they understood each other. She could relax knowing that he wasn't expecting to take her to bed at the first chance he got. There was, and would be, the temptation, but knowing that he understood her decision to wait, a decision that put her in the minority for women her age, made her feel closer to him in a way that she had never felt with any other man. Natalie shook her head to think how they'd only met one another a little over a month ago. It seemed like much longer.

"You know," AJ told her after they'd exited the train back where they'd begun, "I think you're my favorite person I've ever traveled with." He winked at her.

She laughed. "I wonder why?"

"Not just that. I mean, kissing you is always great," he took her hand and held it in his own as they walked, his thumb gently stroking her fingers. "More than great. It's amazing. Out of this world. But after that, before that, the rest of the time...I liked it. All day, the bus and the train."

Natalie knew what he meant, but felt an unfamiliar stirring in her chest, like she wanted to cry or laugh or sing or sob. She wasn't sure what it was, so she kept the emotions to herself. They approached the hotel, but kept on going, walking past it toward the waterfront shopping center.

"Was there anyone you enjoyed traveling with when you were overseas?"

"Not 'enjoyed' in the same way I just enjoyed my time with you on the train," he said, giving her hand a squeeze.

She slapped his arm. "That's not what I meant!"

AJ laughed, and they dodged the crowd around the shops. He didn't speak again as they wound through the shoppers and tourists. Natalie worried she'd brought up something he didn't want to talk about. This was supposed to a fun trip...well, as fun as tagging along with a bunch of senior citizens to Branson can be.

But as they neared an empty stretch of sidewalk that bordered the lake, and he went to stand at the railing, both hands clenched around the post, she could see he was preparing to speak, almost like she could watch the thoughts passing through his mind by the changing expressions on his face.

"I had a good buddy. We were in the same company, so we traveled together quite a bit. He was always laughing, the eternal optimist. If it was hot, he'd say how at least we had water to drink. If we were dirty and stank to high heavens, he'd say how we were lucky our girls weren't there to smell us. When he was missing home, he'd say—" AJ broke off, looking away from where Natalie stood next to him. He cleared his throat. "He'd say at least his family had him over there looking out for them, keeping them safe. Better him than someone else."

Natalie watched as AJ swallowed several times, cleared his throat again, and wiped his cheek with his palm.

"He died?"

AJ didn't speak. Instead, Natalie listened to the sounds of a boat going past in the distance, then heard the gentle lap of the waves as they hit the footings below. The buzz of the shoppers behind them joined in to the noise. She wasn't sure if he even remembered she was next to him. The look on his face made it seem like he was thousands of miles away.

"It was a suicide bomber. We were driving from one part of Baghdad to another. We didn't even see the guy. One minute we were driving along, watching the street and buildings ahead of us, and the next thing we know, we're flying through the air, our truck turned over and fire everywhere."

AJ reached out for her hand, taking it in his.

"He died instantly." He closed his eyes. "He would've said that...at least he didn't suffer."

AJ cleared his throat loudly, and Natalie used her free hand to brush the moisture from her cheeks.

"What was his name?"

"Randy."

"Is he the reason you got out of the service?"

"Not directly. I stayed in for a while after that, finished up my tour. But when I got back stateside, I saw a lot of guys I knew struggling. PTSD, post-traumatic stress disorder, is a real monster. They were being given all kinds of medicine to help them deal, but I didn't want that for myself. The pressure to take the drugs is unbelievable, and it works for some people. For me though, I guess...I guess I went back to my roots in psychology, but I just wanted to talk about it. I didn't want to forget about it, or drown it in meds, I wanted to deal with it."

AJ shrugged.

"Who did you talk to?"

"I had a counselor. He's a great guy. A veteran. He's actually my mentor now, part of finishing up my degree. I also talked to Gramps a lot. He was in Vietnam. Different time, different country, but war is war, you know."

Natalie shook her head. "I don't really know. Not like you do."

AJ looked at her for the first time since they'd come down to the waterfront. He put his arms around her and pulled her close, pressing her into his chest.

She felt AJ kiss her head and heard him say, "Better me than you."

Natalie hugged him back, her face pressed against his chest, which was a little damp from the humidity and the heat. She closed her eyes and said a prayer of thanks that AJ had returned home safely, even though she hadn't known him then.

The bus to the music show was supposed to meet at 6, so Natalie and AJ timed their arrival with a few minutes to freshen up before they had to be back in the lobby. As they neared the hotel, the flashing lights of an ambulance parked outside the front entry caused them to quicken their pace. Natalie's sandal's slapped the sidewalk as she rushed toward the hotel. Images of Gigi with a broken leg from who-knows what shenanigans she could have gotten up to...dancing on tables, sliding down banisters, trying to rock climb up the fireplace. Nothing would surprise Natalie at this point.

Or, what if it was Henrietta? What if Gigi and Charlie had given her too much of the laxatives? Natalie should have checked on her again, made sure she was drinking plenty of fluids. What if she had spent the last several hours sitting on the commode? What if the sweet little lady had passed out and they'd only discovered her when she hadn't met up with them for the bus to the show?

Running past the ambulance, which was waiting and empty, and into the front lobby, the person on the stretcher wasn't anyone Natalie had thought about being sick or injured.

Charlie Jackson lay, strapped down to a stretcher, an oxygen mask over his colorless lips. His skin was so white, it was nearly transparent. His eyes were closed, and his hands resting motionless at his sides. Two EMT's, a man and a woman, wheeled him toward the waiting ambulance.

"Gramps?" AJ cried out at the sight. "What happened? Gramps? Is he—?"

"He's stable. We need to get him to the hospital. Are you family?" An EMT spoke to him, but didn't stop their forward movement. AJ walked quickly alongside them.

"I'm his grandson. What happened?"

"I'm not dead." The voice was weak, but not unnoticed.

"We got a call about an elderly man having chest pains. He hasn't lost consciousness. His oxygen levels are good, but we're going to take him in to get some tests. Stand back."

They had reached the glass doors, which were being held open by hotel personnel. The stretcher was pushed out into the balmy summer air. The male EMT pulled open the back doors of the ambulance, and the stretcher, along with Charlie, was loaded into the back of it.

"I want to go with him." AJ stood tall and rigid, looking like he'd fight anyone who got in his way.

"Of course." The female EMT showed him where to sit inside.

Natalie watched as the door were shut and secured, the lights turned off, and the vehicle pulled out of the parking lot. It was then that she thought to search for Gigi. Why wasn't she here? Knowing Gigi's penchant for dramatics, she ought to be right here in the lobby, wailing and calling for smelling salts.

Pastor Matt was there, as were Mr. and Mrs. Dewey, Mabel, even Henrietta, who was looking as fit as ever, obviously recovered. Natalie approached the group, searching for her grandmother.

"They are taking him to the hospital, which is right down the road, only a few miles away," the pastor was telling them. "There's nothing we can do for him at this time except pray. Do you want to gather up in that corner of the lobby— the one with the couches and chairs? It's a nice area where we can be comfortable, but also lift our voices to God. 'Heal me, O Lord, and I will be healed; save me and I will be saved, for you are the one I praise.' Jeremiah 17: 14 'For where two or three gather in my name, there I am with them.' Matthew 18: 20. Will you come with me?"

The group began to move toward the corner, but Natalie put a hand out and touched Mabel's arm to stop her.

"Have you seen my grandmother?"

Mabel looked around at the group. "I haven't. I assumed she went in the ambulance with Charlie. Did she not?"

"No, AJ went with him. Do you have any idea where Gigi might be?"

Mabel shook her head. "The last I saw her, she was going into her room with you. She's probably still sleeping. That woman can sleep through anything. One of us should wake her up, tell her what's happened. Do you want me to come with you?"

Natalie considered it. Gigi would be beside herself. She had never seen her grandmother in a crisis, and could only imagine what sort of histrionics the woman could produce. Mabel was her friend, but why force her to have to deal with calming down Gigi? No, this would best be done alone, sort of containing the chaos.

"I'll tell her. If I need one of you, I'll phone the front desk and ask them to pass on the message."

Natalie pressed the button on the elevator and watched as the group made their way over to the designated prayer corner. She wished she was going with them. Prayer had always been a part of her life when she was growing up, but she hadn't prayed much lately. Not in several years, in fact. Maybe it was time.

When Natalie walked into her hotel room, she found Gigi curled up on the bed in a bathrobe. She lay in the fetal position, the lapels of her robe pulled up to her chin. Walking around the bed, Natalie saw that Gigi's eyes were open, staring straight ahead, her gaze unfocused and unblinking. Natalie sat down on the edge of the bed, reaching a hand out to her grandmother's. Her nails were perfectly manicured and painted a bright pink, but as Natalie took hold, what she noticed first was the coldness of the older woman's hands. The skin was as soft and thin worn cotton, but was chilled.

"Gigi, are you sick?"

"No. I'm fine, honey."

Her grandmother's eyes stayed on the middle distance, not really seeing anything. She let go of Natalie's hand and brushed a lock of hair from her face. It was then that Natalie saw the tremor in her hands. They shook, twitching gently as Natalie had never seen before. She raised a palm to her grandmother's face and felt her temperature. Her forehead felt warm enough, though not feverish.

"Do you know what's happened?" Natalie asked her.

Gigi nodded. She closed her eyes then, squeezing them shut. Her face seemed to melt in an instant, her lips falling open in a silent cry. Gigi raised her hands and covered her face, chest heaving as she breathed in deeply. Natalie put an arm around her, but Gigi shook her off. She sat up abruptly, dropping her hands, her eyes open and resolute.

"I'm fine. I'll be fine. Don't worry about me. Go see about that man of yours. He'll need you now. And me? Well, I'm going to be alright. I've gone through this before, and I survived it then. Charlie and I weren't even married. I'll bounce back. I just need a minute." Her voice shook slightly, but her jaw was set, whether to steel her courage or keep her tears at bay was uncertain.

Natalie shook her head. "I'm here for you. I'm staying here for you. AJ went to the hospital with Charlie. I won't leave you, Gigi."

"I told you. I'll be fine. When your granddaddy died in the war, I went on, didn't I? I've always done what needed to be done. He went off to Vietnam, and I stayed behind to raise our Dolly Jean. She was just a little thing then. I made it though. We both did. Then when he died, I made it through that." Gigi closed her eyes again, taking deep breaths. "I wanted to fall apart. I wanted to disappear into the grave with him, but I couldn't. I didn't. I kept on going. I told my daughter her father was a hero, and I smiled. I smiled, and I posed in a bikini for an ad so I could get the money to come back home from California. It's a long way from California to Arkansas. A world away. A lifetime."

Natalie took her grandmother's hand in hers, and Gigi held it tightly.

"I came back a poor, pitiful widow at twenty-five with a daughter to raise and nowhere to go but home. I smiled, and I laughed. What was I supposed to do? Wear black forever? Wear my grief on my sleeve? No one wants to see that. Dolly Jean needed me, needed her mama. She'd had enough sadness. She needed laughter and dancing and silliness. So, I gave her that. "

Gigi stood and tightened the belt on her robe.

"I can do it again. I'll be fine. I lost one husband to war, and I lost Charlie today." She nodded. "I'm just not meant to be married, I guess. I don't know why God wants me to be alone, but I know that He has a plan. It's up to me to accept it and to make the most of it." Gigi sat back down on the bed. "But, oh, how I wanted to keep that man, Natalie. I wanted to be his. I didn't want to be alone anymore." She dropped her head into her hands and let out a high-pitched, keening wail.

"No, Gigi, you've got it all wrong. Charlie's not dead. I saw him downstairs when he was going into the ambulance. He was talking. It can't be that bad if he's still talking, right?"

Her grandmother looked at her, eyes narrowed.

"I saw him. I was with him in his room. He grabbed his chest. He was white as a sheet. I called 911, and they came and took him away on a stretcher. I watched them strap him down, and I came back here. I saw him, Natalie."

"No, Gigi. He's not dead. At least, he wasn't when he left here."

Her eyes slid closed again, and she fell to the floor next to the bed. She pressed her hands together and began to pray. The words were mumbled, quietly spoken for only God to hear, but Natalie could make out the words as her grandmother was talked to God, pleading with Him, begging Him. She could hear her asking God to heal Charlie, to leave him here with her. She heard Gigi ask for strength in the coming days.

In those moments, Natalie's world began to come into focus. Where she had struggled with small hurdles in her life, her grandmother moved mountains. Where she had balked at coming home and starting over, Gigi had pushed through even worse. Natalie had been ashamed to return home, but Gigi had cast aside her grief for the chance to come back again, to start again where she had begun. And after experiencing the loss of her husband, she had even had the courage to fall in love again.

Even as the question, *How?* entered her mind, Natalie knew the answer. She saw it right in front of her eyes: Gigi, on her knees.

Natalie slid from the edge of the bed and into the floor beside her grandmother. She clasped her hands in front of her and began to pray, pouring it all out, asking God for guidance, for humility, for courage, for understanding, for Charlie's health.

They stayed like that for a long time, each talking to God. When they'd both exhausted themselves, they eased down to sit on the floor, backs against the bed.

Gigi reached out and gave Natalie's hand a gentle pat.

"Thank you for staying with me. You really are a precious girl." She pulled Natalie into a hug, and Natalie was aware again of how frail her grandmother felt in her arms.

In her mind, Gigi would always be in her late fifties, healthy as a horse and the most gorgeous grandmother at the elementary school's Grandparents' Day lunch, even if she did show a bit too much cleavage for the principal's modest taste.

"Well, if you're feeling up to it, we could go over to the hospital. I'm told it's not far from here." She searched her grandmother's eyes and in them saw a woman prepared to deal with anything. She already had, and would handle anything else that life might throw her way.

"Please." Gigi stood and looked down at herself, the bathrobe falling open slightly at the top. "I should probably put some clothes on first."

"That might be a good idea." Natalie came to her feet in front of Gigi, and saw a bit of red lace sticking out the top of the pink terry cloth robe. "Is that my bra?"

Gigi pulled the lapels closed again. "I don't know what you're talking about."

"Are you wearing my bra? My red lace bra? I haven't even worn it yet. It was an impulse buy. It still had the tags on it! Gigi!"

Her grandmother shrugged. "I saw it in your drawer, and it looked like fun. Kind of sexy. I thought I'd wear it, let Charlie accidentally see a little glimpse of it. I thought it'd make me look like hot stuff." She sighed. "I haven't chased a man since I was in my early twenties. I'm not quite sure how to do it anymore."

"So you turned to theft?'

"I was going to give it back."

Natalie let out a groan, which turned into laughter. "Keep it! I hope it does you some good."

"No way! It's the bra that gave Charlie a heart attack. I was wearing a low-cut top, and I had just bent over to pick up the remote. He got one glimpse of my goodies in this bra, and the next thing I know, I'm calling an ambulance."

Natalie's phone rang. She looked at the display.

"It's AJ." Both women sat down on the bed, their expressions somber and tense, and all laughter gone.

Natalie hit the button to answer the phone and pressed it to her ear, ready for whatever news would come their way.

"Hello?"

"Natalie? It's me." AJ spoke quietly. Hospital noises filled the background. Beeps and voices in the distance.

"I'm here. How is he?" She held her breath. Gigi gripped the comforter between her hands.

"He's fine. He's going to be alright." Natalie let out her breath and smiled at her grandmother, who heaved a sigh and closed her eyes in relief.

"Was it a heart attack?"

"No, not exactly. He has some minor blockage. They're going to have to put a stint in, to open up the spot that's causing him trouble. He'll have to change his diet, eat fewer fried foods and exercise more, but the doctor says he'll be alright."

"Thank God."

"I know. Also, Gramps is asking for Gertie. Do you think she could come down here? Both of you, actually?" The added on request of her, and not just her grandmother, filled her heart.

"Absolutely. We'll be there as soon as we can."

The front desk called a taxi to take them to the hospital, and when they arrived, they were easily directed to the room where Charlie lie propped up on a bed, wearing a blue hospital gown, his legs covered with a white blanket. One arm was hooked to an IV, and the other was holding a television remote control. AJ sat on his left side, facing the door, and he stood as Gigi and Natalie entered the room.

Gigi moved immediately to Charlie's side, where she hovered over him, her hands fluttering about his face and chest like agitated hummingbirds. She alternately scolded him for scaring her and cooed at him for his suffering. Charlie was soaking it all in, basking in the attention, leaning back on a pillow with a smile on his face.

AJ held his arms out to Natalie, who walked quietly into them. He wrapped his arms around her, and held on for dear life. Natalie pressed her cheek to his chest and listened to the rhythm of his heartbeat. She sighed. It felt good to be wrapped up so securely in his arms. After her conversation with Gigi, she felt wrung out, as if witnessing the release of so much pain had sapped all of her own as well. She knew that AJ must be feeling the same way because she felt him sigh into her hair.

"Is he really going to be alright?" Gigi asked from Charlie's side. She held his free hand firmly in her own, the remote control abandoned on the blanket.

"The doctor said so, didn't he? I don't know why she isn't believing me. I told her that all they have to do is put that stent in, and I'm as good as new."

AJ ran a hand through his hair. "Well, that isn't quite what he said, Gramps. The doctor said you will be out of danger, but that you will have to make some lifestyle changes. More exercise. Healthier diet. That sort of thing."

"Aw, that's nothing! I'm a farmer. I get my exercise walking fences and riding horses. I get it lifting hay bales and working cattle. I'm fit as a fiddle."

"How much of those things have you done since I moved here? How many hay bales have you lifted in the past two years, Gramps?" AJ waited for the answer while his grandfather glared daggers at him. "Since I've been around, you haven't been doing much of any of those things you named off. I can't think of the last time you were on a horse."

"I rode in the county fair parade!"

"That was last September. It's nearly July. I don't think that counts as regular exercise."

Natalie cleared her throat and stepped out of AJ's arms. "You could start walking on the treadmill at the senior center. Henrietta and Mabel have taken to working out while they watch their stories."

Charlie's face reddened. "I don't watch soap operas! I just happen to be there when they're on. It's not my fault the women-folk are always putting them on."

Gigi kissed his face. "We know that, dear, and we are so happy that you indulge us and keep us company while we watch." When she faced the younger pair, she winked. "No one here would ever think you watched them willingly. But, we are missing your company during that time. If you aren't around, who will tell us how ridiculous the storyline is? Who will point out when a character isn't acting like a gentleman and tell us what an old fashioned gentleman would do? We're all suffering because you aren't in the exercise room with us during that time."

"Well," Charlie mumbled, "I guess that's true. I could always bring my recliner in there to watch."

Natalie shook her head. "No sitting and watching in that room, I'm afraid. Some of the ladies complained when Al Tankersly did that a few weeks ago. They said he was only coming in there to stare at their behinds, and they made me put up a sign. Exercisers only. No audiences."

Charlie huffed. "Well, shoot! I guess I'll have to get on one of those contraptions then. I don't see why I need to get on a machine to make me walk when I've been walking around on my own for over fifty years."

AJ raised an eyebrow. "Only fifty?"

"Not the point," Charlie countered, teeth clenched. He shrugged. "I'll do it. I see what you're up to here, but I can't fight all three of you. It's not fair."

Gigi kissed his cheek and then used her finger to wipe off the lipstick. "And what about this special diet?" she asked.

"He needs to eat healthier. Fewer fried foods."

Charlie raised up in the bed. "You ain't taking my fried chicken away."

"I am if the doctor says it'll keep you from dying!" Gigi put her hands on her hips. "I don't want you keeling over at my dinner table, Charlie Jackson."

"Life ain't worth living if I got to do it without fried chicken!"

AJ spoke over them, "You'll have to eat more vegetables."

Gigi waved the comment away. "You eat vegetables all the time. Why, we had green beans just last night."

"With butter and bacon in them, Gigi. That doesn't count. They need to be healthy." Natalie lifted her hands up defensively. "I'm only saying the words. I'm not making the rules."

"How am I supposed to cook green beans without butter and bacon? They won't taste right!"

A knock sounded at the door, and everyone turned toward it.

"Did I hear someone asking about how to cook green beans?" A brunette about Natalie's age walked into the room. She was tall and fit, and carrying a stack of white print-out pages. "I'm a nutritionist with the hospital, and it looks like I'm right on time to talk to Mr. Jackson about his food choices."

Charlie rolled his eyes. "Gertie, you'd better stay for this." She grasped his hand, and they both looked like they were about to face a firing squad.

"You want to get something to eat?" AJ asked Natalie, who nodded. They made their excuses and their escape, and the older couple told them to take their time. They intended to listen to the "health nut" and then settle in to watch some television, which was really code for "take a nap".

Chapter 22

Natalie and AJ took another taxi back to the hotel. They wanted to report in with the other members of their group before going to dinner. When they entered the parking lot, they found the seniors gathered around the bus. The moment they saw the pair exit the taxi, the pack descended on them, firing questions about Charlie.

AJ held up his hands. "I'll tell you all at once, if you'll give me a minute!" The crowd settled into a hushed semi-circle around him. AJ went on to tell them all of the news, about the stent and the changes that his grandfather would have to make to ensure that he'd be around for a long while to come.

Pastor Matt spoke up, "When will he be released?"

"I'm not sure yet. I think they'll do the surgery tomorrow morning, and since it's a relatively simple procedure, he'll get to leave day or so after that. Unless there are complications, of course."

"I'll call my mama and daddy. Gigi won't want to leave Charlie, so I'm sure that my folks will come up and stay, then drive him home." Natalie pulled out her cell phone and began to dial the number.

AJ fielded a few more questions while she was on the phone. DeeJay responded with the cool efficiency that was clearly not inherited from her mother. She immediately began making plans, shouting out to her husband to call and tell Jerry that the barbeque plans for the next day were off. They were going to Branson.

Natalie nodded to let AJ know that it was taken care of, and Pastor Matt herded the troupe onto the bus to head out for dinner. Natalie followed them on, taking her usual seat in the middle of the bus. AJ eased himself down next to her.

He leaned his head back and closed his eyes, easing into the instant sleep of a soldier that was a marvel to every civilian.

The mood on the bus was celebratory. Their relief was expressed in their excitement to eat at the home-style restaurant for dinner. Upon arrival, they bounded off of the bus as eagerly as they could manage. AJ came awake as easily as he had fallen asleep, holding out his hand to assist Natalie from her window seat, an old fashioned gentleman— like his grandfather.

As the Big Springs crowd pushed inside the rustic wooden door of the restaurant, a hush fell over them. Jaws dropped, drool pooled on the ground at their feet, and elbows were thrown in a quest to be the first in line.

"Is that a buffet?" Natalie asked AJ, who stood behind her.

"I hope so. I think I see chicken fried steak," he spoke with the awe usually reserved for falling stars and monster trucks.

Natalie giggled.

"I think I see a salad bar in the back," she commented as their group began to be assigned tables.

"You cannot eat salad at a restaurant like this," he said, loud enough to draw a few looks. He didn't notice, instead staring at Natalie like she had dropped down from another planet. "You eat macaroni and cheese or fried okra. You eat either fried chicken, chicken fried steak, or meatloaf. You eat rolls or homemade bread with molasses on it. You have mashed potatoes with gravy. The only choice you have to make is if it's white gravy or brown. But absolutely, no salad."

He spoke with the kind of definitive authority that made it easy for Natalie to see him in a uniform, ordering soldiers to fall in...or whatever they did. Her own military experiences were limited to the movies Stripes and Major Payne.

"I like salad. Besides, after what Charlie just went through, we ought to be eating healthier."

"Gramps isn't here. In front of him, we'll eat like rabbits. But tonight, no salad," AJ informed her just before he pulled out her seat for her.

In the end Natalie had a salad, along with the fried chicken, a few bites of AJ's chicken fried steak—stolen when he was up getting another dinner roll—about a pound of fried okra, and mashed potatoes. White gravy.

"I don't think I can move," she whined, holding her stomach. The bus rumbled toward their hotel, and a satisfied silence had fallen on the nearly comatose riders, broken by only the occasional moan and belch. "Do you think anyone would notice if I unbuttoned my pants?"

"I unbuttoned mine as soon as we got there."

"Did you really?" she asked, watching as his face illuminated by the passing glow of colorfully lit up signs.

"You'll never know." He winked. With a sigh, he leaned up and asked Pastor Matt if the bus could drop them off at the hospital.

"I'll do you one better. We'll drop these guys off at the hotel, and I'll go back over with you two. I'd like to sit and pray with Charlie for a while."

AJ reached his arm out and clasped his hand in hers, their fingers twining together. He squeezed. She squeezed and rested her head on his. Natalie closed her eyes. She said a quick prayer of thanks. This night could've been much different. Instead of going out to eat a gut-busting dinner, she could have been eating a bag of chips in the hospital's waiting room. She could've been in her hotel room holding her grandmother while she struggled not to fall apart. Instead, here she was, sitting next to AJ, who was shaken but not scared, not broken-hearted.

She lifted her head, and after looking around to see that the bus was indeed dark, except for the lights illuminating Pastor Matt and the bus driver as they motioned to the turn ahead, she kissed AJ below his ear along his jaw. He shifted his gaze to her, his eyes weary, and leaned down. He pressed his lips to hers. She lifted her hand to his shoulder, and he shifted one to her cheek. It was a short kiss, no more than a few seconds, but in it she found comfort and the strength to lift herself out of the seat when the bus stopped to go into the hospital again.

Pastor Matt made small talk in the elevator, telling them about all of the hospitals he'd visited during his time as a minister. When they reached Charlie's floor, he excused himself to use the restroom. Natalie told AJ she would wait there and would show the preacher the way to the room. He squeezed her hand and headed down the hall.

Less than a minute later, he returned. Natalie couldn't decipher the look on his face. He was generally unflappable. He'd seen a lot in this world, much of it terrible. The expression on his face wasn't one of horror exactly, but it was something awfully close.

I heard something," he whispered.

Natalie was immediately concerned. "The doctor? What did he say?"

"Not the doctor."

"A nurse?"

AJ shook his head. His expression remained unchanged. Then he shook all over, like a dog coming out of the rain.

"Come and listen. Maybe it's not what it sounds like." He led her by the hand until they reached the closed door to Charlie's room. "Listen."

"I don't hear it now. Maybe I imagined it, though why I would imagine *that* of all things, I don't know. Speaking as someone who is almost a therapist, I think I might need to see one."

"Shhh. I'm trying to listen," she waved her hand at him.

AJ pressed his own ear to the door, several inches above hers, pressing their ears and faces against the cool wooden print on the door. There was the low rumble of voices. More than one voice.

"That's Gigi and Charlie. They're in there," Natalie said. "What did you overhear them say? Wait. Shhh. I think I hear something—" The concern that she had felt before dissipated, replaced with another feeling entirely. It was hung up in the back of her throat and tasting a little like white gravy and bile.

"You mean? Is that sound really what I think it is?" AJ asked in a hushed voice, his face turning sour.

Natalie nodded. She felt ill. Like she needed a bathroom or a trashcan or an ice bucket.

"We're on a church trip, for crying out loud!" she whispered. "It's bad enough that they're getting frisky in a hospital, but in a hospital while on a church trip? That's double bad."

"What should we do? Should we knock?"

"And then what? Throw a bucket of ice on them?"

"Gramps would have a heart attack for sure—Oh, man! I hope he's being careful. If he gets too excited, he might have one!"

"He sounds pretty excited to me," Natalie reported, pulling back from the door and wiping at her ear with the sleeve of her shirt.

"Who's excited?" Pastor Matt spoke from behind AJ. He had come up the hallway while they had been distracted.

Natalie jumped back from the door. AJ took a step in front of it.

"My grandpa is pretty excited that Mr. and Mrs. James are coming up to get him. It's awfully nice of them."

Pastor Matt nodded amiably. He motioned with his hand, "Why don't we go on in? Is he sleeping?"

Natalie shook her head, her ponytail swishing from side to side.

AJ cleared his throat. "I'll just knock and see." He raised his knuckles to the wooden door and rapped three times. The hallway was silent as they waited.

"Come on in," a voice called from within.

"Are you sure?" AJ called out. Natalie moved behind the two men. There was no way on earth she was going to go into that room first. She wanted to be able to duck and cover if need be.

There was no answer from the other side of the door.

"Is it locked or something?" Pastor Matt asked. He stuck out a hand, reaching past AJ to turn the knob. "No. It's open. Let's go on in. I'm anxious to pray with them both."

The door swung open slowly, and Natalie squeezed her eyes shut, expecting to hear exclamations of surprise or shock. Instead, she heard the soft chuckle of AJ's barely restrained laughter. Natalie opened her eyes and peek around him.

Gigi and Charlie were indeed in the hospital bed. They had squeezed in shoulder-to-shoulder in the twin size bed. Charlie's legs were still covered with the blanket, and Gigi's were still covered by her slacks. They sat still, holding hands, eyes glued to the television.

"What are you watching?!" Natalie squeaked, a little louder than she intended.

"Our stories," Gigi informed her. "Now hush up and wait for a commercial break."

Pastor Matt smiled at the sweet picture the older couple made. His attention was drawn to the screen by someone shouting the Lord's name. "Did I hear someone talking about God? Is this a Christian soap opera—" Then a pause, "Goodness! How can they put that on television? Turn it off!" His face was bright red, and he covered his ears.

"Oh, you'd be surprised what they can put on cable these days," Gigi told them. "But it's not rated R or anything, so it must be alright. I'm not seeing anything I haven't seen before. They're all actors anyway."

The older woman patted her hair. It was that motion that drew Natalie's attention to the mark on her grandmother's neck. She had seen marks like those before, never on herself. She thought hickeys were disgusting, but clearly that was a feeling that her grandmother did not share. A large one was forming in the space above her collarbone. Now that Natalie's attention was there, she also noticed that Gigi's shirt was buttoned incorrectly, the buttons and buttonholes not quite matching up.

Natalie rubbed her forehead. Yuck. Oh, some things could never be unseen. She reached up and tightened her ponytail so tight that her eyelids hurt.

Pastor Matt's eyes were glued to Gigi's torso, the hickey and the buttons and the bra. Natalie saw as he turned to look at Gigi and Charlie again, the sweet image of the couple changed forever in his mind. He ground his teeth, and Natalie could tell he was struggling with what to say or do.

AJ reached up and hit the power button on the television. "Maybe we should turn this off for now." The moans and groans that had previously filled the room were silent.

"Good idea," Charlie told him, putting the remote aside on a table. "Miss Gertie and I have some news." He took both of her hands in his, and raised them up to his lips, kissing each one gently. "This little scare has lit a fire under me. I knew I couldn't wait around forever. Enough with courting, we're engaged!"

"Congratulations, you two," AJ said sincerely. "Gramps you are a lucky man. And Gertie, you will be a beautiful bride."

Gigi giggled, and Natalie remembered her anguish of earlier that night. So much emotion for one day. It was turning out well, though. Sort of. Gross, but one person's Happily Ever After is another person's purgative.

"Great news, Gigi. Charlie, we're glad to have you joining the family."

"I would have preferred that you celebrate in a different way, of course," Pastor Matt began, "but if you are getting married," he paused, eyeing the pair, "and getting married very, very soon," the minister paused again, "then I suppose there's no real harm done."

The older couple had lost a little bit of their radiance, but neither moved away from the other. Charlie looked to Gigi for guidance, and she gave him small nod.

"I don't think we want to wait much longer to get married," Charlie told the trio.

"Do they do weddings in Branson? Like in Vegas? Could we get married tonight?" Gigi asked, perking up.

"No," Natalie, AJ, and Pastor Matt said in unison.

Pastor Matt raised a hand, "I would prefer to be the one to do the honors. If I may have that privilege?"

"And you know that Mama will kill you if she doesn't get to be there for it. After all, this will be the first father she's ever really known," Natalie threw in.

"We should have a bachelor party first," AJ supplied.

Natalie elbowed him in the ribs.

"It's all I could think of," he whispered.

"Let us talk about it a minute," Charlie told the group. He promptly raised up the blanket to cover their heads.

"No shenanigans in there, you two," Natalie called out.

AJ groaned. Pastor Matt rubbed his forehead.

The hospital blanket came back down to its previous placement, and all of their clothes seemed to be in place, or as much as they had been moments before.

"One month. That's our limit," Gigi said.

Natalie exchanged glances with AJ and Pastor Matt, who spoke up, "Deal."

The rest of the Branson trip was full of the normal adventures. Charlie and Gigi insisted that AJ and Natalie leave them in peace, and the younger pair had no trouble with that. They shopped in the outlet stores, buying a few items they needed and a lot of items they didn't. They ate three more buffet-style meals, and Natalie was pretty certain she'd gained thirty pounds. AJ, however, looked exactly the same, for which Natalie forgave him. They took an Old Tyme group photo with the seniors, the men dressed up like cowboys and the ladies, regretfully, dressed up like saloon girls. Natalie had asked Henrietta if she felt odd dressing up like a 19th century prostitute, but Henrietta and Mabel had both assured her that they weren't the hooker kind of saloon girls, just the kind who sang and danced and dreamed of better days. In the picture, however, they just looked like streetwalkers with feathered headbands. Clearly the better days were still a long way off.

Upon their arrival in Branson, Natalie stood by while Gigi and Charlie informed her parents of their intention to marry within the month, leaving out some of the details surrounding the original announcement of the engagement. AJ and Pastor Matt had agreed with her that the entire incident should be forgotten and never spoken of again, though Natalie informed her brother in vivid detail. If she had that image in her head, he was sure as heck going to have it in his too. It was only fair.

Charlie's stent went in with no complications. Gigi took full credit, citing her penchant for cooking with bacon grease and butter as the reason, "it was able to slide in there so easy." She wouldn't hear otherwise. The morning of departure, Charlie had been loaded gingerly into the backseat of the SUV, and Gigi had settled into the seat next to him.

AJ and Natalie watched it pull out of the hotel parking lot, Danny driving and DeeJay shaking out aspirin into her hand, tossing them into her mouth with a grimace.

The bus ride home was uneventful. No one had diarrhea in the on-bus restroom. No one shot them dirty looks or acted like AJ was a pariah for "leaving that poor Jamie" for Natalie. It seemed like the entire senior citizen community had accepted them as a couple. Embraced them, even. It was nice, sort of. Natalie still got a funny, tingly feeling in her stomach at the idea that everyone was so happy to see them together. It was the same feeling she got that time she went up in the St. Louis Arch. She had begged and begged to go, but once she got up there and looked down, she just wanted to close her eyes and stand very, very still, not wanting to go back down, but unable to look either.

Chapter 23

"A family dinner!" Charlie exclaimed, "It's been a long time since I've been to one of these."

"If I'd had more notice, we could've had something fancier, but since mother just told me this morning, I didn't have time to put together anything except sandwiches and salads," DeeJay informed her future stepfather while she gave Gigi a pointed look.

Natalie's mother fluttered around the kitchen, stirring a bowl of potato salad and pulling out platters from the fridge. Her brother and father were planted in front of the television casually watching CMT, mainly watching for time to sit down to lunch. Against the concerned protests of everyone, Charlie refused to join them, instead sitting on a bar stool at the kitchen island, his eyes following Gigi as she carried serving dishes to the table. Natalie set the table as quickly as she could and escaped out the backdoor to find AJ, who was hiding out by the barn under the pretense of "checking on something."

"How's that thing that you were checking on?" Natalie asked him. She found AJ sitting on a stack of square bales in the barn, chewing on a piece of straw and staring out at the field.

"It's fine. You know how it is on a farm. Always something or other needing to be looked at, checked on, fiddled with," he said, his mouth turning up on one side. Natalie almost melted. "Speaking of looking at things, did you notice how people were looking at us at church this morning?"

Natalie shook her head.

"They weren't. Nobody thought anything at all about me sitting beside you. Not even when I held your hand when we were walking out. Did you notice that? No dirty looks.

Nothing like that. Nothing at all." AJ grinned at her, pulling her closer with one arm hooked around her waist.

"We're old news already," Natalie informed him. "Trumped by our grandparents."

"I don't mind being old news," he said. "It's more private that way." AJ moved on the hay bale so that he was sitting behind her, a jean-clad leg on either side of hers. He wrapped both arms around her and pulled her back against his chest. "Speaking of private, when do you have some free time? I'd like to take you out. Candlelight and romance and all of that."

She turned to look up at him.

"Going on a date in public? Where anyone could see us together? Interesting idea. I'll have to check my schedule."

"Well, you think about it for a minute," AJ told her. He lifted her ponytail out of the way and began to place tiny kisses around the side of her neck. She giggled. "None of that now! You be thinking of a time you can go out on the town with me. Just the two of us. No old folks allowed." As he spoke, his breath tickled the little hairs on her nape. Natalie tilted her head over to give him more space, and AJ kissed her gently beneath the ear, whispering, "Have I told you today how beautiful you are?" She sighed.

"For crying out loud!" came an exclamation from the doorway.

Natalie turned around, her back pressed to AJ's front. She watched as her brother's face got redder and redder until it was nearly purple.

"A guy can't even walk to his own home!" Brett ran his hands through his hair until it stood on end, creating a lovely just-electrocuted effect.

Natalie held up a hand in protest.

"Three words. Gigi. Charlie. Hickey." She waited as the color drained from her brother's face. "No complaints or I'll start describing what else we saw. Ok?"

Brett stood motionless for a solid minute, his left eye twitching. Finally, he nodded sharply and turned to walk out.

AJ called out, "Did you need something?"

Brett stopped moving, shook his head as if to clear it, and muttered, "Oh, yeah. Lunch. It's ready. If you think you can stomach it. Me? I don't know if I'd ever have an appetite again after seeing Gigi... Let's not talk about it ever again."

"Deal," Natalie immediately answered.

***

The senior center that week was full of energy. The excitement over Charlie and Gigi's engagement put dreams in the eyes of some. Natalie saw winks and flirtatious glances passing between more than just the betrothed. Others reacted in a different way, pointing out that if the couple intended to hold their reception in the center—because, really, where else could they possibly consider holding it—then there was work to be done.

Natalie belonged to the latter group. The sight of her grandmother squeezing Charlie's flat, khaki-clad bottom definitely did not inspire her toward any physical action other than wanting to scour her eyeballs with bleach.

Instead, Natalie bought paint. She enlisted Jamie's hardware store expertise in selecting paint types and all of the necessary equipment to put it on—paint rollers, brushes, edging tools, drop cloths. The hardware store made its largest sale that year. The pair of them taped samples to the wall, held a vote, and then vetoed the vote in favor of a better option. Honestly, whose idea was it to let a bunch of people whose heydays were the seventies choose wall colors?

The day of the painting party dawned beautifully cool for July, inspiring the men to suddenly absent themselves from the chore of painting for the more pleasant atmosphere of the fishing holes. The women didn't mind, as this meant they could wear their grubbiest old painting clothes, wrap bandanas around their hair, and forgo most of their make-up. At least, that's what Natalie, Jamie, and most of the women did. Gigi, naturally, came perfectly coiffed with a tube of lipstick in the pocket of her polka dotted apron.

"Where would you like me, darling?" Gigi asked Natalie, who stood with a clipboard organizing her crew of enthusiastic, but limited geriatrics and the small group of younger volunteers.

Gigi stood in front of her granddaughter smoothing out the bow she had tied on her hip where the strings met.

"Aren't you worried about getting paint on that?" Natalie had worn a pair of old sweatpants, cut off at the knees and a t-shirt advertising a volleyball game from 1998. "That apron looks pretty nice."

Gigi waved her hand dismissively. "I won't get a spot on it. It's strictly for show. Just you see. I'm a very tidy painter."

Natalie shrugged. It wasn't her job to see after her grandmother's laundry. She gave Gigi a small cup of paint and an edging brush and sent her to do the spaces around the windows.

"Are you going to cover up that mural of the children?" Mrs. Talburt asked, scooting up for her assignment. Her walker had been draped with an old sheet which was secured with some cleverly wound twine and a few pieces of masking tape.

"We're going to keep the mural of the mountains and the creek over by the front door, but, yes, I'm afraid we are painting over the one of the children in the cafeteria," Natalie informed her.

"Good. The faces of those little kids always did give me the willies. Their eyes follow you. Make sure you cover up their eyes with a several coats of paint. We don't want them to show through, scaring the daylights out of everyone. It'll be like the walls are watching." Mrs. Talburt blinked up at Natalie, her expression betraying no trace of mirth or sarcasm. Not even the vacant stare of the insane. They were serious, intense, and still fiercely intelligent.

"Alright. That sounds like a good idea." Natalie looked down her list for a task that was easy enough for a woman with a walker. "You want to be the one who paints over their faces? You can make sure their eyes are good and covered."

Mrs. Talburt's face lit up. "Gladly!" She rolled off toward the cans of primer.

Jamie came over to Natalie with her own clipboard, which contained a map of color selections for the different rooms. There were names and check marks written across it.

"Did you find a job for Mrs. Talburt?"

"I sure did, but you should go over and ask her what she's doing in a little while. I'd tell you myself, but it wouldn't have the same effect."

"Sure," Jamie said, no questions asked. "Are we all lined out? Ready to get started on that front wall?"

The pair had decided to do chevron stripes of different colors along the front wall of what was formerly the office, and what would now be referred to as the lobby. They'd taped it off earlier in the week and elected to do the project themselves rather than attempt to explain it to someone else. It also put them right up front to answer questions if anyone needed them.

They settled into an easy rhythm of using smaller brushes and rollers for the detail work, and the larger rollers for the expanses. Jamie's iPod kept played an upbeat mix of songs for them to sing along with, or to ignore and chat over as the case may be. Volunteers came and went, smiling as they returned with pizzas from Luigi's and cookies from Millie's, all donated for the cause.

"I think we'll finish most of it today, don't you?" Jamie asked. Natalie put down her brush and stepped back to inspect their work.

"This part definitely. The rest of it, who knows? We will need to double check their work, see what kind of touch ups we'll have to go back and do. Overall, though, I think we'll be pretty close."

Jamie sat down in the middle of the floor, the only place where she was sure not to lean against a wet wall. She examined the two clipboards.

"It looks like everything is marked off. I could do with a little break this week. Between helping out here and putting in forty hours at the hardware store, I'm beat. How about you?"

Natalie collapsed on the ground beside Jamie, lying back until her shoulder blades rested on the cold tile floor. She heaved a sigh.

"I know how you feel. I've hardly seen AJ at all this week. I mean, it's not like we are used to seeing each other every day or anything, but I'd like to see him more than just once a week."

"You guys are getting pretty close. Is it serious?" Jamie asked. She also stretched out on the floor, and Natalie heard the sound of her sneakers being kicked off.

"If one of those hit our wall, I might murder you," Natalie said.

"Relax. They went over by the doors. Stop avoiding the question."

Natalie closed her eyes, letting the chill of the tile floor seep through her clothes and into her skin. She thought about it. AJ made her feel different than she ever had before. She didn't feel like she had to try hard to impress him or to get him to like her. He just did. She didn't have to work to get his attention or to keep it. He called her every single day, sometimes more than once. He dropped by just to see how she was doing. They laughed together, and never ran out of things to talk about. It was the easiest relationship she'd ever had.

It was also the only she had gone into without a solid plan for their future. With Brantley, Natalie had figured they would date for a year then get engaged. She would work hard and put in more hours than anyone else so she could prove that her professional success wasn't only because she was marrying into the family at Baxter-Wallace, but because she was truly committed to the work. She and Jenn would plan the wedding, going to bridal shows and gown shopping. Then she and Brantley would get married in a grand ceremony befitting his social standing, have a fabulous reception, and then fly off to Antigua for a long honeymoon. After that, she wasn't certain, but she was sure they would do whatever 'happily ever after' entailed.

Only that hadn't worked out so well.

With AJ there was none of that certainty. From the moment she had been called down to human resources to discuss her email assault, her life had been total and complete chaos, the best part of which was AJ. He was calm and secure, so handsome she felt weak in the knees, and he made her think all sorts of crazy thoughts about staying in Big Springs.

"Natalie?" Jamie prompted her.

"I don't know yet. It's complicated, but I think it might be serious. It could be." That was the best answer she could come up with right now. A feeling built in her chest and a smile grew, a small smile no one else saw.

"Lucky girl," Jamie told her.

Natalie nodded.

Then her cell phone rang.

"I'll take the clipboards and go check on the progress while you talk," Jamie told her. "Take your time, but if I pass out from exhaustion, you are the one who has to carry me home."

Natalie laughed and pulled her phone out of her pocket. She checked the caller id.

"Hey, stranger, I was just thinking about you," she said.

Jenn's voice rang out, "Why in the world aren't you back in Memphis yet?"

Natalie groaned. "I told you. I'm jobless, homeless, and nearly broke. Besides, I've been working on a project and haven't really missed it that much."

"You're going insane. You realize that, right?"

"I do, but it's such a nice feeling. So, how are things in the big city? Is it still in mourning without me? Everyone wearing black and whispering about how wronged I was?"

Natalie picked at her shoelaces. They had splatters of blue paint on them. She used her fingernail to scrape at the spots.

"Actually..." the tone of Jenn's voice changed, like she had something juicy she just couldn't wait to tell. "I was in a meeting with Brantley a few minutes ago, and you are not going to believe what he had to say."

Natalie stopped picking at her shoes.

"I don't care what he said anymore," she told her friend. "He's a loser and a jerk."

Silence loomed over the line. It continued, uninterrupted for over a minute, during which Natalie resumed her paint picking. She didn't need to know what he said. He was history. Ancient history. Then again, she'd always really like social studies.

"Ok, what?"

"So I was walking past him, didn't even look his way. I haven't given him the time of day since you left. You know, except in meetings when I had to, but even then I was concise and not at all friendly. I've got your back, girl."

"Thanks, Jenn, now what did he say?"

"He asked about you, what you were doing, if you were still in Arkansas. You should have seen his face. It was awful. His eyes were all puffy, and I think he had a sunburn, but that's beside the point. He wanted to know where you were, what you were doing, and most importantly, when you were coming back."

Natalie exhaled the breath she'd been holding. She closed her eyes and took another deep breath. Of course Brantley was asking about her now. Just when she thought she was over him, over the whole situation, over the hurt.

Jenn continued on. "No one has seen Vanessa at all this week. Gary from the third floor told me that when he'd called tech support about his monitor acting up, they sent up some new guy named Craig. No Vanessa. He asked this Craig guy about Vanessa, and he said he'd never heard of her. What guy who has ever met Vanessa forgets her, you know?"

Natalie blinked quickly and nodded. "She's pretty unforgettable."

"I know. So that leads us to believe that she isn't working here anymore. That also leads us to point number one, Brantley was asking about you."

"Now that Vanessa is gone?"

"I guess. Wait. That's pretty rotten of him, isn't it?" Jenn's triumphant tone deflated. "Hold on. I just put these two facts together. Oh, no. I thought I was calling with good news, like Brantley was finally done being a jerk, and you would get your job back and come home. I didn't realize he was being an even bigger jerk than before." Jenn sounded like she was on the verge of crying.

"It's alright, Jenn. I appreciate you calling. It's good to hear from you no matter what. I'm sorry I haven't called or texted lately. I've been busy." Natalie picked off the last fleck of paint from her shoelace. Now it was the original dingy white, nothing left to pick at there.

"Oh, I know that. I've been sending you emails too. Did you see those? There was a funny one about how Rhonda from down the hall spilled coffee on the carpet in the conference room in the exact shape of a certain part of the male anatomy. She said it was an accident, but everyone keeps teasing her about how it was on purpose. They had to bring in the HR rep to talk to us about passive sexual harassment, but no one got in any real trouble."

"I haven't checked my email in a while. I'm kind of laying off of it, given the current situation. Sorry. I'll go back and look at it when I get home."

"No! No, I never thought. It's ok. I'll just text you the funny stuff instead."

Natalie finished the call by promising she'd let Jenn know when she was coming back to Memphis. The funny thing was, Natalie didn't really feel like Memphis was her home anymore. But Big Springs didn't quite feel like home either.

She sat for a while, picking at the splatters of paint on her arm until she'd pulled out most of them, along with about half of her arm hair. Picking at paint was strangely therapeutic.

"Oh, there you are," Gigi called when she breezed into the lobby. "Jamie says to tell you that we're all done here. Also I'm supposed to tell you that 'Mrs. Talburt got all of their demon eyes,' whatever that means." Gigi shrugged her shoulders. "I'm headed home. Do you want to ride with me?"

"No, I've got my car. I'll just walk through it one time to see the progress, then I'll head out."

Natalie stood up and really looked at her grandmother for the first time since she'd come into the room.   The apron was still tied in its neat little bow.   The polka dots were as white as they had been hours ago.   There wasn't a spot on her.   Even her newly done hair was still perfect.

"Did you paint at all?"

"Of course I did!" Gigi huffed, outraged. "I did all of the edging around the windows in the cafeteria. Then I did the edging around the murals. I even went around the bulletin boards in the classrooms. Well, the former classrooms."

"But you're so clean!"

"And you look like you rolled in blue paint! If you're planning on going out with AJ tonight, you'd better plan on spending at least an hour picking paint out of your hair."

"I don't have any plans with AJ for tonight."

Gigi's mouth dropped open.

"What?" Natalie demanded.

"Oh, dear. I think I may have ruined the surprise," Gigi said. She hitched her purse up higher and started toward the door.

"What surprise?"

"I can't say anything more, but if I were you, sweetness, I'd run out of here as fast as you can so you can get cleaned up. Skirt and heels cleaned up, not jeans and a ponytail like you usually do." With those final words, Gigi rushed out the door.

"I like my ponytail!" Natalie called after her. She ran her hand over her hair and stopped when she felt the rough texture of dried paint. Oh, no.

Chapter 24

Natalie opened the door. She was gorgeous in a blue dress that clung to her skin until it reached her hips, where it flared out, stopping mid-thigh. AJ had a momentary vision of how the bottom would float if she were to twirl around. He didn't dance, but a dress like that practically demanded it.

"She told you, didn't she?"

Natalie patted the bun on top of her head, where her ponytail usually hung. "She didn't tell me anything except that jeans wouldn't be acceptable. I hope I'm not overdressed?"

"You're perfect, but you need one more thing." He held up a red bandana that he planned to use as a blindfold. "Where we're going is a surprise, so if you wouldn't mind turning around."

Natalie raised an eyebrow. "I'm going to assume that it is clean."

"Give me some credit."

She smiled and turned her back to him. The drive to their destination passed quickly. Natalie tried guessing where they were going, but AJ kept her guessing by calling out bogus landmarks. When he pulled the blindfold from her eyes, she gasped.

"You brought me to Knight's? I haven't been here since high school prom!"

"I hope that's not a bad thing," AJ said as he helped her from the truck.

"The restaurant was amazing, but the date was a dud. Boring. I'm pretty sure Brett threatened to beat him up if he so much as held my hand."

The building was designed to look like an elegant old mill at the edge of the spring. The exterior was gray stone with cedar shakes on the roof. Large crepe myrtles blossomed with white flowers on either side of the cobblestone pathway leading up to the wide, wooden porch. Twinkle lights shimmered in the branches of the surrounding trees and bushes. Purple hydrangeas bloomed along the edge off the porch. The night was clear and the moon added its own gentle glow.

"Oh, AJ, it's gorgeous! Even better than it was at prom. Thank you for bringing me here. It was a great idea." She closed her eyes like she was trying to save the memory deep inside.

"We'll come back here, then, every year on this day," he promised her. "I'll be our own personal celebration. The anniversary of our first real date."

Her eyes popped open, and Natalie looked at him with a mixture of puzzlement and alarm. She blinked a few times, and it was as if the spell was broken.

"Let's go in," she suggested.

They ate outside on the back terrace. It was lit by candles and more twinkle lights. The wooden terrace was surrounded by large oak trees and a landscaped path led down to the spring below. Their dinner table overlooked the largest swimming hole at the spring, but the park was closed after dark.

Bringing a date to Knight's was the equivalent of a declaration to the town of Big Springs. A man didn't bring a casual date or a first date to Knight's. It was a place for proposals and anniversaries. It was where you brought your wife when you discovered you were expecting your first child. It was where old men brought their silver-haired wives to hold hands and remember what it had been like to be young and have no idea how much more they could love one another fifty years later.

AJ had brought Natalie here not to propose or celebrate. Not really. He had brought her here as a declaration not to the town, but to Natalie herself. He wanted to show her everything beautiful and great in the world, leaving behind them all of the worst parts of life. There was no place in tonight for memories of Iraq or old boyfriends. This night was meant to be romantic. A new beginning for them both. For them together.

It wasn't working out that way, though. Natalie was acting strange. Distant. Instead of looking around the terrace with the same awe she had expressed upon arriving at the restaurant, she barely noticed it, keeping her eyes on the menu or on her plate. When he commented on the scenery, she nodded absentmindedly. She chewed her bottom lip so hard it looked like it might bleed. She twisted her napkin into knots in her lap. When she wasn't staring at her plate, she stared off into the darkness.

AJ's heart was beginning to pound, and not in the way Natalie usually made his heart pound. He tried even harder to draw her in, making jokes, taking her hand, asking her about the senior center. Nothing penetrated whatever fog she was in.

"Do you want to walk down to the spring?" he asked her when their bill was paid. "We've got a few minutes before they close, but I'm told they keep the pathway lit up for a few hours yet."

Natalie nodded and rose from her seat. She rubbed her arms as though cold, and started toward the steps.

"Would you like my jacket?" He'd worn a suit. Well, the jacket along with a nice shirt and tie and his best blue jeans and boots. It was a Southern man's suit.

"No, I'm fine, thank you." She held onto the handrail as she walked down the stone steps in her heels.

"Why don't you take my arm? I'd hate for you to trip and tumble into the spring."

Natalie took his arm, but didn't move any closer than necessary. Only a few days ago, heck only a few hours ago, she would have snuggled up close to him. It didn't make any sense.

"Did I do something? Are you mad at me, because if you are, you're going to have to tell me what I did? I have no idea what I did or said, but I'm sorry."

"No, I'm not mad," her voice was as cold as the spring water.

"I don't understand then. You're different tonight, just since we came in. Was it what I said before, about us coming here every year? We don't have to, you know. If you don't like Knight's, or whatever."

They came to the bottom of the path where the landscaped cobblestone met up with the grass hillside that surrounded the spring. This was the mouth of the spring, where the water rushed up from underground to pour out, creating the creek and nourishing the plants, animals, and town that surrounded it. The air was cool with a slight breeze that wafted the wet dirt scent up toward them. All the while, Natalie froze him out.

"I'm distracted tonight, I guess. Knight's is lovely."

271

He ran his hands through his hair and stepped in front of her, facing her, forcing her to stop moving and look up at him.

"Tell me what you're thinking. I need to know." His heart was beating fast and hard, as if it knew that whatever she had to say was going to hurt. He said a silent prayer, pleading with God that it would be something simple like a headache or a problem with her grandmother.

"I'm not sure."

"You're not sure what you're thinking?"

"I'm not sure about us, about a year from now, or two years from now, or however many years. I'm just not sure." As she spoke, her voice edged with ice, she stepped away from him and toward the bench that overlooked the spring.

"You aren't sure? I'm sure." He spoke the last words quietly, so quiet he wasn't certain she had heard them until she spoke again.

"I know."

She sat down on the bench, her fingers curling over the seat on either side of her thighs. Her knuckles were white. AJ sat down beside her, pried her fingers loose, and took her hands in his.

"Tell me what happened, what made you change your mind. Let's talk about it."

"I don't know if there's anything to talk about. I might be leaving soon, going back to Memphis. I probably am." She spoke the words like they were a fact, decided and planned out.

"I didn't know you were leaving. I know you'd wanted to in the beginning, but I didn't think that, well, now—"

"That was always the plan. Come home and regroup, then go back."

"When?" Nothing about this felt real.

"I don't know. Someday." She wiped at her cheeks, and AJ saw for the first time that she was crying. It tore him up almost as much as the words she was saying.

"Someday? You don't even know when you're going back? You don't have a plan to leave anytime soon?"

"I am leaving, AJ. Not this week, maybe not even this summer, but this fall or winter, I'll pack up and go." As she spoke, her voice gained strength. She turned to face him for the first time since he'd sat down beside her. "I don't want to hurt you." Though there were tears on her cheeks, her eyes were resolute.

"Too late." He set his chin and stood. He couldn't just sit here while she threw him away like yesterday's trash.

He pulled at his tie. The stupid thing was choking him. He jerked it off and threw it down onto the ground. Next he tackled the top button that was strangling him. He hadn't been this dressed up since he'd been in uniform, and he wanted it gone.

"I'm sorry." Natalie spoke the words, but didn't sound sincere. He could see it now. He'd put too much stock in what they had. Counted his chicken before they hatched. Put all his eggs in one basket. Stupid eggs and stupid chickens.

AJ shook his head. He was burning up. He struggled out of his suit jacket, dropping it onto the grass behind him. That felt better. He could breathe a little easier.

"It's fine. I'll be fine." He cleared his throat. "I got over you once, I'll do it again."

AJ unbuttoned his shirt, revealing a white t-shirt underneath. Now that the jacket and tie were off, he might as well get comfortable. Knight's may have a dress code, but the creek didn't have one. He pulled the tail of his shirt loose, jerked it off over his head, and it joined his jacket on the ground. His chest was bare to the night sky, and it felt good. Free.

"When did you get over me? What are you talking about?"

AJ looked back at her, so beautiful sitting there on the bench. The moonlight spilled down around her, illuminating her blonde hair like a halo. Her skin glowed, but her eyes were sad. She was hurting and there was nothing he could do about it. She was breaking his heart.

"When I was here before, in the summertime when you were still in school, I used to watch you. Not in a creepy way, but in a way that made it hard for me to keep away. You were still a teenager, a few years younger than me, and I was friends with your brother. I couldn't do anything about it, but I hoped and I prayed. I hoped that someday when we were older that I could see you again and that maybe you'd see me the same way that I see you. When I was in Iraq, I used to think about you sometimes. When Gramps would talk about the snow he was getting, I would wonder if you were building a snowman or huddled inside drinking hot chocolate. When he would talk about your grandma's latest stunt, I would imagine you laughing along with her. I thought about you a lot. And I prayed. I prayed that you were enjoying college, having fun, staying safe. I prayed for

274

you to do well and to be happy. And, yeah, every once in a while, I would pray for another chance to see you again. Just another try. And when I saw you again, I thought maybe God had answered my prayers. I guess he did." He chuckled. "I never expected it to end up like this. I'll say that for certain. I guess I should've been more specific in my prayers."

He pulled his belt from his pants.

"Are you going to take off all of your clothes?" Natalie asked, her voice almost timid.

AJ laughed humorlessly.

"I confess that I've been in love with you for over a decade, that I've prayed for you and about you, and that's what you have to say to me?" He turned back to the creek, watching the spring bubble up from underground. It was dark and deep and cool, and looked about as bleak as he felt. "I'm jumping in."

"What? Now? We're having a conversation, and you're going swimming?"

"We aren't having a conversation, not a real one. You're coming up with reasons why you can't be with me. From what I've heard so far, you don't even have a real good reason. You're leaving Big Springs someday. Someday?" He turned back toward her, his voice growing louder. "That's bull, Natalie. You love me too. You just won't admit it."

AJ turned back toward the spring and tugged off his boots. He kicked them over toward the growing pile of his clothes.

Her voice shook when she spoke. "You don't love me."

"Don't tell me what I feel," AJ said, not facing her. He spoke to the darkness. "I'm training to be a therapist. I'm almost a professional in the field of feelings. I know what I feel, and I'm not afraid to say it. I love you, and you know it. You've known it for weeks now."

He unfastened his pants.

"Are you going to take off your pants?" She sounded shocked.

"I'm not swimming with them on." AJ pulled them down and threw them onto the stack. "You're welcome to join me if you want to." He was more vulnerable now than he had ever been, standing before him in nothing but his boxers, asking her to take his hand.

Natalie shook her head. "I don't swim."

"You did when you were a teenager. I remember that pink bikini. I've had dreams about that pink bikini."

"I came down here, but never did more than put my feet in the water. I never learned how to swim. I was too scared."

AJ walked over to her, knelt down in front of her. She turned her head to look off into the distance and to avoid his gaze. He slid one finger along her cheek and gently guided her face until she looked into his eyes.

He pleaded with her, not only with his words but with his whole heart. "Come swimming with me. I'll keep you safe. I'll hold onto you every single second. I won't let you go. I promise you that. I'll never let you go."

Natalie's eyes were full longing, he could see it there. Moisture welled up in them until a few tears spilled over, their tracks glinting in the moonlight. Her lips moved, but not words came. No sounds. She hesitated a moment longer, then shook her head.

AJ dropped his gaze to the ground, stood, and walked to the edge of the spring. There was a rope swing in the trees above, but he made his way to a rock instead. The pool was about twelve feet deep and dark as pitch, but he knew the depths well.

He hit the water smoothly. He stayed underwater for as long as he could, until his lungs burned for air, until he had no choice but to come up and breathe, to come up and live. His heart was broken, but his body was still alive.

When he surfaced, he saw her standing at the bottom edge of the cobblestone path. Her eyes made contact with his, and she shrugged helplessly.

AJ swam over to the rocks at the edge of the swimming hole. He pulled himself up, and climbed up toward the grass at the top of the steep hill by the bench.

"I'll get dressed and drive you home."

Chapter 25

"You look awful," Gigi told Natalie, who was sitting at her makeshift office in the senior center in front of a stack of wedding invitations. Gigi was wearing an elegant combination of pink blouse and capri pants with a beautiful, floral silk scarf. Natalie had on gray sweatpants and her paint-splattered Big Springs Bears t-shirt.

"Gigi, I'm a little busy right now."

"What happened to your face?" Natalie's grandmother sat down across from her and began helping stuff the envelopes. "It looks like you slathered bacon grease on it." She sniffed. "Smells more like dirty socks, though."

Natalie sighed. The morning after her date with AJ she had woken up to a volcano of angry pus on her forehead, and she had used the excuse to skip out on church. And even though that was over a week ago, the zit had just gotten worse every day since.

"It's a pimple cream. It doesn't smell like dirty socks. It's supposed to smell like jasmine and raindrops," she said through clenched teeth.

"I thought you were twenty-four years old. Aren't you too old for pimple creams?"

"I'm twenty-eight, and you're never too old for pimple creams. They're an ointment to treat a medical condition. Eruptions can happen at any age," Natalie informed her. She shoved a stack of invitations and envelopes across the desk.

Gigi shrugged her shoulders and slid another invitation into an envelope.

"Sounds like you watched an infomercial."

Natalie had. She tossed and turned in bed at night until her sheets were wrapped around her enchilada-style, and a few days ago she had started camping out on the couch after Gigi went to bed. She would stay up contemplating purchases of high speed blenders and frightening exercise gear that seemed perfectly logical at three in the morning. The pimple cream had arrived in the mail that morning.

"Is it your time of the month? Your mama always got pimples when she was having her monthlies," Gigi said.

"No. Can we please drop this?" Natalie shoved an invitation into an envelope, crinkling the paper slightly. She mashed down on it with the heel of her hand to smooth it back out.

"Careful there. I don't want my wedding invitations to look like we ran them over with the truck."

Natalie frowned at her. Gigi raised an eyebrow.

"Sorry," Natalie mumbled.

"Now, let's talk about your face. You aren't on your period, so are you pregnant? I had the worst skin when I was--"

Natalie almost fell out of her chair.

"No! I'm not," she dropped her voice to a whisper, "pregnant. I had my period a week and a half ago. Besides which, Gigi, I haven't been...I'm not sure what you think I've been...well, I'm definitely not...that." She ran her hand over her hair and pulled her ponytail tighter.

"And another thing," Gigi began.

Natalie groaned and closed her eyes.

"You listen here, little missy. You're a mess. You pull that ponytail any tighter, your eyelids are going to be stretched clear back to your ears like you got one of those face lifts. Creepy. Between that and your spotted up face, you're starting to resemble some kind of a science experiment gone wrong."

Gigi stood up, brushed her hands together like her work was done, and walked to the door. Before she left, she turned around, her face full of concern and understanding.

"Sweet girl, you know how precious you are to me."

Natalie nodded, her jaw set and lips pursed.

Gigi continued, "I've been so happy to have you with me this summer, but darling, you're making a mistake."

raised her chin. "I don't know what you're talking about."

Gigi gave a little shrug. "I wouldn't tell you if I didn't love you so much, but you messed up." She walked over and stood in front of Natalie. She used her silk scarf to wipe off some of the pimple cream, the ointment smearing in greasy streaks across the fine fabric. Gigi pulled on the band holding Natalie's hair hostage. She loosened it until Natalie's ponytail lay relaxed against her back, only barely containing her hair.

Natalie's shoulders relaxed and the muscles in her jaw softened. She heaved a sigh.

Gigi spoke to her again, "You know I lost your grandfather in Vietnam, only a few months after we'd gotten married."

Natalie nodded and closed her eyes. She'd heard the story of her grandparents' whirlwind romance just before her grandfather had been sent off to fight in the war. He'd been there a little over six months before he was declared missing in action. Gigi had given birth to their only daughter without her husband by her side. It was a year later that the Army had notified her grandmother that her husband had died. DeeJay had never seen her father's face, only pictures.

"I fell in love with that man the moment I saw him," Gigi's voice turned wistful. "He was the most handsome man I'd ever seen. So tall, like your Andrew Jackson, but leaner, almost lanky. My Johnny had a smile that drew everyone to him. We'd walk into a room, and people would flock to him. He never met a stranger, and the women, well, let me just say that I had competition." Gigi's chest shook with quiet laughter. "But Johnny said that after he laid eyes on me, he never saw any of them. He said he took one look at me, and he was mine."

"Oh, Gigi, that's beautiful," Natalie said. Her bottom lip trembled. For the love that they'd had, and the pain of what was lost.

Gigi took Natalie's chin in her hand.

"A person can fall in love in a heartbeat, but can't fall out of love that fast. Why do you think it took me all these years to remarry?"

Natalie shook her head.

Gigi went on. "You won't forget him anytime soon. It's not who you are."

She released her granddaughter's chin and gave her a hard look.

"You made a mistake, dear. Now you need to decide how to fix it. Trust me, a love like that doesn't come along every day."

Gigi pulled her scarf off and wiped her hands on it. She walked over to the trash and dropped it in.

"I don't think I'm making a mistake," Natalie said quietly. "I'm leaving, going back to Memphis."

Her grandmother sighed and threw up her hands.

"I've said what I needed to." Gigi opened the door and walked out into the lobby. She popped her head back in. "Wash that stuff off your face."

Natalie nodded and dropped her head into her hands. She knew Gigi's story was sad, but it was nothing like the situation between her and AJ. No one was going off to war. It wasn't love at first sight. Not really. Not like it was for her grandparents.

She'd made the right decision. She had worked for years and years to get out of Big Springs. Maybe she had lost her job in the city, but that didn't mean she couldn't get another one. She would. She would spend the afternoon looking at the job search websites, see who was hiring. She would be back in Memphis by this fall.

Natalie rubbed her fingers together, the greasy cream smearing. First she had to wash her hands, then she would go about the business of rebuilding her life.

Chapter 26

The moment Natalie walked into the church two days later, an absolute silence fell across the congregation. It was eerie. Eyes looked in her direction, some in open curiosity, some covert behind a hymnal or a neighbor's shoulder, and a few daring individuals didn't merely glance, but glared.

Natalie kept moving, going directly to her family's pew and taking a seat beside her mother. DeeJay, in contrast to the other members of the church, didn't look at her daughter. She kept her eyes glued to the weekly bulletin in her hand.

"Hi, Mama. How are you?"

Her mother shrugged her shoulders.

"It seems a little quiet in here today," Natalie looked around the room, and many of the staring eyeballs darted away, like scared rabbits retreating into the safety of tall grass.

"It wasn't quiet a few minutes ago," DeeJay said, her words clipped. "I got to overhear a lot of things about my daughter and her love life. Your father made me promise I wouldn't say a word, though. Probably for the best." She reached down between the pews for her purse, stuck a hand in and loudly rummaged around.

"This town needs a hobby."

Natalie's mother pulled out a bottle of aspirin. She poured a couple into her hand and offered the bottle to her daughter. Natalie shook her head.

"They do have a hobby." DeeJay popped the pills into her mouth and swallowed them dry. Natalie winced.

"They talk about people. It's what they do." DeeJay dropped her purse onto the floor with a thud.

Her husband leaned over.

"The pot's complaining about the kettle."

"Not now," DeeJay hissed. She elbowed him in the ribs, and he returned to sitting quietly.

Natalie saw Henrietta and Mabel whispering, shaking their heads sadly. They turned to look back at her, simultaneously giving her a small wave. Natalie waved back.

"So where is Brett? Shouldn't he be sitting here enduring this along with us?"

"He's gone. Out of town, probably out of shame," DeeJay whispered. She had returned to staring at the church bulletin, creasing its edges with her fierce grip.

Natalie's father leaned over again. "He goes on a trip every year around this time. Takes a whole week. He should be back by Friday or so. Don't worry about him. He doesn't even know about you and AJ."

Natalie scrunched up her face. "Where does he go?"

Her mother shrugged.

Her father shrugged, then after a minute spoke, "I think it has something to do with that artificial insemination business he's got going. He makes a good living from it, even if he does live in the barn."

Natalie nodded. She could see that. Her brother always had plenty of cash and drove a new truck. Since he wasn't really the drug dealer type, she figured his bull semen sales must be going pretty well.

The buzz of the congregation had risen back up to normal levels when it suddenly went silent again.

"He's here," Natalie's mother whispered. Her knuckles were white. Natalie reached out and took one of the hands in her own. She threaded her fingers with her mother's and gave her a reassuring squeeze.

Natalie leaned in and whispered in her mother's ear, "At least I haven't shown the church my butt."

DeeJay let out a huff of air, as close to a laugh as Natalie could expect.

"The day is early," she whispered back.

True, but Natalie was wearing slacks so the odds were in her favor.

Her mother let out a sigh when she saw AJ and Charlie take a seat in their usual pew.

"Why?" she asked her daughter.

Natalie averted her gaze from the men.

"I had to. I'm leaving. It's better this way." She squeezed her mother's hand again. DeeJay sighed and squeezed back.

Pastor Matt stepped up to the lectern and tapped on the microphone to gain the attention of the beehive of buzzing whispers that had started up again. Natalie spent the entire service focusing on the message. It struck a chord with her. The pastor spoke about how God has a plan for each of us. We may not know his plan. It may not be our plan, but He sees the full picture, the beginning and the end. It made Natalie think, even though she didn't particularly want to.

Natalie spent the next several days avoiding people whenever she could. She went in to the senior center, but stayed in the office working out the details surrounding the unused cafeteria problem. She researched permits and health codes regarding food preparation and commercial kitchens. The good news was that the center was set up for food service, even though it hadn't been used in the past year. Natalie called Tina for recommendations about possible cooks and suppliers. She compiled list after list, made call after call, and created a budget for the project. Finally, she turned over all of her information to Mabel, who knew more about the subject than Natalie ever would. Mabel, pleased to be consulted, promised to look into it and report back.

The wedding plans were coming along as well. Gigi had surprisingly simple tastes. Natalie had expected her grandmother to demand white doves and yards of tulle and twinkle lights. Instead, she wanted a plain wedding held at the church with a reception at Knight's afterward.

Natalie had tried to discourage the use of Knight's. She suggested Luigi's, which was laughed at, though it wasn't a joke. She suggested Millie's or Barb's, which wouldn't work since neither one of those locations was set up for large parties. Natalie almost convinced Gigi to have the reception at her own house, outside with tables and chairs set up around the yard with decorations. Ultimately, Gigi decided against it, saying she didn't want all those people using her bathroom. She'd never get it clean after that many bottoms had sat there.

Knight's was perfect, though. It was romantic and gorgeous. It wasn't owned by any of the couple's immediate friends, so it wasn't an imposition to hire them do all of the catering and clean up. The inside was big enough to hold everyone in the air conditioning, and the outside terrace could be set up for dancing. It was perfect, except that the thought of going back there hit Natalie like a punch to the gut every time she thought about it.

The one aspect off the wedding Gigi was proving difficult about, however, were the dresses. She demanded that both DeeJay and Natalie stand up with her as her bridesmaids. DeeJay was to be the matron of honor. Natalie's mother had insisted that both Lila and Tina be brought along to assist in dress selections, so all five of them trooped down to the local bridal boutique, The White Rose.

"I should warn you," Lila said from the back seat, "I was talking to her about it while I was rolling her hair, and Gertie has some...interesting...ideas for your dresses."

Charlie was dropping Gigi off at the shop, so Natalie was driving her mother and her mother's friends. They had met up for lunch at Barb's after a morning spent at the florist. All of the plans were in place. The only thing missing were the dresses. They only had a week until the wedding, which was cutting it close, but Lila had promised to do all of the alterations on her sewing machine. She was a brilliant seamstress, so no one was really worried about getting the dresses fitted on time.

"What do you mean 'interesting'?" DeeJay asked. She folded down the visor over the front seat to check her lipstick.

"Well, maybe it's nothing, but she had mentioned how much she really loved Dolly Parton."

"I'm well aware of her love for all things Dolly." DeeJay snapped the visor back up. "I've had to explain my name on more than one occasion."

Natalie watched Lila in the rearview mirror. The woman didn't look offended by DeeJay's tone. She nodded compassionately. This was old news.

"What do you mean about the dresses? How does her love of Dolly relate to bridesmaid dresses?" Natalie asked.

Realization hit as soon as the words were out of her mouth. "Sequins?"

Lila shrugged.

"It depends on which era she's going with," DeeJay noted. She had become a bit of a Dolly expert during her lifetime. "We could we wearing sequins and tight skirts, or we could be in tasteful suits with spike heels."

"And tight skirts!" Tina chimed in.

"And cleavage," Natalie added. "Lots and lots of cleavage. No matter what era."

"Well, you both are certainly built for it," Lila said.

Natalie and her mother exchanged a look. They were blessed with an overabundance of boobs, but neither one had embraced the exposure of them quite as much as Gigi had, especially in her youth.

"We will humor her as much as we can, and make the best of it," DeeJay told her daughter. "It's only one evening, after all. We can put up with anything for a few hours."

Lila spoke up again, "And I'll add in extra fabric to cover up your assets after we get them home."

"That's a given," DeeJay replied.

The White Rose hadn't been around when Natalie was growing up. It was one of the few businesses that had been added to the town and had survived, despite the small population. The building was small, a one-story brick structure that had once been a furniture store. It had been abandoned and overgrown when Natalie was in high school, but as she approached the entrance, Natalie noticed how well it was tended now. The landscaping was immaculate, and the windows featured artful displays of white wedding gowns and colorful bridesmaid dresses.

"This is nice," Natalie said aloud as they reached the door. "Who owns this? Anyone I know?"

Her mother froze just before she entered. She turned to look at her daughter.

"I thought you knew."

Natalie frowned. "Knew what?"

"Come on in!" called a voice from Natalie's past. "I haven't seen you since graduation Miss Valedictorian."

Natalie felt the blood drain from her face. Her mother's eyes were wide.

"Oh, now, Jessica, you be nice to my granddaughter. You know she apologized to you about that little mix up."

Natalie forced her feet to carry her into the store. Her brain resisted. It shouted for her to run far, far away, but her feet didn't listen. They walked her right on into the boutique so that she was face to face with her old nemesis.

"Jessica Carlisle," she said. She could hear the icicles in her own voice, but was powerless to melt them. There was too much history to thaw them out now. Natalie had known when she had exposed Jessica's cheating that it would have repercussions, namely herself giving the valedictorian's speech at graduation, but she never pictured it still being a sore spot over a decade later.

"Natalie James. Nice to see you. I thought you lived in Memphis. What happened?" Jessica asked, her tone knowing, taunting.

"I came back," Natalie told her, offering no explanation.

"How are things? Are you here to shop for a wedding dress for yourself? When's the special day?" Jessica's mouth turned up on the edges in what Natalie was sure was the start of an evil grin. She was kind of surprised the woman wasn't rubbing her palms together and cackling.

Gigi stepped in. "Knock it off, Jessica. I'm planning to spend a small fortune in dresses, so you put your claws away. Not that I blame you, of course. Natalie made a mistake, an error in judgment. Leave it be. When we're done here, you can badmouth her behind her back all you want. It's up to you to explain it to Jesus on Judgment Day, not me. But while we're here, you mind your manners."

Jessica nodded, chastised by the reminder of the sale, if not the sin.

Natalie scowled at her grandmother.

Gigi raised an eyebrow.

Natalie sighed. "What do you have picked out for us?"

Fifteen minutes later, DeeJay stood in front of the three-way mirror, turning this way and that.

"This isn't that bad," she said. Tina handed her a hair clip, and DeeJay twisted her hair up and secured it. She pulled a few wisps down by her face. "That looks about right. I'll need some nude pumps, but I've never needed much excuse to buy new shoes."

DeeJay's dress was form fitting, but it was, essentially, a suit. It was sky blue with a knee-length pencil skirt. The jacket had satin on the wide lapels, and the three-quarter length sleeves had jewels on the cuffs, but other than that, it was fairly basic.

"I think I'll change out the white camisole for a pale pink that I have at home," DeeJay noted. "Overall, I'm pretty impressed. When Lila said Dolly, I was worried, but now I see it's not so bad. Kind of like Wall Street Barbie."

"What about you, Natalie?" Tina called over the curtain into the dressing room. "Does yours fit alright? Remember, I can take it up if the jacket is too loose."

Natalie didn't respond. She had peeked out at her mother a few minutes before to see her emerge from her own dressing room looking classy and perfect. Her own reflection didn't show the same. She had started the day with her hair down and free around her shoulders, trying to follow Gigi's advice about loosening up a little, but since putting on her own bridesmaid dress, she had pulled it up into the tightest ponytail yet. The skin on her forehead ached with tension, but Natalie barely noticed.

"Come on, let us see it. Lila's got your grandmother distracted in the other room looking at tiaras. Like my mother needs a tiara to feel like she's queen of the world," DeeJay scoffed. "Come out so we can figure out how to fix it before she gets back."

"It's a suit, so it shouldn't be that bad," Tina added in reassuringly. "Suits are easy enough to fit. Lila's done mine for years."

Natalie swallowed the lump in her throat.

"Mine isn't a suit," she called out.

"Do you have it on?" DeeJay asked.

"Yeah. It's on...sort of."

Without any warning, the curtain was whipped open, and Natalie saw the expressions on the women's faces change. They went from pleasantly curious to shocked. She had seen that look on her mother's face once before—when she'd seen Gigi's thong-clad bottom on display in the church parking lot.

"Oh, dear," Tina said.

"Are those your nipples?" DeeJay asked.

"I think that's a poorly positioned seam," Tina noted. She poked it with an index finger. "That's definitely a seam."

"What happened to the suits?" DeeJay's voice held all of the dismay that Natalie felt.

Gasps from the entrance to the changing area drew their attention.

"Oh, you're wearing it!" Gigi gushed. She rushed over, hands flapping like deranged birds. "I've always loved this style on Dolly. It's so sensual and pretty."

"I think you look absolutely perfect," Jessica Carlisle chimed in.

Natalie glared at her.

"Go stand in front of the three-way mirror." Gigi pulled her over to stand on the raised circle in such a way that Natalie had no choice but to see herself from every possible angle.

The dress was blue, like her mother's, but a shade brighter. If her mother's dress was the color of the sky, Natalie's was the color of the inside of a swimming pool. Where her mother was wearing a tasteful suit, Natalie's dress made her look like a disheveled milk maid. Like the girl just before she steps out onto the saloon stage for the first time, not quite the experienced prostitute in bright red satin, but more like a farm girl not quite sure what she's gotten herself into.

The sleeves, which could have been cap sleeves on another gown, were placed in such a way that they fell down well below her shoulders, like her dress was on the verge of falling to the floor. The bodice held it up, though. It was skin tight with a row of buttons running up the front from the V shape just above her pubic bone all the way up to her breasts, where the entire garment stopped abruptly.

"That ruffle on top of your titties barely keeps you decent," Lila noted. "An inch more and the sheriff would be writing you a ticket for public indecency."

"It covers her up just fine," Gigi protested. "If you'd pull her hair down out of that ponytail and fluff it up a little, I swear, you'd look just like her!"

Natalie's eyes went wide. She reached up and gave her ponytail a good strong tug. Her eyelids widened fractionally.

"Is the V to that bodice right over your...um--" Natalie's mother began, finger pointing well below her daughter's belly button.

Natalie nodded. She felt like crying, but was pretty sure her ponytail was pulling her tear ducts closed.

Gigi beamed. "I always wanted to wear that dress. Now your mama and I are both too old to do it justice, but you, precious girl, you look like a million bucks."

"More like fifty," Jessica Carlisle muttered not quite under her breath.

Natalie's shoulders sank.

"You're sure the hem isn't too short?" Lila asked. "I can lengthen it a little bit if I let out the bottom seam. I could add on at least two inches. It would be a little closer to her knees that way."

"She looks miserable," Tina said. Both of her mother's friends smiled reassuringly, like a person would to someone about face the guillotine. As in, it'll be awful for sure, but we're here for you.

"That's the dress I want my granddaughter to wear to my wedding. I won't hear otherwise. Leave it the way it is." Gigi stood behind Natalie. "You'll see. This dress was meant for you."

"I don't think it was." Natalie spoke quietly, as one would talk to someone who was mentally insane and holding a sharp knife, or in this case, complete control over one's public decency. "I'd be much more comfortable in a suit like Mama's."

"I know you would, darling, but that's not the kind of dress you need. You've got a hundred of those suits. I saw them lined up in your closet. What you need is something to stir you up, push you a little bit. You can't wear this dress and be sad or unsure. To wear this dress you have to have confidence. You have be in control of your own mind. This dress is decisive. This is the dress for you." Gigi squeezed her shoulders.

"Jessica," Gigi called out, "take a picture with that camera phone. That way I can tell if Lila's been messing with it."

Lila protested. Tina winced. DeeJay closed her eyes. Jessica Carlisle snapped the picture, and Natalie wished she were anywhere else in the world.

Chapter 27

"What the heck did you do to AJ?" Brett demanded when he walked into Gigi's kitchen. He wore his usual outfit of worn out blue jeans and a t-shirt with a ball cap pulled down low. It was two days before the wedding, and Natalie was up to her eyeballs in ribbons and tiny bottles of bubbles.

"Well, hello to you too, brother dearest. I'm doing fine, thanks for asking. How are you doing today? Nice weather we've been having." Natalie threaded the ribbons through a hole on the little decorative tags with Charlie + Gertie printed on them. They were adorable, but a pain in the butt.

Brett stood with his hands on his hips, an indignant scowl on his face. He huffed, eyes searching the room for some witty comeback. Not finding one, he pulled out a chair and sat down at the table across from her.

"Hey. How's it going?" His words emerged as more of a grunt, but Natalie let it go. It was progress.

"It's awful. Gigi has me doing all kinds of ridiculous chores. I'm tying these little bows today. Yesterday I was using a rubber stamp to put their initials onto cake boxes. The day before that I was rolling the programs for their ceremony into itty bitty scrolls with a plastic ring around them. I'm ready to jump off a bridge."

He laughed out loud. "You barely get in the bathtub. You're more likely to jump off a cliff than jump off a diving board."

"What's that supposed to mean?" Natalie threw down the ribbons in her hand.

Her brother gave her a look of utter disbelief. "You're a chicken around water. You always have been.

You think no one ever noticed because you would come along and wear a swimsuit, but you never got in. Ever."

Brett gathered up a wad of ribbon and twisted them through his fingers.

Natalie stared at him. She had been swimming before. She knew she had. Who didn't like swimming? She distinctly remembered going out to the swimming hole by the spring with her friends when she was a teenager. That stupid spring.

"I see the wheels turning. No, you never got in. Back in high school, I kept an eye on you just in case you did."

"Why would you keep an eye on me?" she asked. Her brother had treated her like the world's biggest nuisance. He'd avoided her. Any time she had gone to the swimming hole, which hadn't been that often, he had scowled at her and gotten out, preferring to stand out with his buddies at a safe distance than to be caught swimming with his sister, which might be mistaken for hanging out with her.

Brett's kept his gaze on the table, where he was lining up the different ribbons, flattening them out with this fingertips. He cleared his throat.

"You're my baby sister. I wanted to make sure you were alright." He looked up briefly to give her a little smile. "Besides, I always felt bad about pushing you in that one time when we were really little, and I kind of worried that if you did get in, you'd freak out and drown yourself."

Natalie dropped the stack of tags she was holding. Her head was starting to hurt.

"I don't remember your pushing me in. Truthfully, I don't think I ever remember going swimming. I mean, I remember going, but not ever getting in the water." Family reunions, pool parties, trips to the beach, she wore her

296

swimsuit, but at every event, she couldn't ever remember getting wet over her ankles.

Brett took off his ball cap and rubbed his head. He'd buzzed off his hair since she'd last seen him. Not down to the skin, but fairly short all over. And he was clean shaven for once. If he weren't family, and wearing the same outfit he always did, he'd be almost unrecognizable.

"You were probably four or five. We were at the creek. Not by the spring because Mama was still too worried about us going there because of the current. We were at one of the smaller swimming holes. I wasn't much older than you, so don't get mad at me now. I was a little boy." Brett rubbed his head again. He sighed. "You were standing on this rock with one of your Barbie dolls, like having a tea party or whatever you did with those things, and I was mad because you wouldn't play sharks with me. "

Natalie nodded. That sounded about right, well, except for the tea party. Her Barbie games were never that sophisticated. She did remember how mad Brett would get at her when she would ignore him to play by herself instead.

"So, I got mad, and I pushed you off the rock. You must have panicked or something. Even though the water was only about three feet deep, you started splashing around, and your head went under. Dad had to jump in and save you. I got in trouble." He shrugged. "I never talked about it after that, but I watched you just to make sure you didn't fall in or get pushed in ever again. You scared me that day, and I never forgot it."

Natalie shook her head. She didn't remember it.

"And after then, when we went swimming..."

"You never got in. I didn't have to worry about you drowning on dry land, so I never pushed the issue."

297

Natalie stood up and walked to the refrigerator. She pulled out the pitcher of sweet tea and carried it over to the table.

"You want some?"

"You're getting me tea? I just told you that I permanently damaged your psyche or something. Don't you want to hit me or yell at me? I mean, I'm not going to let you give me a swirly, but I would understand if you wanted to dump that pitcher over my head. Go on. I'm ready for it. " He shut his eyes tightly, then raised a hand. "Wait! I want to set my hat down out of the way. I don't want it to get tea all over it. Alright, go for it." He closed his eyes and braced for the cold.

Natalie turned away to grab two glasses from the cabinet. She filled them with ice and brought them to the table and filled them up from the pitcher.

"Are you giving me the silent treatment? You know I can't stand that. I cave every time. Uncle. Mercy. Just talk to me, Nat. Tell me what you're thinking." Brett was nearly begging.

"I'm not giving you the silent treatment, dork. I'm just thinking." Natalie sat down across from him. "You know the funny thing is, I'd never realized that I didn't swim. I don't really ever remember wanting to swim. In terms of damaging my psyche, maybe. It never seemed like that big of a deal to me, though, I guess."

Natalie put her chin in her hand. That wasn't true. There was one time when she wanted to swim, wanted to flip out of her dress and heels and dive into the water. To be fair, though, it wasn't only her aversion to the water that held her back. It was more than that. But she could admit, if only to herself, that she had wanted to jump. In more ways than one.

"That's good. I'd hate to think I ruined your life or anything." He reached for his hat, which he promptly returned to his head.

Natalie scoffed. "You didn't ruin my life. I did that all on my own."

Brett leaned forward again. "What happened with AJ? When I left town, it seemed like you guys were good. Now I get back two weeks later, and it's all frowns and scowls. He treat you ok? Do I need to kick his butt?"

"Do you think you could?" Natalie asked. Her brother might be ripped, at least he claimed he was, but he didn't have the same raw toughness that AJ did. It was probably the Marine in AJ that made him seem so much more masculine than Brett, who possessed a less evident form of masculinity. The ruggedness of a farmer and former football star, as opposed to that of a trained killer—or therapist. Whatever.

"I don't know. I think I could do some damage. It would hurt though." He winced at the thought. "I'll do it if you need me to."

Natalie shook her head.

"No need. I don't think you can beat a guy up because your sister broke his heart. Seems a little mean." Her words didn't come out as flippant as she had hoped they would. She could hear the pain behind them, which bothered her. She'd made her bed, and all that. But lying in it was harder than she'd thought it would be.

"That does seem a little unfair," Brett conceded.

"How's he doing? I haven't seen him in a while."

"He's not too bad, I guess. He's studying for that test that he has to take for his therapist license or whatever it's called. He started his mentoring over in Harrison, so he's going out there most weekdays. I asked him when he was coming back, but he said he didn't know."

Natalie's head snapped up. "What do you mean 'coming back'? Where is he?"

"He's been staying up at Jerry Rasmussen's hunting cabin for the past week or two. That's what Charlie said when I went there looking for him. He wouldn't even answer his phone, I had to go all the way up there to see what was going on with him."

"There cell service up there is kind of spotty," she told him. AJ was at Jerry and Tina's cabin? That didn't make sense. The cabin was nice enough for an extended stay. It had a flat screen TV and cable television, Wi-Fi, air conditioning, and a gorgeous view of the mountains. It was a long drive up there, though. If he was going to Harrison most days, it would add an extra thirty minutes onto his trip.

"I knew he was working on becoming a therapist or whatever, but I didn't know he had started actually doing it. I guess he meets with patients under supervision, like a real counselor," Brett went on.

"I didn't know he was doing that yet either," Natalie said. She wished she'd been able to talk to him after his first day. She wondered if he had been excited about finally getting to start, or worried that he'd do it all right. He would have been dressed up in his professional clothes, maybe even wearing a tie. He looked good in a tie.

"Are you sure you two can't work it out? You guys were good together. You kind of balanced each other out. He got you to relax a little, and you pushed him to finally get that mentoring thing set up."

Natalie shook her head. "He did that on his own. He never mentioned it when we were together."

Brett shrugged. "Still, are you sure? I won't ask again, but I thought I should. You know, just in case."

Natalie looked down at her hands. They were wrapped tightly around the glass of tea. It was sweating on her palms, leaving them cold and damp. She let go of it and rubbed them together, the cool liquid sliding across her skin.

"I'm leaving soon. I have a life in Memphis. As soon as I get another job, I'll go back," she told her brother, who nodded.

"You worked pretty hard to get out of here."

Natalie nodded. "I worked my tail off to get out of here. I liked Memphis, liked being somebody important. Successful."

Brett stood up and put his glass in the sink. He walked behind his sister and patted her on the back.

"You're important here too, you know." He started out of the kitchen, when Natalie stopped him.

"Wait. Where have you been these past two weeks? No one seemed to know where you'd gone."

Brett shrugged. "At a convention."

Natalie scrunched up her nose in disgust. "They have semen conventions?"

He laughed out loud and kept laughing as he opened the door and left. She could still hear him chuckling as he got into his truck.

He never did answer the question.

Chapter 28

"The flowers look lovely," Henrietta said to the group of women gathered at Knight's to make the final wedding preparations. They had made a bargain with the restaurant to pay a little more in order to be able to decorate the terrace the night before. Since Knight's was rented out for all of Saturday, the bundles of flowers and tulle wouldn't be in anyone's way.

"I agree," DeeJay said. She smiled at her mother, who gave her a wink. Natalie watched them affectionately. Despite their bickering, there was a lot of love there.

"What do you say we have some fruity drinks? Make this a bachelorette party?" Gigi asked.

There was a long silence.

"Well, I don't have anything else to do tonight," Mabel noted. She adjusted her fanny pack, which contained all sorts of helpful items like safety pins and masking tape.

"I can call Danny and let him know that I won't be home for a few more hours. I don't want him to worry," DeeJay said. She pulled out her cell phone from the pocket of her leopard-print vest that she wore over black capris and a black t-shirt.

Henrietta bustled off to let the wait staff know they'd be placing an order, and Gigi whispered something in Mabel's ear. The women made eye contact with Natalie, which would have concerned her on any other day.

Today, however, she had made a vow not to worry about anything. Tomorrow would be the wedding. AJ would be there, and she would have to see him again. Natalie could feel the anxiety creeping up inside her mind, like a slow poison on its way to shut down all of her internal organs. She shook her head and pushed the worry back down.

"I'd love something to drink. It's hot as blue blazes out here." She didn't have anyone to call. No one to tell that she'd be late getting home. It was better this way. This wasn't really even her home. Not anymore.

The ladies moved the dozen or so centerpieces from one table to another, and sat down around it. There were several conversations going on all at once. Gigi was discussing lingerie choices with Mabel and Henrietta, who had returned with a stack of menus. DeeJay was talking to Lila about the odds of getting the bride to style her hair in any other way than a basic bob for the wedding day.

Tina turned to Natalie, "I've been wanting to pick your brain, but haven't found the time."

"What can I help you with? Is it something to do with the Chamber of Commerce?" Natalie slid one of the menus in front of her mother's friend and took one for herself.

"I don't want to bother you with details now, especially since this has become a bachelorette party," Tina said. She held the menu away from her to try to get it to focus.

"I don't mind. I don't know if I can help, but I'll do what I can." Natalie snatched the reading glasses from her mother's head and passed them over.

"Thanks, dear. I can't ever keep track of mine." She slid the glasses onto her nose and peered at the menu, talking all the while. "I just wanted to ask you for some input about marketing for some of the events that we've got coming up. We've got the county fair, which has always drawn a decent crowd, but I was thinking we might want to do something a little different with the chamber's exhibition building. Typically we just have the businesses set up booths and pass out business cards and candy and such. To tell you the truth, it's kind of dull, and not many of the fair-goers come though."

Natalie knew what Tina was talking about. The county fair was huge. It was a central part of any Southern summer. The local FFA and 4-H clubs showed animals, farmers brought in their biggest and best vegetables, and once the sun went down, the entire population of the county poured into the midway to defy death by riding on the rickety carnival rides and eating questionable corndogs.

"What have you considered?" Natalie asked. She didn't have any experience with marketing at fairs or carnivals, but it couldn't be much different than any other event.

"That's just it. I don't have any ideas. I tell you what, I'm just about burnt out on the whole business. Don't pass that along to anyone, but between me and you, I'd love to retire. I just hate to leave the town in the lurch."

Possibilities for the fair passed through her mind. A few were immediately appealing and would probably go over well. Gigi snapped her fingers in front of Natalie's face. Clearly, she'd been daydreaming,

"Sweetheart, what do you want to drink? I've ordered some of those fancy nachos for the table," Gigi stated.

The server chimed in, "She means spinach artichoke dip with pita chips."

Gigi continued, "I also got us some of those cheese squares with tomato sauce."

"Toasted ravioli and marinara with sun-dried tomatoes and roasted garlic," the server corrected.

Gigi rolled her eyes. "I said that. Now, we're getting some shrubs. They say that they're a new drink, but I remember my own parents making them. That was probably about ten or fifteen years ago, though, so I can see why they would think they were new." Natalie's grandmother winked. Her great-grandparents had passed away at least twenty years before, and had been teetotalers their whole lives.

"Gigi, stop harassing the poor boy," Natalie told her. "What's in a shrub? I've never heard of it."

Henrietta waved her hand and jumped in before the server could start speaking.

"It's a lovely drink with juice...and seltzer...and a tiny splash of vinegar. They're delicious, though they do make me a little giddy." Henrietta giggled a little.

Natalie winced. Vinegar? Yuck. "I think I'll have a Coke."

The women at the table booed loudly.

"You have to have something more exciting than that, Natalie," her mother scolded. "It a party." She leaned in to whisper, "They're non-alcoholic. Surprisingly good too. But your grandmother likes to act they're some fancy mixed drink You know how she is."

Natalie rolled her eyes. "Fine, I'll have a shrub. I feel like I'm ordering landscaping."

"A strong one!" Gigi declared. "And keep the drinks coming! I'm getting married tomorrow."

The server retreated inside as quickly as he could. Natalie wasn't sure if it was to place their orders, or to escape the crazy old ladies. She would bet money on the latter.

305

He hustled back and retreated just as quickly, the drinks and appetizers on the table, faster than an old lady could ask, "Do you have strippers here?"

Natalie was still running through ideas for the county fair in her head. She had a few that might work, but she'd need to look up a few of the details, check on budgets and such.

"How's your shrub, Natalie?" Henrietta asked.

"It's wonderful. Thanks for making me order it." Natalie took a toasted ravioli and put it on her plate with some marinara sauce. An instant later the platter was passed around and empty.

"I just love these little things," Mabel said. "We should serve them in our cafeteria sometime. I'll have to make sure they're on the menu."

Natalie looked up from her drink.

"What menu? Did something happen with the cafeteria at the senior center?"

Mabel winced. "I had meant to tell you, but you were just so busy with wedding plans. I didn't want to bother you. I took care of the rest of it."

Gigi spoke up. "I told her to leave you be. You'd done enough work for us, for free too. We took all the plans you'd made up, and Mabel showed them to some people. The next thing you know, we've got permits and an anonymous donation of cash to get us started. The first luncheon will be in two weeks."

"These little toasted raviolis are definitely going on the menu," Mabel reiterated.

The chatter rose about menu items and how much intestinal gas each one produced. Natalie didn't follow it. Instead she wondered how all of this could happen without her knowing about it. She had put so much work into that project, hours and hours. It hurt a little to see how it had moved on without her.

"Well, we had to get moving on it," Gigi was saying to Tina. "After all, our Natalie here is headed back to Memphis sometime soon. We couldn't leave it all for her to do, what with her looking for jobs on the internet, and planning on going back anytime now."

They were talking about her like she wasn't even there, like she was already gone.

"Are there any more of the pita chips?" Natalie asked. The women all turned to her at once, as though they'd been watching her, waiting for her to speak.

"I think there are a few left. We were very hungry, though," DeeJay said.

Tina slid the basket over. "Here you go."

There were six chips left. Exactly. Natalie put them on her plate along with the tablespoon of crusty dip that she scraped off the edge of the dish.

"You guys really were hungry. Are we ordering anything else? I haven't eaten since noon, and it's...what time is it?"

"You should have taken a break to eat, honey," her mother said. "We all did."

"When? I didn't see you. I thought we all worked straight through dinner."

"Actually," Gigi said, "we thought we could use this time together. We have some questions for you."

Natalie frowned into her hands. "You guys have been up to something all night. Are you sure you didn't put something in my drink? Some kind of truth serum or something? I know you're not above it."

Her mother spoke up. "I won't say it wasn't suggested, but I wouldn't let your grandmother do that to you. You're welcome, by the way. It was our plan to ply you with too much sugar and not enough food, so that we could bargain with you. Snacks for answers."

"That's crazy. And mean. You guys are looney."

"It's your gene pool too," DeeJay reminded her. "Try as we might to rise above it, it's always there sucking us under again."

Natalie groaned. "So, let's talk. I'm hungry. I'll tell you whatever you want, but I get the whole basket of raviolis when they come out."

The faces nodded. The upper hand felt good, or it would when she was finally able to eat.

"Tell us why you and AJ broke up," DeeJay prompted her. She leaned in. Natalie leaned back and slunk down into her chair.

"I don't want to talk about this."

"Oh, come on. We just want to know what's going on with you. We all care about you so much. Each of us thinks of you like one of our own. It hurts us to see you in pain. Explain it to us," Lila prodded.

Natalie shook her head and crossed her arms over her chest.

Mabel pouted. "You said you'd tell us anything for the whole basket of toasted ravioli. For every question that you don't answer, you lose one. Fair is fair, missy."

Tina spoke up, her tone gentle. "Was he mean to you? I know those overly masculine men can be a bit rough sometimes, even without meaning to. I know he was a Marine, but maybe he didn't know how strong he was, and--"

"No! Nothing like that. He was wonderful. Perfect. Everything a girl could ever want," Natalie protested.

"So why did you two stop seeing each other? What happened?" Henrietta asked this time.

Natalie didn't respond. She took another sip of her drink instead.

"That's one ravioli down," Mabel warned.

Gigi threw her hands up. "Oh, who cares? Let me tell you about this thing that Charlie does when he's kissing my neck. First he--"

"I'll talk about it!" Natalie shrieked. "Just don't talk about that. I'll tell you anything you want to know."

Gigi grinned. "Only if you want to, darling."

Natalie glared. "You're evil."

Her grandmother laughed. "Spill it, or I'll tell you things that would make your hair curl."

"What do you want to know?"

Natalie ended up telling the women all about the last time she had come to Knight's. She told them how she had gotten breathless when she'd seen the place. She told them how she'd been breathless again when AJ had mentioned coming back again years from now, only this time her breath had been sucked out of her lungs by a hard and fast panic. Natalie spilled her guts about how she had sat through dinner unable to eat a single bite. She had visions of being trapped in Big Springs, sucked into the town so far she couldn't breathe. She felt powerless, like her life was happening to her, not by her.

"I worked so hard to get out of here. I gave up so much, and when I finally made it, I get pulled back. Nothing I do even matters. I'll end up right back where I started." Natalie sniffed and gazed out at the sympathetic faces around her.

"You aren't stuck you know," her mother told her when she had stopped talking. Natalie wiped her nose on her napkin. "You weren't forced to come back to Big Springs. Your father and I would have sent you the money you needed to stay in the city."

Gigi reached over and squeezed Natalie's trembling hand. "If I thought you were happy there, I would have moved the stars and moon to make sure you could stay. But were you really, truly happy in the city? Before everything fell apart, when it was at its best?"

Natalie had this vision in her mind of what her life was supposed to be. She was supposed to have a group of girlfriends like in those sexy TV shows. She was supposed to spend her weekends shopping, going on fabulous dates, or running off on quick vacations to a beach.

Instead, she had spent most of her weekends working on her laptop from her apartment—the first apartment that she'd paid a fortune in rent to live in, and then the second apartment that she had shared with Brantley. Her work had made her a prisoner in both. She only had one close friend, Jenn, who she loved but had never felt that close to. Jenn had grown up in the city, and they didn't have a whole lot in common other than their jobs. When she'd been in Memphis, they had been on the phone or texting constantly. But since she'd been home, Natalie found that they didn't have that much to talk about.

Brantley, though, had been pretty great. He was handsome and rich. He took Natalie on those fabulous dates she'd dreamed of—fancy restaurants and art gallery openings. It was like a fairy tale, except that it wasn't. It had felt wrong moving into his home. She was, in her heart, an old fashioned girl, and had considered herself a Christian-- though she hadn't been acting much like one when she'd lived in Memphis. In fact, a lot of what she had done in the past few years hadn't been very Christ-like of her. Truth be told, she was ashamed of herself. Of who she had become.

Natalie had a sneaking suspicion that she had been working for all the wrong things. Money. Status. The bragging rights to say that she was no longer own girl.

Memphis. Natalie didn't really even like the city that much. She was used to mountains and wilderness. She liked being able to see all of the stars, not just the postage stamp of sky that she could glimpse from her window. She had heard cars at night instead of crickets. She'd had to bolt her windows and buy a security system for her car. In Big Springs she usually left the keys in the cup holder and slept with her windows open. The city might be fine and dandy for some, but it never really suited her.

"There's nothing wrong with coming back to where you're from," Gigi told her. "I did it, and I thank God every day that I did."

Natalie nodded. She looked around at the faces of the women in front of her. They were all looking at her with such expressions of love and compassion, like they knew exactly how she felt.

DeeJay cleared her throat. "You know that God has a plan for all of us. He has one for you too, honey. It's just that sometimes our plans and God's plans aren't quite the same thing. But in the end, we if we listen to where He's directing us, it'll all work out."

"I think I need some air," Natalie whispered as she stood, shoving her cell phone into her back pocket. She walked down the steps leading to the cobblestone path.

"Be careful!" Henrietta called out.

Chapter 29

Natalie held onto the handrail as she stepped down. She felt a little shaky, but wasn't in any danger of stumbling around and falling into the spring. She was in danger, though, of admitting that she had made a terrible error in judgment.

She made her way to the bench and sat down, leaned back and stared into the darkness. The trees were outlined against the starry sky, creating a tableau so representative of her childhood that she nearly cried. She remembered going outside and watching the stars, brilliant against the dark frame of the trees. The crickets and frogs were serenading the night. She couldn't hear a single car.

As much as she hated to admit it, she loved this place. Even the spring that was gushing in the swimming hole down below. Its familiar rushing sound was a comfort. She'd never realized that she avoided the water, not until Brett had brought it up. She didn't mind it, in general. She knew she'd put her toes in upon occasion. Looking down into the black current below her, she could understand why she wouldn't want to jump in. Not as a kid, and not before when she'd been here with AJ.

It was scary. She couldn't see what was under the surface. Even though she'd seen people make the same leap hundreds of times before, even though they always seemed to have fun, she couldn't push the worry out of her mind. What if there were rocks down there, unseen dangers? What if there were fish with razor sharp teeth? What if she got turned around and couldn't find the surface? What if she lost herself entirely?

Natalie thought about everything she'd done since she'd come back. Maybe her grandmother had a point. Maybe she was scared. It had a ring of truth to it, and

Natalie groaned aloud. The only cure for a fear was to face it, and she really, really hated having to face her fears.

Her phone vibrated in her pocket.

Natalie reached for it, foolishly hoping that it was AJ. He was calling to tell her he couldn't live without her, to beg her to stay, and she would. She knew that she would, that she wanted to with all of her heart.

Natalie frowned at the name on the screen and let it go to voicemail. She had nothing to say to Brantley, and there was nothing she needed to hear from him now. That was in the past. The doubts and fears she had held onto were falling away.

She wasn't absolutely crazy, though. She listened to the message.

Her former boyfriend began with apologies. He moved on to explanations, none of which amount to anything, not that she cared. She really didn't. He begged for forgiveness and for her to return his call.

Natalie held her phone in her hand and considered his request. Brantley wasn't who she needed him to be. That time in her life had been a mistake. There had been good parts like her friendship with Jenn. She would treasure her always. Her relationship with Brantley? No. She was finished there. She could forgive him. It had been as much his fault as it had been his, so she could let it go. But she would also let him go too.

Natalie scrolled through her contact list, found his name, and deleted him.

Natalie heard a burst of laughter from the terrace. She turned away from the ruckus and sat back down on the bench. It was crazy, really. If anyone had told her that Brantley would come crawling back to her, contrite, she wouldn't have believed it. No way. But it had happened, and she'd turned him away.

It was a beautiful night, not humid at all, which was a miracle this time of year. There was a soft breeze blowing, rustling the leaves on trees alongside the creek. The rope that everyone used to swing out over the spring and fall gracelessly into water was swaying gently back and forth.

She watched it intently. Growing up near the spring, Natalie had seen countless people swing on it. Everyone from grandmothers to preschoolers. Everyone except for her. She had never dared. She was suddenly struck by the absurdity of the situation.

She was afraid to do it because of some event that she couldn't even remember. Who knew if that was even the real reason? Maybe it was some flaw in her personality. She was unable to take risks, to try something new, to stop planning and preparing and just let go for once.

Natalie lay her phone down on the bench and stood up on firm legs. Her steps never wavering, she made her way to the edge so that she was stood looking down into the spring.

"Aren't I just full of surprises today?" she muttered as she picked up the hooked pole that leaned against the tree. She used it to pull the rope back toward her.

"I can do this." Speaking the words aloud galvanized her will. She kicked off her shoes, checked her pockets, and stepped up onto the wooden rungs that had been nailed into the tree.

The rungs had been worn smooth by years of feet climbing them, but the bark of the tree was still rough against her hands. She was grateful she'd chosen to wear jeans for decorating tonight. They protected her knees from being scraped as she clumsily made her way to the topmost rung.

The rope was thick and dry. It felt foreign in her hands. She found the knot used for hanging on and held fast. Against her better judgment, Natalie looked down at the water.

It didn't look as bad as she had imagined it would. It looked almost peaceful, serene. The current didn't seem as fast as she had expected. It didn't gush, but merely flowed. Ripples moved across the surface reflecting the moonlight. It was an image that no photograph could ever capture, no painting ever reproduce. No poem could describe or melody express the wonder and awe that Natalie felt looking down into the spring that she had once feared. She said a prayer of gratitude for the night, the spring, the courage, the moon and stars. For everything that had happened to her in the past few months. For the rotten events and the glorious, knowing that they were all blessings. Her life was a blessing, and as she clung there, arms wrapped around the ancient tree, she felt something big welling up within her.

It was more than the beauty of the moment. It was the step that Natalie knew she was taking. She could feel the change bubbling up inside of herself, as the water bubbled up from earth, some unseen reservoir coming forth and making itself known in such a way that shaped the entire landscape around it. The spring had the power to change history, creating a town from wilderness.

Natalie gripped the rope with all her might, closed her eyes and pulled in a breath. She let it out slowly, opened her eyes again, and pushed off of the tree. For one blissful second she was flying, sailing outward in the darkness, the air blowing across her cheeks.

Exhilarated.

She let go and dropped, then she stopped thinking and concentrated on the water as she broke through the shining surface. It was freezing, breath-stealing cold. There was a reason people swam during the hottest days of summer. Her head submerged, and instead of losing her way as she had once feared, she popped back up a moment later, her face to the sky.

She laughed out loud. Yes, she was cold, but she had done it! She had jumped.

Natalie whooped out loud and threw a fist in the air, then realized that if she stopped moving, she started sinking. She dog paddled awkwardly back to the bank. She pulled herself up onto the grass hill and lay back. She could feel the massive smile on her face. She felt entirely changed. Radiant and new.

"Natalie? You alright down there? We heard a splash. You didn't do something stupid and fall in, did you?" DeeJay called out from the steps.

Natalie grinned and shouted, "Nope!"

"Then come along and get back up here. Your raviolis are waiting for you, and I don't know how much longer I can hold off the old buzzards. They're beginning to circle."

Natalie pushed herself to her feet and looked down at her sopping wet clothes. This was going to be tricky to explain without sounding like a lunatic.

She wrung out her ponytail and flipped it over her shoulder. Nothing to do now but face them. Well, that and claim her food—perhaps in a takeout box.

"Oh, sweet heavens above! What happened to you? I thought you said you didn't fall in!" Natalie's mother rushed to her side the moment Natalie reached the terrace.. "You're chilled to the bone, sweetheart."

"Now that you mention it, I am pretty cold. It felt nice at first. But now I'm freezing."

Gigi piped up, "I thought you were supposed to be my bright grandchild. What happened to you? Don't you know better than to stand too close to the edge down there?"

Henrietta hustled over, carrying an armful of decorative centerpiece candles.

"Are we going to have a séance?" Mabel asked. She wrapped a sweater around Natalie. DeeJay used an arm of it to towel dry Natalie's ponytail.

Henrietta began to set them down in a tight cluster. "No, you smarty. We are going to make a fire for Natalie to warm herself by. Won't that be nice? Who's got a lighter?"

Three minutes later, Natalie found herself huddled over a large circle of magnolia scented candles. It was surprisingly warm. She'd never been much of a fan of magnolia, but she was starting to reconsider it. It was a night for reconsidering, after all.

"How's that now?" DeeJay chaffed her daughter's arms. "You want to tell us how you got soaked to the bone?"

"Not really. It's kind of a long story and a little personal."

"Oh, we don't mind. Go on ahead, the more personal the better." Gigi took a bite of ravioli.

Natalie swung her head around to look at the table behind her, which was suspiciously empty of food.

"Hey! Are those my raviolis?"

The words had barely left her when a scream went out from the crowd. It was the scream that alerted Natalie to the sudden temperature change, the surge of heat in her hair, the ends of which had dried enough to be flammable.

Chapter 30

"Knock, knock! Are you up yet?" a chipper voice called out.

Natalie shook her head from side to side, silently praying for invisibility. If the high-pitched voice couldn't find her, it couldn't make her get out of bed. After the party, she had been up most of the night. She spent some of it weeping over her hair. Though she'd not been burnt, her vanity had taken a hit. Not to mention the tackle from Mabel that would make any linebacker proud. Her hair had been extinguished quickly, but not before several inches had been burnt off.

Natalie had also spent some of the dark hours considering her past, present and future. She had some plans to make and some mistakes to rectify.

And for the first time in her life, Natalie spent several hours in prayer. She'd talked to God, confessed and apologized. She asked for direction and guidance, for the faith to follow the path He had set out for her, no matter where it might lead. She prayed for the courage own up to her mistakes and to make amends, now and in the future. Most of all, she thanked God for his everlasting mercy and for all of the blessings he continued to rain down on her, even when she didn't deserve them. That's what God's grace was all about, though, wasn't it? His mercy through the Son, Jesus Christ. After last night, Natalie felt more assured and confident than ever before. But, she was also exhausted.

A burst of light pierced her dark cocoon of blankets as they were unceremoniously stripped off of her. The light burned her eyes through her eyelids.

"Oh, sweet heavens! Mama, get in here! She looks just awful! You aren't going to believe how terrible she looks." Natalie was hurt both that her mother was killing her slowly with the volume of her shrieks, and that she would say something so unfeeling about her only daughter.

"Good gracious! She can't stand up at my wedding looking like that. I won't have it."

Natalie pulled on the blankets. If she wasn't in a wedding today, that meant she could sleep for a few more days.

"What happened to her hair?" Natalie's mother asked, the pitch of her voice reaching heights only previously heard by dogs. "Where's the rest of it? It wasn't this bad last night."

Natalie's eyes opened. She blinked a few times until her mother's and grandmother's faces came into focus.

"What are you talking about?" she whispered.

DeeJay's hands were over her mouth. Gigi's was hanging open. Both looked horrified. Gigi pointed to the floor next to the bed.

"Is that--" Natalie's mother began. "Oh, no!"

"What is it?" Natalie asked. She was afraid to ask.

"Don't look," Gigi warned her.

Now she didn't have any choice. Natalie eased herself sideways, until her face hung off the edge of the mattress. Below her appeared to be some kind of yellowish rodent. Maybe a guinea pig, curled up sleeping.

Gigi nudged it with her foot. "I think it's your hair."

DeeJay bent down to pick it up by one end. She held onto a black elastic band from which flowed a long, blonde ponytail, the ends of which were singed black and curled up.

Natalie sat straight up in bed, the blankets tumbling to the floor. She reached behind her and felt the back of her head. It was surprisingly light. The hair between her fingers was only a few inches long.

"What? What? What happened?" She sputtered, her tired mind unable to keep up.

"I know you were upset last night, but I didn't think you'd...you'd...mutilate yourself!" DeeJay eyed Natalie's head warily, like whatever had happened to her daughter's hair might be contagious and happen to her.

Natalie shook her head back and forth, missing the whip of a ponytail in her face. She looked from her mother's face to Gigi's. Both stared at her in horror and confusion. It was a familiar expression.

Sometime in the wee hours, that expression had stared back at her in the mirror. She had been overcome with guilt and disgusted with her own vanity. Her eyes had been puffy and red from crying, and the scissors had been right there in the top drawer of the vanity.

Natalie didn't think she could adequately explain it. She barely remembered, much less understood it herself.

"It was a mistake. I did it. I remember now, but it was almost like it happened in a dream."

Gigi cringed, "More like a nightmare."

Finally, DeeJay cleared her throat. "Alright. So, whatever the reason, whether you meant to cut your hair or not, we're going to have to fix this. I know you're hurting, honey, and that your hair looks like you went after it with a pair of gardening shears, but there is a wedding this evening, and we can't just spend all day wailing about how bad it is."

She stepped forward and took Natalie's head in her hands. Natalie let her forehead drop against her mother's stomach, breathing in the comforting scents of home while DeeJay ran her hands over her daughter's hair, assessing the damage.

"I can work with this. We've got to get moving, though. To make this work, I'm going to need a few hours. I've still got to get myself ready for the wedding. Lila will do your hair, of course, mother."

Gigi spoke up, "You can do my hair if you want to, Dolly Jean. I'll let you."

DeeJay was quiet for a few seconds, then spoke, "I appreciate the offer, Mama, but truthfully, since I've got to deal with Natalie's mess, I just don't have time. Besides, Lila does a nice job on it. Thanks, though."

Natalie's mother was on her cell phone before she was out of the bedroom on her way to the front door, asking Lila about bleaches and developers.

Gigi stepped in front of her granddaughter, and once again, Natalie felt her face being taken into gentle hands. She turned Natalie's face from side to side.

"I think you need some coffee. The good stuff. I'll make some." Gigi started toward the bedroom door. "Take a shower. You stink like creek water. I'll meet you outside in fifteen minutes to go to the salon. I'm driving."

The salon was the headquarters for all wedding-related activity that morning. There were people coming and going, picking up and dropping off everything from people to pantyhose. It would have been absolute chaos had DeeJay not been calling out orders with the efficiency of a general from behind her stylist's chair. The only snag in the otherwise flawless system was Natalie's butchered hair. A picture of her ponytail had somehow ended up on the internet, drawing more than the requisite crowd. Susan Appleby was noticeably present, her cell phone snapping pictures of the scene. The woman should've been a journalist.

Natalie sat in her mother's chair and saw a look of glee come across DeeJay's face as she took the shears to Natalie's hair. It was the same look comic book villains got when their evil plan was finally coming together.

"Mama, you didn't cut my hair did you?" Natalie made eye contact with her mother in the mirror. DeeJay looked taken aback, not insulted, but surprised.

"I wish I had thought of it. I would've done this years ago." She gave her daughter a wink and snipped away another chunk of hair.

"Remember to leave some, alright?" Natalie didn't like how much hair was piling up on the floor. Her ponytail hadn't even looked that big. At this rate she'd be down to skin in another twenty minutes.

"Trust me."

As much as she loved her mother, Natalie knew that was impossible. She closed her eyes—to avoid the mirror and the growing mountain of cut hair, but also to ease some of the throbbing behind her eyeballs.

"Drink this." A paper coffee cup was shoved into her hands.

Natalie opened her eyes to see her grandmother standing in front of her with a Coke and a muffin. Her mother and grandmother were taking care of her. Natalie blinked back tears.

"I know. Millie's muffins have brought me to tears before too. They're that good. Now don't cry. We don't need you looking all puffy-eyed. You're bad enough as it is." Gigi winked and wandered back toward Lila's station.

Natalie took a bite of her muffin, closed her eyes, and let the soothing rhythm of combing and cutting lull her into an almost meditative state.

Then her phone buzzed. She had a voicemail. Somehow she'd missed the actual call, probably due to the outrageous volume caused by multiple hair dryers and the voices raised to be heard over them. That combined with the marching band parading through her brain.

"Mama, I've got a message. I'm going to check it really quick. Do you mind?"

Natalie's mother huffed and threw up her hands with all of the drama of a slighted soap opera diva. She pursed her lips and tapped her toe.

Natalie saw the moment an idea sprang into her mother's head. Less than the light a lightbulb coming on, and more like being zapped by an electric fence.

"Can I add color? A few highlights around your face? You let me do that, and you can make all the calls you want." DeeJay's eyes were wide and hopeful.

Natalie shrugged.

"That's a yes! I'll be right back. Use your phone, but *don't* change your mind. You already said yes." Natalie's mother rushed off into the back room, vibrating with excitement.

Natalie rolled her eyes and put the phone to her ear. It was Jenn. She knew it was the big day and was checking in. She wished Natalie good luck and begged for pictures of her in the Dolly dress.

Natalie saved the message. It was a good one, worth listening to again sometime. Natalie had missed Jenn. Jamie was great, but was so different from her bold, gutsy Memphis friend. Like Neapolitan ice cream. Jamie was strawberry; Jenn was chocolate, and Natalie was vanilla. She'd bet that Jamie would like Jenn. Maybe she could talk Jenn into coming back some time. They could all hang out, go out for pizza, or maybe go to Knight's and sit on the terrace, all while keeping a careful eye out for open flames.

The memory of last night hit her. Again, not like a lightbulb, but more like a whole string of firecrackers, one memory rapid-fire right after the other.

"I jumped into the spring last night. In all the excitement from today, I had almost forgotten."

Natalie's mother returned, mixing something in a bowl. She ignored everything but her daughter's hair. All around Natalie, people kept moving, talking, laughing, and never realizing that with that single memory the whole world had changed.

"Mama, I jumped into the spring. The spring." Natalie's voice rose with her excitement.

"I know, hon. I saw you dripping wet. Now keep still."

"I've never jumped in before. Last night was the first time. I did it! I was scared, but I did it anyway. I can't even really swim." Natalie saw her reflection in the mirror. She was beaming, and if she wasn't mistaken, her head was throbbing a little less now than it was a few minutes ago, despite the vigor with which her mother was now working on her hair.

"That sounds like it was a very stupid thing to do," DeeJay stated. Natalie saw her mother watching her now. "It also sounds like it meant something more than getting a little wet. What's this about?"

Natalie shook her head, still hardly able to believe it herself.

"I'm staying in Big Springs. For good."

DeeJay dropped her comb. She never dropped her comb. It was a sin in the world of hairstyling. Nonetheless, Natalie distinctly heard it bounce on the floor.

Then Mama cried. Big, black tears that streaked down her face in inky rivulets.

"I wish you'd jumped in that stupid spring years ago," she blubbered, wiping at her face with a white towel. The sobbing went on for several minutes. She was smiling and weeping all at once. It went on so long that Natalie started feeling guilty for taking so long to come to the inevitable conclusion that staying was better than going. Lila and Gigi and several others came over to see what was the matter, but DeeJay shooed them away.

"Mama, what was it that you wanted to do to my hair before, but I wouldn't let you? If you had full reign, what would you do to it?"

The tears stopped.

"Are you serious? Don't tease me like this, girl. I'll ground you for sure if you're teasing, no matter how old you are."

Their eyes met in the mirror.

"Do it."

Natalie was surprised at how quickly her mother could move when given two of her dearest wishes within five minutes of each other. She immediately flipped the chair around, claiming that her daughter couldn't see until she was finished, like judging a cake before it has been frosted.

Natalie sat and sipped her drink while she was draped in a new cape and while her mother went into overdrive calling out color mixtures to Lila, who stuck Gigi under the dryer and assisted. There was a great deal more snipping, some aluminum foil, a plastic shower cap and a shampoo or three. Oddly enough, Natalie had no second thoughts or regrets at any time. She felt strangely at peace.

When it was finally time for the big reveal, about an hour later, a small crowd had gathered, then dispersed as Gigi insisted that Natalie's make-up be redone before the unveiling. That was the most nerve-wracking part of all, having to sit still while someone put on her eyeliner. It was one thing to do it in a mirror, and an entirely different one to watch your over-excited and highly caffeinated mother bringing a smudger closer and closer to your eyeball.

"Now the dress! She has to put the dress on!" Tina called out. She'd arrived sometime when Natalie was baking under the hair dryers.

It was agreed upon, and Natalie went along. It was amazing how freeing it was to stop fighting the inevitable. She felt like a massive weight was lifted from her shoulders, not to mention the top of her head. But lingering in the background, like the thunder of a coming storm, was the knowledge that even though she was staying, AJ may not take her back, may not want her anymore.

Especially if she looked ridiculous. She couldn't help but add that silent fear.

Gigi declared it to be her right to help Natalie into the dress, since she was the one to pick it out for her after all. Besides, if she wasn't going to be the center of attention on her own wedding day, she wanted some part of Natalie's spotlight.

No one argued with that logic, and Natalie promised her grandmother that after this, all of the focus would return to the bride.

Gigi followed Natalie into the back room that held the washer, dryer, and shelves of beauty products and supplies. There was no mirror in the room. There was, however, a garment bag and a shoe box containing Natalie's worst nightmare.

She sighed and stripped down to the special underwear that the dress required, which she had reluctantly put on before leaving the house. Gigi unzipped the bag and brought out the dress. The bodice retained some of its shape from the boning.

At least there were no sequins, Natalie told herself.

"Step into it," Gigi instructed her. She did as she was told. Her grandmother zipped her up, the dress forcing Natalie to stand straighter.

"The shoes now," Gigi prompted. Natalie slid her feet into the tall nude heels.

Her grandmother stood back a few feet and examined the final result. Her eyes passed from the top of Natalie's head all the way down to the toes of her shoes. Gigi nodded.

"That's you," she said, the words pronounced with a kind of reverence.

"What do you mean? Of course it's me."

Gigi came closer and took her hand. "You've been floundering around for a while, but something's changed. Something more than just your hair and a killer dress. You're different today." She looked into Natalie's eyes. "Today *you* are *you*. At last."

Gigi stood on tiptoe and kissed the younger woman's cheek.

"I think it's more than the dress and hair, isn't it?"

"It is. Last night I spent a little time thinking and a lot of time praying. I came to realize some things about me and the Lord. He loves me no matter where I live or how I earn a living. What makes me a success isn't what other people think of me. It's what He thinks of me and what I think of myself."

"That's exactly right, sweetheart," Gigi agreed. "Oh, I love you so much. You don't know how happy it makes me to hear you say those words. Now, let's go out there and make a scene."

The moment Natalie stepped outside the door into the main room of the salon, all activity stopped. Lila shut off the hair dryer she'd been using. DeeJay stopped teasing her bangs. A group of women from church dropped their copies of *People* and *US Weekly* in unison. Susan Appleby raised her phone to snap a picture.

Natalie hoped that was a good sign.

"Isn't she something?" Gigi commented from behind her. "Now go on and get it out of your systems, because the sooner you do, the sooner this day can go back to being all about me."

"I'm just so happy you're staying," Natalie's mother exclaimed. "I don't care if you shave your whole head." She rushed to her daughter's side and immediately began pulling on edges of her hair to check that it was evenly cut.

Tina, her hair sprayed and fluffed to new heights, stepped in front of Natalie, her expression hopeful. "Staying? As in staying in Big Springs? Not moving back to Memphis?"

Natalie nodded. DeeJay gushed. Gigi winked and left to finish getting ready for her wedding.

"Do you have a job lined up? Any plans?" Tina wasn't blinking. Her black-lined eyes stared, like a simple blink would wake her up from whatever dream she was having.

"I don't have anything—"

"Take my job!" Tina screeched.

Natalie jumped, startled. She nearly toppled over in the heels. Her mother held out a hand to steady her.

DeeJay did a double take to look at her friend. "What will you do for a job, Tina, if Natalie takes yours? That's nice and all, but it's going above and beyond the call of friendship."

Tina's hands came up beneath her chin, clasped together. "Please? I want to retire. The pay is decent, and there are benefits, insurance and all that. We can go over the details. I'll negotiate the moon for you if you'll just take the job."

Natalie put a hand on the woman's shoulder. Tina was trembling slightly.

Natalie considered the offer. There was a lot she could do in a position like that. It would use her degree, the experience she'd gained working for the marketing firm in

Memphis. Now that she saw that her place was in Big Springs, she could see that her heart hadn't been in her work in the city. Not really. The accounts were all just clients, another challenge to accept and another goal to meet. She was good at it, but this...this was home. It was the town she loved, had always loved, despite her brief affair with Tennessee. It was where she wanted to be, and if she could add something to it, make it more than it already was...well, that would feel right.

Natalie smiled. "Let's talk about it some more, but I think I might take the offer."

Tina's squeals of delight garnered as much attention as Natalie's transformation, and the women crowded around to ask questions and congratulate Tina on finding such a perfect replacement and how Natalie was going to turn Big Springs around. Tina was too elated to take exception.

In the center of the circle of well-wishers, Natalie heard her brother's deep voice cutting through the high pitched chatter. Normally disheveled and a little scraggly, Brett was cleaned up. If Natalie didn't know him, she'd think he was a model. No wonder Jenn had said he reminded her of someone famous. His hair short hair was styled artfully, and his face was clean shaven, highlighting his sharp cheekbones and square jaw. Top that off with what looked to be a very nice, very expensive suit, and her brother was almost unrecognizable.

Natalie dislodged herself from the throng and made her way to her brother. She saw him do a double take, and she laughed. He frowned and looked her up and down appraising the changes in the way a brother does, assessing just how much butt kicking he would have to do given how she would turn heads. He sighed and met her eyes. There was more than just the older brother annoyance she'd come to expect any time she was dolled up. In his eyes was amusement, probably because he'd heard how she'd woken up minus one ponytail. There was more still. She'd only seen it directed her way a few times, since it was usually reserved for his prize bull, but Natalie was fairly certain she saw pride in her brother's expression.

She beamed.

"What do you think?"

"You look beautiful, Nat. You'll knock AJ on his tail for sure." Brett nodded. "I like the hair. I'd never have picked it out for you, but it works. It suits you."

She wasn't so sure about that, but she hoped so. She wanted AJ to be pleased with her transformation, to be happy to see her. At this point, though, Natalie was crossing her fingers that he'd talk to her, let her explain. She didn't know what she'd do if he broke her heart the way she had broken his. She'd survive it, of course, but it would hurt. Even more, it's probably what she deserved.

"Speaking of suits--" She let out a low whistle. "You clean up real nice, big brother."

He struck a pose, hip out, eyes squinted with pouty lips, and Natalie was pretty certain she heard a few sighs and the clicking of a camera. She rolled her eyes.

"You look constipated. Don't do that again. Are you ready to head on over? I think Gigi is about ready to go."

The activity of the salon was wrapping up. Women were grabbing purses and shoving lipsticks and combs into the pockets. A few cans of hairspray were being passed around for a final coating before heading out the door.

"In fact, I came here just to see if you wanted to ride with me." He extended an elbow her way.

"What about your date? Don't you have one?" Natalie took his arm as he led her out the door.

"Yeah, I definitely wanted to subject someone else to my grandmother's wedding." He opened the door to his truck for her. "Hop in."

She eyed the distance from the ground to the seat, then assessed whether or not her skirt would let her take the massive step to get in.

Brett sighed, "You're such a pain." He picked her up and plopped her into the seat. "When are you going back to Memphis and getting out of my hair?"

Natalie smiled. "Funny you should mention that—"

Chapter 31

AJ had been anticipating the wedding with the same level of dread most people saved for tax season. It had approached in slow motion, hovering in the near future with its promise of impending doom. Then, quite suddenly, time had sped up in the last few days so that he found himself waiting in the wings of the sanctuary of the church for the event to begin.

When he'd been in Iraq, he had honed his ability to calmly deal with any situation, any crisis that came his way. As a Marine, he was trained not to panic, to control everything from his heart rate to the steadiness of his hands. He could go into the middle of a hostile city without batting an eyelash.

AJ flexed his hands. Steady. If it hadn't been for his years of conditioning, he knew they would be shaking. Instead, he would stand at the front of the church next to his grandfather and watch the woman he loved walk toward him. He would look across the aisle at her, and because he was a Marine, he wouldn't throw himself at her feet.

AJ repeated this and variations of it to himself in the heartbeat it took for the pews to fill with family and friends, essentially half of the town, who had come to see the happy couple tie the knot. In two heartbeats Pastor Matt was motioning for Gramps, AJ, and Danny James to take their positions.

"You ready for this?" his grandfather asked him.

"Me? I'm not the one getting married today. I should be asking you that. You ready? Want me to sneak you out the back?" AJ nodded toward the exit sign down the hall.

Gramps laughed and shook his head. He was happier than AJ had seen him in a long time. They had talked for a long time the other night about his grandma and how she'd be tickled at Charlie marrying Gertie. She'd be pleased, AJ knew, to see his grandfather smile again. Even though he knew that she had gone to be with the Lord, losing his wife had torn Charlie apart, but now he was getting a chance at happiness again.

"I'll be a lucky man if she doesn't change her mind and shows up at all. I'm about half scared she'll bolt part way through her vows."

AJ understood that. He sighed and clasped his grandfather's shoulder. "She'll show up."

They waited at the altar, standing in front of the crowd while classical music played quietly in the background. AJ stood still, his hands clasped in front of him, feet apart. Gramps fidgeted. He waved at people, winked, shook a few hands, pulled at his collar, even bent down to untie and retie his shoe. Danny pulled at his tie and tried to talk to his future father-in-law about fishing, to no avail.

The music changed, and AJ felt his heart stop. It began again the moment Natalie's silhouette appeared at the back of the church. Light spilled in the open doors behind her, creating a brilliant halo, like an angel appearing to the congregation. She took a few steps into the room came clearly into view. There was a collective gasp from the pews. AJ held his breath. She was the most gorgeous woman he'd ever seen. She was exquisite. She was walking his way.

He gazed upon her, taking her in from head to toe. Her hair had been cut. The usual ponytail was gone. Instead, her hair was cut short. It had white blonde streaks around her face, and one piece curled down around her eye. Her lips were glossy. The dress was what did him in. It was short, well above her knees, light blue and looked like it was held up by sheer force of will, while still being decent enough to wear in a church. All in all, he wanted to whisk her out of the church, toss her over his shoulder and carry her off to the nearest quiet place where he could beg her to reconsider, to stay with him, to let him follow her to the city. He would make her all sorts of promises, if only to have another chance.

When his eyes traveled back to her face, having taken in the length of her legs and the height of her heels, he saw the smile on her face. She was watching him. Their eyes met, and their gazes held. AJ breathed again. Neither blinked. She kept up her steady pace down the aisle, and time stretched out once more. Her approach took several lifetimes in which AJ both lived and died. It felt so right to see her walking down the church aisle toward him, until he'd remember she wasn't walking to him, but merely in his direction.

Natalie took her position across from her father, and though AJ didn't notice, DeeJay entered and stood across from him. Then the music changed once again, and Gertie entered and made her way down the aisle. She was radiant in her tasteful suit, surprisingly sedate for a woman whose backside had flashed the entire congregation not two months earlier. AJ was learning, once again, that the world was full of surprises.

Verses were read, and vows were recited. Promises were made, and rings were exchanged. With every new step in the proceedings, AJ couldn't stop himself from wondering if he would ever say these words, make these promises, exchange rings with Natalie. He vowed to do whatever it took to make it happen.

***

Natalie had hoped to have a few minutes alone with AJ after the service. She wanted a chance to talk to him alone, without the entire town—family members included—watching her beg him to take her back. Well, maybe not *beg*. She had some pride after all. At least she hoped she did. She would have to wait and see if it came to that.

There hadn't been time to breathe after the ceremony. Oh, she'd seen him plenty. There had been about a thousand pictures to be taken. She'd stood next to him, in front of him, across from him, all with their grandparents, her parents, and other various members of their families gathered close for a photo. She had done her best to smile for the camera, or at least to look that direction at the appropriate time.

AJ hadn't seemed affected by her presence, though. Not like she was. He was calm and steady. Frankly, it was infuriating. If she was a basketcase, he should be as well.

She had been posed by the photographer, fluffed and straightened by her mother, and pinched by her grandmother for not smiling enough. By the time she escaped the church, Natalie was ready to scream with frustration. AJ had disappeared again.

Without any other options, Natalie hitched a ride with her brother. They stopped along the way at Jamie's house and picked her up. Natalie slid over next to her brother, knees against the gearshift in order to make room. The parking at Knight's was a bit tight, and everyone had been told to carpool. Plus, Brett had volunteered to be their designated driver, despite Natalie's protests that she would never drink again for as long as she lived.

Jamie was wearing a gorgeous green dress of lace over silk. It looked like something out of the sixties, classy and gorgeous. Her copper hair was twisted up on top of her hair with a few tendrils loose around her face.

"Jamie, why don't you have a date picking you up?" Natalie asked her friend.

Brett groaned. "Nat, why do you keep asking about other people's dates? You don't have a date."

Natalie rolled her eyes and stuck out her tongue.

"I kept waiting for Brett to ask me. When he didn't, I was left all alone," Jamie teased. "But, he wound up driving me anyway, so I guess my master plan is working."

The girls laughed when Brett waggled his eyebrows in her direction.

"No, I could've gone with AJ. He asked, just as friends, of course, but I passed. I'm getting a little tired of being the best friend instead of the leading lady." Jamie shrugged and looked out the window.

"Oh, Jamie! I'm sorry if I made you feel--"

Jamie stopped her. "Not you. I did it to myself. It was easier that way. I could go out with guy friends and never think about romance, but I'm starting to think maybe I'd like to give it a try again. To do that, I need to cut down on being the friend-date so much." She didn't turn back to her friends, but instead watched the passing scenery, trees and fields she'd seen millions of times before.

Brett cleared his throat. "Jamie, do you want to go out on a date with me?"

Natalie and Jamie both turned to look at him. He kept his eyes on the road.

"I'll make you a deal, Brett," Jamie began. "If there's ever some kind of apocalypse or nuclear fallout, and we're the only two people left in the entire world, I'll go out with you. Deal?"

Natalie felt Brett let out the breath he'd been holding. His grip on the steering wheel relaxed. He nodded and shot them a grin. "Deal."

The sun was just beginning to set when they walked into Knight's. Natalie had helped set up the decorations, but even she was overwhelmed by how beautiful it looked. The tables were set with centerpieces of lilies and roses. The tablecloths were white, and large tulle and satin bows were tied around the backs of the chairs. Classical music twinkled and flowed from hidden speakers. The lights had been dimmed, and candles were flickering in wall sconces. The brilliant orange and pink of the sunset filled the whole scene with a soft light. It was like something out of an impressionist painting. All the rough edges had been smoothed over, so that only beauty and romance remained.

"Oh, Natalie, it's...it's--" Jamie started.

"I know. It's perfect." They took another moment to stand and appreciate the scene before them.

"You girls get a move on. There's a buffet in there, and I mean to get to it." They parted and made way for Mrs. Talburt to pass, pushing her walker in front of her. The tiny woman's grey curls had been sculpted into a perfect orb around her head, and she had a large purple iris corsage pinned to her dress.

"Can I help you carry your plate?" Jamie asked. She gave Natalie a little wave and followed the older woman to the buffet line.

Natalie looked around, trying to locate AJ. With his impressive height, he usually stood out above the crowd. She didn't see him anywhere. He could be sitting down, or maybe he was helping Charlie with something. She decided to walk around and look for him. Besides, she wasn't hungry yet. Her hangover had finally dissipated, but her appetite hadn't returned. It was probably nerves.

Natalie walked through the large French doors onto the terrace. More tables had been set up out here. Most of the crowd had gone inside, but there were still a few people seated at the tables. She saw her parents sitting close, DeeJay's head resting on her husband's arm. They were taking in the sunset. Natalie smiled. All these years, and her parents still had romantic moments. She didn't want to interrupt and tried to walk behind them.

Her hand was caught in her father's gentle grip. He looked up into her eyes and smiled. He was a man of few words, but they'd always understood each other. He squeezed her hand, and Natalie knew her mother had told him how she planned to stay in Big Springs. Natalie couldn't be sure, but she thought there were unshed tears in his eyes. She bent down and kissed his cheek.

"Who's that? Oh, Natalie, dear, have a seat." Her mother sat up and motioned to the chair beside her. "I was just telling your father the big news. Both of our children in the same town again. You can't know how that feels." She used the cloth napkin to dab at her eyes.

"I've been home all summer, Mama."

DeeJay swatted at her daughter with the napkin. "It's not the same. Oh, honey, we're just so pleased. You'll never know how proud we are of you. Aren't we, Danny?" Her husband nodded and winked.

Natalie's heart felt like it would burst. "That means a lot to me."

"And you hair looks gorgeous, if I do say so myself," her mother went on. "That color just brings out your eyes,

341

and the cut...don't get me started. We should have done this years ago."

Natalie laughed and patted her mother's hand. "It's great, Mama. I wanted to ask...have you seen AJ around anywhere?"

Her parents exchanged looks.

"We saw him get into his truck right after the pictures were finished. He left in a hurry. I don't know where he was going, but he was getting there fast." DeeJay shrugged apologetically. "If either of us see him, we'll let you know."

Natalie felt a lump rise in her throat. He had left. Surely he would come back. It was his grandfather's reception. He was the best man. There was a toast to be made, wasn't there? Maybe he didn't want to see her and had left to keep things from being too awkward between them. He hadn't smiled at her during the ceremony. He'd been so serious, his face hard and unmoving.

She sighed and nodded. "I'd like to talk to him if he shows up." She left her parents to their romantic moment, though the sun was nearly gone now, and only a hint of red remained in the darkening sky. The twinkle lights were flickering on, and the lamp post down by the spring was glowing a soft orange.

After dinner, which Natalie spent sitting next to Jamie and Mrs. Talburt, the cake was cut. Gigi, in her ivory suit, carefully held the piece of cake aloft for Charlie, who leaned in and took a bite. Despite her efforts, icing clung to the side of his mouth. When she laughed, Charlie pulled her into his arms, dipped her, and kissed her loudly. When she was back on her feet, Gigi's mouth was covered in white frosting as well. She smacked her lips and giggled like a young girl.

The tables on the terrace had been moved aside, and the outdoor space had been turned into a dance floor. Upbeat music played from the speakers. It was a mix of newer songs and old standards. Justin Timberlake and Frank Sinatra. Luke Bryan and Ella Fitzgerald. Gigi and Charlie twirled across the dance floor, and Natalie nearly fell over when she saw her grandmother reach down and give Charlie's bottom a squeeze. Susan Appleby snapped a picture with her phone.

Her parents swayed gently, DeeJay's arms wrapped around her husband's neck. Brett taking turns dancing with both Mabel and Henrietta, at one point dancing with both of them simultaneously—switching back and forth between them effortlessly. Her brother had hidden depths, Natalie decided. Jamie was sitting at a table with the Pastor Matt and Jessica Carlisle, who had been invited despite Natalie's protests. They were laughing together over something Jessica had said. Natalie felt the familiar twinge of guilt there, but knew some situations would take years, maybe decades, to repair. Jamie caught Natalie's eye and waved.

It was the perfect moment to slip away. AJ still hadn't shown up, and Natalie didn't think she could spend another minute pretending that her heart wasn't breaking. She took off her heels and carried them with her as she tiptoed down the steps and onto the cobblestone path.

Night had descended, and away from the terrace, Natalie could once again hear the crickets and the frogs and the rushing water of the spring. Luckily, no one else had decided to escape the party by coming down here. She'd bet money that they would later, but for now it was all hers. She dropped her shoes onto the bench and went to stand by the tree that held the rope swing. She had no intention of going in tonight, but smiled at the memory of her leap from yesterday.

"You thinking of jumping?"

Natalie would know that deep voice anywhere. It resonated deep inside of her, and warmth spread throughout her body with just those few words. She waited a moment, caught the breath that had rushed out of her, and turned around.

AJ stood by the bench, the starry sky behind him, and his hands behind his back. He still wore the suit from the wedding, but his hair had become mussed, like he'd run his fingers through it over and over. Natalie took a few steps toward him, and as she got closer, she could see his expression. It was serious, but not the same cold, controlled expression from the wedding.

"I already jumped. Last night." He raised a single eyebrow. "I did! I really did. It wasn't so hard, not after I'd made up my mind to do it."

"Why did you decide to jump? It's not that big of a deal, not wanting to jump into the spring." He shrugged his shoulders and took a step closer. His voice dropped lower, almost a whisper. "I shouldn't have asked it of you. You weren't ready."

"I'm ready now." Natalie took another step closer to him. If she reached out her hand, she could touch him, place her hand over his heart. She held back.

AJ's mouth tilted up in that grin that she loved, the one she'd seen that first day out on the road when she'd been trying to choose which way to go.

"You're awfully dressed up for swimming tonight, but if you want to jump, I'll jump with you." He took the final step toward her and his hand found hers. He laced his fingers with hers, and Natalie looked up to see into his eyes. "Natalie, I've never felt like this before. I'll follow you wherever you want to go. If Big Springs isn't what you want, I'll move. Wherever you go, that's where I want to be."

The sounds of the party, the spring, the crickets and the frogs, all of it drifted away. Natalie could hear only her own heartbeat. It was so much more than she had ever expected. It was like something from a movie, so wonderful it was almost unreal.

But there AJ was, standing in front of her, his hand in hers, his eyes hopeful. She lifted up on her tiptoes and pressed her lips against his. He pulled her toward him, wrapping his strong arms around her waist and holding her close.

Someone on the terrace let out a wolf whistle.

Instead of dropping her and stepping away like a teenager caught making out, he slowly lifted his head and smiled down at her. He eased back a few inches, but kept her fingers entwined with his. Natalie fought to catch her breath.

"Does that mean you'll keep me? Let me come with you?" AJ asked, grinning.

Natalie shook her head. AJ's smile dropped away.

"I'm not leaving. I'm staying in Big Springs for good." She shrugged. "Does the offer still stand? If I promise to love you with my whole heart, for as long as we both shall live? Do you want to stay here in Big Springs with me?"

"I do."

AJ pressed his forehead to hers, eyes closed. At some point, they started to sway to the music, his hands on her waist, hers around his neck. They stayed there, dancing by the spring, well into the night.

Epilogue

Once again, AJ stood waiting in the wings of the sanctuary, dressed in a suit. Gramps stood next to him, almost as worked up as he'd been at his own wedding, pacing back and forth.

"It'll be fine," AJ reassured his grandfather, who shot him a look that could wither the rose pinned to his jacket.

"I don't know how you can be so calm at a time like this." Gramps popped an antacid into his mouth. Ever since his own wedding nearly a year before, the older man had grown increasingly concerned with AJ and Natalie's relationship. AJ suspected his grandfather feared the fallout if he and Natalie never actually made it past the vows. He expected that the older man would sleep a lot easier knowing that Natalie had moved out of her grandmother's old house, where she lived alone, and into the house down the road that AJ had finished building only this past spring.

"You gentlemen almost ready?" Pastor Matt breezed into the hallway, his smile brighter than ever.

"I'm ready whenever she is."

The pastor patted him on the back. "It's a happy day for everyone. It's not every day I get to perform a wedding I had a hand in arranging myself."

AJ had no idea what the man was talking about. He'd been in love with Natalie for ten years.

"The Branson trip, of course. I was the one who suggested that the two of you sit together on the bus, and now look at you...getting married! It's amazing!" He patted AJ on the back again and, noticing the older man's distress, began to reassure him as they made their way to the sanctuary.

AJ entered the door at the side and made his way to the altar. A hush fell over the congregation. Friends, some soldiers and some not, were seated next to family members. The citizens of Big Springs had also come out in force, filling every seat in the church. A few people stood up in the back. Every one of them looked on him with approval and fondness.

The doors at the back of the sanctuary opened, and Brett came in, escorting his mother on one side and Gertie on the other. She insisted that AJ call her Gigi now, just like her other grandchildren did. DeeJay smiled at him as she made her way forward. AJ stepped forward and kissed his future mother-in-law's cheek, before she took her seat on the front row. Gigi pulled him down into a fierce hug.

AJ took his place back at the front of the church, and Brett walked over to join Gramps, who stood up as the best man. Brett had been a huge help in the past six months, assisting AJ with remodeling the storefront next door to the Chamber of Commerce on Main Street. In a few more months it would open as Big Springs Counseling Center, which would specialize in patients dealing with post-traumatic stress. The town had been founded as a haven for veterans seeking healing, and even though it had taken over a century and a half to take off, Big Springs would soon be just that.

Making it all possible, letting the whole world know about the wonders of Big Springs, Arkansas, was Natalie James, soon to be Natalie Jackson. There would be a connecting door between the office of the Chamber of Commerce and the counseling center. To think, after the last wedding he'd attended here, he'd rushed out to meet with a real estate agent about putting his fifty acres up for sale. He'd have done it too, sold everything he owned to follow the woman he loved, heart and soul.

The door at the back of the church opened and the two bridesmaids, Jamie and Jenn, walked slowly forward, their light blue dresses skimming the floor behind them. AJ hardly noticed. His attention was focused on the woman who would come through the doors next.

The music changed, and everyone stood up. Natalie stepped into the room on her father's arm. She was draped in white lace, a veil trailing behind her to the floor.

Their eyes met. They were home.

Author's Note:

The town of Big Springs, Arkansas is fictional. I drew inspiration for this town from both Calico Rock and Cotter, Arkansas. The town's layout is more similar to Calico Rock, except that the real down has the beautiful White River running next to it instead of a creek, though the surrounding area does have plenty of those as well. Cotter, Arkansas has the most gorgeous railroad bridge that I have ever seen. In addition, there is Big Spring Park that holds the real life inspiration for the spring, as well as the name of my fictional town.

My own hometown of Mountain Home, Arkansas sits between these. All three of these real-life towns are dear to my heart.

Thanks

I would like to thank my family for supporting me while I worked on this book: Jake, Thomas, and Peter. My mom, Donna Whitaker, was invaluable. She would talk me through ideas until we were both laughing. I thank my dad, Dennis Baker, for his continuous prayers and guidance. In addition, my first readers: Ashley and Lynda. Your notes and encouragement kept me going. And above all, credit for every breath I take and every word I write goes to my Lord and Savior.

To you, reader, I also say thank you for purchasing and reading my book. If you enjoyed it, please take a moment and write a review. All of your kind words are greatly appreciated.

God Bless!

Misty